KT-215-535

THE
GLASS
BREAKS

ALSO BY A.J. SMITH

The Long War Chronicles

The Black Guard
The Dark Blood
The Red Prince
The World Raven

Form and Void

The Glass Breaks

The FORM &
VOID Trilogy
BOOK I

A·J·SMITH

First published by Head of Zeus in 2019

This is a work of fiction. All characters, organizations, and events portrayed in this novel are either products of the author's imagination or are used fictitiously.

9 7 5 3 1 2 4 6 8

A catalogue record for this book is available from the British Library.

ISBN (HB): 9781786696885
ISBN (TPB): 9781786696892
ISBN (E): 9781786696878

Printed and bound by CPI Group (UK) Ltd, Croydon, CR0 4YY

Head of Zeus Ltd
First Floor East
5–8 Hardwick Street
London EC1R 4RG
WWW.HEADOFZEUS.COM

For Carrie

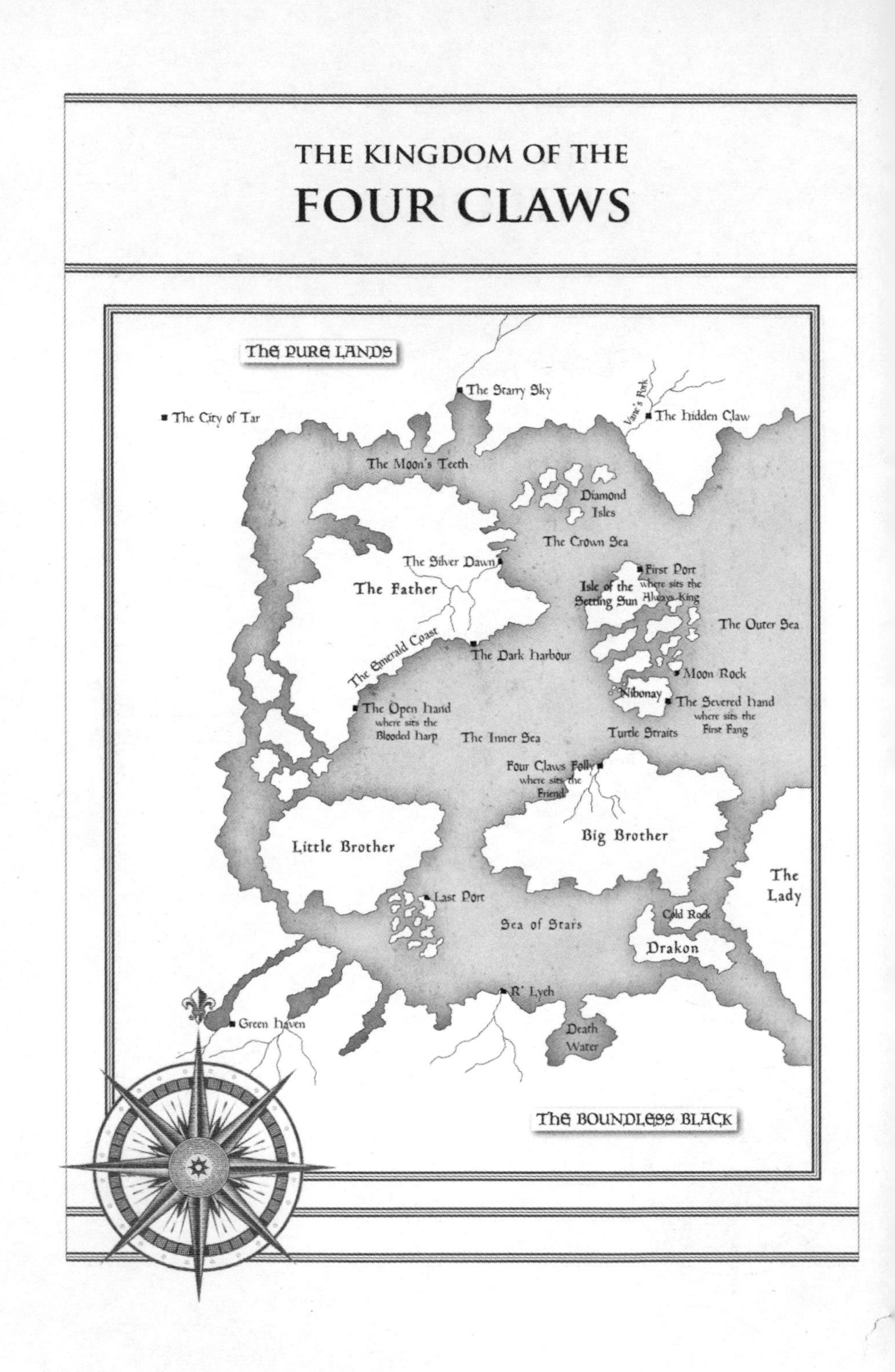
THE KINGDOM OF THE
FOUR CLAWS
The Pure Lands
The Starry Sky
The City of Tar
The Hidden Claw
The Moon's Teeth
Diamond Isles
The Crown Sea
The Silver Dawn
The Father
First Port where sits the Always King
Isle of the Setting Sun
The Outer Sea
The Emerald Coast
The Dark Harbour
Moon Rock
Nibonay
The Open Hand where sits the Blooded Harp
The Severed Hand where sits the First Fang
The Inner Sea
Turtle Straits
Four Claws Folly where sits the Friend
Big Brother
Little Brother
The Lady
Last Port
Cold Rock
Sea of Stars
Drakon
R' Lych
Green Haven
Death Water
The Boundless Black

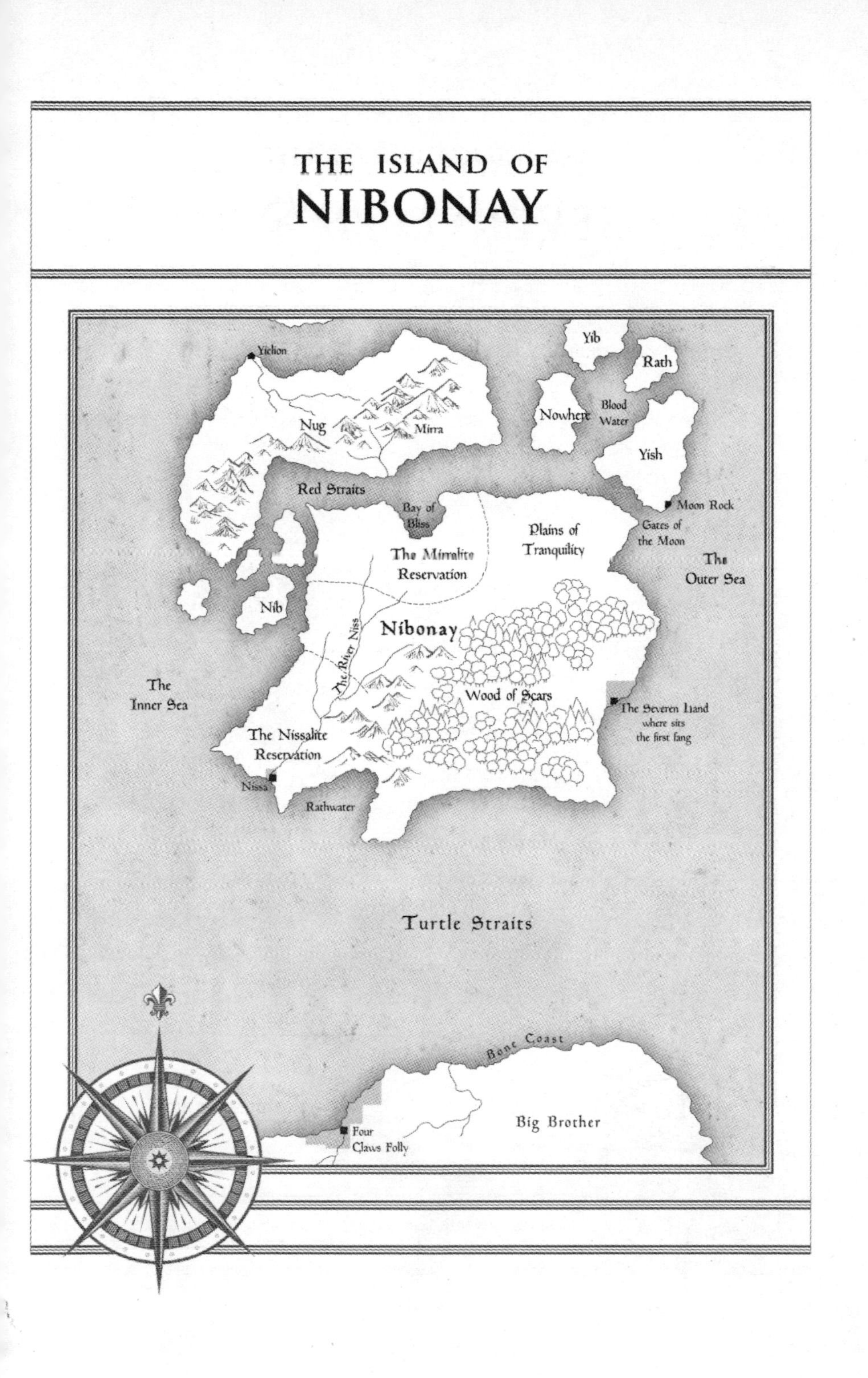

THE ISLAND OF
NIBONAY
Yiclion
Nug
Mirra
Yib
Rath
Nowhere
Blood Water
Yish
Red Straits
Moon Rock
Bay of Bliss
Plains of Tranquility
Gates of the Moon
The Mirralite Reservation
The Outer Sea
Nib
Nibonay
The River Niss
The Inner Sea
Wood of Scars
The Severen Land where sits the first fang
The Nissalite Reservation
Nissa
Rathwater
Turtle Straits
Bone Coast
Big Brother
Four Claws Folly

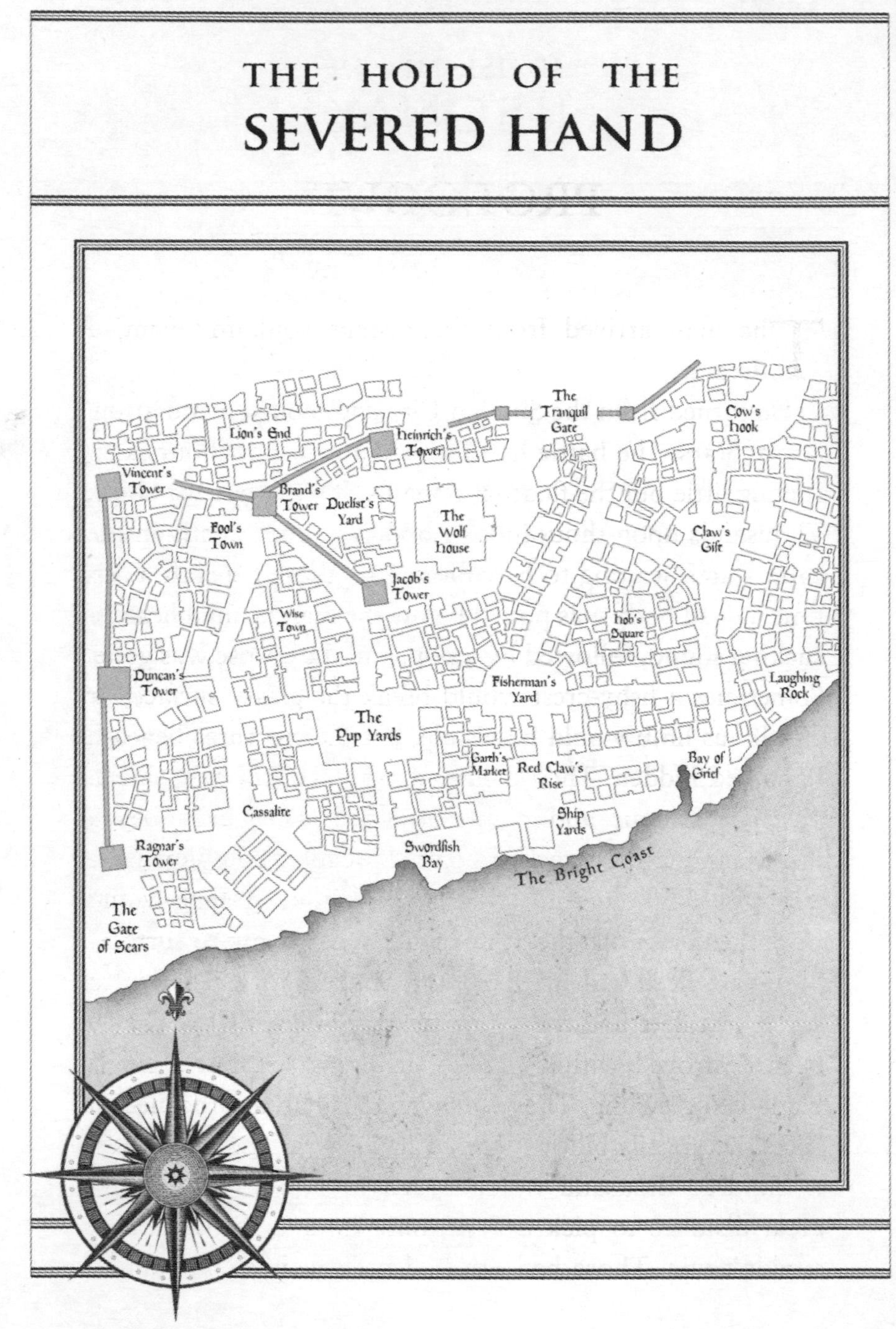
THE HOLD OF THE
SEVERED HAND
Lion's End
Heinrich's Tower
The Tranquil Gate
Cow's Hook
Vincent's Tower
Brand's Tower
Duelist's Yard
The Wolf House
Fool's Town
Claw's Gift
Jacob's Tower
Wise Town
Hob's Square
Duncan's Tower
Fisherman's Yard
Laughing Rock
The Pup Yards
Garth's Market
Red Claw's Rise
Bay of Grief
Cassalire
Ship Yards
Ragnar's Tower
Swordfish Bay
The Bright Coast
The Gate of Scars

PROLOGUE

The man arrived from the distant void, following a dream.

He turned from the Sunken City and looked again at the Sea of Stars. The battle had finished a few short hours ago, leaving little but the floating remains of countless warships. Thousands upon thousands of bodies bobbed gently in the calm water, waiting to be collected by those beneath. Each time a dead body was pulled below the sea, the man heard a sucking sound, followed by a pop, and the corpse was gone. Sometimes a fishy-crest would break the glassy surface, or a bulbous limb would be visible, but the creatures beneath remained hidden. They collected every sword, axe, shield, piece of armour and plank of wood. They even began disassembling the wrecked boats, though to complete their task would take several days. Eventually, everything would be dragged beneath the Sea of Stars, never again to surface.

A vast fleet had attacked the Sunken City. That is to say, a vast fleet had tried to attack the Sunken City. They'd been destroyed within sight of it, dying without a single blade being swung. The swift warships had approached at speed, with sails billowing, and ballistae armed and ready. A hundred thousand warriors, maybe more, had sailed a great distance to pick a fight, only to enter a battle they couldn't win. Those beneath had been waiting, just under the surface. They had strange depth barges of jagged coral and thick, membranous seaweed, able to skewer the hulls of the warships and drag them underwater. Then the sea had boiled, cooking the survivors alive, inside their leather and steel armour. Some had tried to swim ashore, some had clustered together, roaring defiance to quieten the screams, but all had died.

The man had watched from a cliff, invisible to those below. He didn't know who they were, or why they'd come south with such ferocity, but he felt the pain of each departing spirit. Despite their defeat, the dead men and women were creatures of power, and they would be missed. Somewhere else in this realm of form was a kingdom to whom this fleet belonged, though that was all the man could sense. He'd arrived only moments before the battle, and was not even sure where he was, only that he'd been pulled to the Sunken City from far away.

The man stepped back from the cliff and sat against a rock, his eyes flickering between the steaming ocean and the bizarre, cyclopean structures of the Sunken City. The bulk of the metropolis was blessedly obscured beneath the still water, but it was slowly rising, with windowless spires of black stone poking through the water for leagues in every direction. In the centre, dwarfing the surrounding structures, was an immense stone edifice, covered in seaweed and a slick of mouldy green algae. It was a tomb of sorts, though the dead thing within could still dream. It would take decades, perhaps as long as a century, but eventually the Sunken City would be sunken no more. There was certainly enough time for the people of this realm to assemble another fleet. But the man suspected it would meet the same fate as the first.

More than that, when the edifice opened, it would unleash primal chaos on the world.

From along the cliff, he heard footsteps, and turned. He knew nothing of this realm or those that dwelt within it, but he knew he was not in danger, especially not from the old man who approached.

"I have been waiting for you," said the old man. He had wrinkled skin of a light brown, and colourful feathers woven into his waist-length grey hair. He belonged to a different order of men to those of the destroyed fleet, with no armour or weaponry. He had nothing but a wooden whistle, tied around his neck. He averted his deep-set eyes, then bowed his head.

"How did you know I was coming?" was the response. "Does time work differently in this realm?"

"For some," said the old man. "For most it begins in the morning and ends in the night. But for the oldest spirits, it works backwards. I have travelled far to greet you, for the great turtle spirits of the Father remember your arrival, and your deeds not yet done."

A loud creak sounded from the Sea of Stars. The hull of a warship was split in two and pulled beneath the surface, causing bodies to drift away on the sudden waves.

"Do your spirits remember this battle?"

The old man nodded. "In the years to come it will be called the Battle of the Depths, though no tale will recall what truly happened."

"Tell me your name."

The old man tensed his back and stood as upright as he could. He grasped the collar of his thin canvas shirt and ripped it apart, displaying his skeletal chest and the deep scars that covered it. "I am Ten Cuts, speaker of the Rykalite, and I will be your servant. If you will have me."

The man considered it. To accept Ten Cuts would be to accept that he would stay, and care about this realm of men. It would be easier to leave, travelling back to his hall and ignoring the dreams. "Deeds not yet done," he said. "What deeds? What do your spirits remember me doing?"

The speaker of the Rykalite moved past the man and looked at the Sunken City. His eyes widened and his hands began to shake, as his mind recoiled from the impossible spectacle. He was a mortal man with a fragile mind, unable to comprehend what he was looking at. "I have walked for twelve years to greet you," he replied. "I knew of this place, but thought less of it than I did of you. Now I see both, and you give me less pause."

"Answer my question. What deeds?"

"The spirits tell me only what they tell me," replied Ten Cuts. "That they have not told me. But they told me Mathias Blood and the Sea Wolves would assemble a fleet and attack the Sunken City... and they did. And they told me you would be here... and you are here."

"Why did the fleet attack?" asked the man. "Did they know what they faced?"

Ten Cuts rubbed his eyes vigorously, as if to scratch the image from his mind, and stepped back from the high cliff. He walked on unsteady feet, to bow before the man. "The fleet set sail as an act of retribution. The Sea Wolves and their Eastron kin are intractable, and far mightier than my people, but they are relative newcomers to this realm and ignorant of its true nature. They thought they were sailing to a great and inevitable victory. As they had done when they first invaded, forming their Kingdom of the Four Claws from the corpse of the Pure Lands."

The man stood, mumbling to himself. He reached out as best he could, trying to feel the pulse of the world, but it was dim and erratic. He'd not been here long enough to sense anything of depth or texture. To help the mortals of this realm would be the endeavour of decades, and he could not predict the result.

He looked at Ten Cuts, assessing his age to be at least seventy years. "Twelve years to walk here, twelve years to walk back," he mused. "Time may catch up to you before you see your home again." The man smiled and took a breath of air. "But, if you're to serve me, I can't have a trivial thing like old age claiming you. Besides, you have much to tell me, and we have much to do."

The Invaders came from across the sea
    They claimed our rock, our fire, our tree
They followed their Always King and his Claws
    Bringing their steel, their ships, their laws
They had no gods and they had no fate
    They had void and wyrd and they taught us hate

They invaded the Father *and* the Sons
    Killing the Pure Ones

Traditional song of the Mirralite Pure Ones,
written after the First Battle of Tranquillity

PART ONE

Duncan Greenfire at the Severed Hand

1

I was at peace in the void. There was no pain or anxiety, just the gentle caress of the sea, stretching away from me as a blanket of deep blue. It was the world of spirits, beyond the glass of the real world, and the only place I felt no pain. I'd been here for several hours. Soon, my strength would falter and I'd have to leave the realm of void, returning to the realm of form.

I wanted to stroll away from the coast, kicking my bare feet through the warm sea water and the dancing spirits within, but I couldn't move. However peaceful I found the void, I couldn't forget that, in the real world, I was tied to a wooden post by the wrists and ankles, half-submerged in freezing cold water. I'd broken the glass and stepped to the void when the brackish water had reached my chin. The tide would have receded by now, but the temperature would only have gotten worse. I closed my eyes and took a last long breath of pure air, before letting myself slip back through the glass.

I immediately howled in pain. In the real world, night was turning back to day and I could no longer feel my hands or feet. The black sea water was neither gentle nor warm, and the stinging wind forced my eyes to close. I howled again, as my bare chest and face were enveloped by oncoming waves. The water churned, broken only by the rocks of the Bay of Grief, forming a horseshoe around my wooden pole.

"I am a Sea Wolf. I am Eastron from across the sea." It was barely a grunt, but I said it again and again, until my throat was dry and sore. I coughed out sea water and phlegm, retching between heavy breaths.

The rocks around me were muddy green, mottled with seaweed and algae, and high enough to block my view of the hold. But there was no-one waiting for me above and there had been no sound for hours. A day and a night is a long time to wait, and no-one would return until my time was up. I could have drowned yesterday, and my body would not be retrieved until the proper time. Only a Sea Wolf, with strong wyrd, able to stay in the void for hours at a time, could stop from drowning and survive the ordeal. Though no-one expected *me* to survive.

I retched again and shook my head. I could barely open my eyes wide enough to see the air before me, let alone focus sufficiently to break the glass. My strength was gone. I'd used up every ounce of my wyrd to stay alive. I couldn't stop the water rising and I couldn't travel to the void. My only option was to hope that they'd release me before I drowned.

The sun was rising, but only slowly. They'd be back soon. They'd pull me out and I'd be a Sea Wolf. Like my brother, my father, my grandfather and grandmother, like every Greenfire since the Years of Ice. Perhaps everything would be better. Perhaps my pain would end and I'd be free.

"You alive down there?" asked Taymund Grief, appearing on the rocks above me, just as I began to contemplate my death.

"Please, help me," I spluttered. "I can't do this anymore. I'm so tired."

Two more shapes appeared, creating three silhouettes. There was a nasty chuckle from Arthur Brand, but a warm smile from the pup-master. They'd have both reckoned on my death, but had different reactions to my survival.

"You're alive, young Duncan," said Mefford, the pup-master. "Your wyrd is strong, even if your body's weak. Taymund, pull him out. Try to be gentle."

The young duellist was over six feet tall and his shoulders were almost twice as wide as mine. He crouched and sliced his cutlass down through my restraints, making me fall, weakly, into the ice-cold water. His hairy hands then roughly grabbed me by the arms and hefted me backwards. I wore loose woollen leggings, tucked into heavy sailing boots, but was bare-chested and freezing cold. Leaving the water, to cough pathetically on the stone shore, was a massive shock to the system, making my muscles tighten and my lungs empty of air.

"The last man of your age to take the rite drowned the first evening," said Mefford. "Seventeen is too young. Though, for certain families, tradition disagrees. Now, put a blanket over him."

I was too tired to respond. I rocked into a foetal position on the cold rocks, as Arthur Brand reluctantly covered me with a thick, woollen blanket. I grasped it with shivering hands, letting the fabric hug my wet skin. I panted, then coughed, then whimpered. I had no dignity left, and to pretend so would accomplish nothing. But I was still alive. I'd proven my father wrong, and I would be a Sea Wolf after all. I'd proven everyone wrong.

I clenched my fists, slowed my breathing, and started to laugh. I wanted to raise my head and shout *fuck you all* to the world, but I just laughed. It was enough for now.

"If you can laugh, you can stand," said the pup-master. "There is one more thing to do."

They gathered around me. "Your wyrd is strong, boy," said Arthur Brand, a seasoned duellist of the Severed Hand. "Do you have enough left to break the glass? Or do you need me to carry you?"

I stopped laughing and rubbed my eyes. I wasn't strong enough. I didn't want him to know it, but I'd used all my wyrd. For at least the next few hours, until I'd had a chance to rest, I would be just a normal man, with no wellspring of spiritual energy to set me apart.

Mefford grunted. "Did *you* have enough when we fished *you* out? Duncan survived the rite. He's not a pup anymore. He's a Sea Wolf, and he'll be tested no more today. *You* can take him through the glass, Master Brand."

Arthur Brand straightened his stained sea cloak and crouched next to me. He was in his late twenties, perhaps thirty, with black hair and a hard face. He and his twin sister, Adeline, were senior duellists and children of the Battle Brand, elder of Last Port. They'd most recently returned from pillaging Dark Brethren merchants in the Inner Sea. Like most Sea Wolves, he was much larger than me and wore ship-leathers, bonded with steel plates and fitted to the contours of his body.

I sat up on the rocks and faced him, extending my arms and letting him help me to my feet. "How old were *you* when you took the rite?" I asked him, already knowing the answer.

"Nineteen," he replied. "My surname is not Greenfire, Blood, or Red Claw, so I have to wait my turn. Only privileged little pricks like you get to die at seventeen."

"Too young," repeated Mefford, with a shake of his head. "But still, he survived the rite. Now, let's bind him to the Severed Hand."

Mefford and Taymund took a step towards the water, with Arthur moving me into line, facing the Bay of Grief. Each head went back, and each set of eyes turned a crisp white as we broke the glass. Arthur's hand on my shoulder pulled me with him, and an intense feeling of dislocation followed as we stepped to the void.

The four of us stood on shimmering blue rock. The void-air was clear, and caressed my throat as I took deep breaths. The hazy vista of the Bay of Grief now seemed benign, as if I'd survived its torments and was now immune. Even the Outer Sea, flowing away over the horizon, was calm and flowed only gently.

Everything was crisper in the void. The colours were more vibrant, the sounds more acute. The rocks and waves appeared alive, dancing in the glassy air, somehow larger and more defined than in the real world. Nothing dead or artificial existed beyond the glass, just life and the endless tide of spirit and wyrd. Buildings disappeared, roads and walls were nothing but subtle veins of form. It took practice to interpret the language of the void, to read the signs from the real world and orient yourself. But, above all, it was treacherous, and we were taught never to wander far from what we knew.

Each Eastron looked different in the void, their wyrd shining through intense patterns of light. Arthur's arms were a sparkling red, like all duellists, and his head was crested with a dense lump of wyrd, shielding his mind. Taymund's arms were similar, but a jewel of light emanated from his heart. Mefford shone from every inch of his form, though the shine was dull in places.

My wyrd was subtle and layered, like a coiled spring that had yet to be released. I shone far less than the glowing Sea

Wolves to my left, each of whom had moulded their wyrd into forms practical and strong.

"Speak as one," said Mefford. "The spirits are listening."

"To the First Fang I pledge my arm, my head and my heart." I too said the words, but they sounded awkward and felt hollow. "To the Severed Hand I pledge my loyalty and my wyrd." Arthur Brand's voice was the loudest. "To the Eastron from across the sea I claim brotherhood. From the Bright Lands I am come. In the Dark Lands will I prosper." It was called the duellists' oath, but was required of *every* Sea Wolf.

"Step forward, Duncan," said the pup-master. "It is the one hundred and sixty-seventh year of the dark age. The year you became a Sea Wolf."

The landscape around me responded, and wisps of void energy danced from the rocks to envelop all of us. The void rippled, accepting me as a creature of wyrd. My breathing had slowed and my mind was again at peace.

Then, from the ethereal sea, a spiritual wave broke from the glassy surface, rising above us and forming into a shimmering blue wolf, ten foot tall and ravening. I gasped and took a step backwards. Mefford and the others showed equal surprise, though Arthur Brand stood his ground. The enormous spirit eclipsed the calm of the void, like the moon passing in front of the sun on a clear day.

The pup-master dropped to his knee. "My Lady of the Quarter," he said. "We did not expect you."

I'd heard of it. Every young Sea Wolf knew of the spirit, called the Old Bitch of the Sea in tales. It was the totem of the Severed Hand, but rarely appeared unless summoned by the spirit-masters. Each of the great holds had a totem, but ours had not appeared at a rite of passage for decades. I was honoured and scared at the same time. The fear was stronger. I'd never seen so large a spirit.

"Nothing to say, Sharp Tongue?" said Taymund Grief, the young duellist. "I've never seen you lost for words."

"*I've* never seen a spirit that powerful," I replied.

"Both of you, stand up straight," said Mefford.

The Old Bitch of the Sea padded its ghostly feet onto the shore. Each footfall caused blue, foaming water to bubble from its paws. She towered over us, her teeth bared and slobbering. Mefford didn't move an inch as the spirit loped past him to look at me. Not Arthur or Taymund. The spirit was definitely looking at *me*. Its eyes were globes of endless blue light, plunging far into the void and showing me vistas beyond imagination. It's inelegant to admit, but I wanted to be sick. The surge of wyrd from the spirit was almost more than I could bear. *Mine* was powerful, but the Old Bitch of the Sea was made of the stuff, assembled from the boundless tide of wyrd that flowed through the void.

In my head, the spirit spoke. *The glass breaks, the sword falls, the sea rises*. The she-wolf nudged me with her huge muzzle, and I felt soft, warm fur caress my face. Her eyes narrowed, as if she were assessing me. Then she spoke again. *Greenfire must let his wyrd shine*.

Then it was gone, disappearing in a flood of blue, ethereal water, its huge haunches and slavering teeth vanishing in an instant. All that remained was a swirl of lesser water spirits, appearing as snapping wolf pups, but fading slowly from view.

As the void again became calm, my leg began to hurt.

*

I walked with a limp, but I was good at hiding it. When I ran, I dragged my left leg, so I tried not to run; and, as long as I kept an even pace while walking, the limp was almost invisible. On cold days it was worse, but it always hurt, and occasionally made me wince. I was good at hiding that too. I'd learned to suppress the pain and turn the wince into a slight twitch. Only the void provided peace, and it never lasted long.

I couldn't remember a time before the pain. It had been a part of me from the first time my father took a leather whip to the back of my legs. The beating started when I was four or five, and didn't end until I was ten.

On my tenth birthday I was awoken before dawn by a restraining hand over my mouth. "Keep quiet and get dressed," demanded my father, looming over me in the moonlight. "You're coming with me."

I spluttered and wriggled under his hand, trying to free myself. When he was ready, and when I'd stopped struggling, he removed his hand. "Quickly now, boy."

He turned his back and faced my bedroom door, allowing me a modicum of privacy. I grasped my left leg and grunted, trying to keep my weight off it as I turned out of bed. The wound was still raw from my father's most recent displeasure, and even the touch of my hands caused me pain. I limped the three steps to my wardrobe, with the left side of my face twitching rapidly.

I was too afraid to question him, too tired and uncomfortable to think about where we were going and why we had to go there in the dead of night. I just put on my clothes and winced in pain. When my trousers were on, my tunic tied at the neck, and my boots laced up, my father turned.

My father, Wilhelm Greenfire, High Captain of Moon Rock, was short for a Sea Wolf, but his wide shoulders and unwavering glare drew attention away from his height. Members of my family were all short. My elder brother, Kieran, at just under six feet, was judged tall for a Greenfire. My father looked to *him* as his heir. *My* inconvenient presence in his life was embarrassing at best. He beat me to make me strong. But I'd never be strong. I was clever, but weak. So he beat me. Until I was ten, when he woke me in the middle of the night and dragged me from our house.

Moon Rock was built on a slope, from low pastures to huge overhanging cliffs, thrust into the Outer Sea. Two huge jetties formed an arc around the harbour below, and the light from a hundred ships cut through the darkness.

"Where are we going?" I whimpered.

He turned away from me, his fist clasped around my forearm, as we travelled left and right, down the dark, narrow streets of Moon Rock. "We are going to make you strong," he replied. "Or kill you. I have waited ten years for you to show me strength. I am sick of waiting. When your brother was ten years, his arms were already shining with wyrd, and he slept with a cutlass."

I was just a boy. Kieran had tried to protect me from our father, but he was now a Sea Wolf, wearing a red cloak and swinging the blade of the Severed Hand. He could no longer protect me. I was a terrible student, with a weak arm, and no aptitude for combat. My wyrd was volatile and I had no idea how to channel it. And all my father wanted was a warrior.

We stopped at a dingy shack of wood and clay, lying at the top of a winding cobbled street. Below, the harbour was hidden behind buildings, but the sound of waves against wood travelled up to meet us, and the salty tang of the sea caught the back of my throat. The shack had no name and no markings. There was nothing to suggest what lurked within.

My father banged on the door. "Clatterfoot! It's time."

A moment later, the door opened, revealing a slice of light and a thin, bearded face. It was Ronald Blitz, called Clatterfoot. He was a spirit-master, though not one who commanded much respect. He was rarely seen in the hold, and I only recognized him due to his broad wooden leg, ending in a black steel foot. He stepped aside and ushered us into his shack. I was given a firm shove in the back and stumbled from cobbled street to wooden floorboards.

The shack opened into a small room of dust and clutter, with low doorways snaking away into musty darkness. There was a single chair, nailed to the floor in the middle of the shack, but all other furnishings were pushed tight against the walls.

"Put him in the chair," grunted Clatterfoot, hobbling away from the door. The spirit-master wore thick furs, adding bulk to his shoulders, but his face was thin, almost skeletal, with deep-set eyes. The eyes and the face would haunt me for years to come. He'd appear in my dreams as a skeleton wrapped in thorns.

"What? Why?" I spluttered, terrified of some new kind of pain.

My father grabbed my shoulder and turned me to face him, making me shrink under his hateful eyes. He didn't say anything. All I really remember is the hate.

I was seated in the chair, with Clatterfoot walking around me in circles. His metal foot, a single piece of black steel, pounded a dull note, and my father stood back. Whatever was to happen here, was at the bidding of the High Captain.

"Pain is a strange thing, boy," said the spirit-master, grunting between words. "It can be dull or sharp, acute or chronic. It is an axis of thorns, upon which any kind of discomfort can be plotted."

"Is this necessary?" snapped my father. "He's as scared as he's going to get. It doesn't take much with this one. Your flair for intimidation is lost on a sniffling child like him. They call him Sharp Tongue. Not a name to command respect. Just summon the spirit."

Clatterfoot was hunched over, his long face twitching at the interruption. "As I was saying, Duncan Greenfire, called Sharp Tongue, son of the High Captain, pain can be precisely controlled ... by a skilled artisan." He stood facing me, neither smiling nor frowning. He showed an alarming neutrality, as if he could kill a man without his heart-rate changing. "I'm going to hurt you, Duncan," said the spirit-master. "I'm going to cause you more pain than anyone else you will ever meet."

"Enough!" said my father. "Just summon the spirit."

Clatterfoot was displeased, but it only showed in his eyes. He was not fool enough to question the High Captain. He backed away, hurriedly moving to one of a dozen wooden bookshelves. There *were* books, but most of the dusty wood was filled with stained glass jars and alchemical equipment. On the highest shelves were stuffed animals of various kinds, all posed rampant, and facing downwards. The thin spirit-master gathered up a wreath of thorns from a lower shelf, and caressed it sensually.

"The natives of this land, the Pure Ones, can't step to the void," said Clatterfoot. "They'd never heard of the glass until we invaded from across the sea. For thousands of years before us, if they wanted to speak to spirits, they had to bind them into talismans." He remained hunched, as he loomed over me, holding the wreath in his open palms, like some kind of offering.

"Wait," I whimpered. "Father, please!"

"Strength, boy," he replied. "It always was your hardest lesson. You will endure this until you reach eighteen years. In that time the pain will either kill you or force strength into your feeble body. I'd rather my son was dead than weak. If you reach seventeen years and can take the rite, the Bay of Grief will finish you off. But you will *never* be a Sea Wolf and dishonour the name of Greenfire."

Clatterfoot hooked the wreath around my left thigh and connected the ends, forming it into a belt of thorns. He then turned his skeletal face upwards and closed his eyes. The air around him crackled as he summoned his wyrd. Like all spirit-masters, he was taught to reach through the glass, without having to step to the void. It enabled them to treat with dangerous spirits in safety. It was the first time I'd seen it done. A window of blue energy rose in the dark hovel, vibrating at eye-level in front of the one-legged spirit-master.

"The talisman has been built with skill," intoned Clatterfoot, speaking to an unseen presence. "It will be a fine home for you. All we require is pain."

I was just a little boy, who didn't imagine such pain could exist. The spirit-master put a folded length of leather between my teeth, which stopped me biting my tongue off, but the pain, and my father's malice, changed who I was.

When the spirit entered the belt of thorns it was angry and scared, and darted around my body, making every muscle tense with pinpricks of spite. I was ten years old, and forced to understand a father's hatred and a spirit's anger all at once.

But my memories of that day appear with variable clarity. Sometimes I remember *seeing* the pain spirit be bound around my leg; other times I just remember wanting to die. I begged my father to kill me, over and over again, but he just grimaced and shook his head. I spent hours in the spirit-master's hovel, as the bent old man tried to find the perfect balance of pain, but my father said nothing.

Clatterfoot called the spirit *Twist,* and the talisman a thorn clinch. Over the years, I've come to understand the fluctuations in pain that the spirit causes me. Though I never understood why Wilhelm Greenfire had so much hatred for his youngest son, but he never beat me again.

Twist has mood-swings and a chaotic personality. The spirit allows me periods of respite, and punishes me when he feels like it. He refuses to let me even think about removing the thorn clinch, and prefers that I hide its existence. I'm forced to comply. Only in the void is he powerless, as the talisman is bound to the realm of form. But a few hours beyond the glass was the most my wyrd would allow. At first. As I grew, and my father's sneer lengthened, I pushed the limits, staying in the void for longer and longer to avoid the pain. It made my wyrd strong, but my body remained small and weak. I never became the warrior my father wanted, but neither did I die. Somewhere, deep in my form, wyrd bubbled forth, and the stronger it became, the less I could control it.

2

A quarter of a million Eastron and Nissalite Pure Ones lived at the Severed Hand. Far more than at Moon Rock. It was the great hold of the Sea Wolves, raised by my namesake, Duncan Red Claw, when the Always King sent forth his claws. It was only my second visit and it looked larger than I remembered. Growing up at Moon Rock, amidst fishing boats, cobbled streets, and the constant smell of fish, left me ill-prepared for the sprawling hold of the First Fang. It dominated the coast, from the Outer Sea to the Wood of Scars, visible for miles in every direction.

Any native Pure One living on Nibonay need only look at our walls to see the power of the Sea Wolves. The Nissalite had quickly surrendered before Duncan Red Claw, and were allowed freedom, whereas the rebellious Mirralite acted as petty terrorists, living in the wilds and raging against our power. They were only two of the boundless tribes of natives, beaten into submission when the Eastron arrived from across the sea. They were all called Pure Ones, though I didn't really understand why. Weak Ones would have been more appropriate. They outnumbered the Eastron, but had no wyrd, and their military craft was limited.

When we left the void and I could get dressed, my mind didn't care about the water, the Pure Ones, or the spectacle of the Severed Hand. I barely even cared about the Old Bitch of the Sea and her words. All I really cared about was the pain in my leg. The thorn clinch felt tighter than usual, as if Twist was angry that I'd survived the rite. I expected a few hours of insistent pain until the spirit calmed down.

"You look well," said Mefford. "Slightly smug, but well. Your father and the First Fang are waiting at the Wolf House."

"Can I sleep first?" I asked, my left eye twitching. "My father gets cross when I look tired."

Mefford narrowed his eyes. "The High Captain has left Moon Rock to see his youngest son become a Sea Wolf. The First Fang has done without sleep to welcome you to his hold at this early hour. But, if you're too tired, I'm sure they will wait."

"My sister doesn't sleep much," offered Arthur Brand. "But she's waiting in there too. You can piss off your father and Lord Ulric, but Adeline Brand is not to be trifled with. Trust me, boy, you wanna sleep later."

Taymund Grief slapped me on the back. "Don't be a child. You're a short-arsed Sea Wolf with no training, but still a Sea Wolf. Act like it."

I tensed my leg and tried to control my breathing. Taymund had taken the rite last month and tradition dictated that, if he was able, he attended the next time a pup became a Sea Wolf. If *I* was able, I'd be expected to do the same thing in a month's time.

The Bay of Grief cut into the Bright Coast, overlooked by towering shipyards and the dense markets of Red Claw's Rise. Elsewhere in the hold, people were just rising as the sun beckoned them from bed. The night fishermen would return soon and activity would engulf the coast.

I was no longer wrapped in a warm blanket of wyrd, and was glad of my heavy woollen shirt. Mefford helped me button it up, seeing my shivering, red-raw fingertips fumbling at the cloth. He then wrapped my black sea cloak around my shoulders, smiling as he did so.

"It's not the right colour anymore, Sharp Tongue," observed Taymund. "You need some red in it somewhere. You want people to know you're a Sea Wolf."

I hugged the cloak around me, rubbing my chest through the thick fabric. Black or red, it was the warmest I'd been for a day and a night.

"See my cloak," continued the young duellist. "That's Pure One blood. Best red paint there is. It's what every Sea Wolf wants."

The stupid, violent thug had his chin thrust out like he'd said something terribly clever and manly. I felt a twinge in my leg, and a sharp pain travelled up my left side. "How many bodies are there, feeding crabs at the bottom of the Bay of Grief?" I asked, spitefully. "Did *they* want red cloaks? Or did they just want to be Sea Wolves? Idiot."

Taymund pouted, looking at Arthur as if he wanted confirmation that I had overstepped my bounds. Then he punched me in the face. I saw stars behind my eyes and only Mefford's quick reactions stopped me from falling back into the water.

The young duellist smirked. "Ha, what use is strong wyrd if you can't see a punch coming." He punctuated my pained groans with smug laughter.

"Master Grief," snapped the pup-master, "please refrain from beating up Master Greenfire. His first scar shouldn't be from another Sea Wolf."

"He should watch his fucking mouth," mumbled Taymund, storming off towards Red Claw's Rise.

I stood from the cold rocks, nursing a tender cheek. Taymund was typical for a young duellist. He was big, strong, and tried not to think unless absolutely necessary. He swung the blade of the Severed Hand, but didn't care what he swung it at. He'd been taught to use his wyrd to strengthen his sword-arm. With concentration, he could split steel armour or hack through half a dozen Pure Ones.

"Five hundred and twenty-three," said Mefford, inspecting my rapidly-swelling cheek.

"What?"

"Every pup that drowns has their name written in the Wolf House," he replied. "There are five hundred and twenty-three bodies in the Bay of Grief. Each wanted to be a Sea Wolf, and each found their strength wanting. Though only certain families get to try at seventeen."

I wanted to be sorry for my flippancy, but I wasn't. Mefford was just an old man, too consumed with duty to pay me any mind. He hid it behind a friendly face, but he thought no more of me than Taymund or Arthur Brand. If it weren't for my name and my family, he'd not think even to speak to me. But I was a Sea Wolf now, and my world had changed.

The Wolf House was twenty-three storeys high. It was raised a hundred and fifty years ago and had been the seat of the First Fang ever since. It was grey stone, in huge blocks and cyclopean archways, with black murals adorning the higher levels. Pictures of pirate ships, great sea battles, dead

Pure Ones and Dark Brethren, and glory of every kind. But there was also sorrow. Wars lost and enemies yet to be vanquished. The Battle of the Depths, the Sunken Men and their dreaming god, the Year of Slaughter. They were a mournful counterpoint to the Sea Wolves' bluster.

Taymund was waiting by the western entrance as Mefford and Arthur Brand and I approached. The hold was now enveloped in bright morning sunshine and the streets around the Wolf House were bustling. The walk was further than I'd hoped and my left leg was numb by the time we reached the huge building. I'd been beyond the glass a great deal in the past two days, and Twist was making up for lost time. Mefford had to catch me several times, though I had a good excuse to explain my limp. A day and a night in the Bay of Grief tightened the muscles and caused strange aches and pains.

"What's the matter with you, lad?" asked Arthur Brand, as we approached a wide gateway, under a huge portcullis. "Bad leg?"

"The cold," I replied. "It gets into the bones. I'll be alright. If I get some sleep." The last thing I wanted was to see my father, and I clung to the hope that someone would take pity on me and let me find a warm bed first.

Within, on the bottom levels of the Wolf House, there was no great hall or central chamber, just a honeycomb of rooms, both warmed by fires and left cold, with open windows, framing no glass or shutters. The ground floor belonged to the people of the hold, and was used for trials, executions, and challenges too important or private to take place in Duellist's Yard. Pure Ones weren't allowed, and the brown-skinned Nissalite conducted their business in front of permanent tables, set up outside.

The warmer rooms of the Wolf House contained bureaucrats and endless piles of parchment. I imagined that each dusty scroll held some specific importance that the scroll masters could interpret, but to most the words and numbers were as incomprehensible as the weather. Sea Wolves didn't concern themselves with lists of fishermen and the price of grain. That was for Eastron who held no sword, belonged to no family, and lived and died in the security of their hold. At least, that was what we were taught.

The second and third levels were half storerooms and half auction houses. Huge, premium fish were sold in noisy crowds of braying merchants, oft-times coming to blows over the choicest tuna or the largest swordfish. The storerooms were guarded day and night by duellists, chosen for their stoic nature and refusal to accept bribes. In my estimation, people that didn't like eating fish would have been more suited to the role.

Above the rambunctious auction pits were many levels of stored artefacts and woven heraldry. Legendary blades and armour were said to be held in locked vaults, awaiting worthy men to claim them. Some, like Duncan Red Claw's falchion, Greatfang, had been in the Wolf House for a hundred years and would likely never be used again.

The four of us bypassed the scroll masters, the auction house and the vaults, walking up clean stone steps with worn, rounded edges and a whistling downward breeze. Halfway up the building began the Bloody Halls, the rooms of Lord Ulric Blood, the First Fang, with large sections given over to duellists' chambers.

"Straighten your cloak, boy," said Mefford, leading the way into the Bloody Halls. "Only Sea Wolves get in here. Try to look like one."

Before me was a wide, open hall, lined with pillars of red and black stone. Open doorways between the pillars led to winding side corridors and vaulted antechambers. Duellists in red cloaks, wielding cutlasses and falchions, stood in two lines ahead, their weapons held in salute. Beyond the honour guard, facing me from around a circular table, were elders of the Severed Hand, awaiting their new Sea Wolf.

"Duncan Greenfire of Moon Rock!" boomed Lord Ulric Blood, sounding like a giant, gargling rocks. "How flows your wyrd? Untrained, but dangerous, from what I hear."

From the table, my father, Wilhelm Greenfire, chuckled. His long, thin face was neither warm nor welcoming. If anything, his laughter was mocking, and I suddenly felt like a child in pain. Not a Sea Wolf or an Eastron with strong wyrd, but a scolded boy whose father couldn't muster the effort to be proud of his son. Twist tightened around my thigh.

My ascension to Sea Wolf was not an occasion to warrant much ceremony. Five of the twenty-three elders had risen early to see me, but the majority of the hold was likely oblivious to the day and night I'd spent in the Bay of Grief. When Arthur and Adeline Brand became Sea Wolves, the streets were lined with thousands of celebrants. But not for me.

As I walked through the tightly formed corridor of dangerous-looking men and women of the hold, I hoped, beyond the sweat of my brow and the pain in my leg, that I'd be made an apprentice spirit-master and spend my days in the safety and warmth of the hold. Any notions I had of using my wyrd for the glory of the Severed Hand began to wither. I was afraid of everyone, and knew that each of them thought me a freak.

"Slow down, boy," said my father. "Look into the faces of those who guard you. Who guard us all. They swing the blade of the Severed Hand in ways you will never understand."

I was halfway down the line of duellists. Each and every one of them was taller and broader than me. I glanced at their hard faces, looking straight ahead either side of me. I knew a few famous names, a few distantly remembered deeds and faces. Arthur joined his sister, Adeline, at the high table, but others stayed in line to honour *me*. Rys Coldfire, the Wolf's Bastard, a man unbeaten in countless one-on-one challenges; Maron Grief, Taymund's elder brother and a brutal killer. There was no uniform to their appearance, as each duellist functioned independently, protecting the Severed Hand as their wyrd dictated. The Brand twins were never far from Lord Ulric, and were dressed in fine, leather armour. The Wolf's Bastard, most often to be found in Duellist's Yard, wore chainmail under a long leather coat, with wolf designs dyed into the surface. Maron's arms were bare and he wore a simple moulded waistcoat of leather and steel. He was also the tallest amongst them, perfect for lording his considerable strength over those he perceived as weaker than him. People like me.

"Try not to shit yourself," muttered Maron, speaking through gritted teeth so as not to be heard by the elders.

Lord Ulric banged his fist on the table and stood. "That's enough posturing. Get over here, Master Greenfire."

I quickened my pace to get clear of the honour guard.

"Slow down," muttered the last duellist on the left. "It's not unknown for youngsters to trip on the carpet."

I looked at him. He was young, maybe twenty-five, and had curly black hair to his shoulders. He held a heavy, pattern-welded cutlass, pointing upwards in salute. I thought his family name was Ice, but didn't know his first name.

"Thank you," I whispered, clearing the corridor of duellists and emerging before the circular table and the elder Sea Wolves. I walked slowly, keeping my pain under control with small steps.

Lord Ulric Blood, the First Fang, sat in the centre, with his son and heir, Vikon Blood to his left, and master-at-arms, Jonas Grief to his right. My father, still wearing his disapproving sneer, was seated next to Tomas Red Fang, the hold's elderly spirit-master. Arthur and Adeline sat in the two end seats.

I felt smaller than my already limited height. Lord Ulric was huge and intimidating, his son was tall, lean and handsome. Even my father appeared so much larger than life when sitting as an elder Sea Wolf. He made me feel small *and* insignificant, as if my ascension to Sea Wolf was a trial he never thought he'd have to endure. And, as soon as we locked eyes, Twist began to send pinpricks of pain up my left side.

"A name that requires my father to rise from his bed before midday," said Vikon Blood, the Second Fang. "And wyrd that requires our spirit-master's aging presence."

Tomas Red Fang was the oldest man I'd ever seen. To describe him as aging seemed woefully understated. His skin was like folded paper, sharp and creased.

"I'm honoured," I replied, hoping that I wasn't being rude.

"Honoured?" snapped my father. "Stand up straight, boy. At least try to act like a Sea Wolf."

"Sorry ... I ... didn't know when I was allowed to speak, father."

He frowned. I'd seen it a million times. The corners of his mouth twitched, causing his beard to ruffle sideways, and his mahogany brown eyes narrowed. If he was feeling kind, he'd scratch his beard and his eyes would soften. If not, he'd slowly nod his head.

"Always got an answer, boy," he said, nodding his head. "They still call you Sharp Tongue, you know? Do you think that's an honourable name for a Sea Wolf?"

I twitched, but kept the pain under control. "My name is Greenfire," I replied. "You should know that, being my father."

I'd overstepped the boundaries of our relationship. I was seventeen years old and I'd never spoken to him like that before. I'd never come close. He'd heard me swear under my breath once and denied me food for three days. I looked at him, Sea Wolf to Sea Wolf. Perhaps the Old Bitch of the Sea gave me strength, and I realized that his power over me was waning. I wasn't about to kick him in the face, but I was at least unafraid of standing up to him. Though I carried on twitching, as if the thorn clinch didn't care that I'd become a Sea Wolf or that the totem had spoken to me.

Luckily, as his face twisted into a grimace that would, ordinarily, signify a slap of some kind, Vikon Blood spoke. "I heard tales of Wilhelm Greenfire's parenting. Apparently not exaggerated." I struggled to look at the Second Fang. More so even than his father, he was everything that young Sea Wolves wanted to be.

Lord Ulric laughed and resumed his seat next to his son. He was a man of sixty years or more, but was still the largest man at the table. "Don't worry, Master Greenfire," said the First Fang. "You're a Sea Wolf now, you can challenge your old man and kill him. If you want. Your wyrd is your own, and the Day of Challenge is never more than a week away. But if you show respect you'll live longer. Because stronger men can challenge *you*."

My father looked downwards, as if summoning Twist to emphasis his hatred. I was no longer his responsibility, but his disappointment was clear, as if he expected a magical transformation after they pulled me out of the Bay of Grief. Either that, or he was angry I'd survived. Despite the Old Bitch of the Sea, I still found myself remembering Clatterfoot's dwelling at Moon Rock, and my father's indifference.

"Can I speak?" I asked, looking at Lord Ulric, rather than my father.

"Of course," replied the First Fang. "I'm sure great wisdom resides within that wyrd of yours. You're a descendant of Robert Greenfire."

"Yes, my lord. He was First Fang for thirty years."

My father snorted. He was proud of his name, but not of his youngest son. I was a Greenfire, whether he liked it or not, but I'd never be the strongest, the quickest, the biggest, or the most glorious. I may be the cleverest one day, but the stronger the Sea Wolf, the more they distrusted intelligence, and there was much strength at the table before me.

"Robert is the reason you can take the rite at seventeen," offered Vikon.

"And you're the youngest Sea Wolf since my boy here," said Ulric, nodding at his son. "With the strongest wyrd Tomas has seen for many a year."

The old spirit-master nodded, his papery skin wrinkling up. I thought he was looking at me but I couldn't be sure.

His eyes were lost amidst layers of grey, mottled flesh. "You saw thc Old Bitch of the Sea, didn't you, my boy?" he asked. "She spoke to you?"

"I did. That's what I wanted to say. It scared the shit out of me." I paused, looking at the floor. "Sorry for my language, my lords." I glanced behind, expecting a slap from Mefford. Luckily he still stood on the far side of the Bloody Halls, with Taymund. Instead, Twist reminded me to behave, causing further twitching.

Tomas Red Fang waved away my apology. The First Fang and his son both looked at their spirit-master, waiting for his words.

"You're strong, Master Greenfire," said the old man. "But don't be ignorant of how dangerous you could be. *We're* certainly not. Untrained wyrd is like a dormant volcano." He spoke as if he and I were alone in a room somewhere, conversing over a friendly meal. "But our totem is wiser than me, so your wyrd will remain your own." He ignored the ice-cold glare from my father and grinned, his face becoming a sack of loose skin, flowing over an expression of self-satisfaction.

"Let us not speak in haste," said my father. "He is ... erratic. In thought *and* deed. Perhaps we should reconsider allowing him a station ... until we can control him."

"And yet the Old Bitch of the Sea spoke to him. Have *you* ever addressed our totem, High Captain?" asked Tomas Red Fang. "I'll spare you the embarrassment of spluttering out a reply. You haven't."

My father would never attack an old man, but I saw his fist clench, as if he wanted to respond with his blade. If he killed the spirit-master, Lord Ulric would kill him. I saw him think about it, his face showing me a tapestry of internal debate. He just nodded, gritting his teeth. In the past, he'd have waited and taken his anger out on me.

"Tense," I said, more as an expression of my own feelings.

"Indeed," said Vikon Blood. "Perhaps we should merely welcome you to the hold, congratulate you on rising to be a Sea Wolf, assign you to a ship, warn you about getting a big head and ..." He waved his hand. "Send you on your way."

"Put him on a ship," said Lord Ulric. "The totem's presence is enough for me. We shouldn't ignore such an omen. Training or no, let us find out if he can be a Sea Wolf. Cold Man gets back in a few weeks."

My father groaned and I twitched. I didn't tell them what the Old Bitch of the Sea had said, and none of them asked. But the words stuck with me.

3

Two weeks later and I was living in a shitty house at the base of Brand's Tower. I'd been assigned to a ship, the *Dead Horse* under Captain Roderick Ice, called Cold Man, but it was still a week from making berth on Nibonay. They'd been raiding the Emerald Coast for six months, stealing gems and spice from Dark Brethren merchant ships. It was the right of the Sea Wolves to live as pirates, taking wealth and resources from those not strong enough to protect them. Every First Fang since Duncan Red Claw had declared it, and the great hold of the Sea Wolves lived by it. As would I when I left dry land and took my first voyage. I was fucking terrified.

From my window, on the second floor of the building, amidst old Eastron and drunkards, I could see half the hold and more Pure Ones than I'd ever seen. Those of the Nissalite were, on the whole, friendly and eager to please. Most had adopted Eastron fashions and turns of phrase, wearing leather and evoking the Bright Lands when they cursed. Only their light-brown skin and angular eyes gave away their heritage. I'd even heard that the city of Nissa was built in sincere imitation of the Severed Hand. They appeared to be more sensible than other Pure Ones, realizing that only good things came from allying with the Invaders and only bad things came from fighting us.

As I thought of the Impurity Wars, when the Always King brought the Pure Ones to heel, I glanced towards Duellist's Yard. There were no Pure Ones there, just duellists, warriors and fighters. Every day men and women sparred, sometimes friendly, sometimes not, but only ever to first blood. Until the Day of Challenge, when people died. Each week, on Saturday, challenges were heard and answered. Bodies were cleaved and people died over imagined slights and dubious matters of honour. Rys Coldfire, the Wolf's Bastard, oversaw the challenges, making sure every duel was fought with honour. After two weeks of waiting, a week before the *Dead Horse* arrived, I heard my own name bellowed on the Day of Challenge.

"Duncan Greenfire," boomed Maron Grief, from beneath my window. "I name you weakling. Answer me!"

I was away from the window, drawing a picture of the Wolf House in charcoal. It was coming along nicely, but hearing my name caused a pained twitch to ruin the top half of my paper. "Bastard!" I muttered.

"Sharp Tongue, do you hear me?"

I'd seen him glare at me. Since my rite of passage, he found himself wandering past my window with alarming regularity. I met each glare with one of my own, feeling more and more anxious each time we locked eyes.

I craned my neck out of the window. Below, the duellist was dressed in his leather and steel waistcoat, holding a heavy falchion and gritting his teeth. Alongside him, a small gang of hangers-on were showing confident smirks.

"Answer me!" demanded Maron.

"The little boy's scared," joked another young duellist.

"Nah, he's shit in his breaches," offered a third.

They all laughed at me. "Need time to wipe your arse?" asked Maron.

"His mum does that for him." I couldn't even identify the speaker, just that the voice came from a gang of laughing young men. It didn't really matter who'd said it. They were functioning with a kind of hive mentality. There was the blond grinning one, the rat-faced one with a sadistic smirk, the fat one, holding his chest and laughing loudly. Their faces and laughter melded together into a collage of torment, from which I had no escape.

A tear formed in my left eye, made worse by involuntary twitching. This wasn't the Pup Yards of Moon Rock, where I had safe places to run and hide. This was the Severed Hand, and I agreed with Maron's friend. I *was* a little boy, and I *was* scared. Twist certainly thought so, and enveloped my left side with sudden pain, causing me to buckle and fall away from the window. A renewed onslaught of laughter struck me from below, even as I grabbed the thorn clinch, with tears and sweat streaming down my face. They hated me, and in that moment, I hated myself. I was an embarrassment, with no idea how to be a Sea Wolf.

"Fuck me, did he die already?" cackled the rat-faced one.

"I'll get you down here if I have to drag you," snapped Maron, his voice cracking with barely-contained laughter.

Suddenly, the laughter stopped. It was there one instant and gone the next. I heard boots, moving across stone, as if the mob was parting for someone to approach – someone who didn't appreciate laughter.

"Duncan Greenfire," said a gravelly voice, with no hint of humour.

I was beneath the windowsill and couldn't see who spoke, though the man was certainly older than Maron and his cohorts. I extended my leg through gritted teeth, using the wall to lever myself upright. Through the open window I saw Rys Coldfire, called the Wolf's Bastard. The senior duellist was approaching fifty, but still the most feared swordsman at the Severed Hand. I didn't admire him, like I did Lord Vikon, I was just terrified of him.

"Come down, boy," he said. "There will be no more taunts."

I turned away from the window, hiding from the dozens of eyes below. My face was wet from tears, and my fingertips felt clammy. What did I have to do to be a Sea Wolf? Was being tied to a post in the Bay of Grief not enough?

I stayed away from the window, looking at a hardened leather waistcoat and matching greaves. I'd been given them by Mefford, but had not yet worn them, fearing I would look foolish. I had lightweight armour, but no blade. I could use one. That is to say I had a very basic training, but had rarely practised.

My fear slowly turned to anger. I took a deep breath, wiped the tears away, and laced up my armour. Two floors of rickety wood and I emerged onto the street. A space had been cleared below the stained steps of my building, and a loaded silence greeted me.

"This is Duellist's Yard, not a fucking tavern," said the Wolf's Bastard, being the only man to speak. "Duncan's name has been called on the Day of Challenge. He will have a chance to answer."

Two dozen men and women looked at me. Other duels had paused, so that each and every Eastron could hear my answer. Ritual dictated that I either answer and fight, or turn away and be branded a coward. And never be acknowledged as a Sea Wolf. The silent stares were just as bad as the jeering.

Maron Grief had backed away, swinging his falchion in an open section of the Yard. His eyes were fixed on me and his arms began to glow with wyrd. Each swing of his blade was followed by a blue distortion in the air as he summoned his full strength. I gulped, seeing no way I could beat him. Then the tears and the twitching came again. Some of the onlookers sniggered, others sneered and shook their heads. But, worst of all, I saw pity. I felt like a sickly or deformed animal, being put down for his own good.

"I will answer," I murmured.

"Speak up, lad," replied the Wolf's Bastard.

"I will answer," I said, louder, but still choked out through tears.

I was waved forwards, through an emerging gap in the crowd, to stand opposite Maron. My hands were shaking, and the left side of my body was numb. It felt as if Twist was cackling with sadistic laughter, enjoying every morsel of my discomfort. Perhaps the spirit saw death as the ultimate expression of my pain. Or maybe it wanted me dead before I turned eighteen, and would be rid of it.

"Give him a blade," said Maron.

A young boy ran forwards, cradling two swords. One was a heavy falchion, single-edged and more like a sharp club than a sword. The other was a cutlass, lighter, with a slender blade and a basket-hilt. I just looked at them. What was I supposed to do? Defeat a trained duellist, twice my size and ten times my skill? No, I was supposed to die. I was weak and had no place amongst the Sea Wolves.

As I looked at the two swords, my tears began to dry. No blade would help me kill Maron Grief. My wyrd was the only weapon I had, and I so wanted to silence the spiteful laughter, replaying in my head. I turned from the swords, gritting my teeth and glaring up at the bulky duellist.

"Don't think I won't kill you if you're unarmed," said Maron, lunging forwards. "You answered me, you little freak." His falchion swayed across his face as he advanced, before he tensed his shoulder and pushed his wyrd into a mighty blow, more than enough to crush my skull, rend my chest, or sever any limb the duellist desired.

Before the blow landed, I lashed out. My wyrd surged upwards, focusing on my hands, and flowing towards the duellist's head. It was dark blue, crackling like lightning and making every inch of my body tingle. I saw the glass around Maron's head and I grasped it, making him scream in sudden pain, and taking the momentum from his advance. His features and his screams became lost within a vortex of wyrd, as I pushed his head through the glass. His body began to vibrate, dropping his falchion and splaying his arms wide. I didn't allow the rest of him to follow, keeping his body in the realm of form, whilst forcing his head to the void. Blood erupted from his neck and shoulders, and I saw his decapitated head through the glass, falling to the floor and gliding away on a wave of void-stuff. In the real world, all the onlookers saw was his twitching, headless body fall to the floor of Duellist's Yard.

"He's dead!" I cried, letting my wyrd flow back into the recesses of my body. "He called my name on the Day of Challenge... we fought... and I killed him! I'm a Sea Wolf!" The words became a shriek, and the tears became a waterfall.

I'd beaten Maron Grief in a one-on-one duel. I'd not meant to tear his head from his body, but his falchion would have killed me if I'd not acted. If my wyrd had not acted. I'd been called a freak a million times, but this last time was different. Something about Maron's sneer had taken me back to a dark hovel in Moon Rock, and the grim face of my father as he watched his youngest son be tortured. Twist had played a part in Maron's death, but it was my responsibility and I gulped, realizing what I'd done.

"Clear the yard," demanded Rys Coldfire. "All challenges will be answered this evening. Duncan Greenfire, stay where you are."

I fell to the stone and cried, with everyone staring at me. There was no more pity, just surprise. A woman in tight chainmail glared at me, a young man with two cutlasses swore, and everyone whispered.

"Clear the yard," repeated the Wolf's Bastard. With narrow eyes and suspicious chatter, everyone melted to the outer ring of the yard, then dispersed.

Rys shook his head. "Come with me." He dragged me upright, put an arm around my shoulders and led me away from Maron's body, out of the yard and towards the Wolf House. He was a foot taller than me and I struggled to keep up with him, though his arm didn't move from my shoulders. If I'd fallen or stumbled, I imagined he'd just carry me, without missing a step.

We entered the Wolf House, having to slow as we joined the flocked citizens of the hold, heading to the auction houses. Rys led me away from the stairs and towards the isolated duellist chambers. When challenges were answered in the building, they were conducted in private. No onlookers were allowed on the bottom level. Rys flung me into an empty chamber and moved to a weapon rack on the opposite wall.

"Duncan Greenfire, I name you dangerous pup. Answer me!"

Everything was happening so quickly, and I struggled to spew forth a reply. "What?" I spluttered, looking at the blood on my hands.

"Answer me!" he repeated, putting aside his heavy falchion and retrieving a light cutlass.

I stared at him. The Wolf's Bastard was famous, even in Moon Rock. He'd killed hundreds of warriors. Sea Wolves, spirits, Dark Brethren, Pure Ones. His cloak was redder than any Sea Wolf. He had mottled skin and a streaked face. His hair, beard and bushy eyebrows were all muddy grey.

"Your wyrd is too strong to be taken lightly," he stated. "You were warned about this."

He lunged at me, his blade aimed at my chest. I desperately pushed my wyrd at him, moving back in a panic, but the power I'd conjured in Duellists' Yard was nowhere to be found. The lunge was a feint and I nearly over-balanced as my wyrd met no resistance. Before I could refocus, Rys punched me in the side of the head and I saw stars.

"Wake up, Master Greenfire." The voice was old, cracked and indistinct. My head throbbed, my eyes wouldn't open and my leg was numb.

The old man laughed. It was a throaty, knowing chuckle. It was Tomas Red Fang, senior spirit-master of the hold. I felt his wrinkled hand on my forehead. "You'll be okay. He didn't hurt you too badly. As with so many men who have seen death, Rys Coldfire thinks that a damn good hiding is the best lesson. Though he brought you straight to me, so as to not embarrass you publicly. Ripping someone's head off is enough of a spectacle for one day."

It all came back in a vivid flash. Maron was a bully and *would* have killed me, but I'd lost control and done something terrible. I squinted through sore eyes and saw a small, stone room, warmed by a low hearth. We were on the higher levels of the Wolf House, somewhere in the Bloody Halls. "I'm sorry," I whispered.

"You killed the only person you owed an apology," said the spirit-master. "Your first?"

I nodded, scratching at the dried blood on my hands. "It was an accident."

"No," he stated. "Untrained wyrd can have a mind of its own, but to call it an accident is to remove your responsibility. You'll be here for a few hours at least. I advise using it to meditate on your current situation. And, er, try not to violently assault anybody with your wyrd." He walked to the closed, wooden door.

"I can walk," I replied. "Why can't I leave?"

He clasped his hands inside his voluminous green robes and turned back to me, his face becoming a crinkled walnut of pinched disapproval. "Unfortunately, Master Greenfire, you have the rather bad luck to have been beaten up on a day when we have visitors to the Wolf House. Rather important visitors, and I don't want a dangerous young man flailing his way through the Bloody Halls. If it weren't for the Old Bitch of the Sea, you might find yourself locked in here permanently. Please remain until I return. A few hours. No more."

"What visitors?"

He clearly didn't like my manner. "Do you have some authority I should be aware of? No? In which case, please just do as I say." The old man left the room and closed the door behind him.

I lay back down and the tears returned. I wanted to feel guilt for what I'd done, but Twist chided me. Confusion and fear assaulted my mind, with no single thought staying still enough for me to grasp it. I'd torn his head off, and I didn't know how. Was I really so dangerous?

As the thoughts slowed, I began breathing deeply, allowing time to pass. Tomas Red Fang had placed an oil burner next to the bed and a soothing wisp of smoke caressed my nostrils, dampening even the pain in my leg. I fell into a numb, half-asleep repose, taking the time to appreciate that I was still alive. More than that, I'd proved something to everyone who'd seen the duel. I'd proved that I wasn't weak or a coward. I dozed for several hours, letting my revulsion fade, until Twist allowed me a tentative smile. I couldn't swing a sword, but the most powerful duellists might now think twice before calling my name on the Day of Challenge.

I jumped in surprise, as a shadow glided across the room. I was barely awake, and my eyes had wandered to the far wall. I may have been seeing things, but the shadow appeared and disappeared from one stone wall to the other, flickering, as if it walked through a strong wind. The thorn clinch pulsed at the apparition, forcing me to sit up. It felt as if Twist was screaming something at me, but all I could do was grit my teeth and clamp hands to my thigh.

"Okay, okay," I muttered, pulling myself to my feet, and taking a last deep breath of the oil burner.

I moved to the wall, and touched the spot where the shadow had disappeared. I thought that someone was moving on the other side of the glass, but didn't know how I could see him. Beyond that, I could sense focused malice. My wyrd was warning me of something, and it made Twist hurt me.

I didn't really think before opening the door and entering the corridor. I was sore all over, with bits and pieces of me chafing and throbbing in dull pain. Every little movement made my limbs feel heavy and my head swim, like I'd broken the glass and was moving through the thick air of the void.

My room was one of many, either side of a curved walkway, carpeted in deep red, with brass frames on each door. Firelight cast a sparkle across dozens of stone-etched faces. The walls were decorated, from floor to arched ceiling, with screaming mouths and staring eyes, each face cut in intricate designs into the grey stone. I'd never seen it, but the Bloody Halls supposedly contained one face for each Pure One killed by Sea Wolves during the Impurity Wars, when we first invaded Nibonay. Many thousands of stone faces looked inwards at the people who invaded their lands and killed their kind. It was strange to decorate the halls in such a fashion, as if Duncan Red Claw wanted his people to remember what he'd done.

Amongst the screaming faces were horrific images of Sunken Men. No artist knew what they looked like, so the faces were just deformed Eastron, half-drowning, with seaweed tied into their hair. All that was commonly known about them was that they'd defeated an armada of Sea Wolves in the Battle of the Depths, but their imagined faces provided a grotesque centre-point to the decoration of the Bloody Halls.

I followed an insistent pull, down the corridors of the Bloody Halls, along an invisible path left by the flickering shadow. I was well above the auction houses, perhaps only a few twists and turns from Lord Ulric's hall. I felt no excitement as I moved along the corridor, just a sense that something was imminent.

The hall ended at a T-junction. To the left, an archway led to a wide balcony, with the bruised afternoon light casting a circle on the red carpet. On the right was a wider corridor under a vaulted ceiling. It was also the direction from which I heard voices. I hugged the wall and moved towards the sounds. As the corridor opened out and the doors disappeared, I recognized the evenly spaced pillars of black and red that encircled the hall of the First Fang.

Then I saw the shadow again, darting across my peripheral vision. It was just a black shape, moving from a distant corridor as a wisp of smoke. The voices from the hall were now louder, and I spluttered, trying to keep my alarm under control. I moved along the wall, under a high ceiling and intricate wooden vaulting, until I turned to see the edge of the great hall. The pillars blocked most of my view, but I could see the edges of Lord Ulric's table and several Sea Wolves sitting around it. The shadow was gone, and my wyrd gave me no direction to look. I waited, silently spying on the huge hall.

The First Fang himself was on a raised chair – defiantly not called a throne, despite its appearance. He was joined by his spirit-master, who'd told me to stay out of the way, and the twin duellists, Arthur and Adeline Brand. His son, Vikon, paced in front of the elders. Others stood either side of the table, but their faces were blocked from me. The assembled Sea Wolves were chatting, but an edge of anticipation cut through their speech, as if they talked to distract themselves from something.

"Maron will be missed," said Adeline Brand.

"But *Duncan*'s still alive," replied Tomas Red Fang. "So our totem is happy."

She glared at him. "I'd take Maron Grief over ten Duncan Greenfires. Our totem's happiness doesn't move me as it does you."

It occurred to me that eavesdropping is an easy way to hear something you don't like. But I carried on listening, trying to scan the hall for signs of the malevolent shadow.

"The Old Bitch of the Sea speaks only when you listen," said Tomas. "Do you not believe in anything, Mistress Brand?"

She shook her head. "I do not. No gods, spirits or men, hold dominion over me."

"And your First Fang?" interrupted Vikon Blood. "Surely my father holds some dominion over you?"

"I respect him," replied Adeline, "but my wyrd is my own, not his. If he insulted me he'd need to answer for it."

"Shush now," said Ulric, ignoring the duellist's threat. "Our guests are arriving."

I had crept to within ten feet of the high table, crouched in a doorway. No-one was looking in my direction, as the air in the great hall began to twist into a distorted vortex of flowing blue. Figures appeared in a line, approaching through the void. Not the black shape from the corridor, these Eastron arrived from far away, using a void pathway to travel a huge distance in hours rather than weeks. Five figures slowly appeared through the glass, stepping from the void onto the blood-red carpet. I saw Winterlords and a Pure One.

Gold and silver armour, ornate broadswords and flowing cloaks. Two of them wore high-plumed helmets, smelted into the likeness of a bird of prey, with wings sweeping forwards. The smallest, a woman of at least fifty, was clad in tarnished silver chainmail, gathered at the waist and crested with the grasping talons of Dawn Claw, the house of the Always King.

"My lord Ulric, the Severed Hand greets us as warmly as ever," intoned one of the helmeted men, spreading his arms and bowing. "Your fires burn high and bright. Much warmer than First Port. We suffer more during the winter months."

The speaker removed his helmet. He was a huge, clean-cut man with olive skin and thin lips. His armour was bulky, making him appear even larger, and was much heavier than anything a Sea Wolf would wear.

"How flows your wyrd, Prince Oliver?" replied Lord Ulric, in a formal greeting. "I expected your father. He is well?"

"He is," said the Winterlord. "But he does not know I am here. The Always King is no longer healthy enough to travel. As his son I work to secure his legacy. Hence I am here, seeking assurances from an old friend of my family."

The others with him, including the Pure One – a darker-skinned man with thin, canvas clothing – moved forwards and flanked Oliver Dawn Claw. I'd never seen Winterlords and they were larger than I expected. None of them reached the height of Lord Ulric, but each was muscular and fair-haired, with an air of nobility.

"We'll get to that," replied Ulric, raising an eyebrow at the prince. "For now..." he gestured to seats, arranged before the high table. "Sit down."

The visitors waited for Oliver Dawn Claw and then sat in order of seniority. The woman was second, followed by the other man in a crested helmet. The remaining Winterlord, a man close to my own age but hugely built, sat before the Pure One, who bowed to the elders and sat last.

"The Always King is dying," said the prince, locking eyes with Lord Ulric. "His death will lead to a civil war. The Silver Parliament is not what it was. The Dark Brethren have control. The three Cyclone brothers. Santago sits at the Open Hand, Marius at the Dark Harbour, and Trego at the Silver Parliament. It is only my father who keeps them in line."

I'd always been told that the Sea Wolves were apart from the bureaucracy, letting the Winterlords and the Dark Brethren have their Parliament and play at their petty games of move and counter-move. My father called it a bizarre dance, far beneath our concern.

"You want what?" asked Ulric. "A declaration of support? I don't know you, boy. It was your father, Christophe, the Shining Sword, I called friend, not you. The Sea Wolves don't follow easily. You and the Dark Brethren can keep your Parliament. We live and die by our own code."

"This concerns all Eastron, Lord Ulric," said the woman, in a husky purr. "Perhaps you should recognize the authority of the Always King and offer us all possible hospitality and assistance."

"May I present my aunt, Lady Natasha Dawn Claw," said Prince Oliver.

Ulric and the other Sea Wolves exchanged glances. I could tell that the Brand twins were not impressed by the visitors, nor were the assembled duellists. Vikon Blood was smiling, nodding at his father in amusement. I thought that the stiff formality of the Winterlords was causing much humour amongst the Sea Wolves.

"If I may interject," said Tomas Red Fang, his wrinkled face pinching into an expression of annoyance. "I do not see what you intend to gain from speaking to us, Prince Oliver. We will, as I'm sure you appreciate, go as our wyrd flows."

"And a Parliament controlled by the Brethren?" snapped Natasha Dawn Claw. "How will your wyrd flow then? How many years of plunder ... how many years of theft and piracy, Lord Ulric? They have much to pay you back for." Her voice was no longer husky. It cracked into a virtual shriek, showing emotion and anger.

"Impressive," said Adeline Brand, drily. "The passion with which you speak. I respect it. But your pretty face can be eaten by Sunken Men before I pledge to a man I've just met."

The youngest Winterlord stood, his hand going to the hilt of his broadsword. He was clean-shaven, with a floppy fringe of blond hair and light blue eyes. His expression was one of indignation, as if he'd taken Adeline's words personally. "Insult my prince again," he prompted, raising his chin.

Ulric and Vikon smiled, though Tomas shook his head. Before anyone could voice a word of calm, Adeline had risen from her seat and drawn her slim cutlass. "You want to test me, boy? It's the Day of Challenge and we've already had one death."

"Sit down, David," said Prince Oliver. "We are not here to answer challenges, we are here in friendship."

As his words finished, I saw a slight distortion in the air to my left. I was engrossed in the discourse and barely registered the movement, until a crackle reached my ears and I saw the shadow break the glass. The black shape moved in and out of darkness, lunging across the great hall as it left the void. It was a man, cloaked in black, wielding a thin-bladed knife of dull, grey metal. I gasped and stood, ignoring stealth as the figure became clear. The elders of the Severed Hand were arguing, Prince Oliver was attempting to calm the situation, and the other Winterlords were seemingly oblivious to the dark shape. Only the Pure One, his slanted eyes narrow and aware, appeared to register the figure. He stood, but was distracted by my sudden emergence.

The blade was directed at Prince Oliver and appeared silently before he could react. The others saw *me*, but not the assassin, rising from their seats and shouting that I shouldn't be there. I ignored them and dove across the red carpet, past the prince, to tackle the figure.

"Assassin!" shouted Natasha Dawn Claw.

"Duncan!" shouted Arthur Brand.

I pushed the man to the ground and directed my wyrd at his knife. It skittered away from the prince, striking the stone wall, but he was bigger than me and grabbed at my throat. We locked eyes, his face appearing from under his black cowl. He was young, perhaps twenty years, but had a harshness in his sapphire eyes. He struggled, with surprise the only thing that stopped him from gaining the upper hand. Then golden armour appeared above me and the feel of gauntleted hands intruded upon the fight. The assassin was pulled away, to be held in a rough choke-hold by the young Winterlord. I was dragged upwards by steel-clad arms, and saw people engulf the scene with shouted words and swaying steel.

"By the Bright Lands!" exclaimed Vikon Blood.

"This is an outrage," roared Natasha Dawn Claw.

"Shall I kill him, my prince?" asked the young Winterlord, holding the assassin in a rough, steely bear-hug.

"He's Dark Brethren," stated Vikon, rushing to shove aside the older duellist who held me. "Leave him, he's a Sea Wolf."

"Master Greenfire, what in the deepest void are you doing?" snapped Tomas Red Fang.

Vikon straightened my cloak and I breathed in and out a few times, clearing my head. Everyone stood, everyone held weapons. Broad-bladed longswords amongst the Winterlords and smaller cutlasses and falchions held by the Sea Wolves. Only the visiting Pure One and Tomas Red Fang were unarmed. The elderly spirit-master approached slowly with Lord Ulric, inspecting the captive Dark Brethren. He was darker-skinned than a Sea Wolf and his hair was jet-black.

"Sorry I left the room," I said, affecting my best impression of a scolded puppy. "I saw him sneaking around the halls and thought he was up to no good."

Everyone looked at me. Oliver Dawn Claw approached, his broadsword, with its ornate pommel of an eagle, held at the ready. He was enormous. Twice as wide as me, with blond hair parted across frowning green eyes. I suddenly wanted to disappear into a cloak of embarrassment. "You saved my life, Sea Wolf. What is your name?"

"Duncan," I replied in a whisper. "Greenfire."

The cruelty of the Invaders is dependent upon their heritage.

All are powerful, but not all should inspire the same fear.

We saw the Sea Wolves' violence and greed, but we also saw their heart.

We saw the Winterlords' arrogance and short fuse, but we also saw their nobility.

We saw the Kneeling Wolves' submission and cowardice, but we also saw their wisdom.

We saw the Dark Brethren's cunning and treachery, but we also saw their kindness.

Each Invader can be your friend as easily as your enemy.

From "They are called Eastron"
by Snake Charmer, spirit child of the Rykalite

PART TWO

Adeline Brand on the island of Nibonay

4

I'd stayed in my seat. Duncan Greenfire had stopped a Brethren assassin killing the prince, and everyone had jumped to their feet. It was very exciting, but there was little I could contribute. The incident had stopped me following through with my challenge to the young Winterlord, and I decided to let everyone else deal with the aftermath, while I let my anger dissipate.

Arthur, my brother, took the assassin out of the hall, followed by one of the Winterlords, while everyone else argued. Master Greenfire, the dangerous little bastard, was gathered up by Tomas Red Fang and taken away. And the arguing continued. It took an hour of back and forth before anyone returned to join me at the table, and by then the prince had accepted that, despite the attempt on his life, he was not going to get an oath of loyalty from Lord Ulric.

"We'll find out who he is," offered Vikon Blood, trying to placate Lady Natasha Dawn Claw, by far the most agitated of the visitors. "But you should leave. It may not be safe."

"Leave?" snapped the old woman.

"Please," said Prince Oliver. "This changes everything. The Brethren have made their move."

I leant back and put my leather boots up on the table, slowly crossing my legs and smiling at the Winterlords. "Just leave," I said. "When my brother finds out who sent the assassin, we'll tell you. But your presence has no benefit to us, and we will not submit to you."

More arguing ensued. I was largely responsible, but chose not to contribute further. Ulric had called the Always King his brother, but had no reason to follow the prince. We both hated the Dark Brethren, but that was a soft reason to form an alliance. The Parliament *may* change and it *may* affect us, but we'd thrive or we wouldn't. It was not always wise to plan ahead. And no assassin had tried to kill a Sea Wolf.

It was eventually decided that the young Winterlord duellist, called David Falcon's Fang, and his Pure One squire, would remain at the Severed Hand, and represent the prince. Consensus could not be reached on the identity of the assassin, as he wore no heraldry, but Prince Oliver was sure that he'd been sent from the Open Hand, tasked by one of the three Cyclone brothers. His petty, conspiratorial babble barely penetrated my ears, though Lord Ulric and Tomas Red Fang paid close attention, and appeared sincere in their desire to resolve the situation. But I had other things to do, and I didn't give a shit about the Winterlords.

The Wood of Scars was colder than usual, though I was glad to be out of the Wolf House and away from the Winterlords. I felt a sharp breeze, lancing through the trees and flowing over my face. We were on the hunt, tracking Mirralite Pure Ones from the Severed Hand to a lattice of dried river beds, ringing a forest clearing. I thought ten, maybe fifteen men.

"Why don't they learn?" asked Jaxon Ice, the duellist at my side. "Haven't we killed enough of them?"

"They have no wyrd," I replied. "And one hundred and sixty-seven years ago we invaded their island."

The Mirralite would never bend knee to the First Fang. We'd shown them time and time again what we did to rebels, but they appeared determined to die. When I was small, I remember my father whispering tales of the Second Battle of Tranquillity, when the Mirralite rose in open rebellion and were crushed by Lord Ulric and King Christophe Dawn Claw, the Shining Sword. The two Eastron lords declared their friendship on that day and decreed Nibonay to be at peace. The island was ours by the eternal right of conquest and we were nice enough to allow the Pure Ones to remain. My whole life I'd seen the gratitude of the Nissalite and the scorn of the Mirralite. When I took the rite and became a duellist, I gained the power to do something about it. For eleven years I'd swung the blade of the Severed Hand as a Sea Wolf, defending it against Pure Ones, Dark Brethren and all manner of void beasts. Arthur and I had served together on a dozen ships, and our cloaks were red indeed. In blood *and* glory.

"They don't know we're here," I said. "They'd have carried on running. Break the glass and we'll give 'em a surprise. Are we close enough to the hold?"

Jaxon looked up at the sky, then back towards the Severed Hand, assessing whether or not the void would be friendly. "Should be okay," he replied. "Spirit-masters keep this area clear of dangerous spirits. North of here is where things get nasty."

"Okay, break the glass," I confirmed.

I closed my eyes and pushed my mind forwards, flowing effortlessly into the void. Jaxon was already there, several seconds before me, proving once again why we called him the Wisp. He had a knack for moving in and out of the void, and beyond the glass he could travel faster than any other duellist.

Our wyrd was the same, shining in our hearts and arms, but I had a subtle skin of glowing light that covered me from head to toe, setting me apart. Arthur possessed the same light and claimed it was a hereditary gift of our family. We were born one year apart, on the same day, at the same hour. Though everyone thought of us as twins, he was the younger by exactly a year.

"Once more for the Severed Hand," I muttered, drawing my cutlass and moving towards the clearing. The trees were now a shimmering blue and the grass fell away into endless puddles of green, so vibrant they caused me to squint. Jaxon was nice enough to not skip ahead and show me how easily he found void travel.

"Addie, it's quiet tonight," said the Wisp. "The woods are usually more alive than this."

"I haven't been out here for a few weeks," I replied. "Seems colder."

"It is ... it is colder. And not a single spirit."

The Wood of Scars was a dangerous place to break the glass. The Mirralite, in their ignorance, worshipped dozens of nature deities of various kinds, each given a semblance of form in the void. They were hollow compared to our own totem, but nasty when directed by Mirralite shamans, known as varn. But there were none on this night. Varn *or* spirits. It was just quiet and cold.

"Bad omens," I said. "My father said that only a fool ignores bad omens."

"Your father is the Battle Brand, we would be foolish to not heed his advice." Jaxon was smiling at me, affecting an expression of deference.

"And your father is some man of Ice? One of the rebellious ones or one of the dead ones?"

The People of Ice were confined on the island of Nowhere, and few of them sought a home at the Severed Hand. They were acknowledged as Sea Wolves, but had risen in rebellion once too often to be trusted. Jaxon Ice was one of the few to gain station as a duellist.

He laughed, punching me on the shoulder and gliding away, across the treacherous tide of the void.

"What, no advice from old man Ice?" I called after him, before hurrying towards the clearing. The Wisp and I were duellists, equal in all things. Insults and banter would only ever cause shallow cuts. Duellists did not challenge each other, not since Lord Ulric's father, the Bloody Fang, became elder of the Severed Hand.

"Hurry up," joked the Wisp. "There are ten Pure Ones to kill. If you're nice, I'll let you have five of them."

Through the ghostly trees, I could see where a dozen dried river beds met in a shallow depression. A crackling distortion in the void indicated that the Mirralite had lit a fire. The Pure Ones themselves were huddled together, appearing beyond the glass as nothing more than grey husks, devoid of wyrd or any significant power. They were still of the race of men, but different, somehow lesser. Perhaps the Eastron from across the sea would be the same if they'd never harnessed their wyrd.

Jaxon moved to the other side and we flanked them, before taking deep breaths and returning to the realm of form. In a flash of light and wyrd, we struck from the void. Two Pure Ones were driven, as split sides of meat, into the earth. Two more had died before the rest could stand. I whipped my strength into a single point at the tip of my blade and severed a man's head in a blur of movement. Jaxon danced between two Mirralite, slicing one across the gut and throwing the other to the ground.

"Run if you wish," I said calmly, as the remaining Pure Ones ran. "We can run faster."

They were all large men, clad in thin canvas clothing, baggy and adorned with colourful embroidery. Their nature spirits liked bright colours and knotted designs, but not good steel or effective armour. Killing them was like filleting fish.

A single Pure One stood his ground, gritting sharpened teeth at me. He had seaweed woven into his hair, and he licked his lips. I approached, and was about to kill him, when he spoke. "Use your glass while you can, Invader," he growled, with strangely sincere confidence. "I hear the sea, and the Sea Wolves will be deafened by its roar. The glass will break upon the Severed Hand, and in will flood waves of chaos. This I swear on the Lodge of the Rock."

He drew a curved blade and slit his own throat... and he did it slowly, snarling at me the whole time. I'd hunted a thousand Mirralite, and killed a thousand more, but I'd never seen one kill himself. And I'd never seen madness like I saw in his eyes. He meant it, and he believed it, and he'd made sure I heard it before he died. The glass will break upon the Severed Hand – an ominous prophecy, to be sure, but spoken by a worthless prophet.

*

I had a famous name, but I never thought of it as a curse. From my first memories I had been a Brand. My grandfather was *the* Brand. I grew up watching the awe in my father's eyes whenever the Battle Brand spoke or acted. When grandfather died and my parents left for Last Port, my brother and I were made wards of the Severed Hand, to take the rite when we came of age. We were twelve when he left, and I've only seen my father four times in the past fifteen years. The Battle Brand didn't leave Last Port, though Arthur and I were duellists, and didn't need a father.

"What do you think he meant?" asked the Wisp. "About the glass."

We had dealt with the remaining Mirralite and were jogging back to the Severed Hand.

I shrugged. "Pure Ones spout all sorts of meaningless rubbish. If we listened to every one of their doom-laden prophecies, we'd never leave the hold. The Wolf's Bastard keeps track of them. He's got a ledger with all sorts of apocalyptic horse-shit."

"The Invaders came from across the sea," mused the Wisp. "We claimed their rock, their fire, their tree."

I snorted in amusement. "Don't sing that, it bothers me." Even the Nissalite sung the refrain from time to time. Jonas Grief, the master-at-arms, was not above executing Pure Ones cheeky enough to sing it around the Wolf House.

"What did you say about ignoring bad omens?" asked Jaxon.

"The Battle Brand, not me."

"Still, only fools ignore such things."

"Didn't say I was ignoring it," I replied. "I just said the Mirralite are full of portentous crap."

The Wisp was usually right. He had a knack for cutting through the dressing of things and locating the heart. This trait was not liked by my brother, who had taken to bullying Jaxon from a young age. The Wisp usually just smiled, content in the knowledge that his skill in the void was unquestioned. This often made Arthur even more angry and required me to lend a restraining hand. I'd lost count of the bruises Jaxon would have got without me. It made us close friends. The Wisp was far from helpless, but Arthur was the toughest duellist of his generation. Except for his sister.

The trees thinned and the first glimpses of stone appeared across the skyline. The hold of the Severed Hand was a sprawling block of grey and black, dominating the coast for a hundred miles or more. Thick walls connected six huge towers, forming the original western battlements of the hold, and further east, the newer buildings were built from the edge of the Wood of Scars to the Bright Coast.

We approached Ragnar's Tower and the Gate of Scars, leaving the dense forest and feeling the chill winds rolling from the Outer Sea. The land was shimmering and indistinct, sending waves of ghostly mirages across the horizon, each one as real as a painting and as fleeting as a gust of wind. I saw a hundred battles and a thousand people every time I looked at that magical horizon. They were friends, enemies and, most importantly, memories. Each time I looked I wanted to see a mirage I'd seen before, perhaps one from my childhood when a great sea-serpent appeared to devour a boat, or an army of ghostly warriors assaulting an unseen enemy in the distance. Or a more recent memory, of deep green eyes and soft skin.

The glass was thin on Nibonay and allowed visions to leak from the void. Nothing solid or permanent, just flashes of unreality intruding upon the Severed Hand and its Sea Wolves. Two great void battles had taken place here. The two Battles of Tranquillity. Duncan Red Claw had massacred an army of rebels a hundred and fifty years ago, and Ulric Blood had done the same with King Christophe, when I was barely three years old. Each time, the Sea Wolves had attacked en-masse from the void, annihilating the Pure One spirits and fracturing the glass. Since then, powerful nature spirits had reclaimed the void of Nibonay, making it near suicide to break the glass beyond sight of the Severed Hand.

"Look yonder," said the Wisp, pointing to a plume of smoke, seeping above the cliffs. "More ships aflame."

The smoke was distant from the hold and looked like it came from fishing boats or a small jetty. Either way, the Mirralite were stepping up their campaign of sabotage. The last month had seen two dozen such attacks. The Pure Ones skulked to the edge of the woods and flung casks of oil and flaming torches at anything wooden. They were too afraid to mount any serious assaults, but killing them did nothing to stop our boats from burning. They'd stayed clear of Laughing Rock, and any large ships. To the north, the tall masts of the *Dead Horse* were just disappearing over the horizon.

"Why do they bother?" I mused. "They never fire any ships of note or kill anyone. It's barely more than a game."

"Maybe it's the only victory they can get. Either that, or they just fucking hate us."

"Most of them," I replied. "Can you report on your own? I have an errand to run."

He looked at me, a knowing twitch travelling across his narrow eyes. He knew where I was going, perhaps the only duellist who did, but he didn't question me.

"Fine," said the Wisp. "I'll see you tonight. Rys will expect you."

"I'll be there ... and thank you." It was nice to have a friend like Jaxon. A simple kind of luxury, but one I'd bled for.

"Don't thank me, just be careful. And ask the Old Bitch of the Sea to keep your brother from finding out."

I shoved him and clenched my fists. "You should hope he doesn't, for *I* won't tell him."

Jaxon took two large strides backwards and lowered his head in submission. "Addie, you're the only duellist who ever stuck up for me, I'd have to be a cold-hearted bastard to betray you." He looked at me and smiled. "But I think you're an idiot."

"I *am* an idiot ... but I'm a self-aware idiot."

Swordfish Bay stunk of fish. It always stunk of fish. The night boats made it stink in the morning, the day boats made it stink in the evening, and the platforms filled with fish in baskets made it stink throughout the day. I cursed the totem that I was born without a taste for fish. Something about the smell. I could never forget it, even when trying to eat the flesh itself. My brother used to wave salt cod under my nose whenever he felt like a fight. It was the one thing guaranteed to raise my anger. I fought him and I won, I always won.

The only man to ever best me was Rys Coldfire, and he didn't need fish to start the fight. It was enough to call me on the Day of Challenge when I was twenty-one. The next day, when my broken arm and wounded pride were healing, Arthur decided to wave more salt cod in my face and mock me for being thrashed. I kicked him in the balls and shouted that I fucking hated fish.

The smell remained as I turned into the narrow street, south of the Pup Yards. I kept my head low and my sword well-hidden beneath my cloak. Fisherman and Nissalite lived here, but anyone who had been near the Wolf House might know my face. Adeline Brand, duellist of the Severed Hand, would not be seen in such a dark, narrow part of the hold. They'd look at me with wide eyes and ask why I was there. I didn't want to answer them, so I kept my face hidden. It was a risky journey and one I'd resisted for over a week, but something about killing the Pure Ones had driven me to the dark corner of the Severed Hand.

I turned sideways, to squeeze between grey brick buildings, and made my way to the small black door, barely visible next to a secluded fisherman's yard. The door was smooth against the wall and had no handle. I knocked and waited, my hand balling into a fist.

Two bolts were withdrawn from within and the door opened outwards. Just a crack, but enough for a slim, pale face to poke out and inspect me. I grabbed the wood and pulled the door fully open, surprising the man. I held my right fist back, threatening a punch, but giving the man a chance to submit.

"Please, please, I don't want to fight," said the Pure One, a young man, not yet in his twenties.

"Where is he?" I asked.

He looked at me, fearful recognition flowing over his delicate features. "He's not here, noble duellist."

I punched him in the jaw and kicked him back inside the building. I stepped out of the alleyway and closed the door behind me. Within, the building was sparse. It was a shack, with wooden furniture and stairs, leading up and down.

"You're a poor liar," I said. "You know who I am, don't lie to me again. Where is he?"

"Addie," said a voice from the stairs. "Please don't hurt Sky, he's my cousin. He's not been here long, it would be a shame for his experience of the Invaders to start with pain."

He'd come from downstairs and approached silently. He was almost as tall as me and his canvas clothing was loose over his thin limbs, but he moved like a stalking animal. His face was angular and his eyes a deep green. His name was Young Green Eyes, though he was in his early thirties.

The young Pure One, Sky, had started crying on the floor. His face was red and a trickle of blood coated his lips. Now inside, I reassessed his age. He was maybe fifteen. I offered him my hand. "Apologies, boy," I said. "I don't like being lied to."

He wouldn't take my hand, preferring to stay on his arse and scuttle backwards, hiding behind Young Green Eyes. The older man helped him up and ushered him downstairs. When we were alone, I approached, keeping my fists clenched.

"I killed a Mirralite today. He told me to use the glass while I could. What did he mean? What are the varn up to?"

The Pure One didn't back away. He kept his eyes locked on my face. The depths of green plunged into bottomless pits, so vibrant I couldn't look away. Not that I wanted to. The curve of his jaw, the paleness of his skin. He was beautiful *without* his eyes, but with them... I felt a vulnerability I couldn't control. I shoved him backwards. "Answer me!"

He smiled, his face becoming boyish and gentle. "Is it the Day of Challenge?"

"No," I spluttered. "I meant..."

"I know what you meant." He looked me up and down, but wasn't afraid. I hated him for it. "Strange that I didn't run when you knocked on the door. I could have done, I knew it was a duellist."

"Why didn't you?" I asked, forgetting my previous question. "I could kill you and every Pure One in this building. And do you know what would happen to me? Absolutely nothing."

"So kill me," he replied. As if giving me a reason, he raised his chin and stated, "I do not recognize your authority. You are Invaders, unworthy of the Lodge of the Rock. And I am unbound by the Shackles of the Wolf."

We were close now, within touching distance. Young Green Eyes looked like any other Pure One, bronze-skinned and lithe, but he was Mirralite. He belonged to the clan that had never pledged to the First Fang. He was no spy, just a man who didn't believe that fighting the Sea Wolves accomplished anything. To any other Eastron he was Nissalite and compliant.

"I don't want to hurt you," I said, meeting his gaze.

"Try," he replied. "I am not afraid of you."

I grabbed him, balling my hands around his thin tunic and shoving him across a table. He wrapped his arms around my neck and squeezed, minimizing my strength advantage. The table broke as we wrestled back and forth, each grunting as we tried to free our arms. He called me an Invader bitch, I called him a fucking rebel. I kicked and head-butted him, but the nimble bastard managed to keep hold of me in a tight grapple. I thought about kissing him and I thought about killing him. The thoughts had equal weight in my head and provided just enough of a distraction for Young Green Eyes to punch me in the stomach and gain the upper hand. I let go of him and clutched my belly, struggling for breath. The Pure One left me on the floor and stood. His face bled from three small cuts and he nursed a badly twisted arm. I could have used my wyrd and killed him, but I didn't. I'd pulled my blows, though I'd not meant to.

"What was the question?" he asked, through panted breaths.

I sat up against the broken table. In the presence of anyone else, I'd be embarrassed. If my brother could see me, he'd laugh for a week. If the Wolf's Bastard could see me, he'd say I was unworthy of my name.

"I should tear you apart," I snarled, feeling wyrd flow into my clenched fists.

He just looked at me, wiping blood from his cheek. He wrung his hand, wincing at the pain, but he didn't respond. I stood up, ignoring the pain in my stomach and glaring at him. "Why are you not afraid of me?"

Young Green Eyes didn't flinch or turn away from my hate-filled stare. He looked me up and down, and his mouth curled into a smile. He'd never bent his knee to the Sea

Wolves, or admitted that we were superior. To him, we were Invaders. To him, I was ... I didn't know. I wanted him, but I couldn't explain why.

"Last time you came here, we didn't fight before we fucked," said the Pure One. "Is this to replace kissing from now on?"

I grabbed him again, or maybe we grabbed each other. This time there was no hate or anger, just grasping hands and murmured grunts of passion. I tore off his tunic and threw him on the floor. He kept hold of my arm and I fell on top of him.

My brother used to tell me stories of the brothels he'd visited and the whores who waited for his return. Vincent Heartfire bragged about the women throughout the Kingdom who called him husband. Even Rys Coldfire, the Wolf's Bastard, had two mistresses in the hold. Male lust was accepted and celebrated, but when *I* wanted to fuck, I had to do it in secret. Admittedly my choice of lover was questionable, but surely lust was lust.

Young Green Eyes was asleep, his arm draped across my breasts. It was dark outside and the upstairs bedroom was bathed in a grey light. The building was quiet. I knew not how many of his family skulked below, other than Sky, but I imagined they'd keep skulking until I left. I'd broken arms in the past to remind my lover's family that my visits were a secret, and I was confident that their fear of me was enough. If it wasn't, they could only cause me limited trouble anyway. And they knew I'd kill them.

"What hour is it?" he asked. He kept his eyes closed.

I stroked his long, black hair out of his face and leant across to kiss him. His lips reacted, but his body remained still. "Maybe seven o'clock," I replied.

His arm tightened and pulled me close. "Good. Still early."

"I asked you a question," I whispered. "And I'd like an answer."

"Ask again," he replied, still not opening his eyes.

I took a deep breath and stroked my arms across his back. A sheen of sweat coated our flesh, feeling warm and comforting. "A Mirralite warrior told me to use the glass while I could. He said he could hear the sea. What did he mean?"

Young Green Eyes raised himself up on his arms and smiled down at me. "He probably didn't mean anything. If he was at the dangerous end of your cutlass, he'd say anything. Young Mirralite fight the Invaders because the varn tell them to. People like me are rarely listened to."

I didn't believe him. He knew I lusted for him and he used this to distract me, displaying his body and smiling. "You're not telling me the truth. You know I dislike lying."

"Sometimes the truth is worse," he replied.

"Answer me," I repeated.

He looked out of the window and gritted his teeth. "There's talk," he murmured. "A varn called Gloom Scribe has been saying things… and Mirralite are listening."

"What has he been saying? And where do I find him?"

"He's from the Bay of Bliss, but I know not where he lays his head these days. He likes the sea."

"Think harder," I replied.

"Am I just your spy now?" He spat the words and snarled. "If this is rape, tell me. I couldn't fight you off… you could have me if you wanted." He grabbed me and gave me a hard kiss. "I'm not your toy or your inferior. I fuck you because..."

"Because?" I prompted, breathing heavily.

He pressed his lips to mine, but his eyes stayed open. "I think it's time for you to go, Mistress Brand."

5

I was late. I'd run from Swordfish Bay to the Wolf House and I was still an hour late. I tried to convince myself that I was late because I was searching for information. The reality was that I'd enjoyed being naked with Young Green Eyes far too much to remember that I had a prior engagement. I'd not even gained any substantial information. Just a name – Varn Gloom Scribe.

The Wolf House was quiet, with the administration of the hold done for the day. I ran up the stairs and past lesser duellists, emerging into the Bloody Halls to face a dozen questioning looks. Around the high table sat the warriors of the Severed Hand, engaged in a discourse, interrupted by my hasty entrance. I was an equal amongst the greatest duellists of the hold, but fought the urge to blush and apologize. There were raised eyebrows from my brother and Vincent Heartfire. The Wolf's Bastard just frowned at me, gesturing to the one empty seat, and the Wisp smiled, as if he'd won a bet with himself.

"Your face is red, Addie," said Arthur. "Been running?"

"Fuck off," I replied, taking a seat. "What did I miss?"

The Wisp poured me a goblet of wine from one of several carafes on the stone table. I sipped the rich, fruity liquid and quenched my thirst, trying to ignore the disapproving looks. Jaxon knew where I'd been, but the others merely suspected, and they'd not dream that my lover was a Pure One, let alone a Mirralite. They probably thought I'd been snared by a lesser duellist or a particularly tough fisherman.

The only other woman around the table, a tall redhead called Ingrid Raider, was glaring at me, as if I'd spat in her face. She was notoriously promiscuous, but rarely late. I glared back at her until she turned away.

"What did I miss?" I repeated.

Rys Coldfire leant forwards, drumming his fingers on the table. "Well, you missed confirmation that Lord Vikon and young Master Greenfire have left aboard the *Dead Horse*. It appears the Brethren assassin had a second target on Nowhere. Prince Oliver insisted that a Winterlord accompany them, so the young duellist and his Pure One went along."

Ingrid flicked back her curly red hair and resumed glaring at me. "You also missed discussions on the security of the hold, Adeline. Discussions you should have been present for."

"But I wasn't," I replied. "I assume Jaxon told you all about our encounter in the woods?"

"He did," said Rys. "Similar reports have been delivered by Ingrid, Arthur, Vincent *and* Gathin Blood. You are the fifth duellist to tell me the Pure Ones are restless. The other four had nothing further to add. Do you?"

"There's a varn called Gloom Scribe," I replied. "From the Bay of Bliss. He's causing trouble."

Rys lent in. "There is always a varn causing trouble. A different one each turn of the moon. Why is this one different?"

"I've heard of this Pure One," said Vincent Heartfire, a bulky warrior who preferred a mace to a sword. "Gloom Scribe, you say? The name chimes a bell."

"And with me," agreed Ingrid Raider. "A few weeks ago, something about a man who listens to the sea and could charm a snake. Eyes and words that make people pay attention."

"That's it," agreed Vincent. "Just a name that stuck in the memory. I met a Pure One who knew him. He said that this Gloom Scribe spends hours looking at the sea, as if it talks to him. He's from the Bay of Bliss."

Rys took a drink of wine and looked around the seated duellists. His eyes never moved quickly, as if he saw everything in slow-motion. He waited an eternity before speaking. "Addie, take Jaxon and sniff this varn out. Vincent, Arthur, round up some Nissalite – anyone who's been in trouble recently – and ask some pointed questions. Try not to kill anybody unless you have to."

Vincent and Arthur looked at each other. "Just a varn," said my brother. "How dangerous can he be? I've never met one that didn't spend all his time praying at the trunk of some fucking tree, or a damn rock. This one just likes the sea. Is it not a waste of time?"

The Wolf's Bastard glared at my brother. The senior duellist had no mandate to give orders, and anyone around the table could tell him to fuck off if they wanted. Arthur met the glare for an instant, then averted his eyes, looking at me like I could make the nasty man go away.

"Arthur, you can go with Jaxon and your sister," said Rys, deathly quiet. "Ingrid will accompany Vincent in your stead."

"It's not a waste of time," I said. "Burning ships are annoying, but if you burn enough, you burn a fleet. We are best served by stopping whatever this is before it starts."

Arthur scoffed at my words. "Let them summon their nature spirits, let them throw themselves against our walls, let them rant and rave about the Invaders, what *true* victory will ever come of it? *We* are Sea Wolves of the Severed Hand, *they* are lesser men."

"We could have a purge?" suggested Vincent. "Kill a few thousand Mirralite and re-state our seniority."

I hated the idea, but tried not to show it. A purge had worked in the past and *would* solve our immediate problems, assuming our immediate problems were just restless Mirralite and a charismatic varn. Burning ships and raiding parties were nothing new, but Rys Coldfire had a glint in his eyes, as if he suspected more. He smoothed back his silvery-grey hair and shifted position in his seat.

"No purge," said the Wolf's Bastard. "We will do as I have said. I'll know more when I've spoken to Tomas and the First Fang. I have an itch at the back of my mind and I need it scratched." He stood, his heavy falchion striking the stone table. "We are done for now. We meet again tomorrow night."

We all stood. "Once more for the Severed Hand," we said in unison.

Each duellist went their separate way, focusing on the exit and saying nothing. The clank of arms and armour echoed around the hall, but no-one said a word. Tense glances and sullen shakes of the head, but no actual speech.

"Where did you hear about this place?" asked Arthur.

"Never you mind," I replied. "A person I trust said this house is of interest to us."

"And why are we just hiding and watching?" he countered.

The Wisp smiled at him, his face open and friendly in the morning sun. "To see who lives there."

"Wasn't asking you, Icicle," spat Arthur. "If we kick the door in we'll find out who lives there. Though why anyone would want to is beyond me."

He was right about that. I'd never seen so raggedy a dwelling. The edges of Swordfish Bay held hundreds of hovels, dug into the mud and plonked like an incomplete puzzle along the coast. Young Green Eyes had directed me to a series of wooden shacks, loosely placed around a building that I took to be a brothel, judging by the contented glaze on the face of each man who exited. Sailors with a few coins, fishermen looking for some illicit pleasure, but mostly Nissalite. Though I now wondered how many were secretly Mirralite.

"We've been here for an hour," whinged my brother. "And I haven't seen shit. I could sit here for another hour and I still wouldn't see shit."

We were hidden in the shadow of a rock, under the furthest line of shacks. The deep roar of the sea masked our conversation, but I had a good view up to the hovels.

"Tide's coming in," said Jaxon. "Another hour and we'll be swimming. So will half those shacks. They must be used to wet feet."

I took a moment to think. I didn't want to rush in and potentially have to kill sources of information, but neither did I want to wait and give our enemies more time to conspire.

"Who goes to a brothel before breakfast?" mused Arthur.

"Men," I replied. "Come on, let's break the glass and go have a look."

"About time," said my brother.

Jaxon was first, like always, then Arthur and I stretched out with our wyrd and pulled our bodies into the void. It was always easier in the hold, as if the glass was thinner. Tomas Red Fang counselled against breaking the glass in the Severed Hand, but Lord Ulric had decided otherwise. As duellists, it wasn't our place to have an opinion. But I agreed with the old spirit-master.

"You showing off, Icicle?" asked Arthur, as the three of us stood on the shimmering rocks. "You're just a freak."

Jaxon had weathered a thousand such taunts and handled it – as he always did – with silence. He glided away, across the glassy water, his feet causing barely a ripple in the surface. It was a trick few mastered, and I could no more walk on water in the void than I could in the real world. Arthur had tried many times, but always ended up swimming. On this occasion he wisely followed me along the rocks.

In the void, few of the hovels were visible, their temporary nature having little impact beyond the glass. A few buildings, like the brothel, or a nearby tavern, had a vague spiritual reflection, as if enough fucking and alcohol was noticed even by the spirits. The building we'd been looking at was also visible, with a strange texture dancing across its surface. It was spiritually active and somehow important to these Pure Ones. Behind me, those buildings important to the Eastron stood as bastions of shimmering blue light, towering over the voidscape. The Wolf House appeared twice as large beyond the glass, as its true importance could never be conveyed in bricks and mortar.

"Addie, this might be a problem," said Jaxon, standing on the surface of the water and looking up at the building.

We took the long way around, stepping between rocks to avoid patches of sludgy mud. When we stood near the Wisp his cause for concern became obvious. The building was covered in twisted brambles. Sharp, red-tipped thorns jutted outwards, and the building itself was barely visible beneath little spirits, dancing on the surface.

"Pain spirits," said the Wisp. "They've been summoned to protect the house."

"The varn risk much," I replied, "summoning so many spirits within the hold."

"It's far enough from the Wolf House that no-one looks ... or even cares," said Arthur. "Only idiots like us come down here."

What were they protecting? Pure Ones cared nothing for riches, nor did they guard their leaders in such a fashion. I'd never seen so many spirits bound to a single purpose. I imagined their lands to be full of such things, but I hated seeing it in the Severed Hand.

"We can't pass through in the void," said the Wisp. "Those pain spirits are nasty little bastards. And those inside get a warning ... maybe enough to get away."

"So we use the door," I replied.

We found a secluded rock, with crystals of void water lapping against it, and returned to the real world. Travelling through the glass in the other direction was always jarring, as your senses were suddenly filled with light and sound, eclipsing the exaggerated calm of the void. I felt more at home beyond the glass, removed from the trials of the world, and allowed to just be. But it never lasted, and I always had to come back.

Jaxon was already a step ahead as we made our way past the brothel. Our cloaks provided a modicum of anonymity, but any eyes that looked closely would know exactly who we were. Taller, wider, more upright, and likely emanating an aura of imminent violence. Luckily, the muddy streets were mostly empty, though discretion was not helped by Arthur's constant sneer. My brother looked at any Pure One like they should be kneeling before him or throwing offerings at his feet.

"Arthur, try to relax," I whispered. "We are not here as the vanguard of an army. We are making enquiries."

"We are *always* at the vanguard of an army," he replied, not softening his glare. "Don't infect *me* with your sympathies." He lengthened his stride to get past me.

We reached the building, seeing nothing of the twisted brambles. In the real world it was just a hovel, dark with no windows and a slanted roof. Jaxon leant against it, casually surveying the surroundings. It was early morning and those men awake were yawning and rubbing sleep from their eyes. They were either up early or up very late. Either way, most were too addled to give us a second glance.

Jaxon positioned his ear against the wooden walls and listened. "Voices," he whispered. "Maybe five men."

"I feel sorry for them," said Arthur, moving to the door.

"Easy," I warned. "Let us not blunder into anything."

He banged a fist against the door, looking at me like I was being stupid. The Wisp shook his head, indicating that the voices had stopped, and I rushed to stand next to my impulsive brother.

"You open the door or I do," bellowed Arthur.

With no further need to be stealthy, I shook my head and drove my boot into the flimsy wooden door. It shattered inwards, coming off its rusted hinges and bathing the dark interior with sudden light. Figures scattered from our intrusion. Four men, robed in black, ran for adjoining rooms. They said nothing, not even gasps of alarm, and no face was still long enough for me to see it clearly.

I pursued the nearest man. Arthur ran past my left shoulder and went after two more. I lost sight of my brother as I wove through dilapidated rooms and low, musty chambers, in close pursuit of the robed man. There was no space to draw my blade, and I had to duck under most doorways. The man ahead of me paused and I tackled him, smashing through the side of the building and emerging back in the morning sunlight of Swordfish Bay. I pinned him to the muddy ground, locking his arms behind his head. He was a Pure One, an older man with greying hair and weathered skin.

I looked up and saw a dozen curious faces pointed at us. Rolling drunkards, early risers and fishermen. I'd made a hole in the side of the building and planks now fell from the poorly maintained roof, to fall loudly next to me. I pulled the Pure One to his feet and dragged him back into the hovel.

"Addie, got the others," shouted Arthur from within.

I roughly grabbed my captive by the back of the neck and marched him towards the central chamber, swearing to myself. I'd been seen by too many people. Rumours and speculation would travel quickly into the Nissalite slums. A duellist had been seen. My name might even feature in a rumour or two.

The Wisp was repositioning the front door, while Arthur roughed up the other three captives. "Bit of talk out there now," said the Wisp. "We shouldn't hang around."

"Fuck 'em," said Arthur, punching a Pure One in the stomach. "What are they going to do? Attack us? I don't think so."

I threw my captive to the floor, to cower next to the other three. All were pale-skinned Pure Ones in late middle age, fully covered by thin black robes, with ankles and wrists exposed. They exchanged glances and whispered words, but became silent when Arthur kicked the new addition in the head and rendered him unconscious. "No talking," he growled.

I shoved my brother out of the way and righted a small wooden chair, taking a seat in front of the captives.

"We have heard a story," I said, casually, "of a varn called Gloom Scribe. A man who likes the sea. Now, you are in the advantageous position of being able to add to this story. You can open your mouths and let truths spew forth, and your part in the story will be short. It may not even record your names, just that you went home alive." I had their attention, but was surprised that there was little fear on their faces. I drew my cutlass and rested the point against the wooden floor. "And, of course, if you keep quiet, the story will record your deaths... in a dark hovel, your bodies burned for all to see."

The middle captive coughed up some blood and cleared his throat. "We will help you any way we can, noble duellist." His voice was soft and he bowed his head.

"A good start," I replied. "Gloom Scribe, where do I find him?"

"Be careful," said the Wisp, "this one has power." He stepped before the Pure One and looked him up and down. "What's your name?"

The kneeling man did not flinch from us. His cheek and bottom lip were red from Arthur's fist, but he did not blink as Jaxon peered at him. I had no sensory gifts, and could not see things visible to the Wisp, but even I could tell that this particular captive was not just an insignificant Pure One.

"Answer him!" snapped Arthur, punching the man again. "Your name!"

He coughed out more blood and his hands went to his wounded jaw. My brother was strong and he'd rendered more than one man unconscious with a single punch. To see a Pure One be struck twice and not even fall was strange.

"Apologies, most revered Sea Wolves, I forget my place. Gloom Scribe you say? I'm afraid that name chimes no bells. Though I too like the sea."

Arthur went to punch him again, but Jaxon stopped him. The Wisp grabbed the Pure One by the throat and pulled him upright. "Who *are* you?"

I stood next to them, cutlass in hand, and watched in amazement as the man's wounds began to disappear. He didn't smile, and showed no outward defiance, but his eyes betrayed something I did not expect to see in a Pure One. He was using wyrd. It was subtle, far softer that my own – a needle compared to the sledgehammer of a Sea Wolf duellist – but the man was skilled.

"Who are you?" repeated the Wisp, wrapping an arm around the man's throat and holding him in a choke.

The man lowered his chin and twisted forwards, hefting Jaxon off the ground. He carried his weight easily and threw him across the room, to clatter against the flimsy walls. Arthur stood stunned, and I paused, looking at the Pure One's pale face. The Wisp quickly righted himself and crouched. The three of us circled the man, our eyes low and wary.

"You're strong," I said. "Too strong for a Pure One... maybe even too strong for a Sea Wolf. Perhaps a better question is *what* are you?"

He wasn't armed and kept his limbs loose, poised like a cat, not sure in which direction to pounce. He didn't appear afraid, just wary and ready to fight. His eyes pointed downwards, not meeting my gaze or Arthur's snarl. The other captives skulked to the far wall, dragging their unconscious brethren with them, but they showed no sign of action. "The sea calls to us," murmured the oldest captive, his eyes suddenly bloodshot.

"What manner of craft is this?" asked my brother.

"The sea calls to us all," replied the man. "Though few listen." He stopped moving and his eyes dimmed. A subtle mantle of wyrd fell from his face, like a lizard shedding an old skin, and different eyes looked up at the three duellists surrounding him. He was no Pure One. He appeared to be a man, though his face and limbs were hideously deformed. His eyes bulged from his head like a frog's, and thick, flabby lips puckered at us. A layer of sickly-green slime coated his flesh, and his stomach swelled to an enormous girth. I had no earthly idea what he was.

Arthur attacked first, the shock driving him to anger. The strange man parried the cutlass with the flat of his slimy hand and elbowed my brother in the face. He moved quickly, able to outmanoeuvre his opponent in a way I'd never seen. He nullified Arthur's strength with tiny movements and bursts of speed.

Jaxon, still crouched, looked across at me and conveyed his concern. Arthur was outmatched and we both knew it. He was dazed from the elbow and flailing with his blade, trying to overpower the creature, but each swing sapped his strength and struck nothing but wood or thin air.

"Brother!" I shouted. "Disengage!"

A moment later he put all his strength into a single downward swipe. The frog-man side-stepped and grasped Arthur's arms, using his momentum to overbalance him. I saw that he was directed at *me* a moment too late, and was barrelled to the floor by the flying form of my brother.

"Fuck!" I exclaimed, trying to roll to my feet. "Jaxon, subdue it."

The Wisp had already advanced, dropped his blade and grappled the bulbous creature. Arthur and I untangled ourselves and stood, in time to watch Jaxon pinned to the floor with a flabby arm wrapped around his neck. He was gasping for breath as the half-man's bulging eyes flickered around the hovel, looking for a way out.

"Whatever you are, you've got nowhere to go," I snapped. "Release him!"

The creature shifted weight, hefting Jaxon upwards. Its robe now covered only a fraction of its grotesque body. It may have been a man, but a man who resembled a frog, with small suckers on its hands and feet, and mottled patterning of red and green running up its back.

I kept my eyes on it and retrieved my cutlass. I nodded for Arthur to cover the flank and we approached it from both sides. Neither of us knew what it was, but we were duellists of the Severed Hand and would never back down, even to a flabby-limbed creature with abnormal strength. We had both fought void beasts and were not squeamish at the vile or the grotesque. Though this was no summoned spirit, and to see such a thing within the hold was alarming.

"Were *you* why they guarded the house?" I asked.

Its moist lips smacked together, but formed no words. When its gangly arms momentarily loosened their hold around Jaxon's neck, the Wisp sprang upwards and turned, mounting the creature, tying up its arms and allowing us to move in and overwhelm it. It flailed with considerable strength and points of wyrd darted from its extremities, but three duellists could not be shrugged off so easily.

"Stop squirming," shouted Arthur.

"Just hold it," I replied, laying a forearm across the half-man's throat.

I measured the distance and delivered a series of straight punches. They connected on its jaw and its body went limp. I stood, silently looking at its sprawled body. It had nearly bested three of the toughest duellists at the Severed Hand. I felt a momentary flash of fear at what a group of them would be able do. The fear was quickly replaced with anger, as if the sensation had never been there.

6

The three of us sat in the low bar of the Wolf House, nursing bumps and bruises and with many unanswered questions. Arthur had taken it badly. Being defeated was difficult to deal with. Being defeated by a fat frog-man of uncertain origin was bewildering to my brother's worldview. Jaxon was quieter than normal, and had a nasty red and black bruise on his forehead, but he didn't look confused, just thoughtful.

Our captive had returned to the form of a Pure One and regained consciousness within sight of the Wolf House. Despite his arms and legs being bound, he'd smiled at the old building. None of us had asked anything more of him. No questions about what he was. Not even a single petty insult from Arthur. The man had been given to Jonas Grief, the master-at-arms, and was undergoing questioning in the Bloody Halls. The Wolf's Bastard had ordered us away, apparently sensing that at least two of us were shaken by the encounter. He'd suggested alcohol and we'd obliged, sinking a few mugs of ale in the low bar. It had now been several hours and the Severed Hand was bathed in warm afternoon light.

"He must have been a spirit," muttered Arthur, looking out of a narrow stone window, his face illuminated and his eyes pinched. "It's the only answer. New varn, new powers?"

"Wasn't a spirit," replied the Wisp. "Whatever it was, it was a creature of form, not void."

"Fuck do you know, Icicle?" said Arthur. "If you hadn't got in the way, I'd have killed it."

Jaxon was silent.

"Shut up, Arthur," I offered. "You have brawn, I have brains, Jaxon has wyrd. I don't tell you how to fight, he doesn't tell me how to think, and you don't tell him of spirits."

He scowled at me, clenching his fists. My brother was short-tempered and apparently looking for a fight.

"Unclench those fists, brother," I whispered. "Do not take your lack of comprehension out on me."

"What about *him*?" he replied, pointing at the Wisp.

I smiled, taking a deep swig from my third mug of ale. "Do as you wish. I'm neither your mother nor your master. I was just pointing out that if you attack *me* I'd knock out all your fucking teeth."

Jaxon chuckled and rose from his seat, slowly backing away from us. "Well, I no longer think I'm needed here. I'm sure Rys will send for me when our peculiar prisoner has a story to tell. You two have a lovely evening." Before Arthur could protest or throw any more insults, the Wisp had glided out of the stone doorway and left the low bar.

Arthur went back to his mug, grinding his teeth at me. "Didn't mean anything by it. Just wanted a fight. He takes everything so seriously. He was there, it took three duellists to put the thing down. How the fuck does that happen, Addie?"

I moved my chair closer and put an arm around his shoulders. He smiled feebly, and let me give him a hug. I thought that he was close to tears, but he'd never let himself cry around his sister. "It's okay, brother. This is just another thing to learn. We should have been less arrogant ... more considered. No-one died, and we'll have answers soon."

"I don't like being confused," he replied. "It makes my head feel funny."

I pushed his mug under his nose. "So does ale."

He smirked at me and took a swig. "Doesn't make sense."

I didn't have any answers for him. I'd barely had time to consider what it meant. The man – if he was a man – was like nothing I'd seen in the real world. I wasn't confused like Arthur, or interested like Jaxon. I had to place myself above these concerns and see the encounter for what it was: a fight with a deformed man, able to shrug off a duellist with little effort, and who took three of us to subdue. Perhaps he used some wyrd-craft unknown to us, or perhaps he was a familiar foe wearing a different guise. Either way, I needed to be prepared to face such a foe again. That was where *my* concerns lay, the purely practical matter of how to kill a deformed frog-man with freakish strength. Using three duellists per opponent was not a practical solution. I needed time to think.

"Shall we get drunk?" I suggested.

He nodded.

We filled our mugs, drank them, then filled them again. We were alone in the low bar, seated at a stone table, next to a small window. A dozen other such tables, arranged around a fire-pit, were empty, and the bar itself was self-service. Ingrid Raider and Gathin Blood had led men to Swordfish Bay, securing the hovel and questioning the captive Pure Ones. Where the other duellists were I didn't know, but clearly none needed a drink. It was just as well. Arthur's mood was dark and an audience would not help. Even Tomas Red Fang, who had his own mug and his own chair, was absent. The old spirit-master was seeing what he could learn from the pain spirits.

The afternoon stretched and became evening. The sun slowly fell in the sky and ale was drunk. My thoughts gradually flowed back to a pair of striking green eyes and whether I could leave Arthur to drink alone. Or whether I should beat more information from the Pure One before I fucked him. Not today. Today I had to be a sister.

"Wake up!"

I pulled my head from the wooden bar and blinked. I had a headache and a revolting taste in my mouth. Arthur was sprawled in a chair with drool running down his chin. The window showed darkness, and a nightly chill filled the low bar.

"You are needed," said Ingrid Raider, from the open doorway. "But if you feel too delicate..."

I coughed and stood from the bar. My fellow duellist was dressed in leather armour, with a long, black cloak and two cutlasses in her belt. "Who are we needed by?" I asked. "Because there are those I would tell to fuck off at this moment."

"The Wolf's Bastard," replied Ingrid. "Jaxon is already upstairs. Your captive has been encouraged to tell a story."

"Encouraged?" I queried.

"Burned and cut," stated Ingrid. "But still whole. I am not privy to the details. Just that you are needed."

I crossed to my brother and shook him awake. His eyes were bloodshot and his skin pasty. "What's happening?" he muttered. "Are we still drinking?"

"Not anymore," I replied. "Now we're duellists again. We're needed in the Bloody Halls. Perhaps those answers you need."

Arthur groaned and let me assist him in standing. "What time is it?"

"Approaching midnight," replied Ingrid.

She led the way, with my brother and I leaning on each other. By the time we'd reached the second landing of the Wolf House, my head had begun to hurt. As we crested the last flight of stairs and our feet touched the red carpet of the Bloody Halls, my stomach was doing cartwheels and sweat was forming on my skin.

"Rys won't mind if I puke on him, will he?" grumbled Arthur, as pale as me and far more uncertain on his feet.

"He will," I replied. "He will most certainly mind."

Ingrid led the way through the great hall, and up a further level to the dark chambers at the top of the Wolf House. She said nothing to us, though she must have heard our grumbling.

Many duellists disliked the highest chambers of the Bloody Halls. The art-work – in black relief, as the lower halls – was brutal, and depicted vivid scenes of slaughtered Pure Ones and tamed wilderness. The fall of the Lodge of the Rock, when Duncan Red Claw brought the Mirralite to heel and raised the Severed Hand on the bones of the old world. It was where captive Pure Ones were caged and questioned, usually at the point of a cutlass or the sole of a boot. Arthur had kicked, cut and burned his fair share of captives, whereas I disliked torture and avoided the highest chambers of the Wolf House.

Beyond empty cages, and torture rooms filled with serrated implements and iron shackles, we entered one of the largest chambers. Ingrid left us, and we approached alone. The captive was chained to a stone wall, his flabby arms and legs splayed. He appeared to be a man, with all the correct body parts in all the correct places, however his deformities were spread across every part of his body, as if he was only half a man. His huge eyes, though closed, bulged from his sickly-green face, and his wide, puckered mouth dripped slime onto the floor. His belly sagged, like a fleshy sack of meat, with vicious brands burned into the flesh. I studied the creature, finding it hard to turn away, as if a weakness would present itself.

Also in the torture chamber were Jaxon Ice, Rys Coldfire and, surprisingly, Lord Ulric Blood. The First Fang wore only a simple white shirt, with grey chest hair poking through. He sat on a barrel, behind the Wolf's Bastard. My brother and I tried to stand up straight in his presence, pushing our hangovers to the back of our heads and attempting to appear ready for action. We were only partially successful.

"The fearsome Brand twins," said Rys. "Brought low by a few mugs of ale and a chance encounter with a frog-man."

I glared at him, trying to find untruth in his words. When I found none, I averted my gaze, finding my eyes again drawn to the unconscious prisoner.

"What is that thing?" asked Arthur, wisely joining me in not taking offence at Rys's words.

Ulric hopped down from the barrel and approached us. He was taller than me by several inches, but I'd never been cowed by him before, and was not going to let alcohol change that. I stood my ground, meeting his stare. "My lord. I am surprised to see you in the upper chambers."

"I prefer to leave torture to my duellists," he replied. "But this is an exceptional situation." He nodded at the deformed man. "As for what he is, I believe my spirit-master can best answer you."

From a shadowy corner, Tomas Red Fang emerged. The old man had silently broken the glass and appeared from the void. He was wearing armour and looked like an ancient painting of a fallen warrior, too bent and frail to fight as once he could, but still dangerous if taken for granted. I'd never seen him so attired.

"Greetings," said the spirit-master. "You two look worse than me. Have you also been treating with hostile spirits?"

We looked at each other and Arthur lent heavily against my shoulder, any masquerade of sobriety disappearing. "Apologies," said my brother. "Addie wouldn't stop pouring me drinks." I nearly slapped him, but maintained my poise and merely smiled. I'd slap him later and he knew it.

Tomas Red Fang walked up to the captive, still hanging limply from the stone wall on thick iron shackles. The spirit-master looked up at the creature's face and shook his head. "This creature is a part of an old story," he said quietly. "A thing I'd not thought I would see outside of a book, or whispered in a forbidden tale. It is a hybrid. I believe its mother was a Pure One."

"And its father?" I prompted.

He looked at me, his stained breastplate glinting in the torchlight. With a glance at Lord Ulric and the Wolf's Bastard, he chuckled to himself. "You three will hopefully meet his father." He pointed a bent finger at Jaxon, my brother and me. "Our captive is from a village on the Bay of Bliss. He believes his father is still there."

My brother, his head still tilted downwards and his eyes unfocused, clung to my shoulder a little tighter. The Wisp took a step closer to the two of us, and it became clear we were about to be sent on a journey.

"The Bay of Bliss is deep in the Mirralite Reservation," I stated, my forehead creasing up with concern. "Three duellists is hardly an appropriate force for such a journey. The glass will be closed to us. The wild void is too dangerous."

"Let us command an army and raze this village to the ground," said Arthur, his natural aggression pushing through his hangover.

The Wolf's Bastard cleared his throat. "There are ten thousand duellists at the Severed Hand. Most of those are men-at-arms – tough, but not special. There are five hundred who are special, and there are a dozen who I'd want standing next to me in a fight. You three are amongst the dozen. As for why *just* you three, I would have thought that any more may precipitate a war. Do you not think?"

Ulric cleared his throat. "We have considerable stress as it is. Prince Oliver Dawn Claw was nearly killed in my hall. My son may return from Nowhere with further bad news."

The Wisp looked at the unconscious hybrid. "So what are we looking for? A huge frog? Or some kind of varn with unusual sorcery?"

"Both," replied Tomas. "This kind of mating is not done without ceremony. Offerings, rituals... sacrifices. It should be apparent as soon as you arrive."

"Which you will do with all possible stealth," offered the Wolf's Bastard. "While we smoke out this Gloom Scribe. You will assess any possible threat to us and return."

I stood a little straighter and peered at Rys. The senior duellist was cleverer than many knew. He was privy to far more secrets than I or my brother. It was even rumoured that Tomas Red Fang allowed him to use his library. "We need more," I stated. "A stealthy incursion – okay, but what are we looking for? What threat do you speak of? What do you know of this creature?"

Tomas Red Fang backed away and stood next to Lord Ulric. "That is a question I cannot answer without the First Fang's instruction."

Ulric frowned, as if thinking. I didn't want to uncover any great secrets or hear any forbidden truths, but I wasn't going to take Jaxon and my brother to the Bay of Bliss without more information. I was not a servant, and would not follow any Eastron blindly, whether he be First Fang or not.

"Very well," said Ulric. "Tell them."

The spirit-master smiled, as if unburdened. "This creature's father was a Sunken Man. We have not heard of them for fifty years, and thought not to hear of them again. I myself only know this because I have seen pictures. Lord Ulric and Rys know only because I have told them." His smile broadened. "And now *you* know."

Sunken Men. He may as well have said that the creature was fathered by an evil spirit, for that is how the Sunken Men were most often viewed. It was seen as impolite to talk of them, let alone speculate on what they looked like. They were responsible for the greatest defeat of the Sea Wolves, when Mathias Blood lost the entire fleet in the Battle of the Depths.

"I thought..." I didn't know how to finish my sentence. "My father..."

"Yes, the Battle Brand," offered Lord Ulric. "He holds to the same code as every commander of Last Port – they do not need to know of the Sunken Men until the stars are right."

"Commit this creature's face to memory," said Tomas Red Fang, "for you will likely see an abundance of them where you are going. The Sunken Men enjoy appearing to the superstitious and the ignorant, offering tokens and demanding tribute."

"Tribute!" I replied. "You mean the Mirralite hand over their women?"

"Yes, that *is* what I mean," said the spirit-master. "Men *and* women. Something in the nature of these creatures and their dreaming god makes them want to breed with humans. Some manner of base perversion, though no study has been done on the matter."

"Only the weak have gods," snapped Arthur. "Who would want to bow before something they can't see?"

"Who would want to bow?" I interjected.

Tomas considered it. "Perhaps their theology is also worthy of study. When you return. I shouldn't worry about their god, you will have ample to worry about without considering such weighty questions."

"Do we have a name for their village?" asked the Wisp. "Or a more specific location? The Bay of Bliss is lesser than Rathwater, but still no small inlet. There could be a hundred villages there. Should we find Dark Wing and ask him? He's still up there somewhere."

"Our captive relished telling us the name of his village," said Tomas. "We needed no coercion to find that out. The Place Where We Hear The Sea."

"Dark Wing is a good place to start," said Rys. "If he's still there ... and if he's still sane."

By the time my head had cleared and the sun was peeking over the horizon, I was again reclining in the arms of Young Green Eyes. Arthur had gone home to sleep, Jaxon had stayed to learn all he could from Tomas, and I'd come to Swordfish Bay. We would leave at nightfall, keeping to the coast and turning west before the Plains of Tranquillity. We'd reach the Mirralite Reservation within three days, and the Bay of Bliss a day after that.

Nibonay was a wild island and the Sea Wolves rarely ventured far from the Severed Hand. Halfdan Blood, the Bloody Fang, tried to cut down the Wood of Scars and expand inland. He was stopped by the Ice family in a series of destructive civil wars. They believed then, as they do now, that Sea Wolves should not delve too far from the sea. In the century and a half since the hold was raised, several First Fangs had developed plans to expand inland. Each time something had conspired to stop them. Perhaps the Old Bitch of the Sea gets jealous when we look to earth, rock and wood. Only the old duellist, Roland Lahandras, called Dark Wing, made his home outside of the Severed Hand, and he was reputedly rather strange, verging on the unstable.

"You will not see me for a week or more," I said softly. I lay with my back across his chest, looking out of the window, with a thin white blanket half-covering our bodies.

"Where do you go?" he asked, his eyes drooping as he gently fell into slumber.

"The Bay of Bliss," I replied, instantly regretting my candour.

His eyes didn't shoot open, but they opened with enough alacrity for his concern to be obvious. "That's not your world," he replied. "Why would you go there?"

"Once more for the Severed Hand," I whispered, knowing he wouldn't understand what it meant. "Nibonay is ours, we have the right to go where we wish."

He scoffed, turning me around to face him. "You invaded, but you didn't conquer. You just showed enough strength to make us surrender. Your Kingdom of the Four Claws is barely more than a handful of ports and the sea that lies between. The land belongs to other forces. In a thousand years, perhaps your kingdom will have the domination it desires, but not yet."

I slapped him across the face. There was no power, just an insult. He responded by trying to wrestle me flat. He failed and I straddled him. "Do you deny our strength," I barked, holding him down.

"Never," he replied. "Your wyrd is formidable. But if you look into the dark places of the world, you may fall into the wild void, and find things you can't fight."

"Such as?"

"I don't know," he whispered. "I only know that, before the Invaders came, the Pure Ones lived in harmony with the primal forces of this world. We're pure because we are creatures of form, of the land. The void is closed to us, and that makes our lives simple, but safe."

"Did we disrupt your harmony?" I replied, chuckling at his strange view of things. "Is harmony some kind of spirit your varn used to worship?"

His eyes narrowed. "Do you believe in nothing, Adeline?"

"I believe in lots of things," I replied. "I am simply a rational being who cannot be frightened by stories of ghosts and ghouls... or dark places. If the Eastron ever had gods, we slew them and took their power before we left the Bright Lands. No gods, spirits or men hold dominion over me."

"Do you even know where you are bound? A village, a monument, an inlet? You should not blindly wander through the wilds of Nibonay."

"An old duellist has lived up there for years. He hunts and sleeps in your Reservation. I imagine the locals are too afraid to challenge him."

Young Green Eyes stroked a finger across my forehead, tucking a wisp of hair behind my ear. "I know of him. They stay away because he is insane. There are songs about him, The Dark Wing of Death they call him... amongst other things. Last I heard he was trying to depopulate the Mirralite Reservation."

I rolled off him and nestled in under his arm. I wasn't sure which concerned me more – the unknown of the Bay of Bliss, or my feelings for Young Green Eyes.

The Kingdom of the Four Claws was founded by five Invader Lords

Sebastian Dawn Claw lived as a king on a throne

Duncan Red Claw lived as a thief on the sea

Medina Wind Claw lived as an assassin in the shadows

Mathew Lone Claw lived as a friend on his knees

But David Fast Claw lived apart

From "The Seventeenth Book of Law"
by Moon Blood Claw's Bane

PART THREE

Duncan Greenfire aboard the *Dead Horse*

7

The ship wouldn't stop lurching from side to side, apparently determined to throw me from my hammock. The tight mesh swung from dark wooden walls to bump against neighbouring hammocks and snoring people. There were fifty Sea Wolves, tightly packed in the hold of the ship, mostly asleep and uniformly smelling of sweat and grog. I was lucky enough to be at the end of a row and near the stairs, giving me an intermittent breeze of fresh air and a slight feeling of privacy. The privacy was an illusion, but was preferable to bumping between sweating sailors.

Saving Prince Oliver had complicated my life. The assassin, a Dark Brethren called Lugo Eclipse, had been tortured in the Bloody Halls. He'd yielded little, but after having his foot cut off by Arthur Brand, had confessed that he was sent from the Open Hand, and that he had a second target on the island of Nowhere, to be killed once the prince was dead. He had a spirit-whistle, which he'd used to keep himself hidden, commanding a spirit of darkness to cover his passage through the void of the Severed Hand. The whistle would also have allowed him to escape the Bloody Halls, had I not interrupted his work.

For a day or two I'd forgotten about Maron Grief, until I noticed the suspicious looks on each and every sailor's face. They'd all heard what I'd done, and some cared more about the duel than the assassin. An untrained Eastron was capable of anything. Many thought I was a bad omen aboard ship, and they did not keep this opinion to themselves. As for my guilt, with Twist's help, it was gradually morphing into something else. With time, I felt I might even enjoy the suspicious looks. At least no-one was calling me a freak.

I wasn't asleep, but it was still jarring to hear the bell rung from the deck. It was sudden and piercing, indicating that all sailors should wake. Little light penetrated the hold, but I imagined it was early morning, meaning that the *Dead Horse* had reached the Gates of the Moon sooner than expected. I held my hands to my face and groaned, before the violent jolt of the ship's movement sent a wave of pain up my leg and forced me to rise. All around, men and women swung out of their mesh hammocks and barked at each other. This was no-one's first voyage but mine, and everyone adopted a snarl of boisterous aggression. There was swearing, variously directed at being woken, the smell of the hold, or anything else they could think to complain about. In my short time as a Sea Wolf, I'd learned that complaining was an art form. Unlike the more celebrated pursuits of fighting and piracy, it was an unspoken skill that everyone around me appeared proficient in.

The roll of the ship was one of many things I was yet to get used to. Two rows away the young Winterlord who'd accompanied Prince Oliver, came to help me stand upright. "Come on, friend Duncan, this isn't a feather bed and no-one cares for your discomfort." His name was David Falcon's Fang and he was a duellist of First Port. He was also a pompous idiot, and one of the few aboard ship who didn't think I was dangerous.

I looked at him, raising an eyebrow and trying to convey just how little I wanted his reassurance. "Thanks, that is profound advice. I'm surprised your words have not yet found their way into a compendium of great wisdom."

"Is that irony?" asked the Winterlord. "Or are you attempting to be mean?"

"I'm firing shots across your bow," I replied. "So far your hull has repelled my barrage."

He adjusted his silvery armour and assessed whether or not he should punch me.

"You talk too much, Duncan," said William Vane, a Kneeling Wolf from Four Claw's Folly. "You're going to get punched more often than you get answered." He stood in front of David and smiled. "I like your armour, milord."

William was in his late twenties and shorter even than me. Everyone called him Weathervane Will and he spent most of his time in the crow's nest. According to David Falcon's Fang, he was a lesser Eastron, unworthy of an opinion.

"Thank you, Master Vane," said David, raising his head and sneering down at the Kneeling Wolf. "But neither I nor Duncan require your intervention.

"Fair enough," said Will. "I was just saying that a heavy steel breastplate is an odd thing to wear aboard ship. If you take a tumble overboard, your armour will kill you before the sharks get a chance."

"Sharks? There are sharks?" queried David, his smooth features creasing up. He looked at me, steadying himself against a timber as the *Dead Horse* took another lurch. "Are there sharks here?"

I nodded. "We're just passing Moon Rock, the sea's full of them. Lots of swordfish too, but they won't eat you."

"I do not like sharks!" said the tall Winterlord.

Will and I looked at each other. A moment later we burst out laughing. David Falcon's Fang was a towering spectre of Eastron might, but he pouted like a small boy when faced with the possibility of a fin emerging from the water.

"Don't worry, milord," chuckled Will. "They're more afraid of you than you are of them. Better come up on deck now, both of you. Siggy will shout at you." He strolled away, towards the stairs, joining other sailors answering the bell.

"I am not afraid of sharks," stated David when we were again alone. "I am afraid of nothing. I am a duellist of First Port, son of Harold Falcon's Fang."

"Is he important?" I asked. "Your father?"

David gave me one of his more withering stares. He'd given me a wide variety of disapproving looks, though he remained unfailingly polite. "He spent two terms sitting with the Silver Parliament. He is now Lore Master of First Point and sits with the Always King. Yes, he's important. Of all people, *you* should understand what it means to have an important father."

"Neither of our fathers will be able to help us on Nowhere," I warned.

"What do you know about it?"

I shook my head. "Not a lot. The People of Ice live there, under a huge cloud called the Maelstrom."

We were the last to leave the hold, trudging up rickety steps to be assaulted by bright sunshine. The crew were spreading away from me, like ants, crawling over a wooden ant hill. They climbed the rigging and filled every space on the deck of the *Dead Horse*. The sun was still low, but glared across the deck at every man and women, hitting tired eyes and aching limbs. Luckily, the constant roll of the ship made my limp easy to hide.

Behind me, standing by the helm, was Vikon Blood, the Second Fang. He didn't look tired and his feet were firmly planted on the swaying deck. To his right, peering through a looking-glass, was Captain Roderick Ice, called Cold Man.

David and I were ushered away from the downward hatch and shoved to the railing. We were not yet accustomed to life aboard ship and, as such, were deemed useless by Siggy Blackeye, the Mistress of the Boat. Snake Charmer, David's Pure One squire, had it even worse. He wasn't even allowed on deck. It was only David's stern glare that had stopped his friend having to fight a dozen Sea Wolves who objected to his presence. They called him unbound by the Shackles of the Wolf, amongst other things, and bullied him whenever possible. As a result he'd taken to staying in the hold, with barrels of grog for company. But If he'd not been aboard, *I'd* likely have been the focus of their attention.

"Sharp Tongue!" shouted Mistress Blackeye. "Just passing the Gates of the Moon. Want to swim back to your mother? Last chance."

"Nah, he'll fly," offered the bosun. "His wyrd will give him wings."

I looked out at Moon Rock, as a dozen sailors guffawed at my expense. I never realized how small my home was until I woke up at the Severed Hand. The High Captain's holdfast was perched on a cliff, overlooking the harbour, but it was merely a part of the coast, not dominating it like the Severed Hand. Maybe it looked small because I saw it from a distance, or maybe my perceptions had changed. I felt as if my life could be divided into two parts – before I'd torn a duellist's head off and saved Prince Oliver, and after.

"Your home?" asked David. "Quaint."

"Fuck off," I replied. I was too scared to swear at the sailors laughing at me, so I braved a punch to swear at David.

"I meant no insult, friend Duncan," replied the Winterlord. "It's a fishing town. I imagined that *quaint* would be a compliment."

"You see that fort on the cliff? I grew up there. You want to talk about important fathers, mine is probably looking down at us right now. He wouldn't like the seat of the High Captain described as quaint."

"And where is the fabled Sea Wolf fleet? I see few ships at anchor. Maybe a dozen, no more."

I shrugged. "No idea. Last Port, I suppose, or Laughing Rock at the Severed Hand. I know a lot make berth at Rathwater, but the Battle Brand commands the biggest fleet."

"Yes, the Sea of Stars," replied David. "I would love to visit Last Port. So many stories..."

"Kieran's there. My big brother. He says most of those stories are true."

"Indeed?" exclaimed the duellist. "Are we going to talk of Sunken Men and the Battle of the Depths? I thought you Sea Wolves didn't speak of such things."

"We don't," I muttered. "Even Tomas Red Fang won't discuss the Battle of the Depths. My father used to say that it took twenty years for the fleet to recover."

David smiled at me, his face brightening. "Defeat is always an uncomfortable subject." The glare of sunlight shone from his golden hair and warm blue eyes. For a moment I saw why the Winterlords ruled the Kingdom of the Four Claws. Then I scoffed at his pomposity.

"Duncan, David!" shouted Vikon Blood from the quarterdeck. "Come up here."

The *Dead Horse* was rolling from side to side as its topsails were pulled in. The Gates of the Moon was not a narrow channel, but treacherous rocks jutted from the water, and a wise captain knew to respect the sea winds. Whirlpools could appear from nowhere and send ships to their doom if they were not quite in the centre or were travelling too quickly. Cold Man knew his job and the ship had slowed to a crawl as David and I stumbled our way to the quarterdeck.

"Shouldn't you be in the rigging?" asked Cold Man, looking down at me over his broken nose and bushy moustache. He was *certainly* not afraid of me. "Short people should be in the rigging. Siggy's rule, not mine."

"I've not yet found my sea legs," I replied, finding a railing to hold on to. "Weathervane Will's trying to help, but none of the other crew want to talk to me."

"Sailors are superstitious," replied the captain. "You did two things that none of them can do. Vikon says you've had no training, so they don't know who you are or how your wyrd flows." He frowned, looking at me and then David Falcon's Fang. "Can either of you sing?"

"No," replied David, frowning as if he thought he was being insulted. "I am a warrior. My purpose is *not* to entertain you, Captain Ice."

Vikon and Cold Man looked at each other. Even the Second Fang deferred to the captain aboard his ship, but I doubted David's pomposity would elicit punishment. Or maybe they'd send *him* into the rigging.

"None of my crew can sing," said the captain. "I miss singing. Just a nice shanty, something to make the sea less black and the sky less blue. There was a lad called Arn, by the Bright Lands his voice could belt out a storm. He took a Brethren arrow to the head last year."

"I will not be his replacement," replied David, "though my friend Snake Charmer has a haunting voice."

Cold Man scoffed. "Your Pure One is lucky I didn't kill him for *looking* at my ship. The old Bitch doesn't like them standing on a Sea Wolf's deck. It's worse luck than having Master Greenfire aboard."

"Easy," said Vikon Blood. "He's Rykalite, from the Father, not some Mirralite rebel."

"A Pure One is a Pure One," stated Cold Man.

David took his hands from the railing and thrust his chin at the captain. "Snake is my brother ... in blood and honour. I will fight any man who demeans him."

Cold Man and Vikon took a moment to assess the young Winterlord's conviction. Neither was afraid of him and I doubted they'd let the veiled threat pass.

Roderick Ice put a hand on David's shoulder and his bushy moustache twitched. "You're a good lad, Master Falcon's Fang. But a thinly disguised threat is still a threat." He turned from the helm and narrowed his eyes, searching for someone amongst his crew. "Blitz!" he shouted to the bosun. "Get up here."

The man finished admonishing a crewman for an indiscretion I didn't understand, and answered his captain's call. "Yes, captain."

"Take our Winterlord friend to the hold. He'll be confined with his Pure One until we reach Nowhere."

David spluttered and had to grab the railing to stop from falling over. "I will not be corralled like a Kneeling Wolf," he snorted.

Cold Man, on surer footing, strode towards David and grabbed him by the throat, summoning a globe of churning wyrd into his massive hand. "Listen to me, you shiny little cunt. This is my ship, my kingdom, my world. You exist in it because your prince insisted you accompany us. You go to the hold or I throw you overboard. Choose."

I edged along the railing, away from the confrontation, and met Vikon's eyes. The Second Fang was smiling, and winked at me. I wished I could hate him, but I desperately wanted his approval. He, like Tomas Red Fang and the Wolf's Bastard, knew I was dangerous, but had still sent me to Nowhere. His presence was like a comfort blanket, for I couldn't imagine Vikon Blood letting me to get into too much trouble.

"Release me!" demanded David, grabbing Cold Man's arm, but lacking the strength to free himself.

"Choose," repeated the captain.

David's eyes were wide, but he'd stopped struggling. It must have been hard for him, perhaps the first time he'd been cowed in such a fashion. I momentarily worried that he'd start a fight he couldn't win, but luckily his intelligence overrode his pride. "I will retreat to the hold," he whispered.

"Good," replied Cold Man, releasing his grip. "Blitz, escort him below."

"Aye, captain," said the bosun, grabbing hold of David's arm. "With me, young lord."

David paused, looking at me as if he thought I'd see him differently, but he allowed himself to be led away by Blitz.

"The hold is getting full," said Vikon Blood. "A Pure One, a Brethren assassin, now a Winterlord. Luckily only one requires guarding."

"Was that really necessary?" I asked the Second Fang. "Won't it anger Prince Oliver?"

Cold Man peered at me across his moustache.

"The Winterlords will never understand the laws of the sea, Master Greenfire," replied Vikon. "We sometimes need to remind them that the Sea Wolves live by a different code. You're our totem's favourite, you should know that."

I gulped, looking at the deck. I knew I was only on the *Dead Horse* because the Old Bitch of the Sea had spoken to me, but I didn't want everyone else to know that. The crew had enough reasons to be suspicious of me.

Before I could say something clever, the *Dead Horse* lurched to port as its topsails were pulled in. The vessel passed the Gates of the Moon, and when I looked back at the cliff, I could no longer see Moon Rock. All sight of my home had gone and I hadn't even had the chance to get a last look. I had to take weight off my left leg as Twist reminded me how lost I was.

Without David, I had no-one to talk to, and my thoughts turned dark. I wondered who I was and what I'd really accomplished. Surviving the rite meant I was a Sea Wolf, killing Maron Grief meant I was feared, and saving Prince Oliver meant that the elders of the Severed Hand knew who I was and cared about what I did. So why was I still fucking terrified? Twist wouldn't let me feel peace, and constantly reminded me that it was my wyrd, not me, that had accomplished everything. I felt like a fraud, but knew that I would never be in better position to prove my worth.

I stared behind the ship for what seemed like hours, as the coastline angled downwards and became covered in pointed pine trees. The island of Yish was uninhabited, except for Moon Rock, and this was the closest I'd ever been to its densely forested interior. Maybe some Pure Ones lived in the deep woods, but no Eastron or people of note.

The sea channel was narrow until Blood Water and the dark island of Nowhere. Until then, we'd be a lone ship, framed by forested coastlines, and weaving to avoid jutting rocks and whirlpools. It was a treacherous journey, far from friendly berths and allied ships. Even on Nowhere, the People of Ice had few ships and were unlikely to lend aid if we needed it. I knew I shouldn't be worried, but I was. The *Dead Horse* had a crew of eighty Sea Wolves, including two of the greatest warriors of the Severed Hand – Vikon Blood and Roderick Ice – yet still I had a knot in my stomach.

David was confined below deck, and Weathervane Will appeared to be my designated minder. The Kneeling Wolf directed me this way and that, to ropes that needed coiling, tying or loosening. I didn't understand the usefulness of my actions, nor why the *Dead Horse* needed so many ropes, but I was kept busy, and barely registered the frequent glares I received from superstitious sailors.

"What's that?" I asked Will.

The Kneeling Wolf joined me amidships, looking forward off the starboard side. He narrowed his eyes and peered into the distance. "What's what?" he replied. "Can't see anything."

Twist nudged my leg with a jab of pain. Something was wrong. Will couldn't see anything, but I knew something was there, just beyond sight at the edge of the horizon. My fingertips were tingling, as if I'd plunged my hands into hot water.

"The sea," mused Will. "Rocks. Cliffs. Pine trees. What am I supposed to see?" He turned from the railing and shouted aloft. "Lookout! Two points off starboard, do you see anything by the coast?"

The woman in the crow's nest raised a looking-glass and scanned the horizon. "Nothing," came the reply. "Two inlets, a waterfall, trees ... looks like a rocky beach either side."

Weathervane Will put a hand on my shoulder. "You're seeing things, my boy. First voyage. Sometimes the Bitch plays tricks."

I shrugged off his hand. "It's not a trick and it's not the fucking sea. We're in danger, I know it." I winced in pain. It was rare that I let it show, but it appeared to punctuate my point.

Will didn't laugh or make a joke. I wasn't used to people taking me seriously, but that's exactly what he did. "I believe you," he said. "Wait here." He jogged back towards the quarterdeck, where Anthony Blitz, the bosun, was stationed. They exchanged words and returned to me.

"You got an itch, Master Greenfire?" asked Blitz.

"Don't mock him," said Will. "We should listen to him."

The bosun took a moment, scanning both of our faces, before looking to the horizon. "Who's in the crow's nest?" he asked.

"Lydia Hearth," replied Will. "She didn't see anything."

Blitz looked down at me and screwed up his face. "If you tell me your wyrd is warning you of danger, I will believe you."

I stuttered as I tried to reply. I had never had any kind of danger sense, and yet I *knew* we were in danger. Perhaps my wyrd *was* warning me. "I don't know," I stammered. "I just know something's wrong... over there, near the coast."

Blitz nodded slowly. "Weathervane Will, sound general quarters."

"Aye," replied the Kneeling Wolf.

A moment later a loud bell was rung from the quarterdeck, rousing those below. The *Dead Horse* operated a three-watch system on an eight-hour rotation. Two-thirds of the men were usually sleeping, eating, or at leisure in the bunk-rooms. Though it was mid-afternoon, I still felt sorry for those roused from their hammocks by the loud ringing of a bell. Especially as it was my fault they were being roused. All I could do was stand sheepishly at the starboard rail, hiding behind Blitz, as the deck quickly filled up with sailors. The bell still rang, and the crew moved to their appointed battle stations. The ballistae ports remained closed, but their crews stood ready.

Cold Man, Vikon Blood and Mistress Blackeye emerged from the forecastle and strode along the deck to where Blitz and I stood. "What is it, bosun?" asked the captain.

"Two points off starboard," replied Blitz, "Master Greenfire's wyrd is warning us of something."

All three looked at me, but before I could read any reaction on their faces, a shout sounded from the crow's nest.

"Contact!" shouted Lydia Hearth from high above us.

"Whereaway?" boomed Cold Man.

"Two points off starboard," replied the lookout. "War canoes, coming from the inlets."

Vikon shoved past me and reached for a looking-glass. The captain did the same, and Mistress Blackeye ushered Blitz and me back from the railing.

"Ten boats," said Vikon. "No, twelve ... bloody hell, twenty."

The captain looked up at the sails, then at the opposite coast. He frowned at the lack of wind, and chewed on his thick moustache at the high cliffs on the port side.

"Prepare for battle," whispered Cold Man.

"Prepare for battle!" boomed Siggy Blackeye, emptying her lungs to be heard by everyone on deck or in the rigging. "Ports open, cutlasses at the ready, bowmen aloft, wet down the deck ... move your fucking arses!"

"Twenty war canoes," shouted Blitz to the ballistae crews. "Starboard side."

Then I was alone. Everyone knew what to do and where to stand except me. I stood, like a confused statue, as the crew of the *Dead Horse* got ready to fight. Vikon and Captain Ice went to the helm, Blitz went to the forward ballistae, and Mistress Blackeye shouted her way from one side of the ship to the other. With no-one telling me what to do, I simply stood there, looking at the coast.

I'd never seen war canoes before, though I'd heard stories. Each one held ten Pure One warriors, paddling forwards at a frenzied speed, cutting through the water like an arrow. They didn't beat drums or ring bells, and were prized for their speed and stealth – enough to overwhelm many ships not expecting an attack. I hoped I'd given Cold Man enough warning to defend his ship. But I still felt that something was wrong.

There was a hand on my shoulder and I turned to face Weathervane Will. "Not to worry, there's only two hundred of them."

"There's only eighty of *us*," I replied.

He smirked, making him look like a mischievous child. "I'm no Sea Wolf, Duncan, but even I'm a match for two or three Mirralite. Shouldn't you be rattling your cutlass, ready to get bloody?"

"I don't want to get bloody, but I'm a Sea Wolf." I was breathless and my fingertips still tingled, even as I was shoved out of the way again. This time, one of the ballistae crew felt that I was in his way. The twenty war canoes were getting closer and their warriors – bare-chested men with blue tattoos and pale skin – made no sound as they bore down on their prey.

"Wait," I said to Will. "It's not them I can feel. It's not the war canoes. They're no danger. It's something else. Something in the void."

My hands were now burning and I felt that my life was in imminent danger. My wyrd was talking to me and I listened, grabbing Will and moving to the left, just as the low sun was obscured by a thrusting blade. The air shimmered all across the deck and slices of light cut through the glass. Dozens of Eastron appeared, dressed in black, wielding straight swords. They attacked from the void, killing twenty Sea Wolves in one strike.

I was stunned. Will and I were now lying on the damp wood of the *Dead Horse*, with a cloaked man standing over us, ready to strike. We'd avoided the initial attack, but the man now advanced.

"Roll to the left," barked Weathervane Will.

I did as he asked and narrowly avoided a downward thrust from a strange blade. Will kicked out and connected with the stranger's groin, sending him to the deck. He then grabbed me and hefted us both upwards.

Across the deck, the Sea Wolves were fighting back. Rig-rats jumped from the masts, wielding cutlasses, and the ballistae crews left their stations to engage the intruders. I saw our enemies' faces only as fleeting glimpses, but they were Dark Brethren, using their mastery of the void to overpower the superior skill and strength of the Sea Wolves. They danced through the air, appearing and disappearing, using their wyrd-craft in a way I didn't understand. The Brethren used their straight swords as foci, lashing out with their wyrd and taking the crew off-guard. Upon their black armour was the Night Wing, a lord of the quarter and the totem spirit of the Open Hand. It was a black owl, looking with scorn from a haughty, circular face.

Then I heard a roar as Vikon Blood, the Second Fang, appeared by the centre mast. He didn't break the glass or play the Brethren at their own game. He filled his extremities with wyrd and used superior strength and skill to batter his assailants to death. I saw him drive two cutlasses into the head of a man, then throw another overboard with a casual backhand swipe. I stared at him with my mouth open. He was everything I wanted to be.

"Duncan, look out," snapped Will.

I turned and saw a spear, inches from my face, and a Pure One, clambering over the starboard rail. His face was scarred, with blue dye streaked across his eyes and mouth. I lashed out with my wyrd. There was no focus or direction, just a panicked sense that the Pure One should leave me alone. The sense left my mind, travelled to my hands, and entered the air as a solid wall of shimmering wyrd, breaking the Mirralite's neck as if it were a twig, and sending his body flying backwards in a spin.

"By the Bright Lands!" exclaimed Will, looking with amazement as I flung two more Pure Ones from the *Dead Horse*, both with broken bodies.

"There are more," I replied, pointing along the railings. From all directions, Pure Ones pulled themselves aboard the ship. Some died at the point of arrows, but most joined the Dark Brethren in slaughtering the crew.

I dragged Will away from the starboard railing and we headed towards the helm, dodging thrown spears and Dark Brethren void legionnaires. I saw them as shadows on the other side of the glass, and could easily avoid their attacks, though every moment I felt Twist get angrier. I was killing people, and I couldn't control it. I felt as if I had senses in the back of my head, allowing me to defend myself from all angles at once.

"How the fuck can you do this?" asked Weathervane Will, still clinging to a small cutlass.

"I don't know!" I snapped, as vibrating layers of wyrd pulsed from my arms.

I saw Cold Man, standing tall behind the helm, swinging an over-sized axe. His feet were planted on the deck of his ship and he described a circle of death with his axe. Standing over his shoulder was Siggy Blackeye, the Mistress of the Boat. She still shouted, telling the remaining crew to stand together and give their lives for the Severed Hand. They were true Sea Wolves, even when faced with overwhelming odds.

I thought the ship was lost and I started to panic. There were more attackers than defenders. The Sea Wolves were now little more than pockets of resistance, spread across the deck, as a bloody wave cut them down. The Mirralite were little threat on their own, but in threes and fours they could overwhelm the warriors of the Severed Hand, and the Brethren were like shadows, using their wyrd to confuse and disorient.

I suddenly realized that Will and I were surrounded. My wyrd wasn't subtle, quiet or even under control, and this made me a focus of attention. I wished I could dampen it, but Twist wouldn't let me. For a moment, the cork had been pulled from the bottle, and most people aboard the *Dead Horse* – attackers *and* defenders – were looking at me. It created a pause, forcing me to look into the dead faces of dozens of Sea Wolves. I involuntarily decapitated a Dark Brethren when I saw the cleaved body of Anthony Blitz. Tears of exertion and fear flooded from my eyes, but the globe of crackling blue wyrd only grew in size. I couldn't fight, but I could kill, and I was a Sea Wolf.

I screamed, as Twist stabbed my flesh with a hundred thorns, and forced me to kill anyone who wished me harm. There were too many of them, and all I could do to stay alive was to send an explosive shockwave of wyrd across the deck. As I lost consciousness, I heard dozens of death rattles. My last hope was that my eruption of wyrd could differentiate friend from foe.

8

I opened my eyes and saw blue sky. My head throbbed and my leg was numb. My mouth was dry and my skin was covered in sweat. I could feel rocks beneath my body. I was lying on a beach, with the sea tickling my feet. I tried to sit up, but my hands and legs were bound with rope. I felt drained and thin, as if I'd been pulled from the deepest sleep.

"You are lucky to be alive," said a calm voice. "Such exertion is dangerous for your people."

I turned my head and saw Snake Charmer, David's Pure One squire. His arms and legs were tied, and his face was badly beaten. For a moment, I forgot the enormity of what I'd done and why the Dark Brethren would attack us, and wondered why the Pure Ones would beat one of their own. "Are you okay?" I asked.

"Mostly," answered Snake. "David and I were in hold when you ... ended the fight. When the Brethren brought us up on deck, everyone was either dead or unconscious. Your doing?"

I looked at the rocks beneath me, wanting to say no. "Did I kill any of the crew?"

Snake nodded along the beach. I blinked tears from my eyes and tried to orient myself. Everything was foggy, like a sheet of mist across my field of vision. Gradually, I regained focus, and saw ten or eleven restrained Sea Wolves.

Vikon Blood was amongst them, as was the Kneeling Wolf, Weathervane Will.

"They're alive," said Snake. "As I said, you *ended* the fight, you didn't win it."

Beyond the surviving crew, Mirralite Pure Ones, directed by Dark Brethren, were piling bodies. I gulped, and felt vomit in my throat. The dead were formed into three distinct piles on the rocky beach. The smallest was of Dark Brethren, mostly mangled into fleshy pieces. Then came the cleaved bodies of tattooed Mirralite. But the closest pile, and by far the largest, was comprised of Sea Wolves. "How many of them did *I* kill?" I asked, terrified by the sheer scale of death.

"I think... most of the Brethren and Pure Ones," replied Snake. "You just knocked the Sea Wolves insensible. If the attackers had not had reinforcements you might have won the day. Though many warriors fell."

"And the assassin?" I asked.

"Freed," replied Snake. "Taken away by the Brethren. Though I don't think that is why they attacked the *Dead Horse*."

From close by, opposite the growing mounds of corpses, four Dark Brethren realized I was awake and encircled me. They wore black armour of different tones, with a faded owl on every tabard. They held high-tension short bows, and quickly pointed four arrows at my head. I tensed my legs and tried not to piss myself. Twist was asleep, and my wyrd felt like a damp rag. I was totally helpless, and feebly put my hands in the air.

Off the coast, I saw the *Dead Horse* aflame. The sails were sheets of fire, dancing downwards and catching the wood of the deck. The ship would burn to the waterline in a matter of minutes. My first voyage as a Sea Wolf had ended in an explosion of wyrd, with the crew utterly defeated by their oldest enemy. I'd tried to help. I'd desperately tried to help. But I had no control, and I'd just lashed out.

A strange mixture of revulsion, fear and confusion overtook me. I looked at the warriors I'd killed and felt as if my mind was crawling up a mountain of dead bodies, becoming heavier with every step. Was I really as dangerous as everyone thought? Or was the Old Bitch of the Sea right to show me her favour? I wanted to be a Sea Wolf, but I was just a freak with a pain spirit.

"Your life is in the balance," said one of the Dark Brethren, a clean-cut warrior with a young face. "My name is Loco Death Spell, and I will end you if you disobey me. You may have killed a hundred warriors, but Inigo Night Walker and the third void legion now control your fate."

The bodies were burned. Around seventy Sea Wolves were surrounded by wood and set alight. On top of the pile of bodies, posed with no reverence, the broken body of Captain Roderick Ice was thrown. Cold Man's eyes were open and bloodshot, though his neck, chest and arms were riddled with deep slice marks. He'd died fighting. Any one of his wounds would have maimed a lesser man, but it had taken dozens to put him down.

The survivors were allowed to say no words over the departing spirits. Hoods were placed over our heads and we were hefted onto war canoes by the Mirralite, whilst the Dark Brethren used their void paths to go on ahead. It was a subtle use of wyrd, not practised by Sea Wolves, allowing swift travel through a hostile voidscape. I didn't know how it worked, but they must have found a way to conceal themselves from the darker denizens of the wild void. They'd used their craft to assault the *Dead Horse* and kill the Sea Wolves. But I didn't know why.

I saw David's limp body be hooded just before me. The Winterlord had been divested of his armour and was badly beaten, but he was still alive. I couldn't say the same about most others.

As the canoes left the beach I picked up two bits of information. Somehow Siggy Blackeye had escaped into the forest by pretending to be dead, and the Dark Brethren leader was called Inigo Night Walker. Neither piece of information improved our immediate prospects, but I was glad a Sea Wolf had escaped.

With my arms tied behind my back, and my head resting against wood, I fell into a strange world of dislocation. For hours, I was twisted into a hundred different shapes, as the war canoe negotiated the Red Straits at high speed. I couldn't tell east from west, let alone see where we were going. I wanted to fall asleep, but I couldn't stop twitching. I tried to focus my wyrd, but I was too agitated. All I could do was wait and get angrier. I waited for hours that felt like days, rolling the same few thoughts around my head. Why would the Dark Brethren be so bold as to attack a Sea Wolf ship so close to the Severed Hand? But mostly that I didn't deserve to be alive, when so many better Sea Wolves had died. I always hoped that, when I was tested, I'd find a way to shine. But, so far, everything I'd done had been spontaneous, chaotic, and undeniably dangerous. Why couldn't I wield a sword, join the battle and contribute? I might have died, but I'd have been a proper Sea Wolf, fighting alongside the Second Fang, if only for a moment. I cried.

When the canoe finally stopped, I could hear sea birds and smell grass. The grating of wood on rocks and the stomp of heavy feet told me that the boats were being hefted up a beach. I was still crying, with tensed limbs, covered in pins-and-needles, and I wailed in pain as I was lifted from the boat and dumped on the rocks.

My hood was removed, revealing a crisp, blue sky that hurt my eyes. I was scared to know where we were, but looked anyway. Inland, I saw wooden structures and an encircling wall. Further away, over dense woodland, was a murky black cloud, belching forth rain and flashes of lightning. It was the island of Nowhere, and the cloud was called the Maelstrom. I'd never been here, but pictures of the Maelstrom hung in my father's hall on Moon Rock. It was the ancestral home of the Ice family, ruled by Xavyer Ice, called the Grim Wolf, and the churning cloud was a void storm. The glass on Nowhere was chaotic. It was fractured in places, like a stone wall in others. It was said that only the practised or powerful could summon their wyrd on the island, and breaking the glass was impossible. Though falling into the void, if you got too close to the Maelstrom, was a very real danger. I wondered if the Brethren void paths would still work. The only ones I could see were Loco and the three others tasked with pointing arrows at my head. And beyond that was a larger question. Why would the Grim Wolf allow the Dark Brethren to berth on his island?

"Why are we here?" I asked one of my guards. "This is a Sea Wolf island."

"Some Sea Wolves are wiser than others," replied Loco Death Spell, moving to stand behind me, with a heavy short sword in his hand.

Along the coast of Nowhere, a hundred Pure Ones stood guard over eleven survivors of the *Dead Horse*. They were conscious and heavily restrained, and most were wounded. All of them, including Vikon Blood, were looking at me. Snake Charmer and David Falcon's Fang were the only ones not glaring. In Sea Wolf eyes I saw hate, pity, anger and revulsion. Cold Man had said that they didn't know who I was or how my wyrd flowed. I wanted to make them understand that *I* didn't know either. I thought I knew who I was, but I'd *never* known how my wyrd flowed.

Then a crackle in my fingertips alerted me to something beyond the glass. I looked up and saw a flash of white light, and two void paths opened along the beach. In lock-step, appearing from nowhere, came fifty void legionnaires.

"Lord Inigo returns," observed Loco.

The Mirralite who guarded the few survivors took a step away, allowing the Dark Brethren to take over custody. They were smaller than Sea Wolves, barely larger than the Pure Ones, though their movements were quick and precise. Their armour was all black, made of segmented steel and thick fabric. Each warrior wore the same tabard, showing the haughty Night Wing.

There were now fifty Brethren and a hundred Pure Ones, guarding a broken group of eleven survivors. A Winterlord, a Kneeling Wolf, a Pure One, and eight Sea Wolves.

A Dark Brethren, older than the others and wearing no armour, was staring over the wounded form of Vikon Blood. His skin was a deep bronze, and under his heavy black robe he wore loose clothing of thin fabric that fluttered in the wind. He had two straight swords, belted at the hip, and soft boots that made little sound on the rocks. He approached the Second Fang.

"We are both Eastron," said Lord Vikon. "As a defeated warrior, I demand to know your name." He was in pain, struggling to stay upright. There was blood at the corners of his mouth, and bruises across his cheeks and neck. I wanted to help him, but I was too far away to do anything useful.

"As a victorious warrior, I give it," replied the Brethren. "I am Inigo Night Walker, Sentinel of the Dark Harbour and commander of the third void legion. You are my prisoners and will be treated with respect, whether you live or die."

"A sentinel?" queried Vikon. "A position of note amongst your people. Not the leader of a raiding party of cowards. Have we hurt the Stranger's feelings?"

Inigo Night Walker turned his dark eyes to the other survivors. "Accept my apologies, Lord Vikon. We did not know you were aboard, and underestimated your prowess. We thought to kill a few and capture the majority." He fixed his eyes on me. "Then your young wyrd-master killed dozens of my warriors. That was unexpected."

"This will mean war," replied the Second Fang, shifting position and looking at me out of the side of his eye. "Trying to kill Prince Oliver, trying to kill me. And why the fuck are you on Nowhere? Scouting the assassin's next target? Two hundred ships will descend upon the Open Hand and hang Marius Cyclone by his entrails."

"You don't listen!" snapped Inigo. "I told you, I am Sentinel of the Dark Harbour, not the Open Hand." He turned away, gritting his teeth. "Please try not to be too much of a Sea Wolf, howling at the moon whenever your feelings are hurt. All Dark Brethren are not the same. We sent no assassin to the Severed Hand, and we attacked the *Dead Horse* out of necessity. We had to stop you returning to your father. This island *must* remain secure."

The other survivors moved in closer, edging towards the Second Fang in muted solidarity. I rubbed my eyes, trying to focus enough to join them, but was stopped by the four Brethren guards. Loco reacted to my small movements by holding his bulky short sword to my throat. "*You* will not be contributing," he said. "I see one flicker of wyrd and you lose more blood than you can spare."

The majority of the void legionnaires were in loose formation behind their commander, being faced down by the battered survivors of the *Dead Horse*. Eleven warriors, their hands tied and their weapons taken, refused to submit to fifty well-armed Dark Brethren. I so wanted to be with them, to be able to think and act like them. I wondered if they were as confused and afraid as me. I wanted to stop time and speak to Lord Vikon. I wanted to say sorry and ask him if I could ever really be a Sea Wolf. But all I did was stay seated and scratch at my thorn clinch.

"You won't believe me," continued Inigo Night Walker, "but I am not your enemy. If you'd not set sail for Nowhere, we would perhaps have met under more formal circumstances. But your people are not ready for my words, or the words of the Stranger. Perhaps in a year or two, when the sea has risen."

Vikon Blood laughed at the Dark Brethren, keeping his pain under control. "You will never understand us. You've conspired against the Winterlords and now you've conspired against us. That was a mistake." He did his best to stand, but fell back to the rocks. Weathervane Will and Lydia Hearth helped him upright, so he could face Inigo Night Walker. "Our code demands open war. You would do well to prepare yourself. Run back to Marius Cyclone, where your dishonour may be celebrated."

Every Sea Wolf who could stand, did so. We'd all heard of Marius Cyclone. He was the youngest of the three Cyclone brothers and, as the elder of the Dark Harbour, was called the Stranger. My brother, Kieran, talked of him often, as if he were our greatest enemy. It was ships from his hold most frequently targeted by Sea Wolf pirates. By invoking his name, Inigo had given the survivors all the reason they needed to thrust out their chests and remain defiant. For the first time since I'd boarded the *Dead Horse*, they had something other than me to focus on.

I tried to slow my breathing and feel my wyrd, but there was nothing to hold on to. Twist was scratching at my leg, but the glass of Nowhere muted the pain. I couldn't do anything. I couldn't protect the Second Fang or even lash out at the Dark Brethren. Focusing the slightest bit of power required leaching it through the glass, like drinking water from a tiny hole in a dam.

"We're going to take the boy," said Inigo, directing Loco to bring me closer. "The rest of you will stay here as prisoners."

"No!" shouted Vikon Blood. "We. Will. Not." He locked eyes with me and tried to smile, as if he knew how much I admired him. We were both sons, living in the wake of our fathers, and I again found strength in his presence. "He is Duncan Greenfire, and he is a Sea Wolf. He stays with us. Do as you will, but he'll be with us when you do it."

The word of the Second Fang was enough for the other survivors, and I felt goose bumps as they all looked at me. The hatred was gone, and every man and woman used me as a focus for their defiance. A freak I may be, but I was *their* freak, and was infinitely more worthy than any Dark Brethren. I wished things were different. I wished I'd not unleashed my wyrd aboard the *Dead Horse*. I wished I was normal. But, for a moment, I felt like I was a Sea Wolf.

Unfortunately, Inigo Night Walker didn't care about sentiment. He slowly walked over to me, his thin, black clothing swaying in the wind. "Someone may have a use for you, boy," said the Brethren. "But these others..." he shook his head. "If *you* hadn't complicated things, we would have taken forty prisoners. We killed many Sea Wolves out of vengeance, after you erupted. What are you? Some kind of spirit child?"

I shook my head, but couldn't speak. Hearing that I'd been responsible for killing the crew made me feel sick. Behind my eyes, I saw the stern face of my father, shaking his head, as if he had been proven right.

"Speak, boy," said Inigo. "How does your wyrd flow?"

"I...I don't know. I stopped one of your assassins in the Bloody Halls and we brought him here. He had a second target on Nowhere. Then *you* attacked us. But, my wyrd...it's, it's...I don't know." I babbled the same few sentences, until the commander of the third void legion waved his hand and made me shut up.

"Leave him alone," shouted the Second Fang. "He's one of us."

Inigo Night Walker rolled his eyes. "Lord Vikon, I promised you would be treated with respect. Please remain silent and accept your fate, or that may change. You have lost, you are helpless. Remember that."

I struggled to think of a worse thing he could have said to a group of Sea Wolves. We'd been defeated in battle, albeit with subterfuge and trickery, but to call us helpless was like lighting a short fuse. I stood apart, but I felt everything *they* did. My blood rose, as all eleven survivors, their hands still bound, took a stride forwards, forming a line behind Lord Vikon. None could summon their wyrd, and dried blood covered their exposed flesh, but their bravery gave me strength.

Inigo grunted, shaking his head, as if he fought an internal conflict. His legionnaires moved slowly to flank him, but they kept their blades sheathed, unafraid of a dozen battered Sea Wolves with their hands tied behind their backs.

Then the commander raised his head and took a deep breath. "It's easier if I kill you," he stated, frowning at Vikon. "If open war is already inevitable, why would I keep you alive, Lord Vikon Blood, Second Fang of the Severed Hand?"

I tensed my arms and held my breath, wanting to summon a dagger of wyrd to drive into the commander's throat. But there was nothing there. Even the pain of the thorn clinch was dull, and my wyrd didn't appear to care that I was a Sea Wolf. If ever there was a chance to prove myself it was now, at a time when swords and strength were irrelevant. I could summon all my chaotic power and decimate the Dark Brethren with a surge of wyrd, but the glass of Nowhere wouldn't let me.

"Kill him," ordered Inigo Night Walker. "*And* his Sea Wolves. Subdue the rat, the Winterlord and the Pure One."

Fifty void legionnaires drew wide-bladed short swords and advanced. I panicked, feeling more helpless than I thought possible. I was pulled back to a dark dwelling in Moon Rock, where I'd first known pain and helplessness. I saw my father, and I saw Clatterfoot, as if they were presiding over my torment. It was them, as much as Loco Death Spell, who kept me captive, and stopped me rushing to help Lord Vikon.

None of the Sea Wolves retreated. Nor did Weathervane Will or David Falcon's Fang. They were all wounded, exhausted and restrained, but each and every one of them ran forwards to meet the void legionnaires. The Second Fang growled, baring his teeth as if he could bite his way to victory. None of them could summon their wyrd, but they didn't care. I wanted to be one of them, and I saw their hopeless charge in slow motion, with each face burned upon my memory. They knew they would die, but it didn't occur to them to accept their deaths. Only Snake Charmer, David's Pure One squire, remained behind, bowing his head as the survivors of the *Dead Horse* ran onto fifty Dark Brethren blades.

I couldn't do anything. I was forced to watch. I was a volatile, dangerous little bastard, and I'd killed a hundred people without meaning to, but I cried like a child as I watched them all die. I didn't even feel pain. I just felt empty.

David Falcon's Fang was beaten unconscious, William Vane was choked out, but everyone else was cut down. Vikon head-butted the first man and drop-kicked the second, but he was overwhelmed. Lydia Hearth screamed herself to death, as a contemptuous swipe opened her throat. Another man was kicked to the ground and had his head stomped to a pulp. Most met their end at the point of a short sword, driven into stomachs and chests. The void legionnaires may have been highly skilled, but this was simple butchery, and Loco's blade stopped me reacting. Even when the Brethren began to laugh, all I could do was hold my head upright and cry.

"You fucking cowards," slurred Vikon Blood, rising to his knees as the last surviving Sea Wolf. He was cut from head to toe, with blood seeping from every crease of skin, but still he smiled.

"Hold," said Inigo, drawing his own blade and striding towards the dying man. "Are they your last words?"

Vikon's bloody face contorted into a huge grin. His eyes sought me out, and he blinked to clear his vision. With deep breaths and a look of peace on his battered face, he smiled at me. "She spoke to you, Duncan. She spoke to *you*. She never spoke to me, or my father. The Old Bitch of the Sea knows more than all of us. More than me, more than these fucking Dark Brethren. She sees you, and she sees what you can become. Live, Duncan. Live and honour us. Honour the Sea Wolves."

Inigo Night Walker held his sword to Vikon's neck. The Brethren glanced back at me, frowned, and delivered the killing blow, opening the Second Fang's throat. Vikon Blood's battered face was calm, even as he took his last breath and fell dead onto the rocky ground.

9

Kieran told me stories of the Dark Brethren, and the hundred and fifty years of attritional warfare we'd fought against them since Duncan Red Claw first spilled blood along the Emerald Coast. But *I'd* never pillaged one of their ships, or raided one of their settlements. The first one I'd seen had tried to assassinate Prince Oliver in the Bloody Halls. Then they'd destroyed the *Dead Horse* and killed one of the few men I admired. It was hard not to hate them, though these Brethren claimed not to have sent the assassin. What that meant, and why the Grim Wolf allowed them to remain on Nowhere were open questions. Questions that Twist obviously didn't want me thinking about.

The pain in my leg was such that the image of Lord Vikon's dying face was painted behind my eyes. I was bound and hooded, given from one pair of hands to another, as I was led from the rocky beach. I wailed, cried, wrung my fists, and spluttered, barely able to take the pain of the thorn clinch. But I deserved it. My father had been right, all those years ago. I'd never be a Sea Wolf. I'd tried, but had just caused more death. And, when I *could* have made a difference, I was helpless.

"*Honour us.*" I didn't know how.

I still felt Loco's blade at my neck, and the young Brethren took his duties seriously, allowing me minimal movement.

Even when the pain made me retch, I was forced to stay upright. Inigo Night Walker wanted me closely guarded, and my hood only partly obfuscated the four warriors standing around me. If only the void legionnaires knew how weak and confused I truly was.

Somewhere nearby, David Falcon's Fang, Weathervane Will, and Snake Charmer were also captives, but I could hear no defiance from them. I imagined we were held separately, and I worried that there was no reason for Inigo to spare them. *I'd* done enough to pique his interest, if slaughtering a hundred of his warriors could be categorized in such a way, but the others seemed to be alive purely because they weren't Sea Wolves. Perhaps the Dark Brethren hated us as much as we hated them. Could that alone have driven them to prowl the Red Straits, waiting for a ship to attack?

After several hours of sweat, pain and raging self-doubt, my hood was removed. We were beyond the coastal wall, and had entered a settlement of thatch and bound planks, well south of the Maelstrom. The Grim Wolf and his People of Ice lived in the centre of the island, directly under the void storm, though they were not so idle as to miss an incursion of Pure Ones and Dark Brethren. They were still Sea Wolves, despite their rebellious reputation, but had allowed Inigo to kill the Second Fang.

The majority of the Dark Brethren moved to a series of large, circular pavilions in the centre of the camp, while the Mirralite spread out around the edges, tending to cook-fires, forges and stables. My four guards and I went to a smaller hut, on the northern edge of the settlement. At no point did Loco's blade leave my throat, though I was allowed to sit down, albeit on a rickety, wooden bench. The young void legionnaire sat behind me on a single chair, with the other three, their short bows held loosely, standing in front of the single door.

"Get comfortable, boy," said Loco Death Spell. "They'll take time deciding what to do with *you*."

"My name's Duncan," I murmured. "I'm not a boy. I survived the rite." I couldn't bring myself to say that I was a Sea Wolf. I turned as much as his blade would allow, looking at him over my shoulder. "Your assassin didn't think I was just a boy ... when I stopped him killing Oliver Dawn Claw."

Loco's clean-cut face was humourless. "Had it been *our* assassin, a whelp like you, wyrd or no, would not have been able to stop him. But I don't know who tried to kill the Winterlord prince. It wasn't Inigo Night Walker or Marius Cyclone. Whatever you and your people may believe, those of the Dark Harbour are not your enemies, nor the enemies of the Always King. We attacked your ship out of necessity. To keep this island secure."

I scoffed, rubbing at my thorn clinch to relieve soreness. I could imagine what Kieran would say, what the Second Fang would say, what every warrior at the Severed Hand would say. But I wasn't them, and I didn't want to chance that the void legionnaire's stoicism had a limit.

"You're small for a Sea Wolf," observed Loco.

"I'm a Greenfire, we're all small. Are all Death Spells humourless?"

"I can only speak for my father and two sisters ... but, yes," replied the Dark Brethren. "And keep your eyes facing forwards. I may have to kill you, and you shouldn't greet your Old Bitch of the Sea with *my* face as the last thing you saw."

I gulped, and Twist tightened around my leg, causing a dull throb that made me wince and grit my teeth. I'd been too confused and distracted to realize that piquing Inigo's interest might not be enough to keep me alive. I'd caused so much death, and everyone was afraid of me, but I could still be killed, as easily as Lord Vikon and the other Sea Wolves. Why would they keep me alive? I was a complication, and war with the Severed Hand might already be inevitable. I imagined that the pain was Twist rolling his eyes, exasperated that I'd finally accepted how much danger I was in.

"She spoke to me," I replied, with the pain making me light-headed. "Our totem. When they dragged me out of the Bay of Grief. I was fucking freezing, and Arthur Brand had to drag me through the glass. But she appeared from the void, a beautiful blue wolf, and she spoke to me. She was the only reason I was on the *Dead Horse*. The First Fang trusted the Old Bitch of the Sea and gave me a chance to prove I could be a Sea Wolf." I took a deep breath, scratching at my leg. "That was three weeks ago. How do you think I'm doing so far?" My light-headedness quickly flowed into exhaustion.

Loco sensed that it was a rhetorical question, and simply grunted, acknowledging that he'd been listening. "You can sleep if you want," said the void legionnaire. "But summon no wyrd, or I *will* have to kill you."

The wooden bench was narrow and flimsy, but it was large and secure enough for me to curl up and sleep. The cold metal of Loco's blade remained against my neck but, as I shifted position to get comfortable, I felt it slowly move to rest across my back. Then I felt nothing, as exhaustion overtook me.

In my dreams, Twist and I relived the attack on the *Dead Horse*, and the end of Lord Vikon Blood. The pain spirit directed me left and right, like it also held a blade to my throat, telling me what I should be looking at. I saw the warning I'd delivered, the battle on deck, and the eruption of wyrd that ended the fight. Then I saw my unconscious body, sprawled amidships, and Twist directed my eyes elsewhere. Someone had been watching me. Someone pale and hard to see. Perhaps close by, able to view the fight from a position of safety. It was a strange sensation, accompanied by the thin whine of a whistle. The prickly feeling of being watched, and the sound of the whistle remained, as the dream showed me my helplessness, while the Second Fang and the surviving Sea Wolves were killed. I wanted to talk to Twist, and ask him who had been watching, but the spirit could only communicate with pain.

"Stop screaming, boy. Wake the fuck up!"

I shook my head, saw Loco's face, and fell off the bench. It was night-time and the small hut was now illuminated by a single brazier, next to the door. My leg was numb, as Twist danced up and down, shouting something at me. The other Brethren, alarmed by my screaming, all pointed their arrows at my head. "It's okay," I winced. "I'll be okay. Please don't shoot me. I won't summon my wyrd." I massaged my leg and took deep breaths, until Twist quietened down.

"A nightmare," observed Loco Death Spell. "A battle will often bring a troubled sleep. And *you* killed more than any blade or bow. Perhaps a bad dream is the start of your punishment." The young void legionnaire, with his clean-cut face and high cheekbones, didn't change expression, and it was impossible to discern whether I was being mocked. "Get up. Lord Inigo requests your presence."

I delayed as long as I could, gritting my teeth and scratching at the thorn clinch, until I was sure I could stand. No-one offered to help me, even when I leant heavily on the bench, with a muted grunt of pain. For the first time since the beach, I didn't have a blade against my throat. A situation that Loco remedied, as soon as I was standing.

"You'll excuse me," said the void legionnaire, gently resting the edge of his short sword against my chin. "You appear to be a feeble runt, but I know you're more than that. If you are a mighty wyrd-master, you should drop the act. We will treat you no differently."

I balked, pushing away the sword. I heard three short bows tense, and saw Loco's eyes widen, as he pointed the blade at my face. They thought I could erupt at any moment. I didn't know if the Dark Brethren agreed with the Sea Wolves about untrained wyrd, but my four guards were certainly afraid of me.

"Sorry," I muttered, spreading my arms in submission. "I'm not what you think I am. I don't know what I am, but I'm no wyrd-master. Whatever that is."

Loco grasped my shoulders and spun me around, placing his sword across my neck. The other three retreated from the hut, keeping their arrows aimed at me, as I was led into the crisp night of Nowhere. I was tired, and my leg hurt, but the fresh evening air was like a slap to the face, forcing me to be alert.

I was led away from the hut, under close guard. Other structures covered the low ground, over a sandy rise from the southern coast of Nowhere. Some buildings were of wood, with coned roofs of thatch. Others were formed of framed canvas, with temporary fires and forges. Mirralite Pure Ones filled the open ground, with the Dark Brethren confined to a few of the larger tents. There was no heraldry on display, nothing to signal Inigo Night Walker's rank, nor the presence of the void legionnaires.

"Look yonder," said Loco, nudging my head in the direction of a wooden pole, buried into the earth, next to the largest pavilion. Around the base was a mound of earth, and a pool of dark liquid.

I squinted through the darkness, unable to see what was tied to the pole. With Loco's permission, I approached the mound of earth and gasped. It was Lugo Eclipse, the assassin I'd last seen being dragged out of Lord Ulric's hall by Arthur Brand. The Dark Brethren was naked, and suspended well above the ground, his arms stretched out, and his wrists bound by rope. His legs hung limply from the pole, and blood covered every inch of skin. It was unsettling to see him again, and even more unsettling to see that he'd been tortured and killed by his own people. Then I gasped a second time, as I realized that both of his feet had now been cut off, and the pool of dark liquid was his blood.

"Why have you done that to him?" I mumbled. "Why defile him like that?"

Loco pulled me away from the mutilated corpse. "It's a rite of punishment. He will have to crawl as he greets the Night Wing."

My stomach did a somersault, and I vomited in my mouth. I'd killed this man as much as the void legionnaires who'd cut him. He'd tried to kill Prince Oliver Dawn Claw,

I'd stopped him, and he'd been tortured to death by his own people. But it all started with me and my stupid fucking wyrd. And I still didn't know who'd sent him to the Severed Hand. Loco and Inigo insisted it wasn't them, and their treatment of the man added weight to their claims. It also made it impossible that they'd attacked the *Dead Horse* to free the assassin.

The guards led me away from the dead man, and towards the largest tent. Around the canvas pavilion stood void legionnaires, but no Pure Ones, and my nostrils caught the scent of rich, hoppy ale coming from within. It was a smell I knew well, and filled many streets of Moon Rock, competing with fish and salt to be the dominant smell of the hold. I'd not expected the Dark Brethren to be drinking such liquor.

"Speak when spoken to, boy," said Loco, his back suddenly straighter and his demeanour more professional, as he parted the tent flaps and pulled me within.

I blinked and let my eyes acclimatize to the dark interior. The canvas was black, as was the interior carpet, with a single, small brazier in the centre.

"Apologies," said a voice from the gloomy pavilion. "We did not know what to do with you while we discussed your fate. Leaving you isolated appeared the sensible decision."

It was Inigo Night Walker, his face gradually becoming distinct as I stopped blinking. He sat, cross-legged, on a plump cushion, wearing casual clothing of black satin. To his left were other Dark Brethren, standing at-ease, but still dressed for war.

"Duncan Greenfire," said a deep voice from the right.

Loco pushed me further into the pavilion, and I gasped. Slouched on cushions, holding mugs of pungent ale, were four Sea Wolves. They wore leather armour, with tarnished metal breastplates, displaying a shard of blue ice. They appeared unkempt and barbaric next to the clean-cut Brethren, but something in their eyes made me homesick.

The oldest amongst them had spoken. He stood from his cushion and approached me. He was an imposing man, though advancing in years, with a bushy grey beard and wild, blue eyes, flecked with red. My mind conjured the image of a great, grey bear, barrel-chested and savage. "Do you know me, boy?"

"You're a man of Ice," I spluttered. "A Sea Wolf."

His blue eyes narrowed and his bearded face creased up. "I know your father," he replied. "My name is Xavyer Ice, I'm called the Grim Wolf of Nowhere."

He paused, allowing me a moment. I'd heard much of him and his people. The Years of Ice were over a hundred years ago, but they tore the Severed Hand apart, and were far from forgotten. My ancestor, Robert Greenfire, had ended the civil war, but the People of Ice were distrusted to this day. Though they were still Sea Wolves. Why did they so casually converse with the Dark Brethren? Had they helped them attack the *Dead Horse*?

Then my eyes were drawn to another figure, partially hidden in shadows behind the rest. I saw a pale-skinned man, then wondered if I'd seen anything at all. The pavilion was dark, and the exterior moonlight created strange mirages through gaps in the fabric. The pale skin, the bone-white hair, the pink eyes, could it all have been a trick of the light? Certainly no-one else registered the man's presence.

"Duncan," said the Grim Wolf, "I'm sorry for what happened to the *Dead Horse*." He gritted his teeth. "If we'd known it was Cold Man's ship or that young Vikon was aboard..." He looked at Inigo Night Walker, but left his sentence unfinished.

"The Second Fang was an unexpected bonus," offered the Dark Brethren.

"No," I murmured, before Xavyer Ice could respond. "You killed him. You killed him like he was nothing. You killed all of them. You started a war." Loco grabbed me by the collar and wrenched me backwards before I could say anything else. Again, my guards flexed their bows, anticipating a spontaneous eruption of wyrd.

Inigo and the Grim Wolf looked at each other. No hostility passed between them, just a series of complicated questions and doubts, none of which I understood. At least they were too involved with each other to be concerned by *my* outburst.

Then I saw the pale man again, gliding in and out of shadows at the rear of the pavilion. No-one looked at him, but everyone paused, as if their thoughts had been interrupted. I heard the same thin whistle, and suddenly felt frustrated at my helplessness.

"Why am I still alive?" I asked, unable to conjure any more profound question.

Inigo stood from his cushion. He was far younger than the Grim Wolf, and several inches shorter, but his movements were precise, suggesting a warrior of impressive skill. "Will *you* answer the boy?" he asked the man of Ice. "Or should I?"

The Sea Wolves all stood, setting aside their ale and flanking Xavyer Ice. One of them, a woman of middle years with braided black hair, straightened her breastplate and approached Inigo Night Walker. "Be careful, Brethren," she warned. "This is our island. An island upon which you are a guest."

Inigo spread his arms in supplication, but a sly smile never left his face.

"Duncan," said the Grim Wolf. "We travel inland tomorrow. Back to Cold Point, under the Maelstrom. We needed to decide whether or not you were too dangerous to bring with us."

"He *is* coming with us," said someone from the rear of the pavilion. The voice was strange, clipped at the edges, but deep and commanding.

I gasped, but I was the only one. For an instant, I saw a pale man with wide shoulders and long, braided white hair. The glare of his pink eyes reached me across the tent, but they were gentle, as if their power was unintentional. He melted back into the shadows, but the eyes stayed with me. Twist was wary, coiling around my leg like a threatened animal.

"You're coming with us," said Inigo, as if he'd not heard the strange voice, and the idea had been his own. "Nowhere must be protected, and you should get some rest, we leave in the morning."

"Someone has a use for you," added Xavyer Ice. "You and your wyrd are special."

I was special. I didn't feel special. I felt confused and alone, held captive by a strange people on a strange island. For the first time in my life, Twist was the only thing I could cling to. The pain spirit was as confused as me, and the insistent fluctuations of pain that caressed my leg suggested he was dealing with his own torment. I couldn't speak to him, and ask if *he* knew why the Dark Brethren and the People of Ice had conspired to kill a Sea Wolf crew and execute the Second Fang. Perhaps he had some wisdom as to who the pale man was, and why no-one appeared to see him but me. I suspected he knew as much or less than *I* did.

I tried to feel the glass, and retreat to the peace of the void, but there was nothing to grasp. The island of Nowhere was like no place I'd been, like no place I'd heard of. Venture too far from a hold, and the void was like a treacherous sky, into which a careless traveller could fall, or be torn apart by wild spirits. But the Grim Wolf's island was different. It was as if the Maelstrom sucked up all the energy, leaving no void for the Eastron to step into. Certainly my wyrd, the only thing about me that appeared to matter, was muted to the point of uselessness. I'd been leeching small slivers of spiritual energy since I arrived, but my wyrd felt like a half-empty glass of water. I had a small reservoir, but the power I'd used aboard the *Dead Horse* was nowhere to be found.

Happily, my captors appeared to have realized that I wasn't going to erupt and kill everyone, and Loco was content to guard me from outside the hut. It was still dark, but I was no longer tired. I was alone for the first time since I'd left the Severed Hand, with nothing but a thin whistling sound to keep me company. The sound wouldn't go away, no matter how much I rubbed at my ears, and the pale man wouldn't leave my thoughts, no matter how much I scratched at my head.

"I just want some peace," I stated, more a series of quiet grunts than actual words.

Peace, replied a distant growl. *No peace for you.*

The words were felt, rather than heard, and I was surprised at my lack of alarm. Even Twist, still nudging my leg in agitation, reacted to the growl with interest rather than fear.

Greenfire must see something. Must know something. Must see it and know it before it is too late. The glass breaks, the sword falls, the sea rises.

I felt soft fur against my hands and face, but couldn't see the creature to whom it belonged. I heard the gentle wash of a calm sea, and looked up, excepting to behold a huge, blue wolf, but all I saw was the dark hut.

"You said that to me before," I replied. "I don't know what it means. *Or* why you spoke to me."

I stood up and was somewhere else. One moment I'd been in the hut, scratching my head and rubbing my ears. The next I was outside, under a low moon, as if by standing up I'd also walked through a door. A gentle sea breeze caressed my face, and low-hanging fog surrounded me. I hadn't broken the glass. I was still in the realm of form, on the island of Nowhere. My leg throbbed, as if Twist was mumbling with interest. The pain spirit directed my eyes left and right, confirming our location. At our back was the expansive camp, filled with small, circular huts and large Dark Brethren pavilions. At our front, over a craggy rise, was the beach where Lord Vikon Blood had died. And at my side, was a huge, invisible presence. The Old Bitch of the Sea emitted a deep growl, and the unmistakable aroma of wet dog crept up my nostrils.

Greenfire will follow. And see. And know.

The voice was impossibly deep, yet gentle, with each utterance causing a subtle aftershock of spiritual power, made no less awesome by my inability to actually *see* the totem of the Sea Wolves. I followed, feeling a strange calm envelop me. Even when the thin, whistling sound returned, it didn't make me scratch at my ears. It made me curious. I didn't *need* my wyrd, when I strode in the wake of the Lady of the Quarter. She'd chosen me. I didn't know why, but in that moment I didn't care.

Ahead of us, the moon poked through the fog, creating a glow across the gently rolling ocean. The whistle came from along the rocky beach, where a single dark figure sat on a thick piece of driftwood. I heard the paws of the huge wolf, striding slowly ahead of me, towards the whistle. Her tail swayed, causing a ripple in the air. My nostrils and throat were filled with the soothing caress of the sea, as much from the spirit as from the Red Straits.

As the figure came into view, I saw an old Pure One, dressed in robes of faded red and black. He had dark skin, wrinkled at the cheeks, and pinched around the mouth and eyes. His whistle, held against thin lips with cracked and bent hands, was wooden, with feathers tied around it.

The Old Bitch of the Sea stopped before the old man, and I sensed that she had lowered herself into a crouch on the rocky beach.

"My name is Ten Cuts," said the Pure One, removing the whistle from his lips. "Your wyrd is powerful, young Invader. We will answer your questions, and those of this Lady of the Quarter."

With a grumble, and a subtle gnash of her teeth, the spectral wolf told me what to say. "How does the sea rise?" I asked, not understanding the question. "We *know* it will rise. We have felt it in black tides of the void. Every ebb and flow speaks of an end. And then ... nothing but chaos." I could feel the distress of the totem. She was terrified of something she knew. Something she remembered, from a time long before the Eastron invaded. She feared it had returned. Whatever it was, however the question was answered, she wanted me to know. She wanted me to bear witness.

I gasped and the wolf growled, as a pale spectre passed across our field of vision. The image ghosted behind Ten Cuts, looking at me with indistinct, pink eyes. Whoever he was, he appeared to walk in and out of the moonlight, never staying still long enough for me to get a clear look.

The old man blew his whistle again, holding the note, and my fingertips began to tingle with wyrd. "Tell me, young Invader," said Ten Cuts. "Know you of the great turtle spirits of the Father? It is said that they see history backwards. The Rykalite have ever revered them as agents of prophecy. Mightier, in their own way, than even the Lords and Ladies of the Quarter."

The Old Bitch of the Sea curled around me on the rocks, letting me feel her fur against the back of my neck. The ancient sea spirit was impatient, and she made *me* impatient. "How does the sea rise?" I repeated.

As if prepared to answer my question, the shadowy figure reappeared, moving slower now and allowing me to see the outline of wide shoulders, within a black robe. Ten Cuts didn't acknowledge him, and slowly returned the spirit-whistle to his lips. "We will show you what we have shown others," he whispered. "What we have shown Marius Cyclone and Xavyer Ice. Witness what has happened before ... and what will happen again."

The pale man moved his shadowy arms in the air, weaving an irregular circle, and I left the beach. At least my mind did. I was enveloped in a blanket of wyrd. Or was it wyrd? It was certainly power, but not filtered through any recognizable prism. It was raw and unfiltered, and showed me the outline of an enormous sea turtle, perched in the waters of the void. It was three or four times larger than the Old Bitch of the Sea, but there was nothing hostile or warlike in its countenance.

I closed my eyes, knowing that both Twist and the totem were with me. When I opened them, I stood on a high cliff, next to an unfamiliar coastline. On one side was a glittering ocean, as calm as a glass of water; on the other was a sprawling city of impossible construction. Bizarre angles joining strange surfaces and illogical platforms, it was half-submerged in the still water, and crawling with bulbous, frog-like creatures. In the centre, towering over all within sight, was an immense set of grey doors, etched in silvery markings of intertwined spiral designs. Around the doors was a giant, stone edifice, draped in a thick layer of seaweed and dripping with slimy water. The doors were five times taller than the Wolf House, and half of Moon Rock would have fit within the huge building.

"You'll want to look away," said Ten Cuts. "Try not to. You may one day have to describe what you saw. Remember, or you'll have to look again."

The doors moved outwards. Gradually at first, they creaked and threw forth a mist of fetid air. Then they were flung open and something emerged from the darkness beyond. A mountainous form walked or stumbled forwards, its ankles scratching through seaweed and salty water, to reach the open air. The light of three aligned stars shone across its bulbous form, and I saw flabby arms and legs of immense proportion, dripping with sickly fluids. The head was swept backwards and a mass of pulpy tentacles reached from the face.

As it limped from the door, straightening to its full immensity, the sea rose, forming tidal waves that eclipsed the city and the landscape, yet barely reaching the shins of the enormous creature. Small, polypous creatures fell from its body, as toothy, tentacled amoebas, shrugged off with every movement of its titanic form. Then the earth churned, and chunks of rock and soil fell into the sky. Each of its strides was as wide as the Severed Hand, and whatever its webbed feet touched they destroyed.

"It cannot be fought," said Ten Cuts. "It cannot be reasoned with. It is an Old One from before time as you understand it. It ruled this world before the mountains rose and the continents formed. It has been dead, but dreaming, in its Sunken City, until the stars are right. For, at the right time, even death can die."

Then jutting pillars of jagged lava penetrated the surface of the ocean. The water boiled and the forests caught fire, sending waves of smoke and ash into the air. I saw man-made structures shaken to pieces, with chunks of stone and masonry falling into the sky. The land itself fell from the earth and tumbled upwards. Mountains cracked, lakes boiled, mortal creatures were turned into dust, and an era of pure chaos began. All that remained was the sea, rising higher and higher, until it broke as a wave of absolute despair.

Greenfire must let his wyrd shine. Greenfire must honour us all. The Sunken City awakens. I return to my den. Must find Alpha Wolf. She will lead fight back. There is no time. Need time to save Eastron.

The Impurity Wars lasted nine years
  And thousands of Pure Ones died.
The great cull of Nibonay lasted three months
  And thousands of Pure Ones died.
The Second Battle of Tranquillity lasted two hours
  And thousands of Pure Ones died.
If nothing else, the Invaders are getting more efficient.

From "Nine Years, Three Months,
Two Hours: a meditation"
by Heart Song, Speaker of the Nissalite

PART FOUR

Adeline Brand in the Mirralite Reservation

10

The story goes that Mathias Blood had to do no persuading to get the Sea Wolf fleet to attack the Sunken City. On the contrary, it is told that he had to turn warriors away who wanted to join the armada. Fishermen and blacksmiths; shield maidens and pups, each wanting to be a part of the largest fleet ever assembled. But still, he had tens of thousands of warriors across numerous ships. Why would he think he needed more? Last Port had been attacked by Sunken Men and strange depth barges, and we had to respond.

They set sail from the Severed Hand in 91DA – seventy-six years ago – and arrived at the Sunken City a year later. No-one survived the Battle of the Depths and nothing is known for sure about what happened once the fleet left Last Port. Not a plank of wood or a cleaved limb has ever been recovered. It took twenty years for the Sea Wolves to recover. And that's the end of the story. At least, it's the end of the commonly known story. We now knew more, but I did not feel any wiser. I felt bound, as if knowledge of the Sunken Men held me in some vice of responsibility.

Arthur had accepted the knowledge, saying that it would stand him in good stead as a future Battle Brand. I let him believe so. It was as good a coping mechanism as any. Certainly better than Jaxon's method of silently brooding on what *might* happen when we reached the Bay of Bliss. His mumbling ranged from a village of frogs, to a hundred different kinds of craven altar and a cadre of mad varn. As for me, I tried to keep my focus, letting the Wisp worry about this and that, while I kept my mind calm and my heart as ice.

We were far from the Outer Sea, and north of the Wood of Scars. We'd passed into the Mirralite Reservation a day ago, and seen nothing of note to mark the border of our two worlds. It seemed the Pure Ones didn't know or care that we had given them a portion of Nibonay. The rugged terrain was dotted with rocks and occasional pinnacles, splitting the earth and jutting upwards. Jaxon believed that they were a remnant of past battles, when the varn used spirit-whistles to drag spirits of the earth into their service against the armies of Duncan Red Claw. Many pinnacles were broken, as if felled by the wyrd of long-dead duellists. Now they were just rocks, covering the landscape like a thin forest of stone. We camped amongst them, our small fire the only light in any direction. It was cold, but not windy, and there were no signs of rain. We would sleep under the sky, using the rocks as cover, and wrapped up in blankets of our wyrd. It was suicidal to enter the void here, as powerful nature spirits prowled beyond the glass, free from the restrictions of being close to the Severed Hand and our spirit-masters.

"If I remember correctly," said Jaxon, leaning against a rocky pinnacle. "There's a dead forest to the north of here. We'll find Dark Wing somewhere around there."

"How do you know so much, Icicle?" asked Arthur. "I understand that you know how to reach the Reservation, but the dead forest? Did you come here on holiday when you were a pup?"

Jaxon ignored him and drew a line in the mud. "That's a dry riverbed, the Mirralite believe that it houses dark spirits." He drew a few triangles next to the line. "That's the forest. And I know because a spirit told me. Well, showed me. It was an air spirit, drifting around the Wolf House. I think it just wanted a chat, but it had been as far north as the dead forest."

Arthur chuckled to himself. To my knowledge my brother had never spoken to a spirit in his life. He deemed it beneath him, and thought little of any duellist who disagreed. Such work was for Tomas Red Fang and his spirit-masters.

"You trust the spirit?" I asked.

"Air spirits are flighty," replied the Wisp. "Though the concept of lying does not occur to them. No, the information is reliable. A Sea Wolf lives near here. A Sea Wolf who scares away any spirits that get too close. It appears that Dark Wing likes the void around his shack to be empty. The air spirit certainly remembered him. The Place Where We Hear The Sea is a distinctive name, hopefully he knows of it."

"Hopefully," I said. "Arthur, you have first watch. Eyes to the north and west. Wake me in two hours."

"Once more for the Severed Hand," he muttered, standing and securing his cutlass belt.

The dead forest began where the pinnacles ended, as if the varn used tree spirits when their earth spirits failed. I could almost see the rampaging duellists, charging into rock and wood, fighting to tame the very land, before the Pure Ones were forced to surrender. Young Green Eyes would no doubt have some poetic description of the Sea Wolves' campaign. How we crushed their harmony under our steel blades and stone walls. To me, the pinnacles were just old rocks, and the dead forest was only a dead forest.

The trees were huge, though gnarled and split. Grey veins ran from the rocky earth to the points of skeletal branches, reaching into the air with neither leaves nor fruit. The bark was white, though green mould crept across the trunks in places, and patches were blackened and burned. As we crossed the dry river bed and entered the forest, I saw a subtle mist of fungal spores, clustered around the roots. The trees might be dead, but they provided a home for exotic mushrooms and virulent mould, much of it likely poisonous.

The forest occupied low ground, a day's walk from the Bay of Bliss. The terrain was too barren to farm, and there was no natural water source. It was practically a desert compared to the lush ground around the Severed Hand. We'd seen no Mirralite and I couldn't imagine anyone living here.

"Hold!" snapped Jaxon, crouching next to a tree, his hand reaching for his cutlass.

Arthur and I flanked him, drawing weapons and holding position. "What do you hear?" I asked, scanning the thinly spaced trees ahead of us.

"I hear feet coming this way. Maybe ten or more."

"Cover," I ordered, and the three of us spread out, standing ready behind trees. Ten Pure Ones were no real danger to three duellists, but I wanted to see them before we struck. I couldn't break the glass, but a tree was just as good under the right circumstances.

Jaxon's hearing was exceptionally acute, and it was a minute until I could hear the sound of running feet. Mirralite wore thin, canvas boots, tied around the ankles with leather thongs, and the sound was a dull thud. Along with the footfalls came a series of grunts and coughs, as if the Pure Ones were running *from* something. I poked my head out from behind the tree.

Appearing from the dead forest, their legs blurring across the ground, were a dozen Mirralite. I saw flashes of red and green across dusty, grey cloth; long, decorated strains of dark hair, and florid tattoos on exposed limbs. They carried spears and hand-axes, with two short bows. Several were wounded, though not severely, and I recognized the snarl of warriors fresh from battle.

"Once more for the Severed Hand," I muttered, stepping from behind the tree and summoning wyrd into my limbs.

Arthur and Jaxon did the same, and we blocked the path of the fleeing Mirralite. They slowed, shouted at each other, then shouted at us, then hefted their weapons and prepared to fight. Perhaps they had never met duellists before, or perhaps their blood was up from their recent conflict. Either way, they attacked us ferociously.

A man crouched before me and thrust his spear at my head. It was powerful, but ill-disciplined, and I stepped aside, grabbing the wooden shaft in my off-hand. I wrested his spear from his hands and cut off his head with a single swing of my cutlass. Arthur had caught an arrow in mid-air and driven it into the head of another Mirralite. The Wisp had sliced a throat and tripped a man to the rocky ground. We advanced.

My brother took the lead, duelling four Mirralite with contemptuous ease. He barely needed to parry their clumsy attacks, preferring to duck and dodge, while lashing out with fatal darts of movement. All four died in as many blinks of an eye. I advanced right, while Jaxon took the left. We covered Arthur's back, killing three more Mirralite as the last Pure One was driven to the ground by my brother's boot.

"Stay still!" barked Arthur, placing his cutlass at the throat of the only survivor. He then turned to me. "I assume you wanted to question one of them?"

I smiled and kicked a dead Pure One out of my way. "You look like you needed that. Is a week without killing anyone too much for you?"

Jaxon cleaned his cutlass and stepped beyond where Arthur held the Pure One. "There's someone else out there."

"Should I be scared, Icicle?" mocked Arthur, nodding at the dozen dead Mirralite. "I doubt there's anything within a hundred leagues that could make me sweat. Even your fucking village of frogs."

I shoved my brother out of the way and stood next to Jaxon. "Dark Wing?" I asked. "He can't be *that* terrifying"

The Wisp looked through the trees with narrow eyes, scanning the white trunks and mouldy roots. I trusted his eyes and ears, but didn't like being ignored. "Jaxon! What is it?"

"A dog," he replied. "More than one. I can hear them growling."

Then a howl sounded through the forest. The dogs did not rush us, like the Pure Ones. They approached slowly, letting us see them gradually. They were of all sizes and breeds, from thick-muzzled hounds to slender terriers. All had matted fur and red eyes, as if they were possessed of some collective power.

"I don't want to kill any dogs," said Arthur, his brow furrowed in confusion.

"Nor me," I replied. "Jaxon, what is this?"

The Wisp sheathed his blade and held out his hands in supplication. "I have no earthly idea."

The dogs looked at us, a dozen rows of bared teeth forming a line between the dead trees. I couldn't imagine that they lived here. There was no foliage or game, and the fungus was not edible.

Suddenly, the last surviving Pure One scrambled backwards, trying to flee from the dogs. Even when Arthur kicked him in the ribs, he continued to crawl away. Two of the largest dogs bounded after him, ignoring the three of us and snarling at the terrified Mirralite. They were Yishian Mastiffs – wild hounds with thick, toothy muzzles and broad forelimbs. We stepped away and let them have the man, sheathing our blades as they latched onto him with powerful jaws. Both hounds got a mouthful of flesh and shook vigorously, causing blood and screaming to fill the air.

"I like dogs," said Arthur, turning away from the dying man. "But that's a bit strong."

The screams became gurgles. One of the hounds tore off a chunk of flesh from the man's shoulder and raked his claws across the man's face. The other, smaller dogs advanced slowly, surrounding us and the two hounds. When the man was dead they circled us, but no longer bared their teeth.

"Do you have a home?" Jaxon asked one of the red-eyed terriers, letting it sniff his hand. "You can't be all alone here."

"They don't like Pure Ones," I said with a smile. "Shall we adopt them?"

The terrier nuzzled against Jaxon's hand, wagging its tail.

Just as the atmosphere lost its tension, and the dogs became more friendly, a slash appeared in the glass and a man stepped from the void. He was close to Arthur in height, and a mane of knotted brown hair fell from his head and face. Extra bulk was added to his huge frame by a wolf-skin cloak, providing a fury mantle on each of his shoulders. He was Eastron, with a wild, unfocused cast to his eyes. Certainly a Sea Wolf, though his cloth was mismatched and poor, and he wore no armour, just layer upon layer of patchwork fabric, hanging in folds to the tops of steel-shod boots.

"Stand down, sir!" I barked, unsure if the wild-man was stable enough to respond, or aware enough not to simply attack us.

He looked at the dead Pure Ones, his left eye twitching and his hairy hands balling into fists. The dogs clustered around him, standing at heel, as if their master had appeared. He didn't pet them or speak any commands, but his authority was clear.

"Sea Wolves!" he rumbled, his red tongue licking at the air over his bushy beard. "You have made a mess of these men. How can I display their heads now? *This* one has an arrow through his eye-socket."

"Yeah, that was me," offered Arthur.

The wild-man lumbered over to my brother, his dogs still clustered at his feet. He was wider, hairier, and far smellier than Arthur, but he was also unarmed, and moved like an ox rather than a warrior.

"Step back," said Arthur, gritting his teeth at having so large a man standing so close to him.

The man grunted at him and the dogs growled.

"You are Dark Wing?" I enquired. "We are here to talk to you, not fight you. We are bound for the Bay of Bliss."

He squinted at me. There was a wily glint in his eyes, but also a madness and much barely contained rage. As our eyes met, I felt a surge of wyrd from him, flowing across his limbs and making him seem even bigger. His power was unfocused and raw, lacking the refinement required of duellists, but profound, nonetheless.

"Who do you wish to test?" I asked, nodding at his now-glowing fists. "Yourself or us?"

"Things are never as simple as they appear," he replied. "My name is Roland Lahandras, I am called Dark Wing. Now, fuck off out of my forest and I won't have to feed you to my dogs." In unison, each one of the beasts bared their teeth at us.

Arthur, without showing much thought, shoved Dark Wing away from him. My brother reacted to the threat in the only way he knew how, but he had no such confidence with a pack of dogs. The wild-man took several steps backwards, but didn't fall.

"Hold!" I commanded. To my surprise, both Arthur *and* the dogs obeyed me. They had been ready to pounce, crouching on their back legs, with slavering teeth. But now they all sat, looking quizzically at the strange woman who'd shouted at them. "I said we are not here to fight. However, you cannot expect us to be cowed by a threat. Do *not* threaten us again!"

"We are duellists of the Severed Hand," announced Arthur, standing in a wrestlers' stance with his legs wide and his fists ready.

"I know what you are, boy," said Dark Wing. "I know more of what you are than you do. I know what you are and I rage for what you are…you and your wolves, cowering behind stone walls like those who kneel. Only ever seeing half a world. Not even that. And all that you *do* see is given to you by arrogant old men, sitting safely in tall, stone towers." He growled at the three of us, clenching and unclenching his fists as he tried to control his anger. "Just leave me to my dogs." He shook his head and marched off, followed closely by each one of his animals.

I watched the thick folds of raggedy fabric flow and move in the wind as he left, striding between white trees like an angry cart horse or some kind of rabid oxen. He had been a duellist once, but if there was a story behind his solitude I had not heard it. His name, Lahandras, marked his ancestors as Sea Wolves who'd interbred with Pure Ones. Eastron blood was always dominant and there was little discrimination, but these days it was uncommon. Most Sea Wolves with his name had allied with the People of Ice, and now lived on Yish or Nowhere.

"Strange fellow," said Jaxon.

"Addie, let me subdue him," said Arthur. "He's big, but slow."

"And the dogs?" I replied. "How will you subdue them? No, we'll follow, but there'll be no subduing." An errant Sea Wolf and a pack of wild dogs was not enough to turn me around, nor sufficiently intimidating to make me fear for my life. The three of us, if the situation demanded it, were more than a match for any wild duellist and any pack of dogs. His manner and his lack of respect were more concerning.

We kept our blades sheathed as we walked, following in his wake, though keeping our distance. "Is he as tough as I think?" I asked Jaxon.

He considered it. "He was. Maybe twenty years ago. I think he's spent too much time alone, his wyrd is all over the place. Not to say he's helpless ... I certainly wouldn't want to bet on the outcome if Arthur went for him."

"Fuck you, Icicle," spat my brother. "He's a fat old man."

"But he's not a frog," I barked. "So we aren't here to hurt him, spy on him or kill him. He's a side-trip. Hopefully an informative side-trip."

We had no sight of Dark Wing, but the sound of dogs barking kept us in the right direction. North west, deeper into both the dead forest and the Mirralite Reservation, but away from the Bay of Bliss. I'd hoped that our blind wandering would get direction from Dark Wing, perhaps a way of sneaking up on the village, or intelligence on what we would find. However, since meeting the wild-man, I feared we'd get little more than pissed on by a pack of dogs; perhaps a brief fight before our wandering continued. But I had to pursue him to find out.

"Addie, I smell blood here," said Jaxon, coming to a stop before an unusually large tree. "Up there." His eyes rose, focusing on a high branch, upon which were hung a cluster of severed heads. Their hair was long and braided, with seashells and stones woven into the strands.

"They're Pure Ones," I observed. "Dark Wing doesn't believe in subtlety."

"More over here," said Arthur, a little way ahead.

We joined him, where a line of skulls were staked into the hard ground. Beyond, nailed to more wooden stakes, were dozens of rotting heads. Some were barely more than skeletons. Others were fresh, with blood still pooled in the eye sockets and upon the lips. It seemed wrong to display death in such a fashion, and butchery of this kind was no longer practised at the Severed Hand. Many years past, Lord Ulric's father, the Bloody Fang, displayed two thousand heads from Brand's Tower, leaving them to rot so that the Nissalite knew their place. Such brutality had not been necessary for a long time.

"Sign of weakness," said Arthur. "Strength speaks for itself. It doesn't need such ... crutches."

Jaxon looked at me, shaking his head as if to condemn Dark Wing. The Wisp disliked the severed heads for a more prosaic reason than my brother. He simply didn't think that any man, Pure One or Eastron, should be degraded so.

"He must live somewhere," I said. "Let's find it."

Neither of my companions replied. Nor did they nod or remove their eyes from the dead Pure Ones, but they followed me as I moved deeper into the forest, past more severed heads, and fence-lines made of bone. It appeared that Dark Wing was a craftsman as well as a butcher. The macabre structures must have been the work of decades, costing more life and labour than I could imagine. The fences became arches, and the arches became tunnels, each one rendered skilfully out of bone and sinew.

"How many Mirralite has he killed, do you think?" mused Jaxon, as we entered a tunnel of bone.

From ahead of us, echoing through the structure, came a response. "Four thousand. A few more, a few less. I lose count."

Ahead of us was a low spire, built in the fashion of a Pure One house. Several tunnels led to it, and the pointed, circular roof was equal parts bone, wood and mud.

"Shall I welcome you as old friends?" mused the wildman. "Invite you in and pour us each a mug of ale?" We still couldn't see him, and his voice appeared to come from several directions at once. "No, I think not. I have asked you to leave, you have chosen not to."

We reached the central chamber and saw where Dark Wing lived. The interior room was lined with animal skins and furs, with a stone fireplace against the far wall. A dozen baskets, woven from twigs, provided homes for his dogs, and the huge man himself sat cross-legged before his hearth. The whole room stunk of death, and skulls were being boiled in a huge cauldron.

"You're right, we ignored your request. We chose to follow you," I said. "If you wish to fight us, I invite you to do so now. If not, may we sit and speak?"

He grunted at me, then looked around at his dogs. All of the animals were slumped in their baskets, though many now wagged their tails at him. They did not appear aggressive.

"You're lucky my dogs like you," said Dark Wing. "If it was just your men, they'd have already attacked. But you're a proper bitch and they know it."

"Thank you, what a lovely sentiment. May I sit?"

Arthur scoffed. "You're gonna let this fat old bastard insult you, Addie?"

I patted my brother on the back. "I think it was meant as a compliment."

"Sit," said Dark Wing. "Just you. Those two can stand."

There were no chairs, just layered animal skins; some deeply furred, others no more than tanned leather. I selected a moderately clean skin, and pulled it under me, sitting opposite the wild-man. "The Bay of Bliss," I began. "You have been there?"

"I have," he replied.

"There is a village there. They call it The Place Where We Hear The Sea. Do you know it?"

"I do," he responded.

"Good. Thank you for your candour. Now, tell me of this place."

He scratched at his wiry beard, pulling a twig from the mass of hair. Even seated, the layers of his clothing made him look anything but human. Perhaps an enormous toad, squatting on its hind legs. He swallowed, though his throat sounded dry, and his eyes had suddenly narrowed. He reached under one of his larger rugs, to where several wooden boxes were placed in a rocky hole. The dogs began to whine as he reached for the largest box. It was made of dark wood and brass, with dusty hinges and a strange, circular latch. He placed it on the floor between us.

"And this is?" I asked.

"Careful, Addie," warned Jaxon. "Whatever it is, he's afraid of it."

I looked down at the box. Upon the latch was a macabre engraving. A face, wreathed in tentacles, with glowing green gems for eyes.

"Press the eyes to open it," said Dark Wing.

I considered Jaxon's warning, but could not imagine anything within a box to be of genuine concern to me. I pressed against the green gems, surprised to feel they were warm, and the latch clicked open. Inside, the box was lined with green quilted fabric, and a small, black statue lay on its side within.

The two Yishian Mastiffs began to bark. Not as if warning of danger, but as if afraid. Each bark ended with a mournful whine, picked up by the smaller dogs and rising to a cacophony.

"What is this?" I asked.

"Look at it!"

I reached into the box and removed the statue. It was warm in my hands, and made of some unknown black rock, chiselled along a silvery grain to resemble a creature, sitting atop a crude altar. The creature brought to mind an octopus, a frog, and a man. A pulpy head, somehow iridescent, even through the black rock, was framed by a beard of tentacles, creeping across a grotesque, scaly body, with stumpy reptilian wings. Its form was unnatural and made the hairs on my arms tingle.

"What is this?" I repeated.

"*That* is the Dreaming God," replied Dark Wing. "When you listen to the sea, you hear his dreams. The village you seek has been listening for a long time. No Pure Ones go there, and I have only seen it from afar."

I dropped the statue back into its box and contemptuously kicked the lid closed. "Fascinating as that is, I need to know more temporal matters. For a start you could tell me where the fuck we find this village. And then you could tell me who the fuck lives there."

11

Legend says that the Eastron killed their god. Before we left the Bright Lands, we rose in force to show that we would never kneel to an absent spirit who claimed dominion over us. But it was not an often-told legend. At the Severed Hand, the idea of worship had been cast upon the fire long ago. The very concept offended our sense of self. We had no fate, we had wyrd. We made our own destinies and fought our own battles. No gods, spirits or men held dominion over me.

But we were not ignorant of the divine. Pure One legends tell of gods, distantly removed from man, striding through the void as giants. At Green Haven, a now-forgotten Tassalite trading port, they worship a gold giant, said to demand tribute in the form of greed. South of Four Claw's Folly, a coven of Kneeling Wolves betrayed their kin to worship a flesh giant, who supposedly appeared to them from the distant void. Such tales filled the Kingdom of the Four Claws. There were as many gods as there were men to invent them. But the Sea Wolves would never stoop to such servitude.

But even *we* had legends. As vague as history was when it concerned the Battle of the Depths, it certainly recorded that Mathias Blood and his warriors believed the Dreaming God to be a genuine threat. Tomas Red Fang concurred, and the old spirit-master had instilled in me a subtle fear of the Sunken Men's god. Not that I would admit this to Jaxon or my brother, but I feared a thing that I could not fight. A thing of flesh and blood could only pose so much threat to me, but a god? I didn't even know what a god was. Did it have a heart I could pierce or a head I could sever? The statue suggested a being with limbs and a body, but was it a true representation of the creature? Or, more likely, simply a grotesque token used as a focus for worship?

Dark Wing had taken the statue from a small settlement, now uninhabited, that the Mirralite had tried to establish north of his forest. He'd attacked from the void, killing a hundred men and women across two days. He described hunting the last ten with his pack of dogs, each of whom he'd trained to hate Pure Ones. His philosophy was simple – invaders should not stop until they become conquerors. He still fought the Impurity Wars – the old conflict started by Sebastian Dawn Claw, the first Always King, and ended by Moon Blood Claw's Bane, when he and his Pure Ones surrendered on the Isle of the Setting Sun.

Even given his wildness, Dark Wing had seen much of the world. He'd delved into dark places never reached by other Eastron, and learned more than he wanted about those places. To hear him talk, we now approached one of the darker things he'd seen.

We were nearing the coast. The smell of salt water had been present for the last few hours, and grew stronger the closer we edged to the rocky cliffs. Behind us was the edge of a twisted forest, comprised more of brambles than trees. Ahead of us was the Bay of Bliss – a horseshoe of basalt cliffs, with dozens of villages nestled amongst the rocks.

Some were on the water's edge, others positioned away from the sea on inland pastures, but all were in the low ground, and crawling with Pure Ones.

"I didn't know there were so many Mirralite," said Arthur, looking down on the numerous settlements below us. "Where's the village we want?"

"The eastern point of the bay, beyond the forest," replied Jaxon. "We can't see it from here. Dark Wing was vague about the approach, but we should drop down from the cliffs and keep to the furthest pasture. With luck, we can get there without passing another village, or getting too close to a farmstead."

"After you, Icicle," offered Arthur, sweeping his hand towards the eastern cliffs.

Jaxon picked his way through a thin bramble-framed pathway and began to drop down from the high cliff's edge. The Bay of Bliss was before us, a glittering sheet of blue and black, undulating gently as far as the eye could see. The Mirralite had picked a beautiful part of Nibonay for their dark worship. As we walked downwards, I wondered how widespread the infection was. The Place Where We Hear The Sea was our destination, but there were so many other villages, each with hundreds of Pure Ones. Most looked like they made their crust from fishing or farming, but ignorant natives could be swayed in a hundred different ways, and our enemies could be hiding behind every fishing net or pointed cottage.

We'd taken animal skins from Dark Wing's bone palace, and each of us wore them as a cloak, covering our armour and weapons. At a distance, we'd just be three travellers, braving the brisk sea winds that churned up from the Red

Straits. No-one knew our faces or names this far from the Severed Hand, but I'd guess that any Eastron would be treated as enemies, and, contrary to what Arthur might believe, the three of us were not capable of fighting the entire Bay of Bliss.

We dropped below the wind, tracing a zigzag path through widening mountain trails. There was much game here – deer runs, rabbit holes and pheasant nests. The Mirralite had plenty to eat if, like me, they hated fish, but we saw no hunting lodges, nor any obvious footprints. When we reached a wooded fissure in the basalt cliffs, I saw why. There were solid wooden walkways, weaving between high branches and leading to the pastures beyond. It appeared that the Mirralite preferred hunting from bough platforms in the trees.

"Addie, danger!" barked Jaxon, listening to his wyrd and scanning the trees.

A whistling sound raced along the fissure and a red-fletched arrow struck Arthur in the thigh. "Fuck!" he shouted, dropping to the ground and grabbing his leg.

"There," I said, pointing to a young Mirralite, half-hidden in the trees. Jaxon sprang from the path and dropped his shoulder into the trunk of the tree. I followed, adding my strength to his. We wrenched the trunk back and forth, shaking the bowman from his platform. He fell heavily to the moss-covered rocks below, dropping his bow and emptying his lungs of air. He'd landed on his back, and a spurt of blood erupted from his mouth.

"Arthur, can you stand?" I asked, while Jaxon went to the coughing Pure One.

My brother groaned in irritation and sat up, testing his leg. The arrowhead had emerged through the back of his thigh and he pressed down firmly, trying to stem the flow of blood. He hobbled to his feet, but howled in pain and fell back to the floor. "Shit! No, I can't," he growled.

"We just made a lot of noise," said the Wisp, holding his hand over the Pure One's mouth to stop him screaming. "Stealth is easier when things are quiet. We should go to ground."

"Agreed," I said. "Finish him off, we'll move."

Jaxon wrapped an arm around the Pure One's neck and choked him to death while I helped Arthur to stand. The wound was crippling, but not fatal, and could be healed with a few surges of wyrd and a few hours' rest. But for now it was a complication. He leant against me and grunted.

"Put me in a bush and come find me later," he said.

"Shut up," I replied. "Jaxon, come on, if we cut across here, we can get lost in the woods." I pointed to the low ground, between two cultivated fields. The wood was on the coast, between us and The Place Where We Hear The Sea.

Another arrow hit the dirt near my foot. The Pure One that fired it was on the edge of another platform and darted away as soon as he'd fired, disappearing inland, likely towards the nearest village.

"Okay, let's move," I said, helping Arthur off the path and towards the low ground.

"Three more," said Jaxon, covering the rear. "We made a noise *and* we were seen."

We couldn't run. The ground was uneven, and Arthur gritted his teeth every few steps. Even when we reached the flat land between the two fields, I was carrying almost half his weight. To the left, over a bramble fence-line, was a field of corn, rising as a wall between us and a distant farm house. To the right, the field was ploughed, but devoid of a crop, meaning that anyone looking in the right direction would easily see us. The forest had appeared close as we walked down from the cliffs; now, as I helped my brother hobble onwards, it looked dangerously far away.

Across the bare field, I saw three more Pure Ones – an adult woman and two young boys. The woman wore a simple grey dress, and the boys scampered behind her when they saw us. They'd appeared out of nowhere, and were more surprised than afraid, as if they'd heard of the Invaders, but never seen them. Our height, our size, our weapons, our curse words – we must have appeared as nothing more than monstrous outsiders. Luckily for them, the woman and her children fled, disappearing across the field. I had no desire to kill three such Pure Ones, but would have been forced to, had they lingered or cried for help. Though the image of their faces stuck with me as I carried my brother onwards.

"Jaxon, check the forest. We need somewhere to lie low."

"Aye," replied the Wisp, leaving Arthur and me, and sprinting towards the trees. He kept his head low, but his eyes aware, scanning the farms on either side of us.

"Addie," grunted Arthur. "The bastard mangled my leg."

"A poor start to our glorious invasion of the Bay of Bliss," I quipped, taking as much of Arthur's weight as I could. "You've had worse."

"Why me? Why didn't he shoot you or the Icicle?"

"Shut up," I replied.

We edged forwards, with my brother hopping across the bare earth, keeping weight off his wounded leg. Jaxon had disappeared into the trees, leaving the two of us to limp our way to relative safety.

"When they attack – leg or no leg – I bet I kill more than you," said Arthur with a pained smile. "Twenty at least before they overwhelm me. Not a bad way to go."

"Shut up," I repeated. "You're not going to die just yet. We've got a job to do."

I heard shouting from the rocky fissures behind us, and the sound of running feet on wooden platforms. It appeared the local Pure Ones were quick to react when their land was threatened, as arrows began to thud into the ground behind us. Thankfully, we were beyond an aimed shot from the platforms and getting hit would be a matter of bad luck.

Jaxon reappeared from the trees and sprinted back to join us. "The forest is wild. No paths, just animal runs. With a head start we can get lost in there easy."

"*If* we get there," grunted Arthur, motioning to the Wisp to come and help him.

With Jaxon on one side and me on the other, we broke into a laboured run, carrying Arthur between us. Arrows now flew over our shoulders, as the pursuing Mirralite reached the level ground. I couldn't turn to confirm their numbers, but they were a large gang, shouting at each other to cut us off.

The trees loomed ahead. Tall and green with a dense canopy, and leading up to the treeline, a mass of thick bramble bushes and felled tree trunks. We weaved past the first few bushes, keeping foliage between us and our pursuers, but it was clear we'd not outrun them.

I let go of Arthur, positioning as much of his weight on Jaxon's shoulder as he could stand. "Take him into the trees, I'll catch up."

The Wisp nodded and started to move off.

"Fuck off!" snapped Arthur. "If *you're* standing here, I'm standing too."

I looked back along the dirt path, between the two fields. Ten or more Pure Ones were approaching, with dozens more holding back with drawn bows. Those at the front were heavily marked in blue ink, and swinging long-spears.

"You can't fight," I said. "Unless I kill the first few, they'll overwhelm us before we get you healed. You and Jaxon find a place to hide. I'll buy you time." I drew my cutlass and appropriated my brother's.

Arthur wasn't happy, but the wound in his leg was now bleeding heavily, and he wasn't so stupid as to ignore his big sister, especially when she was right. They hobbled away, past the bushes and into the trees. I turned to face the oncoming warriors, making sure I had relative cover from the archers. Bramble thickets would not stop a blade at close range, but did wonders when faced with long-range arrows.

"Once more for the Severed Hand," I whispered, crouching out of sight and edging along a fallen tree trunk. My wyrd was already tingling along my limbs as a consequence of having to flee, and it was a simple matter to flood my extremities with power. Ten men was a lot, even for Adeline Brand, and I squeezed every ounce of strength from my body. I'd need to sleep to recuperate from the expenditure of wyrd, but it was preferable to dying in such a pitiful fashion.

The spearmen slowed as they reached the edge of the forest, clustering together to pick their way through the bramble bushes and fallen tree trunks. When I broke cover, it was behind the lead man. I cut his throat and threw him backwards, into the path of the nearest two. I then hopped over the tree trunk and engaged three more. With two cutlasses I could parry their weak spear thrusts and kill them with minimal effort. Their arms and shoulders were bare, giving me ample room for a killing or crippling blow. As long as they flailed individually to get to me, I was safe, able to tackle them in ones and twos, using the natural cover to my advantage.

"Invader!" they shouted, as if I was their worst nightmare, conjured from a dark pit to end their lives. Each man was frenzied, with tears of anger flowing down their faces. But still they died, unable to match my strength or speed.

My limbs began to burn as wyrd bubbled to the surface. I unleashed a ferocious thrust at a man's head, driving the blade clean through his face, and wheeled to engage another.

Then I was cut on the cheek by a stray arrow. It turned me sideways just long enough for a glancing blow to strike the side of my head. I tumbled backwards, into a thicket, and struggled to stand, as the remaining Pure Ones surrounded me. I wasn't sure how many were left, but four spears were being driven downwards. Two were deflected by my leather armour, one missed the mark, just to the left of my head, but the last found a gap between my breastplate and my belt. The steel bit into my side and I howled in sudden pain.

The wound was bad, but a split-second later my wyrd numbed the pain, allowing me to grit my teeth and wrestle the spear from its wielder. More thrusts came in, but I used the spear to pull myself upright and out of the thicket. I rolled forwards, thinking of escape. Behind me, a handful of Pure Ones were still alive, with many more approaching. Jaxon and Arthur had made their escape, and it was time for me to leave.

"Stop them!" bellowed a man at the rear.

"For the Lodge of the Rock!" screamed another.

I had to kill a final man who was quick enough to cut me off, but after he fell from my blade I was amidst trees and thick brush, running north as best I could, whilst holding my bleeding side. Arthur had been shot from cover, wounded by a cowardly attack; *I* had been cut in a stand-up fight, and gritted my teeth in anger that I'd been so sloppy as to disregard the distant archers.

My pursuers slowed, forming up into a single mob before they entered the forest. I paused next to a gnarled oak tree, and ran my hand down the bark, looking for a sign from Jaxon. Two horizontal cuts formed an arrow, pointing to the left, and I followed the sign, deeper into the trees.

The Mirralite made an almighty racket, stomping and cutting their way into the dense forest. I heard wails of anguish as men reached the bodies of those I'd killed. They were not eager to follow their brothers in death, but neither would they accept Invaders in their lands. And there was something else. They were afraid we would reach something. Some barrier beyond which they felt powerless. They kept saying *don't let them pass the vale*, though it meant nothing to me.

They floundered at the treeline, arguing about where I was and the dangers of pursuing. I was well hidden and moving quickly away by the time they'd finished arguing. A good thing too, for my wound made running impossible. If it weren't for the trees, providing support as I fled, I'd be crawling, with a hand pressed to my wounded side. Luck was with me and the Pure Ones followed only slowly, taking their time and spreading out, and I had a chance to tear a piece of cloth from my belt and soak up the seeping blood.

I moved past trees and around bushes, following marks from Jaxon and staying ahead of the cautious Mirralite, until a wide game trail crossed my path. A large beast hunted the area, and it'd trodden all foliage into a channel of mulch. On the opposite side, hanging on lines of woven rope, suspended on the low branches, were thousands of seashells. A salty smell hit my nostrils, and seaweed, hanging from the branches as ropey tentacles, barred the way ahead. I paused, before crossing the game trail and pushing my way past falling strands of seaweed and dangling seashells.

"Addie!" snapped Jaxon, crouching in the brush, between two fallen trees. "Keep low."

I ducked into the brush, half vaulting, half falling over one of the tree trunks. Arthur lay opposite me, clutching his wounded leg. They'd removed the arrow and bound the wound. A subtle glow of wyrd swirled over the leg, and I saw my brother wincing as the wound was healed. It would take time, but he'd be fine. My own wound felt like a punch to the heart as I hit the ground and took cover.

"What happened to you?" asked Arthur, sweating from exertion.

"Shush now," said Jaxon, poking his head over the log and scanning the wide game trail. "I want to see if they'll cross the line of seashells. I think it's a warning."

I pulled myself to my knees, joining the Wisp in looking behind for our pursuers. "A warning from who?"

"I don't know," he replied. "But the spirits here are restless... hostile even. Just wait, we'll see."

From a little way down the game trail, a gang of Mirralite appeared. They broke the treeline, but wouldn't cross the barrier of shells and seaweed. They looked both ways, but said nothing, though several clutched at private tokens or made signs of protection in the air. Grimly, the pursuing Mirralite stowed their weapons and gave up the pursuit, turning back towards their pastures and wooden hunting platforms.

"That answers one question," said Jaxon. "They're afraid of something. Now we just need to know what."

"One tribe hates another," offered Arthur, still clutching his leg. "Maybe an argument about who gets to fuck the village goat."

I turned around and took a seat, pulling back a section of my leather breastplate. "Maybe," I said. "But they looked afraid, not angry."

Jaxon crouched next to me and prodded at the spear wound in my side. "Nasty," he said. "Did you lose concentration, or perhaps you let one strike you to make the fight more interesting?"

"Just seal the wound," I muttered, aware that my brother was smirking at me.

The Wisp placed his palms on my skin and the wound quickly became numb. As my own wyrd receded and exhaustion took over, I felt the gentle touch of healing energy, flowing across my skin. Jaxon put one hand against my forehead and smoothed back my hair. "Sleep, Addie, sleep. Rest in the arms of your wyrd." I only distantly heard the words, as I fell into a deep sleep.

12

It was approaching dusk when we first spied the village. A night spent in the dense forest had healed our wounds and recharged our wyrd, and we were now within sight of our destination. The Place Where We Hear The Sea was a horseshoe of wood, facing a jagged reef, just off the coast. It had streets of mud, and homes of stone and thatch, though many were in bad repair, with cracked walls and exposed roof frames. It looked old, far older than any other Pure One settlement I had seen. It was like a piece of the landscape, a rock or some-such thing, pressed into the mud of Nibonay a thousand years ago. Yet it was missing the touch of nature that I associated with Pure Ones. There were no trees in the settlement, and the earth had long turned to mud. All that stood out was the square stone building, half-poking out from the shallows of the Bay of Bliss. It was of strange design, different to the rest of the village, with sharp angles and deep recesses.

"What kind of village is that?" asked Arthur, as the three of us looked down from the encircling cliffs. "Is that a building in the sea?"

"It's not part of the reef," replied Jaxon. "How many people live there, do you think? A few hundred?"

"I can't see anyone," I said. "Looks empty."

"No, a few hearths still burn," observed Jaxon, pointing to a series of thatched halls, emanating a dull, golden glow. "Though this is like no village of men I have seen … or felt."

I looked at him with a raised eyebrow. "Felt? Speak plain, Jaxon."

"The glass is thin here," he replied. "As if some great weight presses on it from the void."

"Spirits?" queried Arthur.

Jaxon nodded. "Many. Multitudes, but … I don't know. Something. I don't want to step to the void and find out, but I think there are more than nature sprits, lurking beyond the glass."

Arthur scoffed, resting a hand on his cutlass and marching down a steep mountain trail, towards The Place Where We Hear The Sea. The approach was wooded and bathed in deep shadows, allowing us plenty of time to look at the sinister village, though my brother made no effort to be stealthy.

"Sea Wolf confidence works best at the Severed Hand," said Jaxon. "In the rest of the world it may appear as arrogance." He looked at me with a sheepish grin. "Ragnar Ice said that."

"What a pity he's dead," I replied. "Such a wise man of an Ice is a loss to the world. Come on, let's stop him blundering into a fight he can't win."

We hurried after my brother, trotting down the mountain trail. Though it was still afternoon, there was heavy cloud cover, and the vales leading to the village soaked up little light. The trees gave way to knotted thorns, and the grass turned to mud and rock.

We reached Arthur, and made sure the three of us approached together and quietly. My brother nursed a slight limp, and it had made him grumpier than usual. Using wyrd to heal wounds was difficult, and Jaxon, though powerful, was no expert healer. The Wisp had patched us both up as best he could, but we were not at our best. The remnant of the spear wound in my side was simply tightness with occasional pain, that would endure until we returned to the hold. But it was a small complaint, and both of us were still able to fight at near-peak efficiency. Arthur just wanted an excuse to be grumpy, as if the sinister village and being so far from home was not enough reason.

We reached a broken wooden fence, encircling a churned patch of mud. Nearby was an old stable, with no beasts or partitions. It was as if these Pure Ones had started farming crops and keeping livestock, but long since lost the inclination. Or perhaps the need. The same was true of the first proper building we reached. It was made of irregular stone bricks, but the mortar was rotten and dusty in places, and the holes were filled with moss and weeds. There were no signs that it was a house, or fulfilled any practical function.

"Tread carefully," I whispered, as we entered the village. "There'll be people here somewhere, let's make sure we see them before they see us."

"This place stinks," said Arthur, edging along an angular stone wall. "Rotten fish or something."

We skulked between two equally dilapidated buildings, approaching a larger building with a pointed roof of muddy-brown thatch. At the intersection, we paused, Arthur looking one way and me looking the other. The street was equal parts stone and mud, forming a strange cobbled pattern that would require hopping, rather than walking, to stay clear of mud. With the streets clear, we advanced into the shadows of larger buildings, where hearths still burned, sending thin slivers of smoke through rickety chimneys, and rusty golden glows through shuttered windows.

We paused again. Jaxon and Arthur held position behind me as I moved to one of the glowing windows. There was no sound but the crackle of a fire. Nothing to cover my movements, so I crept as slowly as I could to the shuttered windowsill. It was waist-high and the light came from a low angle. I crouched into a small shaft of light and looked within.

The light came from a single steel brazier on the floor of a dusty room. The walls and surfaces were low and rotten, as if neglected for years, and no recognizable furniture or comforts lay within, though there were four figures, hunched around the fire. They ate hungrily from a basket of raw fish, filling the air with a frightful smell and making it hard to see their faces, though all of their eyes bulged and their bellies swelled. Their deformities were not as extreme as the creature we'd captured at the Severed Hand, but they were cut from the same abominable cloth. Their full lips smacked together around fish bones, and greasy oils seeped from their mouths.

I took a moment to think, wondering how out-of-our-depth we were, before leaving the shaft of light and returning to the others. "Frog-men within," I whispered. "Not *as* fucked-up, but fucked-up enough."

"Do we give them steel?" asked Arthur.

"No," I replied. "We need to see more. A few hybrids are no threat. And don't forget that it took three of us to incapacitate one of them."

"When not expecting the fight," countered Arthur. "A prepared duellist is a different opponent to a surprised one. If I was aware, I'd beat any fucking frog-man."

Jaxon was distracted, looking towards the sea. I prodded him in the ribs. "Wake up," I snapped. "Unless you sense something worth mentioning, you listen to *me*."

"I sense too much," he replied. "It's as if we're passing under a cloud. I've never felt anything like it." He looked at me and I saw fear in his eyes. I'd known Jaxon all my life, and rarely seen him afraid. He played the part of a sensitive spirit-master, but he was as much a duellist as Arthur or myself. "Addie, I think we should leave."

"Fuck off, Icicle," said my brother. "I've yet to see anything worthy of fear. It's all mist and mystery, nothing real."

"If we leave, what do we tell Lord Ulric?" I asked. "Add that to my curiosity, and we have ample reason to push on. Let's get to the large building and see what dwells within. If it's just a dozen hybrids, we have little to worry about. But I won't leave until I know if there is threat here. Can you tell me of a threat?"

"Nothing specific," replied Jaxon. "But the void here scares me. It should scare you too."

I moved away, cutting across another deserted intersection, and approaching the tall, central building. I also approached the coast, and the low wooden platforms that snaked towards the blocky structure in the bay. Even close to the water there was no-one abroad in the strange settlement, and we passed without impediment through empty streets of mud and stone. There were racks of fishing rods and splayed nets, long since abandoned and gone rotten. The jetty held splintered and broken boats, oars dangling in the water, hanging limply from their moorings.

Jaxon skipped silently next to me. "A sentry," he whispered, casting his eyes upwards. I followed his gaze to an open window, two storeys from the ground, where stood a cloaked figure, looking out across the jetty. His form was bulbous, but blessedly obscured by fabric and shadow, though a hooked spear was visible in his flabby hands. He stood away from the hearths within, but directly in our path.

I nodded to my brother, and drew a fingertip across my lips to indicate silence. Arthur disappeared into a shadow at the base of the building, holding a heavy throwing knife across his chest. He moved to a good position opposite the sentry, but well hidden, and took aim, sighting along his arm. His throw was precise, striking the hybrid in the throat and sending him backwards with barely a grunt.

"We move," I said, darting across the street to where the dead creature's feet extended. Jaxon followed and pulled the corpse down from the open window, laying him in shadow and pushing back his cloak.

"Fuck me," I exclaimed, as the frog-man was revealed. Arthur's knife was wedged between rippling folds of flab, below a wide mouth and above a greasy chest. The creature's eyes were wide, and bulged from distorted eye sockets. He was at least as grotesque as our captive at the Severed Hand, as much frog as he was man.

"See, a blade in the throat and they die like a pig at slaughter," said Arthur.

"A lucky shot," I replied. "An inch up or down and you'd have hit nothing but blubber."

"What kind of weapon is this?" he asked, ignoring my assessment and inspecting the hybrid's strange spear. It had a shaft of hard wood, wrapped in green twine, with a hooked blade at one end. He tested the edge and winced. "Damn, it's sharp. Not steel, I don't know what it is."

"Ditch it with the body," I said, helping Jaxon move the bulbous creature further into the shadows. "I don't think the sun ever shines here, so it'll remain hidden long enough."

The Wisp frowned at me. "Let us hope we're treated with similar reverence if we are to fall." He wasn't happy, but I didn't want to take the time it would require to mollify him.

"Let's see what is within," I replied, frowning back at him.

Arthur threw the hooked spear onto the dead creature's chest and led the way to the nearest source of light – a low window, emitting the same rusty glow as the previous building, and containing the same mismatched shutters. This time all three of us approached, looking into the large building through three separate slivers of light.

Within, our eyes were shown a great assembly of hybrids, each one more grotesque than the last. The curses, etched upon their flesh, ranged from simple bulging eyes and full lips, to those who were almost entirely frog-men. The more human-looking wore clothes and had thin, greasy hair; the more frog-like were bald and wore only robes, barely covering their bloated limbs and swollen bellies.

There were dozens of them, all removed from us, a good distance below street level, on a rotten wooden floor. They clustered around a circular well of thick granite blocks, poking up from the ground. Some – the most deformed – held hooked spears and stood around the edges of the chamber, while most crouched or squatted around the well.

There were no interior walls or ceilings, and the building was hollow from the mouldy floor to the pointed rafters.

"Not an army," I whispered. "Some kind of worship perhaps."

"They worship a water well?" scoffed my brother. "They live on the coast, there's water everywhere. Fucking heathens."

The Wisp was still frowning, but he did not look on the abominations within. His eyes were focused on the dark coast and the angular building in the bay. "We're too far from home," he said. "I can hear the sea." My brother and I turned from the hybrids and looked at him. "It sings a dirge, but I can't hear the words... just the sorrow... and the madness."

Arthur was about to insult him, when a sound from within the building caught our attention. Through the slivers of light we saw the stagnant water of the well begin to churn, even as the hybrids within gargled a shrill prayer to their dreaming god. From the well rose a large figure, displacing the water and replacing it with oozing slime. It was greyish-green with a sickly-white belly. Shiny scales crept up its back, rising to a red crest behind its swollen head. A long tongue flopped from a puckered mouth, and membranous webs linked each of its long fingers. I saw parts of a frog, parts of a fish, but nothing of man or anything I understood.

It wasn't a hybrid, it was a Sunken Man, and I recoiled from it, and saw my brother do the same. It was at least ten feet tall and wider than two men. In one suckered hand it held a vicious-looking weapon, comprising a wooden shaft between two pincers. In the other was a chalice of black metal.

"Addie!" murmured Arthur.

I ignored him. The gangly creature was pulling itself from the well to tower over the hybrids, each of which was now screeching with euphoria. I couldn't see a way of killing the creature. It was just too big. A solid thrust would barely pierce its mass, and even its head was pulpy, and protected by layers of slime and blubber.

"Addie," repeated Arthur. "What do we do?"

The Sunken Man thrust out its rippling belly, sending slime and grease all over the floor. The screeching hybrids threw back their heads and the females exposed their bodies, beckoning the creature to take them. It strode amongst them, its webbed feet flopping as much as stepping across the wooden floor, inspecting the offered bodies. Without their robes, I saw that several were already heavily pregnant.

My mouth twitched, and I felt a surge of wyrd enter my hands. I tried to push it down as best I could, but anger was often the hardest thing to control. "I see a threat," I snarled. "A threat too much for the three of us."

"We should leave," warned Jaxon for the second time.

"I believe you're right," I replied. "This is enough for Lord Ulric *and* my curiosity."

A screech sounded from the nearest wooden jetty, and I turned to see a heavily deformed hybrid staring at us. It could have been there for some time, peering into the darkness to discern whether we were a shadow, whilst our attention was taken by the Sunken Man. Its screeching extended and rose in volume, echoing through the silent streets.

As I tried to focus, calm my anger, and assess our next move, Arthur stood and rushed past me, drawing his cutlass and bearing down on the hybrid. Sight of the abomination had affected him more than it had me, and I could feel his prodigious wyrd flowing through his tensed limbs. He had enough control not to growl or shout a challenge, but his footsteps were not light and he paid no attention to staying in the shadows.

"Too much noise," said Jaxon. "We must stop him. We must leave. The sea rises."

I stood, leaving the shadows at the base of the large building, and pursued my brother. The Wisp joined me, though he hung back and took a stealthier route. Arthur held his cutlass above his head, charging his wyrd for a powerful strike at the startled hybrid. The creature was female, with sagging, wrinkly breasts and a distended belly, poking through an open robe. She held a canvas sack, but no weapons, and gave me no indication that she was preparing to avoid my brother's blade.

"Once more for the Severed Hand," grunted Arthur, bringing his cutlass and his wyrd down on the hybrid's skull. The blade bit into the creature's flabby head, and a gout of sickly fluid oozed upwards. My brother was using too much power and would exhaust himself quickly, but with three more strikes he proved his point that an aware duellist was more dangerous than a surprised one. Layers of slime and flesh made the hybrid resilient, but Arthur hacked through its natural defences and split its grotesque head down the middle.

"Arthur, time to go," I snapped, through gritted teeth.

He looked at me. He was panting and his eyes were red and moist. With a flick of his wrist, the creature's ichor left his cutlass and flopped onto the twitching corpse at his feet.

Then the sea began to move. It had been still and black, barely more than a background to our visit. But now it rose and fell, as small waves broke against the wooden jetty. Gently at first, the water churned and boiled, throwing forth spray that made me close my eyes. Around the angular structure in the bay, I saw seaweed writhe and dance in the air, thrown upward by the waves and looking like black tentacles, framing the square building. Everything smelled of salt and fish, even the wooden jetty and the strangely cobbled street on which I stood. Suddenly, from the water, fins appeared, a few at a time, displacing the waves. Arthur turned in time to see a dozen Sunken Men rise slowly from the bay. Their fish-like crests were flushed to a bright red, and each huge creature held the same spear, topped with a vicious pincer. They wore belts and sashes, adorned with seashells and other flotsam, but were largely naked, flopping out of the water like bipedal fish. They were smaller than the previous one, though still two heads taller than any man.

From behind, I heard gargled shouting and running feet. I looked back and saw hybrids filling the street behind us. From the large building came the flabbiest and the most grotesque, wielding their hooked spears and staring at the three duellists who had invaded their fucked-up village and interrupted their worship. They spread out behind us, hissing to each other, and slowly cutting off any means of temporal escape.

We were trapped against the coast. Jaxon was to my left, crouched in the shadow of a rotten fishing boat. Arthur was vibrating with anger a few feet in front of me, his eyes focused on the Sunken Men. All three of us were in the open, but Arthur stood out, silhouetted against the sea. I didn't know what to do. In that moment, I felt fear, and knew that my blade and my wyrd were not enough. No gods, spirits or men held dominion over me, but defeat was still defeat and death was still death. East or west would take us deeper into the village; north were a dozen Sunken Men, south were more hybrids than I could count. The only option was the void.

"Jaxon, Arthur, the glass! Now! Or we'll be nothing but fish-food."

"I'd rather die here than in the void," snapped Jaxon, his eyes wide and bloodshot. "For death will come either way."

Arthur heard me, but didn't reply. He was too busy roaring curses at the Sunken Men who pulled their flabby bodies out of the wash towards him.

"Break the glass!" I repeated. "We survive this problem, before dealing with the next one."

Jaxon's jaw tightened, but he pushed back his head and his pupils turned white. I took a few large strides and clamped my hand onto Arthur's shoulder, before reaching out with my wyrd and dragging us both to the void.

The Wisp was already beyond the glass, but my eyes were drawn elsewhere. The Bay of Bliss, the strange settlement, even the approaching monsters, all were eclipsed by a roiling mass of spirits. It was as if we stood in dense fog, with thousands of eyes looking at us through the mist. The globes of wyrd, surrounding our bodies, kept the spirits at bay, but only because they were startled. Within moments the mist closed in.

"Addie, these are chaos spirits," said the Wisp. "The spawn of something greater."

Arthur still held his cutlass and took a wide stance, but tears fell from his eyes, as if he couldn't understand what was happening to him. As I opened my mouth to command we move away through the void, the mist began to take form. The eyes were now attached to reaching tendrils, and each tendril was attached to a bubbling mound of flesh and mouths. There were thousands of spirits, twisting and turning, like a tornado of skin and ichor, surrounding us and getting closer. I hesitated, as mouths reached for us, snapping with thin, gnashing teeth.

The Wisp found his voice before me. "Back through the glass. Now!" he shouted, his voice cracking with fear.

I reached for Arthur again, but my arm was snared by a fleshy tentacle. Puckered mouths covered its length, and it gripped my skin, biting in pin-points of pain across my forearm. I howled, trying to fling the spirit aside and reach my brother. He swung his cutlass in frenzied circles, hacking at anything that got within his range. The last thing on his mind was retreat. They could die, and he cut down several, making them blink out of existence as they were killed. But dozens of spiteful mouths pierced his body. His mind had recoiled at the sight of a foe he could not match with steel and wyrd, and I saw him enveloped by fleshy lips and razor-sharp teeth. He disappeared in agony, with an insane shriek on his lips, carried away on a endless tide of flesh.

"Arthur!" I roared, as Jaxon's hand reached my shoulder and pulled us both back through the glass.

I fell to the muddy street, staring up at the cloudy sky with Jaxon sprawled next to me. Before I could sit up or scream in anguish at the loss of my brother, my neck was held by a pincer and my arms were restrained by slimy hands.

Will men remember the Icelords?

Will they know we came with the Always King and his Claws?

Will they know of our wisdom and our kindness?

Will they know not all Eastron came to the Pure Lands as invaders?

No, they will not. The Sea Wolves did their work well.

For now we are People of Ice, and Icelords no longer.

From "The Lament" by Valen Ice, First Fang 50–52DA

PART FIVE

Duncan Greenfire on Nowhere

13

We'd arrived at Cold Point the previous evening, in a tight convoy of horses and carts. Every hour of travel we'd crept further under the Maelstrom, until the sky disappeared and only the churning black vortex remained. It was a vast cone, cut into the glass, deep enough that I couldn't see its end. Strange tunnels of black cloud rippled downwards as typhoons, striking the earth a distance away and bridging the gap between the realm of form and the realm of void. I kept expecting to be sucked upwards by some void storm, and pulled into the depthless layers of infinity and wyrd that assaulted my eyes. The undulating rocky landscape was minuscule in comparison, as if the world had broken to show us just how insignificant we were. Even Cold Point, the Grim Wolf's town, was barely an interesting feature on a tiny canvas. I didn't even notice it at first. Not until the encircling wall became impossible to ignore.

The town of Ice was well distant from the centre of the Maelstrom, and built predominantly of huge granite blocks. Three rivers plunged towards it, each meeting a sluice gate and a high arched gateway. It looked nothing like the Severed Hand or Moon Rock, both of which were sprawling affairs, plonked within a high wall, designed to keep everything nasty outside. Cold Point had dozens of high walls, criss-crossing its streets and creating small forts at each intersection. Nothing was ramshackle or in need of repair. Simple doors were framed with iron struts and were flush to the granite walls when closed. Every street, every turning, every crossroads could be locked up and defended. It was a town built to make an attacker bleed. But those that lived here were forced forever to look at the Maelstrom.

I certainly struggled to turn away as Loco Death Spell led me through the largest of the three gates. The Brethren dismounted outside the walls, tying their beasts in low granite stables, tended to by Mirralite Pure Ones. The other captives – David Falcon's Fang, Snake Charmer and William Vane – were held in individual carts, closely guarded by Inigo Night Walker's duellists.

I had only Twist for company, and the pain spirit was evidently lost in thought. He'd experienced the same things as me, and had just as many questions. Neither of us could recall the vision with any clarity, but the Old Bitch of the Sea and her words were felt as strongly as the death of Lord Vikon. *Greenfire must let his wyrd shine. Greenfire must honour us all.* I still didn't know how, but despite my own feelings of inadequacy, I knew that the Old Bitch of the Sea accepted me as a Sea Wolf. For now that was enough, though simpler considerations still plagued my mind. What was Inigo Night Walker doing on Nowhere? And why had the Brethren attacked the *Dead Horse*?

The man was Xymon Ice, called Blade Smile, and he wouldn't stop staring at me. He was the Grim Wolf's eldest son and looked at me like I was some kind of strange logic puzzle. That perhaps I needed decoding. He may have been right, but his staring was not making a good first impression. He shared the wild and twitchy eyes of his father, but was much smaller. He verged on the slender, with thin, muscled forearms and tight jaw bones. I'd been delivered to him by Loco, with no explanation as to why we needed to speak. Blade Smile held no sword to my throat, but he gracefully twirled a knife through his fingertips, as if he could bury it in my forehead with a flick of his wrist.

"Do you know who built this town?" asked Blade Smile, after an eternity of silent staring. "Do they teach that at the Severed Hand?"

"No," I replied, not sure whether I was being tested. "I didn't even know it existed."

"A woman called Velya Ice. She came across the sea with Sebastian Dawn Claw, but is not widely remembered. She was lover to David Fast Claw and Maven Bright. But the three of them spoke of peace over war and were exiled. Maven's people became the Defiants. David's people became the Sundered Claws. And Velya retreated to Nowhere." He was being very serious. His angular face and wild eyes made him look like a painting of a mad man, and would not be out of place etched in black stone in the Bloody Halls. "She raised Cold Point in 10DA, four years before Duncan Red Claw raised the Severed Hand."

"That sounds like cow shit to me," I blurted out. Luckily he didn't take offence. In fact, he smiled, as if accepting that his statement *was* hard to believe. The island of Nowhere had its own identity, and it was strange to learn that the People of Ice lived in one small town in the centre.

"Stand, Master Greenfire. Come to the window."

We were in a grey stone room, towards the top of a high tower, built into a thick granite wall. Like the rest of Cold Point, the tower was not a separate structure, but more like an appendage of a single huge block of stone. Most towns and holds rose up over years – a fort here, a hall there. A market and stable would appear over time, and a defensive wall was added when the settlement got big enough. Not the town of Ice.

I joined Blade Smile by the window and saw the tightly organized town, languishing under the eternal black and grey of the Maelstrom. It was larger than it appeared from a distance, and the streets were bustling with men and women of Ice. Further west, outside the town and spreading across the overcast plains, were a hundred pointed buildings of Mirralite design. The army I'd seen on the coast was now camped under the edges of the Maelstrom, a few miles from the vicious tornadoes of void energy. Perhaps Ten Cuts was amongst them, with the pale man still over his shoulder.

"Why here?" I asked. "Seems a stupid place for a town. And who were you fighting that you needed such defences?"

He didn't turn his wild eyes from the window. "Cold Point was here before the glass fractured. That happened later, under the foolishness of the Sea Wolves. We fought your people for so long." His wild eyes sparkled, as if he remembered old stories of adventure and loss. "These walls were all that stopped them annihilating every one of us. Well, these walls and the Maelstrom they'd caused by treating the glass as a tool."

"You speak like you're a Winterlord or a Brethren," I replied. "Are you not still a Sea Wolf? We're all the same, and these bastards killed Lord Vikon. Why don't you just talk to the First Fang, I'm sure he'd…"

"He'd what?" interrupted Blade Smile. "He'd take our counsel? If that is the case, Ulric Blood must have softened as he's aged. His father, the Bloody Fang, struck our names and our history from your Wolf House. His son will no sooner hear our words than he will accept us as equals. He is a barbaric fool."

I shoved him away. It was spontaneous, and had little power, but caused the young man of Ice to pin me against the wall with a blade against my throat. I felt Twist react, poised to defend me if he felt we were in actual danger. My reservoirs of power were still low, but I'd amassed enough to send Blade Smile flying if I so chose. "Careful," I warned, fighting fear. "I can't always control my wyrd. But you shouldn't insult the First Fang like that."

I could imagine what Arthur Brand or Rys Coldfire would do, though I couldn't force myself to feel their rage. I was a Sea Wolf, but I wasn't like them. I didn't know why the totem had chosen me, but it certainly wasn't for my strength, or for my sword-arm. Shoving him had been stupid.

Blade Smile removed his knife, and stepped away. I tried to hide my relief, and appear confident, though I doubted how successful I'd been. True confidence took time, and I'd only felt like a Sea Wolf for a day.

"Sorry," I said, with little humility. "I've seen a lot of my people die in the last few days, and I'm a captive of yours and the fucking Dark Brethren. I'll try to remain calm." I surprised myself by locking eyes with a man who could probably kill me, or order me killed.

Blade Smile frowned, his angular face turning into a series of creased triangles. "You're feeling fragile," he observed, seeing through my fledgling confidence. "It will pass. My father wasn't right for days after *he* conversed with Ten Cuts. And he's Xavyer Ice, the Grim Wolf of Nowhere. You're just a pup."

I stared at him. "What?"

"Ten Cuts," he repeated. "And the great turtle. A spirit of time's memory. They say Marius Cyclone wouldn't leave his chambers for two weeks after *he* saw the sea rise. But he's a Dark Brethren, they can be soft. I've not been honoured with the vision myself, so you must be far more important than you look."

Twist jabbed at my leg, causing rapid spasms of burning pain. I tried to howl, but I lost my breath and just coughed, doubling over against the windowsill and retching. The pain spirit was angry, and felt like we were part of an eldritch game, the rules of which we'd not been told. I couldn't fully remember what I'd been shown, just that the sea was rising. I may have joined a select group, but I was still captive and ignorant. Could the spirit-whistle of Ten Cuts truly have made the Grim Wolf ally with the Brethren and betray the First Fang? Marius Cyclone may not have tasked the assassin, but it was difficult not to see all of them – Inigo and the third void legion *and* Xavyer and the People of Ice – as enemies of the Severed Hand.

Blade Smile made no effort to help me. His wild eyes just changed position, following me as I curled up into a ball beneath the window. "Bad leg?" he asked, unmoved by his own understatement, but apparently glad that he could sheath his knife.

"Just leave me alone," I wailed, talking to the spirit *and* the man.

"As you wish," replied the man of Ice. "I'm just charged with killing you if you summon your wyrd, while my father assembles enough men to get us north. Travelling under the Maelstrom is getting harder. All manner of void beasts have flooded the interior of the island. But that's where we must go. We need to show you something. Why Nowhere must be protected."

I panted, willing Twist to understand that I was as confused as him. He'd not felt my renewed confidence from the Old Bitch of the Sea, and our torment was out of sync, like one of us was recovering quicker than the other. When we'd killed Maron Grief, saved Prince Oliver, and fought to defend the *Dead Horse*, spirit and man had been of a single mind. But captivity and helplessness affected us differently. We'd both been shown something terrible, but neither of us remembered it.

The door opened and a woman of Ice entered. My head was pressed against the stone floor and I could barely move, but I recognized her from Inigo Night Walker's pavilion. She'd chided the Dark Brethren for his arrogance.

"What did you do to him?" she asked Blade Smile. "No-one told you to hurt him. Apparently, the Old Lady spoke to young Master Greenfire."

"He just fell over," was the reply. "His leg started hurting. Duncan, this is Zia Lahandras, my aunt."

She crouched next to me, flicking a long braid of black hair behind her shoulder. "You have a lot of blood on your hands," she said, putting a finger under my chin and pulling my face upwards. "I know you've suffered, and that your wyrd is strong, but in this moment you need to do what you're told. *Someone* may have use for you, but *we* are well prepared to kill you if your wyrd becomes a problem... or a danger. But my brother says you need to see something."

I dug fingernails into my left thigh and panted. Gradually, my breathing slowed, and I wrestled the pain into a dull thud. Twist was annoyed, wanting to lash out and make the woman of Ice tell us everything. *Who* had a use for me? And why had the Grim Wolf conspired with Inigo Night Walker to kill the Second Fang? Was the reality of the rising sea enough? With a deep breath, Twist and I agreed not to waste our small amount of wyrd on Zia Lahandras.

"We're taking you under the Maelstrom," continued Zia. "To the very point of the void storm. If you can't stand, you can't run... and you'll need to run."

She was far more intimidating than Blade Smile, with deep brown eyes and a sharp face. I could barely bend my left leg, but she pulled me to my feet, not appearing to care about my pain. With Blade Smile behind us, I was dragged from the square room. She gave me no chance to ask any questions, or even open my mouth.

Beyond the room were closed steel doors and spiral stairs. The passageways were all of grey granite blocks, mirroring every other building in Cold Point, and making the structure appear as if it had been carved from a mountain. I gritted my teeth and tried to shut out the pain, as we walked down the narrow stairs and emerged on a floor, three storeys below. The tower widened and we continued across a large, circular room, carpeted in black, and adorned with archaic weaponry. Swords and axes; spears and shields; bows and arrows. The People of Ice were reputed to be peaceful until roused, but the large room showed a rich tradition of war. I wondered how much of it had been used fighting other Sea Wolves.

Blade Smile was ambling next to me, looking with curiosity at my leg, as we walked down more stairs and crossed more rooms of black carpet and ceremonial weaponry. Around each room beyond the first were duellists, wearing the same tabard, displaying a chip of blue ice. They stood guard before rooms and corridors, and said nothing as we passed.

At the base of the building, my vision was filled with armed warriors. The courtyard was bounded by four tall towers and the high walls between, and the warriors wore as many different kinds of armour as they did faces. People of Ice, in their blue tabards, stood next to Dark Brethren, wearing the haughty Night Wing on their chests. Mingled amongst them were Mirralite, wearing no armour and carrying fragile-looking spears and blades. The courtyard had been buzzing with conversation a moment before we arrived. Now it was silent.

Twist calmed, allowing me to assess my situation without grabbing my left thigh and wincing. I'd kept from crying, determined at least to *appear* as a man. They might not yet see me as a Sea Wolf, but they didn't need to see any more of my weakness. I had an obligation to the Old Bitch of the Sea and to Lord Vikon. Appearing to be a helpless child might make my immediate situation more comfortable, but it no longer reflected who I was. If Twist and I were to penetrate the mysteries around us, we needed to quieten our internal squabbles.

From the press of warriors came three men. Inigo Night Walker and the Grim Wolf caused all warriors to form a channel for their approach, while an elderly Pure One followed. It was Ten Cuts, though his heavily wrinkled face was now painted with blue streaks down each cheek. The speaker of the Rykalite wore red feathers, woven into his long, grey hair, and held a ceremonial spear. Around his neck was the wooden spirit-whistle, and my burgeoning confidence faded, as I struggled to remember what he'd shown me.

"It may appear strange," said the Grim Wolf, "to travel under the Maelstrom just for you. But you must see something. You must see why we protect this place. Hundreds of warriors and spirit-masters hold the centre of Nowhere, trying to stem the flow of void beasts. The Maelstrom opens a little more each day. Though I'd not thought to show a Sea Wolf… we didn't think you were ready. Not until the sea begins to rise."

"You've seen it?" I grunted, trying not to look at Ten Cuts. "The… vision?"

Xavyer Ice nodded and, as his honour-name suggested, his face remained grim. "Marius Cyclone needed my island and he needed the Maelstrom, so Ten Cuts showed me what was at stake. What you call betrayal, I call wisdom, perhaps even survival. Inigo and I agreed that those of the Severed Hand were too… stubborn to recognize that some enemies can't be fought."

"Hopefully you are different," added Inigo Night Walker.

Twist and I were equally confused, and the pain all but disappeared, allowing me a few moments of clear thought. I narrowed my eyes and shrugged off the gently restraining hands of Zia and Blade Smile. "I'm a Sea Wolf," I stated. "*I'm* of the Severed Hand. You need me for something. What?"

"Not *us*," replied Inigo.

"But *someone* has a use for you," said the Grim Wolf, his eyes glazing over, as if he wasn't in complete control of his words. Similarly blank expressions flowed across everyone within earshot, though they only appeared for an instant. Even Inigo Night Walker slumped, nodding in agreement, before his military bearing returned a moment later. Only Ten Cuts and I were unaffected, and the distant note of a thin whistle sounded in my ears. I wondered if their minds were even their own, or if the strange pale man had woven a spell over them.

"Time to go," said the Grim Wolf, as if nothing had happened.

"Be gentle," offered Ten Cuts. "The young Invader has known pain. I think it may be *all* he has known."

The Grim Wolf addressed Blade Smile. "Xymon, look after him. It's a short run to the caves. Carry him if you need to. Watch his wyrd, it might start to misbehave."

"Yes, father," replied Blade Smile.

"Loco will assist," said Inigo, waving behind him to the clean-cut void legionnaire. "You haven't seen what Duncan can do. There is much power within that feeble frame."

"That's what we're counting on," replied the Grim Wolf. He glared at me. "If he's not as powerful as we think, there will be no reason to keep him alive."

I had no chance to respond. Loco Death Spell and Blade Smile held me between them. They were of a similar age and size, but one was wild and the other stoic. Loco's humourless glare and Blade Smile's manic grin clashed in front of me, as I was led from the wide granite steps, to join the mass of warriors. They thought I was powerful, but would kill me if I wasn't powerful enough. Twist and I wrestled with the strange conundrum, though we remained compliant.

"Form up," snapped Zia Lahandras, following after us.

A hundred warriors, mostly People of Ice, picked up swords and shields, and assembled into ranks. Inigo and the Brethren stayed at the rear, as Blade Smile and Loco led me to the front of the group, across tight cobbles, to the shadow of a huge gate. We were not at the edge of the town, but the gate formed one end of a well-covered road, leading between tall towers, from the middle of Cold Point to the northern walls. The gate was opened with a woody creak and a groan of metal, and the wide avenue appeared.

"Why do you need to take me under the Maelstrom?" I asked Loco Death Spell.

He didn't answer right away, but kept his hand balled in a fistful of my shirt, making sure I didn't stop walking. The resonant snap of metal on stone followed us out of the gate and along the avenue, as a column of armed men and women prepared to leave the safety of Cold Point.

"If I told you we were going to save the Eastron from annihilation, would you think me joking?" replied Loco, as the company increased its pace, enveloping me in marching men and women.

"You told me Death Spells are humourless," I countered.

"We are," said the young void legionnaire.

Blade Smile scoffed, staring at me with his wild eyes. "Just do as you're told, Duncan. The realms of form and void are smashing together out there, it'll do strange things to your wyrd. It'll hopefully show us how powerful you actually are." He twirled one of his knives in front of my face, as if to remind me that many outcomes included my death.

Zia Lahandras bellowed a command to the gate-guards, and the huge outer doors began to move. They were larger and thicker than all the interior gates, and were covered by dozens of murder-holes across the two adjacent towers. I felt as if I was witnessing the unveiling of a new world. Certainly the Maelstrom had been obscured by the walls, and was now all I could see.

The column of warriors didn't slow, and we were smoothly swept up in their marching, out of the gate into the northern half of the island. Beyond the curtain wall, the terrain was rugged grassland, much the same as the rest of Nowhere, but the grass, trees and shrubs were all low to the ground, or withered, as if the Maelstrom robbed the land of life-giving nutrients.

Then my senses were assaulted by a broken landscape. We crossed a rocky outcropping, and the air became a shimmering blue, with black veins crossing the scrubland, like lines of spider silk. Chunks of earth and rock hung at impossible angles, and trees danced in the air like insane creatures. It was as if the pieces of the world had all been mixed up and put back together in the wrong order. Form and void were smashing against each other, as the Maelstrom churned overhead, too deep and layered to see with any clarity. The painting of it in my father's hall at Moon Rock was impressive, but did it no justice. I had no idea the glass could fracture in such a way.

I wondered why tales of the void storm were not told at the Severed Hand. But most of all I wondered again why we needed to travel under it. As I wondered, Twist stirred against my leg. The pain spirit flexed, and I felt a rush of wyrd. Nowhere was a strange place. One moment I'd been banging my head against a stone wall, the next I was diving into a warm, blue ocean. Every inch of my skin tingled, sending a warm blanket across my body. I suddenly felt powerful again, as if my reservoirs went from half-empty to overflowing, but Twist and I agreed not to lash out... for the time being.

"Stand ready," boomed the Grim Wolf. All around me, Dark Brethren and People of Ice pulsed with wyrd, as their might returned. The glass was barely a membrane, and every Eastron summoned their full power, appearing as a mass of flame-handed warriors.

Blade Smile grabbed me around the neck. "Don't do anything stupid, boy. You should be feeling pretty strong, but I can break your neck before you kill anyone. Keep it under control."

The company fanned out, approaching a pit of craggy low ground, directly under the point of the Maelstrom, and I saw why everyone was so wary about travelling into the interior of Nowhere. The immense, rumbling void storm crackled through tones of black, grey and blue, sending forth wave after wave of potent spiritual energy. There was no solid barrier between form and void, and massed spirits tumbled to the ground, appearing as twisted distortions of nature. Swarms of brightly-coloured insects, bizarre many-legged balls of flesh, and huge, scaled serpents. Spirits of the wild void infested the low plains, kept back from the approaching cave system by a perimeter of wooden bulwarks. I'd never seen anything like it. The void I knew was a place of calm, but all I saw, thrown downwards by the Maelstrom, was chaos.

As we got closer, the warriors of Ice broke into loose formation, tackling any spirits that clustered across our path.

Duellists and void legionnaires summoned torrents of wyrd into their limbs and hacked at the spirits with methodical ferocity, clearing our way to the caves.

Loco and Blade Smile kept me tightly between them, as if expecting me to erupt at any moment. But they needn't have worried. Seeing the wild void flow, like abominable waves, was enough to keep me and Twist compliant. I could feel immense, pulsing wyrd, but kept it all internal, and was the only Eastron present not to shine with spiritual energy. I'd not been trained how to marshal such strength, and if it weren't for the pain spirit, I feared I'd *literally* erupt.

As the company ran towards the barricades and the caves beyond, I saw a swarm of grotesque, segmented wasp spirits consume a squad of void legionnaires. I saw a rampaging rage spirit – made up of a thousand mismatched arms, legs, torsos and heads – barrel a dozen Pure Ones out of its way. But the company reached the low ground more or less intact.

By the time we'd crossed the barricades, and hurriedly entered the largest of a dozen cave mouths, I'd seen at least ten warriors die to get me under the Maelstrom. And I still didn't know *why* or what they wanted me to see. My wyrd had returned, and was stronger than ever, but I had nowhere to point it. My customary tactic of lashing out seemed infantile, as if Twist and I had gained a modicum of maturity … and control. If there was a way to honour Vikon Blood and the Old Bitch of the Sea, I was determined to find it. If that meant hiding my power and remaining a captive, so be it.

14

Twist was dancing around my leg. The pain spirit vibrated against the many layers of wyrd that now thrummed within me, using them to perform somersaults and gleeful cartwheels. The centre of the Maelstrom gave me more power than I'd ever known, though I was in excruciating pain as a result. It was the only way Twist could communicate, and he made it difficult to stand. Luckily, I was propped up between Loco and Blade Smile, both of whom had glowing arms. In fact, every Eastron I could see in the well-lit caves, pulsed with the pale blue glow of wyrd. Every Eastron except me.

The small company had rushed into a complex of caves beneath the Maelstrom. The tunnels were well used and clean, with carpets and wooden structures. I could sense dozens of spirit-masters, using their collective craft to keep this small area free from the chaos belched forth by the Maelstrom. The Grim Wolf and his people were expending considerable power to protect a few caves, directly under the point of the void storm. There was something here of great value. Something that Marius Cyclone wanted. Something that drove the People of Ice to betray the First Fang, and the Dark Brethren to assault the *Dead Horse*.

The ninety warriors who had survived the journey north began to fan out into the cave complex, clustering into groups of Pure Ones, Dark Brethren and People of Ice. They didn't mingle, and relied on Inigo Night Walker, Ten Cuts and the Grim Wolf to coordinate their efforts.

"What's the matter with you?" asked Loco, frowning down at me. "Where's your wyrd? Why does it not shine?"

The Grim Wolf and Inigo approached, sheathing their weapons. The man of Ice was chewing on his lips in concern, and the commander of the third void legion had narrow, questioning eyes.

"We've seen nothing, father," said Blade Smile. "The boy didn't show so much as a trickle of power the whole journey."

"How flows your wyrd, Master Greenfire?" asked Xavyer Ice, flexing his glowing blue shoulders. He still looked like a bear, but now appeared twice as wide, as if his wyrd gave him a second skin. "Where is your power?"

Everyone was taller than me. Blade Smile was the shortest, and slowly held his small knife to my throat. Inigo and Loco were of similar size, and stood mere inches from my face. The Grim Wolf was far and away the tallest, though he stood back, regarding me warily.

"I don't know what you want me to say," I replied, straining against Twist to stand upright. "My wyrd is untrained, I can't control it." It was an easy thing to say, for I'd heard it all my life, but it was no longer completely true. It felt like a lie, for I could feel huge gouts of spiritual power, bubbling just below the surface. But I somehow kept it all internal, as if the impulse to prove myself was softening. "I'm a Sea Wolf," I stated. "I'm also your prisoner, but I'm not your fucking pet. My wyrd is my own."

Inigo glared at me. "I saw what you can do, Duncan. Don't pretend you're weak. Show us."

Blade Smile's knife pressed against my throat. "But don't get carried away," said the young man of Ice. "Just show us your wyrd."

They all stared at me, expecting a show of strength, or perhaps just an acknowledgement that the Maelstrom had affected me the same as it had them. But I didn't give them anything. I knew I was playing a dangerous game, but I wasn't going to honour the Severed Hand by being a coward. My wyrd had never shone brightly, and it was easy to hide it from them.

Then Inigo punched me in the face. It was a restrained blow, aimed at my nose, and made my eyes water. I fell backwards, and Twist flared against my leg. I summoned no wyrd, but had to grit my teeth to stop lashing out at the Dark Brethren. I groaned and curled up on the floor, gingerly touching my nose. I muttered under my breath, trying to stay calm.

"Is this a fucking joke?" snapped Inigo, kicking me in the stomach. "You killed a hundred warriors aboard the *Dead Horse*. And now you whimper? Where is your wyrd, Sea Wolf?"

He kicked me again, and I coughed violently, hugging my knees so as to protect my stomach from further punishment. My pain tolerance was astonishing, but the raging void legionnaire may have caused some internal damage. Added to which was the extreme effort it took to keep Twist from using my wyrd to do something violent. I was gambling that they wouldn't kill me. If a blade was swung at my head, I'd have no choice but to act, but a few punches and kicks I could endure.

"Stop kicking him," said the Grim Wolf. "Xymon, help him up."

Blade Smile sheathed his knife and grabbed my shoulders. With a heave, he pulled me to my feet, though I couldn't stand fully upright.

The Grim Wolf shoved past Inigo and Loco, to direct his wild, blue eyes down at me. "I warned you," he rumbled. "If you're not powerful enough to be of use, we have no reason to let you live. If you have anything to show us, now would be the time." His words were ominous, and far more threatening than being kicked repeatedly. I was also now aware that dozens of other warriors were looking at me.

Twist scratched at my leg, as if to ask if I was sure of what I was doing. The reasons for my deception were numerous but I wasn't sure of any of them. I was sick of being ignorant, and wanted some plain answers. I had gained some control for the first time in my life, and was eager to use it. But most of all, these were my captors, and a Sea Wolf would never submit to his captors. If the sea was truly rising, and a pale man was pulling their strings, I would stay defiant until I was told the truth. Until I saw a way to honour Vikon Blood, the Old Bitch of the Sea, and the crew of the *Dead Horse*.

I straightened, looking up at the Grim Wolf. The pain abated, though I gulped, and my face twitched. "Then you should kill me," I stated, amazed at my own bravery. "But I'll die a Sea Wolf."

The man of Ice scratched at his matted beard. "You wear your fear well," he observed. "*And* your pain. But how are you with the pain of others?"

"I've got nothing more to say to you," I replied, gritting my teeth.

He nodded, and put an enormous, hairy hand on my shoulder. "It's okay, lad. I know you have power in there somewhere. Perhaps threatening *your* life is not the way to unleash it. Zia, take him to the cells. Watch him closely."

"Yes, brother," replied Zia Lahandras.

The line of cells was built into the cave wall. Old, dark wood with black iron fastenings. Each door was a slightly different size, dictated by the slanted cave ceiling, and contained a barred window at head height. We were deeper in the cave system, far from the central chambers and the massed warriors. I was closely guarded by Zia and three men of Ice, though no blade was held to my throat. They still believed me to be powerful, but perhaps not an immediate danger.

"Down the end," said Zia Lahandras, shoving me along the line of cells. "Follow the cursing."

A few steps along the corridor and I could hear a mumbled voice. Halfway down, and the words coalesced into swear words. As I reached the last two cells, I heard Weathervane Will spitting curses through the hole in his cell door. The Kneeling Wolf was on tiptoes to be seen through the bars.

"... and fuck your mother's mother, and fuck her stupid fucking face. I kneel, but not to you ... Duncan?"

From within the small cell, Snake Charmer stood from a low bed and approached the barred window. "Friend Duncan!" exclaimed the Pure One. "I am glad to see you safe."

I smiled, feeling genuine happiness at seeing them again. I was not the only survivor of the *Dead Horse*. They would be as confused as me, and confusion, like misery, was fond of company. "I was certain they'd have killed you."

"Not me," said Will, with a vicious grin. "I'm just a rat. The legionnaires aren't allowed to sully their blades, and Valen Ice made a vow to the Friend a century ago. I've been insulting them for days, it appears there is nothing I can say that will make them kill me."

"I can vouch for that," offered Snake, looking down at the diminutive Eastron. "As we were hooded and dragged north, he focused his attacks on our captives' parentage. His language has been most colourful."

"You didn't see the Maelstrom?" I asked.

"Felt it," said Will. "But we've had hoods whenever they moved us. The beach to Cold Point, Cold Point to the caves. And *you*? We haven't seen you since the beach. Since they executed Lord Vikon."

"They want my wyrd," I replied. "I don't know what for, but... I've seen things. The sea rising." I coughed and shook my head, scratching at my leg. "I can't really remember it... it's... like the part of a dream you can't recall."

The Pure One and the Kneeling Wolf looked at each other. As Will was about to speak, Zia grabbed my neck and pulled me away from the cell window. "That's enough," she commanded.

"Hello, sweetheart," said Will, winking at the woman of Ice. "Why don't you come in here and tickle my balls?"

Snake coughed in embarrassment, but Zia barely reacted. "The wolves that kneel will ever be our friends," she replied, with a respectful bow of the head.

"Oh, fuck off," said Will, sneering in irritation and backing away from the cell door.

"The Winterlord is in *there*," said Zia, ignoring Weathervane Will and pointing to the last cell. "He won't submit to imprisonment, so requires more substantial restraints than those two."

I swallowed, and took a few tentative steps along the corridor. The last door was small, barely taller than me, and the cell was tiny, certainly not large enough for David Falcon's Fang to stand. He was chained and gagged, seated in an awkward crouch against the far wall. His plate armour was nowhere to be seen, and his huge form was clad in nothing but bloody rags, with bandages tied around his thigh, forearm and neck. Though his blue eyes were narrow and focused, and his breathing was slow.

"We don't want to hurt him," said Zia. "We have no quarrel with First Port *or* the Always King." She bowed her head, and pushed a braid of black hair behind her shoulder. "But we feel you would be more compliant if he was in pain…and you had the power to stop it. We could hurt the Pure One or the rat, but Master Falcon's Fang…he's a Winterlord. Perhaps the enormity of his suffering will make you realize what is at stake – the very future of the Eastron from across the sea."

I locked eyes with David. Looking back at me was rage and defiance. The young Winterlord duellist appeared even bigger when squeezed into a tiny cell, with his muscles tensed against the steel chains and stone walls. It suddenly occurred to me that none of us would be here if I'd not killed Maron Grief and snuck out of my room in the Bloody Halls. But then Prince Oliver Dawn Claw would be dead, and the war would have already begun. I was conflicted, and Twist punctuated my torment with an insistent spasm, travelling up my left leg, and assaulting my capacity to think clearly. The pain spirit didn't understand why I kept my power shackled, and in that moment, neither did I.

I glared at Zia. "You're going to hurt David to make me show you my wyrd?"

The three men of Ice who'd accompanied us encircled me, holding heavy-bladed cutlasses. "Is the threat not enough?" asked Zia. "If you agree to use your power to aid us, there is no need to hurt anyone."

I sneered at her, fed up with being kept in the dark. "You've not even told me what you want. Inigo and your brother are apparently now best friends, and have only said that *someone* has a use for me, and that you attacked the *Dead Horse* to keep Nowhere safe. But my wyrd belongs to no-one else, and I'll use it when and where *I* choose."

Honour us, Duncan.

I looked at David's unmoving, defiant eyes. Then at the small cell window where Weathervane Will craned his neck to see us. Finally, I stared down at the stone floor. "Okay, Twist," I muttered. "I think I've been a prisoner long enough."

Zia was frowning, wondering who I was talking to, and the three armed men kept their blades close to my neck, but I didn't care. With a deep breath, I unleashed my wyrd. It was like every inch of my body surged into a new skin of dark blue light. I roared, as the surge reached my head, flowing from my eyes and mouth, and becoming a violently crackling mantle of energy. The Maelstrom removed my shackles like the breaking of a dam, allowing me to shatter three cutlasses with a thought, and fling their wielders into the walls. I broke their necks, backs, and limbs. I crushed

Zia's head into mush with a wave of my shimmering arms, sending a spray of blood across the cell doors. I killed them and it was all so effortless. Zia's headless body fell, much as Maron Grief's had on the stone of Duellist's Yard, but this time there was no-one here to reprimand me.

Then I couldn't catch my breath. My wyrd was surging beyond the limits of my body, and I screamed in pain, trying to pull it back. I could feel the void, pulsing through me, as if the glass was malleable or transparent. I feared I'd kill myself, until Twist began stabbing me in the leg, forcing my wyrd to retreat. I slumped to the floor, panting heavily and fighting to stay conscious. There was blood everywhere, with broken bodies, posed like depraved statues, against the cell doors.

"Duncan!" snapped Will. "The key-chain. On her belt."

I shivered and curled up into a ball, wanting the world to leave me alone. The Kneeling Wolf had seen me use my wyrd twice, enabling him to focus on his freedom, rather than the four people I'd killed.

"Duncan, you just made a lot of noise. They'll be coming. The key-chain!"

I had no strength. My whole body was tensed and my bones weren't moving properly. All I could do was slump at Zia's body, trying not to look at her, as I rolled her towards Will's outstretched hand. The Kneeling Wolf reached through the barred cell window, pulling the key-chain from Zia's belt and fumbling with the keys. Snake was standing behind him, though his face showed no anxiety or shock. At the end of the corridor, shouts of alarm told me that other warriors were arriving.

Will tried two keys in the lock of his cell door, swearing loudly as each did nothing. The third made a heavy click as it turned, and he shoved the door outwards, pushing Zia's body away from the cell.

"Snake, get to David," snapped the Kneeling Wolf, lobbing the key-chain to the Pure One.

Snake grabbed a cutlass from Zia's belt, and disappeared quickly inside David's cell, whilst Will raised his arms and moved to greet the three approaching warriors of Ice. "Wait, wait," he shouted, bowing his head in supplication. "I kneel to you, noble Sea Wolves. It's all a mistake." He looked down at me, and realized I wasn't going to be any further help. Not until I'd had time to recover. I was barely awake, and was unable to move without extreme effort. Even Twist was exhausted, and curled up within the thorn clinch, like an animal falling asleep after the exertion of a successful hunt.

The three warriors recovered quickly, but Will had bought just enough time for Snake Charmer to unchain David Falcon's Fang. The huge Winterlord emerged from his cell with Zia's cutlass in his bloody hand. His feet were bare and his grey rags hung from his body. He spared a moment to survey the people I'd killed, before summoning wyrd into his arms and charging at the warriors of Ice.

Will dove to the side as the first man died. David was a skilled duellist, despite his youth, and skewered his target through the throat, before pulling back and holding a low stance. "You will die here," he said, addressing the two men who remained. "Fast or slow, it *will* come."

They attacked as one, going for his head and legs at the same time. David parried the high blow, and kicked away the other. He was clearly not accustomed to fighting with so slender a blade, but his superior strength and skill compensated for any of his shortcomings with a Sea Wolf cutlass. The next man of Ice was killed with a backhand slice across the forehead, and the last had his head smashed against the wall.

When it was done, after no more than ten seconds of violence, David leant against the wall and caught his breath. "Snake, check the corridor. You, rat, arm yourself." He then looked down at me, and the broken bodies either side. "How flows your wyrd, friend Duncan?"

I managed to sit upright, breathing heavily, against the stone wall. I spluttered a few times, but couldn't form any actual words. I just looked up at him, like a wounded child who'd made a huge mistake. I couldn't look at the four people I'd killed, but I knew they were there, twitching either side of me. I'd killed many more aboard the *Dead Horse*, but I'd not seen *their* faces. This was different. This was worse. My control was an illusion. I could keep my wyrd caged or I could unleash it, there was nothing in between. And I couldn't stop it from killing people.

"You need to stand, Duncan," said the Winterlord. "We have to move. Now!" He grabbed me and I was pulled to my feet. My legs were wobbly, but David let me lean on him, and we stumbled away from the cells.

Weathervane Will acquired a cutlass from a dead body, and Snake Charmer darted forwards, to check the T-junction at the end of the prison corridor. The Kneeling Wolf stared at me, while the Pure One remained calm and precise.

"To you I kneel, noble Sea Wolf," said Will, with a reassuring smirk. "I think we should go home now." David handed me off to the Kneeling Wolf, who wrapped an arm around my shoulder. "I got ya. Just take it slow."

"The way is clear," said David, striding ahead to join Snake Charmer.

With the Winterlord in the lead, we skulked along the stone corridor, away from the dead bodies and towards the main caves. Will kept me moving at an even pace, but said nothing. The thorn clinch was burning, and I felt like I was walking through water, with no strength and heavy limbs. Had I honoured anyone? Or had I just killed more people? I'd helped the other survivors from their cells, but we were far from free.

At the end of the stone corridor, the walls flowed back into craggy rock, as the caves expanded away from us. Voices and movement echoed through the chambers, though direction was impossible to discern.

"Duncan, which way?" whispered David.

Will helped me limp past Snake, to peer into the caves. Other hewn corridors went left and right, with the central passage an irregular cave. "We came from there," I replied, pointing to the large cave. "That's where all the warriors are."

David frowned, glancing around the passages. He kept his own counsel, not thinking to ask for advice. His wyrd was flickering along the length of his arms as he pondered his situation, as if he was reminding himself that it was still there. The glass of Nowhere made it difficult to trust your wyrd, even under the Maelstrom, though the young duellist would likely never confess to any doubts.

Before he could decide what to do, two Pure Ones emerged from one of the side corridors. Will and I hugged the wall, but David just looked at them, refusing to hide from lesser men. They looked back at him, gradually registering his bloody clothes and fierce expression. All at once they started running, and David leapt forwards in pursuit, with Will and Snake close behind. I was left, leaning against the cave wall, struggling to stand. The two fleeing Pure Ones made for the large cave ahead of us, shouting that the prisoners were free. David tackled one from behind, whilst Weathervane Will dragged the other to the ground by his long, black hair.

I hobbled along the wall after them, as the Pure Ones' echoing shouts filled the caves. "Should we hide?" I suggested, feebly.

Will choked one unconscious, and David knocked the other one out with a single punch, but the damage had been done. The words faded slowly, but had travelled far in the open cave system. I feared that we'd be swarmed by warriors within moments, though David showed no signs of hiding. The Winterlord moved from the two unconscious Mirralite and stood in the centre of the cave entrance, as if to greet anyone who came to investigate.

"Duncan's right, milord," offered Will. "We can't fight a whole army down here."

"We can and we will," replied David, hefting Zia's cutlass. "Though we will likely fall, honour will have been sated. The Dawn Claw will mourn our passing." He shared a respectful nod with Snake Charmer and took a deep breath, pulling prodigious wyrd into his arms.

"Honour?" I blurted out. "What has honour got to do with anything? I thought we were going to escape. How can we honour anyone when we're dead?"

Will stepped gingerly into the shadows, encouraging Snake and me to do the same. Running footsteps reached all our ears, though it was still impossible to tell where they came from. David Falcon's Fang didn't appear to care. He faced the largest cave entrance and scowled.

"Snake, come stand by me," said the Winterlord. "If we die, let us die side by side, as brothers."

If I'd been less panicked, I'd have been amazed at the way David spoke to his squire. He appeared to see all other Pure Ones as inferior, whereas Snake Charmer was worthy of being called a brother.

"They're coming," observed Will. "Sounds like a lot of them."

I backed away, hugging the wall next to the Kneeling Wolf. Both of us were scanning the passageways and cold, stone corridors, looking for the easiest place to run away. The way back to the cells was open, but glowing lights and echoing footsteps vibrated down all other corridors.

Will looked at me and smiled. "I think we're fucked, Master Greenfire."

He was right. The echoes were replaced by armoured warriors, emerging with confusion from most angles before me. From the largest cave, in front of David, came a mob of Eastron. A few Dark Brethren, amongst People of Ice, coming in response to the shouting. They saw the huge Winterlord and Snake Charmer, but Will and I were lost in shadows.

"Come to your deaths," announced David.

The warriors stopped moving, puzzled by the blood-soaked duellist before them. From other corridors came dozens of Pure Ones and People of Ice, destroying any hope we had of retreat. I suddenly felt like a fool. I was responsible for Vikon Blood's death, and now I would be responsible for David's. My already laden conscience might also have to bear the weight of William Vane's death, perhaps even Snake Charmer's.

From behind the press of warriors in the large cave, came insistent commands in a deep voice. David took a stride towards the People of Ice and Dark Brethren, daring them to attack him. Instead, they parted, revealing the lumbering figure of Xavyer Ice, the Grim Wolf. Barely visible over his left shoulder was Ten Cuts. Will and I had now stepped into the cave, seeing no reason to remain hidden.

"Easy, boy," said the Grim Wolf, holding his arms out and grinning at David. He narrowed his eyes when he saw me, but didn't stop grinning. "This isn't your time. This isn't a glorious last stand. There's no glory, there's just death. Return to your cell and live another day, Winterlord." He paused, his wild, blue eyes narrowing and his mouth closing into a frown. "Where did you get that sword? It's my sister's. I gave it to her."

David glanced at the bloody cutlass, but didn't turn and acknowledge me. "Your sister kindly freed me," replied the Winterlord. "If you want me to answer for her death ... well, I'm standing right in front of you."

The Grim Wolf bowed his head and closed his eyes. He rubbed his face, paced back and forth, grumbled under his breath and shook his head. I was again reminded of a distressed bear.

After a moment, the grieving man turned his back on David, and addressed his people. "Zia Lahandras, called Freeze, my sister, is dead. She was killed by *this* entitled prick." His voice vibrated with madness, as if the death of his sister overrode all other concerns. "We should kill all four of them." He spoke coldly, stating our deaths as a matter-of-fact.

Everything slowed down. Swords seemed to appear from every conceivable angle, and Twist howled in the recesses of my mind. The pain spirit wanted to lash out, but our wyrd was nowhere to be found.

The endless line of swords advanced, and the Grim Wolf faced David. The huge man of Ice theatrically drew the two cutlasses in his belt and dropped them to the stone floor. Now unarmed, he crouched, as if preparing to charge, and summoned a thick layer of wyrd across each shoulder. The line between man and bear was hard to see, as the Grim Wolf pounced at the Winterlord.

Xavyer Ice was wider, but David was taller, and the two massive men clashed with a surge of rippling, blue wyrd. The sword proved ineffectual, skittering away as soon as it struck the Grim Wolf's body, and the Winterlord was forced to grapple the ravening man of Ice. David was pinned to the floor, his legs locked together in a powerful mount, and his neck restrained with a forearm. The Grim Wolf hefted his full weight into David's neck, slowly crushing his windpipe.

Warriors now advanced on Will and me. The Dark Brethren weren't involved, but that made little difference. I backed away, but every direction was covered with swords. I saw Snake Charmer, standing impassively, with his gaze focused on David, but his reluctance to fight didn't matter to the approaching warriors. All four of us were about to die.

"Do *not* kill them!" commanded Ten Cuts.

Everything stopped.

15

I was in a square room, made of uniform bricks of grey stone. Two windows were shrouded in red curtains, with no breeze or light coming from either, and I was seated in a soft, leather armchair. It was warm, but a pleasant breeze appeared to rise from the thick carpets. I didn't know where I was or how I got there. One moment I was preparing for death, the next I was free of pain, and sitting in comfort. I heard Ten Cuts speak and I saw everyone stop moving, but then nothing. Just the square stone room. I thought I was in the void, but couldn't be sure.

A table appeared next to me. It was small and wooden, of strange design, and appeared out of nowhere. Upon its surface was a mug, filled to the brim with frothing ale. I trusted nothing about my new environment, but licked my lips nonetheless. My mouth was dry, and the ale was unnaturally appealing. Bubbles of condensation crept down the mug, and a rich smell of hops caressed my nostrils. I reached for the ale and held it under my nose, before taking a deep drink. It was beyond refreshing, and tickled my tongue with fizzing points of richness and warmth. I'd drunk ale before, furtively behind my father's back, but had never really liked the taste. Now it was nectar, bringing me back to consciousness.

"It's called Sixth Hill Reserve," said a strange voice, out of nowhere. "You have nothing like it in the Kingdom of the Four Claws. At the Dark Harbour they drink stout. It's not bad, but too bitter for my taste. I hear you Sea Wolves have good ale. But I also hear you are uncultured brutes, too blind to see beyond your rage. I've heard many stories in which your people are the villains."

I took another drink, surprised at my lack of alarm. A strange stone room and a disembodied voice were merely the latest in a long line of obscure things I'd yet to grasp. I even considered that I was hearing voices that weren't there. But I didn't feel tormented. I didn't feel pain either. But then I could have been going mad. It was a very real consideration. Perhaps everything since I'd killed Maron Grief had been a hallucination.

"You're not going mad," said the voice. "I have a use for you, but you shouldn't have killed Zia Lahandras. You have caused me considerable stress. The Grim Wolf is powerful when *not* grieving his sister. His mind does not open as easily as others'."

I was unfamiliar with the accent. It was precise, with clipped edges, but each word was enunciated clearly. It seemed to go with the square stone room, as if one was a part of the other, and I was caught between the two.

"*Your* mind surprised me," continued the voice. "You're one of four mortals in this realm to have seen me. And the first to do so without my intention. Ten Cuts is my closest ally, and Marius Cyclone was the first Eastron I trusted. Rage Breaker of the Sundered Claws was a necessity. And then there is you, Duncan Redfire."

"Greenfire," I corrected. "I belong to the house of Robert Greenfire, First Fang of the Severed Hand between the fifty-seventh and the eightieth year of the dark age. He brought peace after the Years of Ice. My father is Wilhelm Greenfire, High Captain of Moon Rock … and you're the pale man, aren't you?"

There was no reply. I scanned the room furtively, looking for something that might indicate a trick, or an illusion. But everything looked real. "Are you controlling their minds?" I asked. "How many of them? Are you controlling *me*?"

"Not you," replied the voice. "You're too powerful. But many others, yes. It's the only way to save your people. How else do you imagine the People of Ice would ally with Marius Cyclone and the Dark Brethren? Old enmities run deep in your kingdom … as in all human realms of form. Telling them they are all going to die should be enough, but it rarely is."

"Are you a spirit? Some kind of old totem summoned by the Stranger?" I took another deep drink of ale, and sunk further into the leather armchair.

"No," was the reply. "If I told you who I was you wouldn't understand the answer. For now just accept that I am *trying* to help you and your people. Few of you know it, but the Eastron will soon become embroiled in a war they can't hope to win. The sea rises, young man."

I tried to recall the vision in detail, but everything was remembered through a haze, as if my mind was protecting me from reliving the eldritch spectacle of the Sunken City and its dreaming occupant. "Do I have *you* to thank for knowing what I don't want to know?" I looked at the carpeted floor, and gritted my teeth. "And are *you* the reason a crew of Sea Wolves is dead?"

"Regrettably," was the reply. "I sought to keep Nowhere isolated until the time was right. I made Inigo attack your ship in the belief it would be an easy victory against a crew of brutes. Nowhere must be protected, and I couldn't risk the Sea Wolves sabotaging my efforts, but Vikon Blood was a truly mighty warrior... and then there was you, young Invader. It was an unexpected turn of events."

I threw the mug of ale against the stone wall. It didn't break, or splash across the carpet, but simply phased out of existence when it hit the brickwork. It was not a satisfying display of anger, so I kicked the chair over, and upended the table. "An unexpected turn of fucking events? Do you know what you've done? You killed someone I liked. Someone who was kind to me. And you've started a war."

"Hmm," replied the voice. "I think Santago Cyclone did that when he sent an assassin to kill the Winterlord prince. Marius and his elder brother parted ways shortly after they saw the vision of the Sunken City."

"One Dark Brethren is the same as another," I grunted. It was the sort of thing Lord Vikon would have said.

"If only that were true," said the pale man. "All three of the Cyclone brothers were shown the vision, and the three reacted very differently. Santago saw a chance for power, Trego went mad, only Marius saw it for what it was – the annihilation of the Eastron. He agreed to help me gain access to the Maelstrom. For only on the island of Nowhere, under the point of the void storm, can your people be saved."

My anger gradually disappeared when it became obvious that the pale man didn't care about my petulance. I righted the chair, and perched on the edge of the leather seat. "There's something of great value here, isn't there? Why else would you, Inigo and the Grim Wolf go to such efforts to keep it safe and secret?"

I didn't get a response straightaway, and wished I hadn't thrown away the mug of ale. I scratched at my thorn clinch and couldn't feel Twist, confirming that the square stone room was somewhere in the void.

"Apologies," said the voice, after what felt like an hour. "My attention is elsewhere. It has taken considerable effort to undo the damage done when you killed Zia Lahandras. Controlling so many mortals at once is draining, so please try not to kill anyone else. I may have to let you die next time. I don't like my influence to be too overt."

I only really had one question left. Everything else branched off it, like tiny rivers, flowing from an enormous lake. "Why me?" I asked. "I'm just a Sea Wolf freak. Why go to so much trouble over *me*?"

"I have a use for you," was the maddening reply. "You're going to help me. Together we can save the Eastron from slavery under the Sunken God. We can give them a future. We can honour them all."

I was dragged back through the glass. The voice disappeared, as did the chair, the table and the square, stone room. The temperature dropped suddenly, and a whistle of wind travelled sharply through the caves of Nowhere. The realm of form was frozen in place, like a three-dimensional painting. David Falcon's Fang was still sprawled on the rocky ground, his throat held firmly by the Grim Wolf, and his face locked into a mask of rage-filled defiance. Weathervane Will was cowering under three cutlasses, his eyes wide and his mouth open, as if he couldn't believe that he'd die like this. Around me were a forest of unmoving figures, mostly holding blades and wearing anger on their faces. It was surreal to walk amongst them, unfettered by whatever held them in place. I stood face-to-face with Snake Charmer, looking up into his calm, light-brown features. There was no alarm or fear, just a passive acceptance of his fate.

Ten Cuts approached through the frozen warriors, looking at me with narrow eyes. The old Pure One had a thin smile on his drawn face, with his wrinkles forming an arc around a subtly-curved mouth. It felt as if we were alone, viewing a past scene that both had experienced. We silently circled around David Falcon's Fang and Xavyer Ice, like it was a bizarre sculpture.

"What happens now?" I asked. "Are *you* going to answer my question?"

"Soon," he replied, pointing to the stone floor next to Weathervane Will.

I frowned, unsure of what he was suggesting.

"I believe you were crouched next to the Kneeling Wolf," said Ten Cuts. "Please resume crouching. Time will continue its march in a few moments."

I swore under my breath, feeling like I was riding a runaway horse that kept getting faster and faster. Then Twist woke up and I was dragged to the stone floor. The thorn clinch felt as if it were on fire, burning my flesh black. The pain spirit had not experienced the stone room, or the pale man's voice, and he was trying to catch up. As always, this was expressed through pain.

Ten Cuts extended his hand and helped me to stand upright, keeping his dark eyes soft. I focused on the spirit-whistle around his neck, silently begging him to blow it and make Twist go back to sleep. But he didn't.

"Listen to me, Invader pup," whispered the old Pure One, helping me into position next to Will. "You have been chosen by a benevolent power, who will be the salvation of both our peoples. In the centuries not yet lived you will come to worship him as a god. And your power will shine brightly over your people for eternity."

Everything happened quickly, but no-one was killed. As one, acting as mindless drones, the warriors of Ice sheathed their swords, and Will and I were gathered up in restraining arms. The Grim Wolf's rage turned quickly to amusement, and David's defiance became contrition. Our escape was suddenly a matter of amusement, as we were bundled together. Snake was barely touched, and allowed to stroll next to Will and me, whereas David was kicked several times, pulled to his feet, and held in a choke-hold by the Grim Wolf.

"You're a funny little fucker," said Xavyer Ice, slapping the Winterlord's cheek. "But you need to know when you're beaten. Return to your cell and live another day, or keep struggling and I'll kick you to death."

I shook my head, wondering what had happened. I'd killed someone, but couldn't remember who. I'd been terrified for my life, but now I just felt tired, as if I carried a huge weight. I'd helped David escape, but I knew how foolish that had been. We were all lucky not to have been summarily executed by the Grim Wolf and his warriors of Ice.

Ten Cuts stood next to Inigo Night Walker, behind the Grim Wolf, and the old Pure One was whispering in the Dark Brethren's ear.

"Easy," said Inigo, placing a slender hand on the Grim Wolf's huge shoulder. "I think we should accept some blame here, Xavyer. Young Duncan must be awfully confused. By freeing the Winterlord and the rat, he was merely trying to take control. Is that not so, Master Greenfire? You remembered you were a Sea Wolf?"

Everyone looked at me. There was still some fear, but most people now smiled, as if there was a general agreement with Inigo Night Walker's assessment of my state of mind. *I* certainly agreed with him, and was glad that the atmosphere had softened, and that I wouldn't be responsible for getting anyone else killed.

"Well," conceded the Grim Wolf, loosening his choke-hold and allowing David to stand upright. "You weren't foolish enough to kill any of my people, so I believe I can overlook your glorious escape attempt. Just don't try it again, my lord."

David didn't flinch, though I could tell his mind was whirring. Perhaps he was reassessing his combat prowess, or perhaps he was lamenting that he had no blade and had been forced to wrestle the huge man of Ice. "I will submit to imprisonment," said the Winterlord. "But I will not wear chains."

"Agreed," rumbled the Grim Wolf. "Though there are easier ways of making that point."

"I'll take the boy," said Inigo, grabbing me by the arm. "I won't allow him to cause any more trouble. We should show him. Perhaps if we'd done so in the first place, he would be more willing to use his wyrd to aid us."

I felt as if I was remembering a dozen different things at the same time. I forgot things, recovered them, then forgot them again. My mind was rebelling, making me feel like I was seeing everything from afar, a distant dream of form, unconnected to reality. I was quite definitely going mad.

I'd used my wyrd again, and killed four people, including the Grim Wolf's sister. I'd released David and seen three more men of Ice die, but no-one recalled this but me. If the Grim Wolf ever had a sister, he no longer remembered her, and the six dead warriors had disappeared, as if they'd never existed. The only eyes that had seen what truly happened were mine, and those of Ten Cuts. Snake Charmer, William Vane, even Inigo Night Walker and Loco Death Spell – they'd all been tricked, shown a false reality that none of them questioned.

"Things are complicated," said Inigo, leading me away from the cells and deeper into the caves of Nowhere. "But you already know that."

David and the others had been placed back under lock and key, and we were surrounded by a squad of void legionnaires, led by Loco. Ten Cuts was trailing behind, and we'd entered a series of strange caverns, with jagged stalactites falling from the ceiling.

"It's a terrible thing to know the sea will rise," continued Inigo, his eyes narrowing as he recalled the vision. It was strangely reassuring to know that others had seen the spectacle of the Sunken City, despite their ignorance of the pale man and his mind control.

"Who else has seen it?" I asked, my face twitching.

The Dark Brethren glanced behind him, smiling at Ten Cuts. "The Stranger has placed the authority in the honourable hands of this Pure One, and Ten Cuts plays his whistle to whom he chooses. Xavyer Ice and I, Santos Spirit Killer, Jessimion Death Spell, a scattered few others. Marius Cyclone will be the salvation of the Eastron."

I grunted in exasperation. "What the fuck does that mean?" I asked, more tired than angry. "I'm sorry, but I think I'm going mad. I need to hear something that I understand."

Loco Death Spell slapped me. "Manners, boy."

"At ease," ordered Inigo, casually. "He deserves something more, so we give him something more." He positioned me in front of him, stalactites hanging over our heads. "Some foes cannot be fought, Master Greenfire. Some foes can annihilate you without acknowledging you exist. Without a sword being swung, or a ballistae being fired." He ordered a halt, and the void legionnaires stood at-ease. "If the Eastron cannot win, what can we do?"

He was waiting for an answer. I'd gotten used to people asking me rhetorical questions, assuming that *their* wisdom would trump any contribution *I* might have. I was, after all, just a Sea Wolf pup, a freak who had survived the rite at seventeen and stumbled his way into prominence. Nothing I'd done, from killing Maron Grief and saving Prince Oliver, to erupting aboard the *Dead Horse* and killing Zia Lahandras, had been properly thought out. It had all just happened. But at least my eyes were open. I knew that someone or something was controlling the minds of everyone here.

"You actually want an answer?" I replied. "From me? You don't even know why you've kept me alive. You know half of the puzzle and I know the other. So tell me what you're protecting here."

Inigo took two strides backwards, motioning for me to follow. "I'll answer my own question," he said. "If the Eastron cannot win, all we can do is retreat. But to where do we flee?"

"I don't know," I mumbled, with an exhausted sigh, realizing that his question had in fact been rhetorical. "Where do we flee?"

"The void," replied Inigo, knowingly. "Every single one of us. Even the Sea Wolves. The Eastron invaded from across the sea, but we will retreat into the distant void. You've seen what we face, and you know we can't win. We need to leave before it's too late."

"Are you mad?"

He laughed. "This is not a hasty plan, Master Greenfire. My lord Marius has thought this through. From the day he saw the vision, to the day he learned of a distant realm and the way to get there." He kept moving backwards until we stood in the centre of the cave. "If our route to survival had not been on the island of Nowhere, we would not have come here. Nor would we have attacked the *Dead Horse*. This place *must* be protected."

Ten Cuts approached, ignoring Inigo and me, looking up at the forest of stalactites. He placed his spirit-whistle to his lips and let forth a single note, which echoed gently around the large cave. From the ceiling, appearing in black waves, I saw the glass break and I saw the Maelstrom. My wyrd tingled and I felt the presence of the great turtle spirit, but this was not a vision. The Dark Brethren formed a circle around us, and a spiral of the void storm descended to ground level.

"The Stranger was visited by an old spirit," said Inigo. "The spirit told him of a doorway to a distant realm."

The Maelstrom formed an archway between Ten Cuts and me. It was three times taller than me and framed a crackling vortex of void energy. The fractured glass of Nowhere had thrown forth mighty void serpents and all manner of spiritual chaos, but it appeared also to have thrown forth a doorway. I could feel the power beyond and my wyrd pulsed, like the door had a magnetic pull. From the assembled Dark Brethren, small tendrils of light-blue wyrd snaked towards the centre of the cavern. Everyone except Ten Cuts showed their wyrd. The old Pure One moved to face me. He tried to smile, but it didn't reach his eyes. He knew both halves of the truth, more so than me, and held some authority I didn't understand. He and his spirit-whistle had shown me more than I'd wanted to see.

"Where does it lead?" I asked Ten Cuts.

"To a hall beyond the world," he replied. "Large enough for a civilization to make a home. And beyond are realms of form beyond count. The Eastron are mighty, and they do not deserve to fall into the sky when the sea rises."

"Who is the pale man?" I mumbled, ignoring the Dark Brethren. "And what does he want from me? Forget all the shadowy shit and just tell me the truth."

Inigo and the others were focused on the shimmering break in the glass, perhaps musing upon what lay beyond. They were not listening to us talk.

"You are still alive because your wyrd is wild and powerful. You have resisted training and learned nothing about how to cage your might. The Invaders are a conundrum with a single great weakness – they twist what makes them special into petty displays of strength. They think that swinging a sword is the answer to every problem."

I smiled. "It's the answer to most. The Pure Ones had no questions it couldn't answer."

"We lived in harmony with the world," he replied, his weathered face only a few inches from my own. His light-brown skin was loose and made it hard to tell what expression he was wearing. "Perhaps this world needs harmony more than it needs swords. But no people deserves annihilation, even the Invaders from across the sea. If you do not take this single avenue of escape, you will all die."

I glanced at Inigo Night Walker. He and the other Dark Brethren were staring at the doorway, seemingly blind to everything else. I felt as if I was seeing the world from a unique perspective, removed from reality. Or at least reality as I understood it. Only Ten Cuts existed in the same space as me. The strange voice had described the old Pure One as his closest ally. But then he'd also described Marius Cyclone as trustworthy, so his judgement might be suspect.

"You are not a warrior," continued Ten Cuts. "You are not a leader, a scholar, or a rogue. Your power is unique, and… as the world needs harmony more than swords, it needs you more than it needs your fellow Sea Wolves. You are the only individual we have found with the power to widen this doorway. If you agree to help, this single slice of void can become a gateway, through which a thousand mortals can march, side-by-side, to safety." He looked at me, his earnest eyes conveying layers of complex emotions. "But our time is now short, for your people will soon come looking for their lost ship. We sought to *guard* the doorway, keeping it safe and secret as we worked, an inch at a time, to make it larger. Then we found *you*… and salvation seems closer."

It appeared so elegant. A simple solution to thwart the Sunken God. I didn't know if it would work, and I was certain the Sea Wolves would view it as running away, but, for the first time since I'd left the Severed Hand, I felt I knew what was expected of me. At least in part. Saving the Eastron from extinction would honour Lord Vikon, the Old Bitch of the Sea, everyone who'd died aboard the *Dead Horse*.

"Word from the coast," said Loco, slicing through my introspection. "Warships sighted."

"How many?" replied Inigo.

"Four. Three from the Severed Hand and one from the Folly." Loco had already begun ordering the other Brethren out of the cavern. "They're moving quickly, my lord, we can't take them at sea."

The commander of the third void legion waved me and Ten Cuts away from the rapidly disappearing doorway into the void. "Tell the Grim Wolf we're braving the Maelstrom and moving back to Cold Point, then to the coast. We'll greet the Sea Wolves at the beach."

Ten Cuts shook off Inigo's hand and frowned. Then he spoke, directly at the commander. "We have no time for this. Once the young man and I have travelled beyond, we can work fast. We may yet be able to greet the Sea Wolves as friends and saviours." His manner was commanding, and made the lesser Dark Brethren avert their eyes and appear contrite, though Inigo remained imperious.

"Not yet," replied the commander. "That boy may be the only chance we have for a diplomatic solution. A few extra days won't harm our chances of escape, but it may save the lives of many Eastron. He's coming back to the coast with us."

I swore under my breath.

The world came into being and it didn't change.

From its first moment until its last it will have a master. When the master blinked, men appeared.

Men grew, warred, learned and existed all within that blink.

One day the master will see again, and our blink of the eye will end.

Manos Bowyer, Spirit-Master of Four Claw's Folly

PART SIX

Adeline Brand at the Bay of Bliss

16

Arthur and I had never been taught to fear. From our first days of training in the Pup Yards of the Severed Hand, we were taught to kill, to focus our wyrd, to use our arms, our power and our wits to defeat any foe. But never to fear them. What was there to fear for a duellist of the Severed Hand? The Eastron were superior men, the Sea Wolves were superior Eastron, and the Brand twins were superior Sea Wolves. Tomas Red Fang and his spirit-masters could speak for hours about the threats of the void, but *I'd* never seen anything to fear. As long as my mind and my blade remained sharp, the world would do well to fear *me*. But I'd never truly seen the world. I'd seen the great hold of the Sea Wolves, I'd seen Moon Rock, and I'd seen the void around both. I'd seen the Inner Sea, the Outer Sea, and the decks of a dozen ships. But I'd never seen the world. Young Green Eyes was right – the Kingdom of the Four Claws was little more than a handful of holds and the sea in between. I was a few days' travel from the Severed Hand, and a million miles from the world I knew.

Jaxon and I had been restrained, and beaten into unconsciousness. I think I'd hurt several of the hybrids before my eyes closed, but it didn't change the outcome. When I awoke, I was being dragged through cold, brackish water, with irregular stone blocks overhead. A passageway of some kind, with the salty water and pungent smell of fish all around me. The hybrids hissed and babbled, their voices coming to my ears as a series of pops and sucking sounds, containing no meaning. I was struck unconscious several more times, and awoke each time with cloudier vision and a more painful headache. The hybrids appeared incapable of punching me hard enough to send me to a longer sleep. Or maybe they enjoyed beating me. Certainly their frog-like murmurings rose in pitch as I was struck. Perhaps it was laughter.

When the passageway ended, and I regained enough wits to maintain a facade of torpor, we entered a huge square stone edifice, and were thrown onto a wet floor, riddled with mould and seaweed. The Wisp was next to me, his body quivering and his eyes staring. Two dozen hybrids came with us and spread out into the dark chamber, their grotesque heads held low, as if in reverence. Ahead, we were greeted by the maniacally smiling face of a Pure One. He was no hybrid, but appeared to be a normal man of the Mirralite. He wore sickly-green robes and stood before a rippling pool of water, dug into the centre of the chamber. Elsewhere, standing silently before open doorways, were more Pure Ones, in the same robes and with the same smiles.

"The Devils of the Sea," said the Pure One, noting that both of us were conscious. "Mighty beings brought low... and brought to me." His smile widened into a grin, showing black teeth. "Do you know where you are?"

I was pulled upright by slimy hands, and shoved into a seated position, with my arms bound behind my back.

"Answer me!" cackled the Pure One, in mockery of our customs.

I looked at Jaxon, and saw that he would not be answering. I feared that his sensitive mind was overwhelmed. We knew what was in the void. We'd both seen the chaos spirits kill Arthur, and the Wisp was unusually attuned to terrors beyond the glass. If anyone was going to speak for us, it would be me. I'd seen my brother be torn apart, but I wouldn't let myself dwell on it when other lives were at stake. He'd never forgive me if I gave in to despair.

"We are far from home," I replied, unable to conjure any bravado.

"You are in the Lodge of Dagon, girl. You will hear the sea and you will taste madness. But you will be mother to mighty beings. In time, your offspring will join their cousins and rule this world. You are strong and will survive many couplings and many births."

A little vomit appeared in my mouth, and I spat it onto the damp floor. Out of habit, I looked around, assessing the enemies arrayed against us. More than I could fight, even if I had Jaxon to help me and we both had blades and free hands. There were no Sunken Men, just armed hybrids and robed Mirralite. Then I realized I was distracting myself from the thought of being raped by abominations from the sea. "Fuck you," I spat, letting anger eclipse fear. "I am a duellist of the Severed Hand and I may not be free, but I believe I have strength enough to choose death over violation."

I began to focus my wyrd, pooling it in my hands and channelling every ounce of my strength. I intended to send it to my head in one concentrated burst and end my own life in a surge of power that would kill me, Jaxon, and perhaps the mad Mirralite. I didn't know if it was possible, or if I was strong enough, but it occurred to me and I tried it, all in one moment.

"No," said the mad Pure One, waving his hand in a slow circle, and elongating the word. I felt the wyrd drain from my limbs, and my strength wane to nothing. "You cannot choose death. You can choose only violation."

"How can you do this?" I uttered, finding myself too weak to remain sitting. I fell on my side and a spray of water hit my face. I looked at Jaxon and tried to convey fear, but he didn't see me. His eyes were focused in mid-air, and sweat was pouring down his face. "You are just a Pure One."

"I am the Nether One, varn of the Dreaming God... and I hear the sea," he replied. "As you will in time. If your ears are not consumed by your own screams." He cackled again, his mouth wide and his eyes crazed. "Take the female to the pens. Take the male to the Temple. Let the First Fang rage until all Nibonay shakes."

I remained conscious, but was as weak as a child. Jaxon and I were separated and my limp body was carried over the shoulder of a bulbous hybrid, through stinking passageways, past cells of screaming Pure Ones, to a dank chamber. Water sloshed across the floor, and vile images were carved into the walls. Three cages of dull, black steel lay in the stagnant water, with hunched occupants in two of the cages. Both were obviously women, though only the middle one showed signs of movement.

"Rest in cage, Sea Wolf," grunted the hybrid. "Will need strength." Again, the throaty, gargled laughter.

The left-hand cage was opened and I was flung inside, my face immersed in a foot of water. My strength slowly returned and I was able to sit upright, but I could feel no wyrd within my limbs. The mad Pure One had somehow robbed me of my power. Or perhaps it was this place, or the madness all around me. It didn't matter. I could stand if needed, and I could still fight like a rabid wolf, but I had no advantage of wyrd. And my eyes were newly opened to fear. It was as if the glass around me had broken when I saw Arthur be dragged to his death, and I now looked upon a new world of terror and madness. I wanted to see an avenue of escape, rescue Jaxon, and flee this place. But I wasn't even looking. My senses were rebelling against me, letting me feel only fear, and see only hopelessness.

"You're just in time for fish," said a sing-song voice from the adjacent cage.

I didn't look up. "I don't like fish," I muttered.

I heard the other captive shift position, as if she was looking at me, but my eyes were staring at the tepid water in which I sat. I didn't care who she was or what she looked like.

"Just a saying," said the woman. "My ma used to say it before dinner. *Just in time for fish* she'd say ... then plonk a bowl of vegetable soup in front of us. Not that these froggy-folk serve vegetable soup *or* fish. Nope, it's gruel and hard bread I'm afraid."

"Until we die," I grunted, through a scratchy throat and a dry mouth.

I heard a few grumbles and disapproving snorts, but the other captive didn't reply. Perhaps she'd sensed that I wanted to be left alone. Or perhaps I was wallowing in my fear. I shook my head and sat up, wiping greasy water from my face. Between our cages was a few feet of water, and through the wide bars I saw a young Eastron woman. I guessed we were about the same age, though her dirty face and matted hair made it difficult to tell. Her pale blue eyes were wide and she stared at me without blinking.

"You're a Kneeling Wolf," I said, coughing to relieve the scratch in my throat.

"To you I kneel, noble Sea Wolf," she replied. "Yes, I cough a lot too. Cough, cough, cough. It's probably the food."

I rubbed my eyes and turned in the cage to face her. I struggled to focus on anything beyond her, but I was at least able to discern that there were two exits from the watery chamber.

"It'll be along in a minute," said the Kneeling Wolf. "Gruel and hard bread. *I* think it's awful, but it'll be nice to have a second opinion. Do you know what my old ma would say about now?"

I frowned at her. "Just in time for fish?" I offered.

"That's right," she excitedly replied. "Just in time for fish."

I shook my head again. A part of me thought I was hallucinating, and the Kneeling Wolf was merely my spiritual punishment for getting Arthur killed. Another part of me didn't care and just wanted to sleep, in the desperate hope that all this was a fever dream. But it wasn't a dream, and I wasn't hallucinating.

"What's your name?" I asked. "I'm Adeline Brand."

She smiled warmly, seemingly amazed that I was real enough to have a name. "Pleased to meet you, Adeline, I'm Harriet, Harriet Mud."

"How long have you been here, Harriet?"

She drummed her muddy fingertips against the bars. "Not long. But long enough. I suppose I'm luckier than some. Yes, luckier than some."

I took a few deep breaths. Strangely, having a vulnerable young woman to talk to was not the worst thing under my current circumstances. She was weak and had likely seen things that would always be behind her eyes. Things that would no doubt also fill *my* future.

"Harriet, I'm not going to let you fall any further if I can help it. I can't get you out of here, but I can talk to you. And you can talk to me. And we will have each other. For as long as we have anything." I stretched out my hand, and found that the cells were close enough for two prisoners to touch. "Take my hand, Harriet, and tell me how you came to be at the Bay of Bliss."

She looked like a timid puppy, all eyebrows and chin, as she reached a slender arm through the bars of her cage and took my hand. "They'll be here soon with hard bread and gruel. You must be hungry."

"Harriet," I prompted, "why are you here?"

"Well," she bleated, "it wasn't just me. There were five of us. I think Tasha and Lucas escaped. They're strong swimmers, I know they made it. Hector was cut open by a frog-man, and me and Zorah were brought here." She released my hand and gestured over her shoulder to the other cage. "I think we've been here two weeks or more."

I looked at the third cage and saw no movement. The figure within was curled up in the still water at the base of the cage, wrapped in layers of muddy cloth. "They kept you for mating?" I asked, revolted at my own question.

She laughed, with tears streaming down her dirty face. "Not me. They don't want me. Not for *that* anyway." She placed a hand on her shoulder and pushed her cloak aside, revealing an arm riddled with sores and flaking skin. "I've had it since I was a girl. We call it the withering. It's just on my arm and my foot, but the Pure One said it made me unclean. I'm lucky. Luckier than some."

"And Zorah?" I asked, reaching out again through the bars.

This time, Harriet didn't hold my hand. She just averted her eyes and looked at the rippling water. "Zorah has been taken from her cage six times. When they brought her back... the first time, she just screamed. After that... she wouldn't talk. The Pure One kept saying that the seed wouldn't take."

I tensed my arms and gripped the bars. My breathing came heavy, growled from the pits of an empty stomach. I thought that being helpless was worse than being beaten. I doubted my own strength, and I thought a thousand thoughts of what was to come. I felt a tear fall on my cheek and I realized I was silently crying.

"Why did five Kneeling Wolves come to the Bay of Bliss?" I repeated, this time in a whisper.

"Same reason as you, I suppose," she replied. "The Friend sent us here to find out if the Sunken Men had returned. I just hope Lucas and Tasha get back with the answer. Or sent a spirit."

The Friend was Isaiah Leaf, the elder of Four Claw's Folly, and the inheritor of Mathew Lone Claw, who'd arrived with the Always King. He was pledged to the First Fang, and usually derided as a good-natured little brother or some such. Though the wise amongst us knew that the Kneeling Wolves were more worthy than most Eastron.

"You should have come to the Severed Hand," I said. "We could have used your counsel."

"If we had, you'd have done exactly what you've done. But you wouldn't have me to talk to."

From the right-hand exit, a huge shadow was cast across all three cages. I wiped my eyes and turned to glare at the hybrid who entered. It was heavily deformed, and bulged at the belly and neck. Its globular eyes were green and white, and it blinked at us, before loping across the chamber with a large wooden bucket in its slimy hands.

"Just in time for fish," said Harriet Mud, still looking at me.

I said nothing as the hybrid approached. I thought about the range of my arms through bars and I thought about grabbing the bucket. But neither would release me from my cage, so I just watched.

"Eat!" grunted the creature, grabbing two bowls and filling them with thin gruel from the bucket. He didn't get close enough for me to reach him, nor did he place the bucket within range. He just dumped two bowls of gruel on pillars, raised above the shallow water, and placed a hunk of hard bread in each bowl. Then he grunted and left, giving me no opportunity to do anything but watch.

Harriet swept up the bowl and hungrily gulped down the gruel. She tore off chunks of bread and dunked them in the liquid, eating as quickly as she could. I took the bowl and sniffed. There was a fishy odour and the earthy notes of root vegetables. I put the bowl back and ate the hard bread. It was dry and bereft of flavour, but was at least food.

"We weren't put here straight away," said Harriet between slurped mouthfuls of gruel. "They didn't have any Eastron, so they just put us in their breeding pens with the Mirralite – men *and* women."

"How many?" I asked. "How many breeders?"

She shrugged. "More than twenty, less than a hundred. Half the women were pregnant, and spared further ordeal until they birthed. Half the men were barely sane. I don't know what they do to breed with the men, but it took its toll. Some of them wanted to please their dreaming god, but most just screamed."

"Mated to a Sunken Man. A fate no warm-blooded creature should have forced upon them."

"Oh, no," exclaimed Harriet. "They were mated to the frog-men, the inbreeds. The ... other creatures, they're the ones that took Zorah."

Another voice joined our hushed conversation. From the left-hand exit, a robed Pure One exited the shadows. "And they will take you also, Sea Wolf. Your belly is far riper than this one's." He waved a sinewy arm at Zorah's cage. "The seed will surely take."

I moved suddenly, crouching in his direction and grabbing the bars that stopped me reaching him. He gasped, startled by my sudden movement. Whatever else these Pure Ones were, they still felt fear, however fleetingly. The man recovered quickly, but kept his glaring eyes pointed at me.

"They have never coupled with a Sea Wolf," he said, licking his lips. "It will be a glorious step in dispelling the past, before we consume your people entirely."

"What past?" I queried, tightening my fists around the bars of my cage. "Your dreaming god and his creatures are barely a myth at the Severed Hand."

He held his hands together in front of his face, as if praying. "But the Dreaming God knows *you*, whether or not you know him. The Devils of the Sea attacked his city. An army of ants believed themselves strong enough to attack a mountain. But even ants must be taught their place."

"He would do well to fear us," I replied.

"No!" he shouted. "To feel fear for an instant does not mean you understand it. It has always been a closed book to your people, whose pages need to be pried open. But for your insult, you will be the first to fall. He remembers you. Of all the ants upon this rock, he remembers *you* and your boats. You attacked his resting place with a hundred thousand insects. He remembers everything."

A thousand insults, curses and challenges rushed through my head. Then a thousand reasons why each was pointless. I wanted to scream and shake the bars, but I pushed my rage into the pit of my stomach and said nothing.

"Are you taking her again?" whimpered Harriet, still slurping from her bowl.

"Indeed," replied the Pure One. "We have a young, virile male for her this time. The seed will take if we have to nail it to her belly."

I gritted my teeth and saw my knuckles turn white against the bars, but I remained helpless as the Mirralite sloshed across the chamber towards Zorah's cage. Two large hybrids followed him, wearing cloaks that were little more than sacks to cover their bellies, and wielding their strange pincer spears. Harriet, holding her bowl to her lips, followed their movements, her eyes wide and eager, as if waiting for something.

The Pure One opened the cage with a heavy iron key and directed the hybrids to remove Zorah, who was still motionless. They grabbed her with flabby arms, though grunted and showed irritation that she wasn't moving.

"Ha, fuck you," cackled Harriet. "She's dead! She died two hours ago. You can't hurt her anymore. You'll never hurt her again." She dropped her bowl and clapped excitedly. "We're not fishermen you know, we're Kneeling Wolves of Four Claw's Folly, and we will fuck you any way we can. If we have to die, we'll die!" Her cackling rose in volume, becoming high-pitched and manic.

As I watched her revel in the most macabre of victories, I thought that the Pure One intended to kill her. His eyes showed rage, as if he felt he'd been humiliated. It would pass, but in that instant I knew he was about to order her death.

As any good big sister should, I quickly decided to protect her. "Mirralite!" I shouted. "Answer me."

He wrung his fists like a petulant child, looking between me and Harriet. Perhaps deciding which of us he hated more. The Sea Wolf? Whose people had attacked his god's city in the Battle of the Depths. Or the Kneeling Wolf? Who had been a compliant puppy an instant before.

"You won't answer because you are a coward," I snapped, keeping his focus on me. "You fear me because I am a Sea Wolf. My people didn't run, they fought. They didn't cower before your Sunken Men, they attacked. We lost the Battle of the Depths, but we never surrendered."

"Silence!" screeched the Pure One.

"Or what?" I roared. "You'll have me fucked to death by Sunken Men? You're gonna do that anyway. What do you have to threaten me with?"

He vibrated with incandescent rage, clenching and unclenching his fists as he stared at me. "Remove the Sea Wolf," he ordered. "We will teach her humility."

Suddenly, a spark of defiance returned. I'd made him angry and he was going to try and punish me. I couldn't identify my next move, but getting out of the cage would hugely improve my options. I kept cursing him, keeping his anger bubbling on the surface of his dusty face.

My cage was opened, and flabby hands grabbed my arms. The bulbous hybrids were stronger than me, and my petty attempts at resistance did nothing, but at least I was out of the cage. They flung me into the water, at the feet of the Pure One, and I spluttered as the brackish liquid filled my mouth and rushed up my nose.

"Stand her up," said the Mirralite.

The two hybrids pulled me to my feet. I struggled to focus and keep my rage in check. Defiance would get me so far, then it would get me killed, and I tried to remember that a duellist with no wyrd was just a warrior. But wyrd or no, I still had my mind, and my mind was focused on the man before me and the two exits either side of him. "Do as you will," I grunted. "You will not break me."

"I won't need to," he replied. "You will be broken by the passage of time. Not by any individual moment or particular torture, but by the accumulation of hours, days, weeks and years."

I tried to wrestle free, but the blubbery hybrids gave me no room to move. I looked across at Harriet, who was no longer laughing, and tried to smile at her, but the expression got lost before it reached my eyes. I may have been out of my cage, but I had no avenue of escape. I hung my head.

"Just kill me," I grunted from a scratchy throat. "You've already killed my brother, and sent my closest friend mad. I'll never…"

"Enough!" he interrupted. "Your stubborn belief that you still have power is making me weary. And, from what I understand, it was not us that killed your brother. If you'd not been so arrogant as step to the shadow, your brother would be alive now…slowly being consumed, along with your closest friend. *You* killed your brother, not us." He didn't smile or gloat, he just stated the facts and let me crumble back to the watery floor. "Now, you will be beaten for your insolence. After which, you will be placed back in your cell."

The pincers were nasty weapons, but they used them only to bludgeon me into unconsciousness. If they'd wanted, they could have snipped off my limbs with little effort, but perhaps they didn't need to. Perhaps I was truly no threat to them.

I took the Sea Wolf rite when I was twenty years old. I could have been tied to a post in the Bay of Grief a year earlier, but I waited for Arthur. Everyone thought we were twins, so it made sense to drown together, and those who knew we weren't never questioned my decision. By the time we were taking the rite, I'd already fought three duels on his behalf, killing people who I'd overheard insulting him. The first man targeted his intelligence, the second his skill beyond the glass. The third, whose name I'd called just before my seventeenth birthday, was a seasoned duellist. Unluckily for him, he was also a loud-mouthed prick who'd questioned

Arthur's short temper, and dared to suggest that this was a failing of all Brands. I made a show of killing him, and never had to defend my brother again. Years later, Arthur told me he'd fought *five* duels in defence of me, and had made a show of killing the last. We agreed that we should just have mutilated the first one and saved ourselves some unnecessary fights.

When we were strapped to wooden posts, freezing, half-naked and trying not to drown, we laughed and joked, teasing each other for our shortcomings. I thought too much, he didn't think enough. I disliked our family name, he was far too proud of it. But we were both made of the strongest steel, and would be the greatest Sea Wolves the Kingdom of the Four Claws had ever known.

Since that day we'd rarely been apart for long. We'd fought together a thousand times or more. He was my anger, I was his calm. We thought we were one person, divided down the middle by the Old Bitch of the Sea. My mother always said I spent my first year of life waiting for something. She said I wasn't really there until Arthur was born. What kind of woman would I be now he was gone? Was I now half a person?

17

Time meant nothing in the Lodge of Dagon. We couldn't see outside, and it was always dark in the stone chamber. The only regularity was provided by the twice-daily offerings of hard bread and gruel. My beating had not been severe, and I'd weathered far worse. I did wonder how many times a woman – even Adeline Brand – could be beaten unconscious before brain damage ensued, but for now I felt little more than an insistent headache. Harriet gave me a daily update on how red and bruised my face was, and by the tenth bowl of gruel I was apparently back to normal. Though normal was certainly relative. We'd seen multiple different hybrids, and the Nether One had returned twice more. Once to assess how damaged I was, and once to remove Zorah's body, but no schedule had been forthcoming as to when my violation would begin.

"I think there's actually a bit of flavour in this," said Harriet, sniffing her bowl of gruel. "Or maybe my taste buds have died."

I prodded in my own bowl, and saw only black grains of some kind, and limp carrots, floating in the thin, brown liquid. It was all I'd eaten for days, and I felt tired and thin as a result. The bread helped, but was not enough for me to maintain any kind of strength. Nor was the cage big enough for me to exercise. And I was struggling to conjure reasons to stay sharp and combat-ready. I'd been released once, and had been just as helpless. Perhaps I should give up and accept that I would die in the Lodge of Dagon.

"You're grumpy today," said Harriet in her sing-song voice. "You look down at the water when you're grumpy. You look up at the exits when you're not. Come on, what's our plan of escape for today?"

"No plan," I replied. "Not today."

"Oh, come on, grumpy-guts, I liked yesterday's plan. We both throw our gruel in the face of the frog-man and hope he stumbles close enough for you to grab him and get the key."

"They're too strong," I replied. "And we don't know what's in the next chamber."

"I told you," giggled Harriet. "The Mirralite pens are to the left, and they took Zorah to the right."

"Hardly a detailed map of the Lodge. They brought me from the right also." A thought occurred to me. "If the pens are to the left, why do we not hear them scream?"

"There's a long corridor. You can hear water sloshing above. I think this place is quite big. It must stretch under the Bay of Bliss." She sighed, looking up at the bare stone ceiling. "I miss the sky."

"And I miss my brother," I whispered, too quiet for her to hear.

"We can't leave without your friend anyway. What was his name? Wispy?"

I smiled. "The Wisp. Jaxon Ice. Last I saw him, his mind was struggling to deal with the chaos spirits in the void. I fear that he'll only have fallen further without me. They took him to the Temple, wherever that is. I don't even know if he's alive."

"All the more reason not to stop our daily escape planning," announced Harriet, her unblinking eyes showing complete trust. "How about our spoons? They're wood, we could fashion weapons."

I shook my head, trying to smile. "The wood's rotten. Everything here is rotten. Except these cages." I shook the bars and found them as unyielding as when I'd first been imprisoned. "No, we only get out of these cages if someone lets us out."

"So, it's trickery then," stated Harriet, excitedly. "My speciality. You know, I've convinced these froggy-folk that I'm quite mad. So, what do we do? Gain their trust?"

I rubbed my eyes. The headache was moving to the front of my head and becoming sharp. Harriet's voice was soft and did nothing to worsen my pain, but I struggled to take an active part in the conversation, preferring instead to look down at the murky water.

"Adeline Brand, are you ignoring me?"

"No," I grunted. "Sorry... I... my head hurts. I think I should try and sleep. It's a few hours 'til food."

"Oh, you poor thing," said Harriet. "Don't you worry, we'll have another plan tomorrow."

I turned away from her, nestling into the corner of the cage as best I could. I had bruises and scabs from sleeping against the metal, and could only just stretch out my legs, half-submerging them in water. My leather trousers and boots had held up well, though they were not water-proof. My armour had been taken and the thick, black shirt I was left with was constantly getting wet, half-drying, then getting wet again. As least it wasn't cold.

In the days I'd been here, I'd determined that the water level changed with the tides. This meant that the water in which we sat, though brackish and foul-smelling, was at least replaced daily by a fresh tide from the Bay of Bliss. And something in the Lodge of Dagon heated the water and kept the chamber at a constant temperature.

As my eyes closed, I heard sloshing, and groggily looked up. Two hybrids appeared from the left exit, followed by the Nether One. They walked quickly, parting the water in small waves.

"You, Sea Wolf!" stated the Pure One. "Your wounds have healed and it is now your time. May it be the first of many couplings."

My stomach did a somersault and I suddenly felt light-headed. They had the patience to wait, and the confidence that I was completely helpless. Two hybrids was more than enough to keep me compliant *before* confinement had robbed me of my edge. Was there truly anything I could do? A lifetime of lessons and experience came crashing down into a single moment of helplessness. For the first time in my life, I was just a scared woman.

I could barely hear Harriet trying to talk to me as I was roughly dragged from the cage. I put up no resistance, being little more than a dead weight in their greasy, bulbous arms. The Kneeling Wolf shrieked and shook the bars of her cage, but I couldn't hear her words. I just let them take me from the cage and drag me through the tepid water. The sound of Harriet's indistinct shrieks slowly disappeared, to be replaced with the thunderous rumble of my heart and the slosh of water.

I was taken out of the chamber and along a corridor with a high ceiling. My legs were dragging in the water, with the hybrids carrying all of my weight. It may have been the way I was brought in, or may have been towards the breeding pens. I couldn't be sure. My wits had left me, and the thought of escape was now as distant as Young Green Eyes or the Severed Hand.

The corridor widened, then shrank, then turned left. I heard screaming and I saw caged Mirralite, slumped against iron bars and rotten stone walls. Mostly cowering men, with a few heavily pregnant women. Water was everywhere. Some flowed in through narrow slits in the wall, to drain away down rusted gratings. Some collected in pits and holes on the floor, to be displaced by moving feet or the constant flow. Mould and moss covered everything, with sickly-white crabs scuttling through the water.

Beyond the cages, the passageway widened again. Here there were sunken pools in the stone floor, leading into deep water beneath the Lodge of Dagon, and high above, I saw the sky for the first time in days. There were two openings in the square ceiling, poking above the Bay of Bliss. It was dusk, and I could just see the last blue tinges disappear from the sky.

Before I could sigh, or say an internal goodbye to the light, I was thrown forwards, to land in a foot of water, before a half-rotten wooden door. I had not seen any other doors within the structure, and I could tell it held some special significant. There were three huge bolts, securing it closed, and its hinges were hidden behind iron facings.

The Nether One unbolted the door and turned to me. "Rejoice, Sea Wolf, for you will be the first casualty of the war. The last war your people will ever know."

My hands shook and a sharp pain enveloped my head. As the door opened outwards, I saw a circular chamber. It was full of water, and a shard of darkening light came from an irregular hole in the ceiling. I didn't resist as the two hybrids held my arms and legs, and flung me through the door. My head caught the door frame, causing dull pain, and I landed heavily in salty water. As I spluttered and tried to sit up, the door was slammed shut and I was alone with a bleeding forehead.

My feet didn't touch the bottom, and I had to scramble to the sides of the chamber. There was a wide hole in the middle of the floor, leading down into black water, and I moved away from it, hugging the walls. I reached the door and banged on the wood, but heard the last bolt clank into place, and sloshing footsteps as my captors moved away from the door.

I began to panic. Blood crept into my eyes and I felt my forehead. It was a deep cut, but all I cared about was clearing my vision. The hole in the ceiling was too high to reach, the door was too solid to break, and I was too weak and too scared to fight. As the water started to churn, all I could do was cower against the door.

"To the First Fang I pledge my arm, my head and my heart," I muttered, reciting the duellist's oath. "To my hold I pledge my loyalty and my strength. To the Eastron from across the sea I claim brotherhood. From the Bright Lands I am come. In the Dark Lands will I prosper."

Before I'd finished speaking, a bright red crest had poked through the water. A vile smell, metallic and salty, filled the chamber, as the Sunken Man rose from a frothy swell. It stayed waist-deep in the water, showing its swollen belly but keeping its muscled legs hidden. I was face-to-face with it, barely a few feet away, and its greasy black eyes were fixed on me. It was more fish than frog, but had the qualities of both; an elongated, slippery head, with a gummy, thick-lipped mouth. It was four times my size and naked, with a layer of slimy grease dripping from its barely humanoid body.

"Once more for the Severed Hand," I whispered, too terrified to think.

It reached a sinewy arm towards me and I saw malevolent lust on its wide face. I was to be violated. I was to be used as a breeder. I thought about how to kill myself. How to bash my head against the door, or dive underwater until I drowned, but my limbs wouldn't move. My mind was no longer connected to anything. It just floated in the air, waiting for the Sunken Man and some kind of pained oblivion.

I couldn't move, but I could still see, and something caught my eye above the approaching creature. From the hole in the ceiling, I saw a face. It was a moon-faced Eastron with closely cut black hair, his head and upper body clearly visible in the dusk sky. He looked down at me and frowned, then at the Sunken Man and screwed up his face in revulsion. He'd made no sound and the creature had not seen him, nor did it see the female face that appeared on the opposite side of the hole. They were both Kneeling Wolves and had a silent conversation above me, gesturing to the creature and mouthing words of alarm.

I tried not to gasp or shout, even as the Sunken Man stretched its frog-like limbs and pulled its whole body out of the water to loom over me. It took its time, licking a pink tongue across slimy green lips, and stroking at the air between us with suckered hands.

The male Kneeling Wolf disappeared beyond the edge of the hole, and the female waved at me, mouthing *hello*. She then tried to convey something with her waving arms. She seemed to be saying *get ready to move*, but I couldn't be sure. Then the male reappeared with a wooden bucket. He smiled and waved me away from the Sunken Man, then held his nose, as if he shared my discomfort at the smell. My limbs began to respond when the female produced a small flaming torch, and the male poured lantern oil all over the creature and the surface of the water. The Sunken Man puckered his flabby lips and looked up, as the thick black liquid flowed down his face.

"You wanna fuck?" challenged the man.

"Fuck this, you greasy bastard," growled the woman, throwing the torch at the Sunken Man's head.

I flung myself backwards, grabbing the wall, as the creature was enveloped in muddy fire. It started at the head and formed a crackling mantle down to the water, where it flared and pulsed on the surface. The Sunken Man flailed its arms and gargled, but the volume of its voice didn't rise above a murmur. Its mouth was wide, but it seemed unable to generate much sound. Its tongue rolled out, to flail at the air as bubbles of melted flesh appeared and popped across its torso.

Both Kneeling Wolves produced short bows and buried red-fletched arrows in the creature's head. They reloaded quickly and put two arrows each in and around its eyes. The Sunken Man groped at the wall, vomiting sickly-green fluid into the chamber. It slumped downwards, trying to immerse itself in water and put out the flames, but the lantern oil wouldn't be extinguished so easily, and the creature was already half-dead.

"Out the way, love," said the male Kneeling Wolf, hopping down into the chamber. He was short, wore ragged brown fabric and held two heavy knives, with the short bow slung at his belt. The woman followed, trailing a heavy rope-ladder behind her.

"Come on, it takes a while for them to die," said the woman, taking me by the arm and leading me to the far side of the chamber. "The fire does for them, but always aim for the eyes. That greasy skin is tougher than it looks."

The creature was now bent over against the wall, trying to put the fire out with its hands, but its movement were jerky and pained. The male Kneeling Wolf stood between us and the creature, holding his knives ready. When the Sunken Man finally slumped to the waterline, the man rushed in and stabbed it repeatedly in the head. Even with its body burned to a muddy black, the knives didn't penetrate far. It took several heavy thrusts to breach its skin, after which the man stabbed its head to a pulpy mess.

"Tasha Strong," said the woman. "This is Lucas Vane. We're very pleased to see you."

"I prefer Lucas Frog Killer," said the man. "You okay, love? Must've given you a fright."

I didn't reply, and couldn't tear my eyes from the dead Sunken Man, smouldering as a mound of charred flesh in the corner of the chamber.

"It's okay," said the woman, "escape is more important than talking. Come on, let's get out of this nasty water."

The man placed a boot on the bottom of the rope-ladder and steadied it. The woman eased me to my feet, but I fell back into the water, unable to make my legs work properly. "Can't stand," I muttered.

The man came to our aid, and they took an arm each, half-carrying me to the rope-ladder. "You're in shock, love," said Lucas Vane. "Happened to me too. First time I saw one up close."

"He pissed himself," offered Tasha Strong, placing my quivering hands on a smooth wooden rung of the ladder.

"I did, I pissed myself," agreed Lucas. "Up we go now."

I clenched my hands around the ladder and hung on.

"That's it, one step at a time," said Tasha, easing my left foot into place.

I panted heavily and blinked water and blood from my eyes, but I managed to coax enough life into my limbs to climb upwards. Lucas held the rope-ladder and Tasha shoved me towards the light as best she could. They muttered to each other beneath me, assessing how long until the dead Sunken Man would be discovered. They didn't seem in a huge hurry, but once I was secure on the ladder, Tasha hopped over to the door and pressed her ear against it.

I found some strength and pulled myself to the hole in the ceiling. It was vaguely circular, with irregular edges, but was solid enough for me to grab the stone and heft myself out of the Lodge of Dagon. The darkening sky had just enough blue for me orient myself, and I looked down at a huge complex of interconnected stone structures, poking above the water. Everything was angular and square, like a spider's web of seaweed-covered stone, floating just above the surface. The water broke over the structures, flowing down into the Lodge through holes and grating, and depositing frothy waves of seaweed and crabs over everything. I sat at a high point, within sight of the cliffs, but I couldn't see the Mirralite village or any signs of life.

"Down to the boat, love," said Lucas Vane, appearing out of the hole.

"What boat?" I asked, through a dry mouth.

He showed me a rope that fell down the side of the structure upon which we sat. At its other end was a small rowing boat, wedged in a corner between stone walls. "*That* boat. Unless you wanna swim."

"Don't tease her," said Tasha, joining us in the open and pulling the ladder up after her.

Not really knowing why, I lashed out and grabbed Lucas by the throat. My strength was slowly returning, and I easily restrained him. "Don't fucking tease me," I growled.

He grabbed my arm, but was far weaker than me. He tried to speak, but I'd cut off his air.

"Easy," said Tasha, putting a gentle hand on my shoulder. "You can kill him once we've got out of here."

I released him and suddenly felt terrible. The man had rescued me, and I'd threatened him. "I'm so sorry. I… don't feel myself."

He rubbed his neck and gave me a thin smile. "S'okay," he grunted, before sliding down the rope towards their small boat. "To you I kneel, noble Sea Wolf."

Tasha unfastened the rope and we followed him down. The boat lolled in the water as Lucas extended the oars and pushed us away from the Lodge. He manoeuvred us towards the cliffs, past the huge structure's jutting stone arms.

"Rest," said Tasha, helping me recline against barrels of lamp oil at the back of the boat. "You can tell us your name when you wake up. And if you've seen Zorah or Harriet."

I hadn't intended to fall asleep. Once I'd left the Lodge and regained some of my wits, I had hundreds of questions, but my body had other ideas. The gentle slosh of water eased me into an exhausted sleep, while the quiet babbling of the Kneeling Wolves provided a lullaby. I awoke briefly as we reached a gravel beach, surrounded by vertical cliffs, and the boat was pulled out of the water. I was aware that Tasha covered me with a blanket, but I was quickly back to sleep.

Then my eyes saw bright blue sky and I sat up. My head hurt, but my hands were steady and I could feel my wyrd, as if a vile fog had been lifted. I blinked, coughed, felt the throbbing cut on my forehead, and tensed my muscles. I still had some strength, and more would return.

From the gravel beach I couldn't see the Lodge of Dagon or the Mirralite village, though the high cliffs looked familiar.

"Morning, noble Sea Wolf," said Tasha, approaching with a earthenware plate. "Nice bit of smoked bacon, nestled lovingly between two thick slabs of soft bread. Is there truly any better way to start the day?" She passed me the plate and the smell of cooked bacon made me sigh with involuntary pleasure.

"Thank you," I said, taking the food and shovelling it down in big mouthfuls.

The Kneeling Wolf perched on the edge of the boat and waited for me to finish eating. She then took the plate and smiled. "Do you have a name?"

I nodded. "Adeline Brand, duellist of the Severed Hand."

"Me and Lucas didn't know there were Sea Wolves here. We were looking for our mates when we heard a door slam. Your door. It looked like... well, I assume the frog had unpleasant intentions."

I wiped bacon grease from my chin and stood up. My legs were stiff and my back delivered a lance of sharp pain, but physically I felt far better than I had in days.

"They wanted to mate a Sunken Man with an Eastron, to produce offspring. They tried with one of your friends. I'm sorry, but Zorah is dead."

Lucas Vane appeared from the mouth of a shallow cave and stared at me. "Dead? Are you sure?"

"I'm sure she's sure," said Tasha, her face dropping into a frown of grief. "And Harriet Mud? Did you see her?"

"I did. She helped keep me sane. Alive when last I saw her. She has the withering and they won't use her as a breeder. I don't know what they intend for her. A friend of mine is in there also. He was taken to the Temple."

Lucas began to cry and the two Kneeling Wolves met in an emotional embrace. They wore rough-spun woollen clothing and no armour, though their boots were heavy, steel-shod leather, rising to an ornate buckle at the shin.

"We can't leave without them," I said, a note of calm authority returning to my voice. "You must have some idea about this place by now. The ways in and out. And why have they not pursued us?"

They finished their embrace and Tasha motioned for me to follow them. "More comfortable in the cave. We have a fire and some supplies."

They led me within, where two bedrolls were arranged around a small campfire. Sacks of food, blades and arrows showed that the group had travelled light, and the placement of their camp showed that they were far from careless.

"They won't follow," said Lucas. "But it's safer out of the open." He sat down and offered me a bottle of liquor. "And there's rum in here, love."

"Why don't they follow?" I asked, swigging from the offered bottle.

Lucas smiled, seemingly impressed at the size of my swig. "No idea, but they don't have a sense of urgency. It's like we're no threat to them."

"It's true," offered Tasha, placing more bacon in a small frying pan. "We must have seen half a dozen of the frogs, and given them every reason to chase us. But we get a distance away and it's like they get bored. When we return, they act as if it's the first time they've seen us."

Tasha made three more bacon sandwiches and we ate between shared gulps of rum. For the first time, I assessed the two Kneeling Wolf duellists who'd saved my life. Lucas was late twenties, around my age. Tasha was a little older, with sharp worry lines at her temples. Neither was much over five feet tall, though they both had a solid build and an elegant way of moving. Whatever training they'd received at Four Claw's Folly, it gave them the appearance of seasoned duellists.

"I told Harriet that you should have come to the Severed Hand first. If you knew what was here we could have come with a larger force."

Lucas was wolfing down his sandwich and spoke through a full mouth. "We didn't know."

"We suspected," added Tasha. "Isaiah Leaf just wanted confirmation. It took a long time, following clues, before we even knew to come to the Bay of Bliss. Sorry we didn't come to you first."

I showed a genuine smile for the first time since before Arthur died. "You saved my life. There is little you will ever need to apologize for."

"To you we kneel," said Tasha, returning my smile.

I took a few deep breaths and tried to relax, pushing thoughts of Jaxon and my brother to the back of my mind. If I was to survive, if I was to rescue my friend and avenge my brother, I would need a mind at rest. If I was to return to the Severed Hand and warn the First Fang, I would need to stay alive. I rubbed my eyes and struggled to keep my thoughts in order. "There's a lot to consider," I grumbled. Looking out of the cave, I blinked at the bright blue sky. "Where are we? Exactly?"

"Down the eastern coast," replied Tasha. "Once you leave that freaky village, the rest of the Pure Ones just fight or run away. They're as scared of the Sunken Village as we are."

"I am not afraid," I growled, more out of habit than truth. "So they don't range far from The Place Where We Hear The Sea? That gives us an advantage."

Lucas finished his sandwich and wiped his chin. "Sorry to be blunt, sweetheart, but what do you expect us to do with that advantage?"

"Don't be rude, Frog Killer," chided Tasha. "I think what he means is that we were rather lucky to find *you*. We were searching for Zorah and Harriet and heard a door slam. Unless you know the layout of that place..."

I looked down at the fire and tried to remember the Lodge of Dagon. I was carried in along a square tunnel; I met the Nether One in a large square chamber; I was imprisoned in a smaller square chamber; and I was carried out through more square chambers. I didn't know anything useful about the place. "Do you know where the Temple is?" I asked, trying to focus on Jaxon.

"Aye, we do," replied Lucas, sharing a worried glance with Tasha. "It's the big box-thing in the bay. The one you can see from the village."

"Why would they take him there?" I asked. "And is there a way in?"

Tasha, eating her sandwich with more delicacy than Lucas or me, politely coughed. "There are narrow slits in the roof," she said. "You can see in when they light the torches inside."

"And?" I prompted.

"Varn," said Lucas, draining the bottle of rum. "Lots of them. Doing unnatural things. You ever seen a chaos spirit?"

I shuddered, remembering the whirling miasma of flesh and teeth that had consumed Arthur. "I have. The void there is full of them. More than I could count."

"They're summoning them," he replied. "Have been for years it looks like. Thousands upon thousands of them."

"We only glimpsed," said Tasha. "Just a glimpse through the glass, on top of the square building in the bay. And we didn't glimpse again. It was when we first got here, a few weeks ago, before Hector died and we lost Harriet and Zorah."

"Show me," I said, looking around for a suitable blade amongst their supplies. "If that's where they took Jaxon, that's where we'll go."

The Kneeling Wolves looked at each other as if they *would* follow me, but only reluctantly. They both showed awareness, and I wasn't so arrogant as to ignore their counsel, but I couldn't conceive of retreat without first trying to rescue Jaxon Ice.

"Before you advise me against it," I said, gently, "remember that you yourselves were trying to rescue your friends when you happened upon me."

Lucas smoothed crumbs from his lap and looked at me. He didn't share his companion's smile and appeared unsure how to speak to me. "Sorry, love," he muttered. "I suppose we've been over this a hundred times since we came here. Tasha and me have talked and talked and talked about what to do. Then we find you ... and suddenly we have more things to talk about. Just when we'd decided to stop talking. We heard your door slam as we said our goodbyes. We were gonna have a final look for our friends, then head for Four Claw's Folly and warn the Friend of what we'd seen."

Tasha smiled warmly, the worry lines at her temples curving into an expression of trust. "We'll show you what you want to see, noble Sea Wolf, but you did ask another question – why would they take him there?"

"And the answer?" I prompted.

"In the Temple we saw them feeding Pure Ones to the chaos spirits," said Lucas. "It was enough knowledge to take back home. As we left, we got careless and they ambushed us on the shore."

"How is that possible?" I exclaimed. "Pure Ones can't step beyond the glass."

They exchanged another look. "You'll need to see for yourself," said Tasha.

18

Returning to the Bay of Bliss was strange, and I kept thinking about the Mirralite family we'd passed in the field. From the beach, the Kneeling Wolves and I had climbed a steep game trail and crested the encircling cliffs. I kept scanning the farmsteads that littered the horizon, searching for the one by the woods, where the woman and her children had fled, but they all looked the same. Each had a pointed roof of dusty gold thatch, and adjacent to each was a field. Some had wheat, others cattle, and some were overgrown or ploughed, waiting for a crop.

The Sunken Village was as removed from them as it was from us. And yet they'd lived within a spit of it for centuries and done nothing but cower. The line of seashells in the woods was the barrier between two worlds and it appeared that neither side wanted it breached. Though my resolve and my wyrd had returned, I still felt like an ignorant outsider, blundering, sword-in-hand, through a field of toxic flowers, as if my strength and my blade would be enough to fight off the toxins.

I smiled, thinking how bewildered Arthur would be. And how he'd chide me for thinking too much. I couldn't yet bring myself to wonder what Jaxon would say. I still hoped that I'd hear him say it himself.

"This way," said Tasha, turning from the cliffs to a steep downward path.

In the distance, partly hidden by the woods, was the Sunken Village. We were at a high point, overlooking much of the bay, with fishing villages and small jetties filling my field of vision. There was a clear gap, filled with dense forest, between our destination and the rest of the Mirralite settlements. The path we took plunged downwards through the woods and ended at a rocky cove, close to the Sunken Village. It was a covert approach and much better than the route I had originally taken.

"It's not yet midday," said Lucas Vane, who still insisted on being called Frog Killer. "The seas will be calm. Bit of a swim, but the frogs don't like the light, so we should just get wet… not dead."

All three of us looked up to the sky. The village was still shrouded in crackling clouds, but the surrounding vista was blue and clear, pushing light into the edges of the storm.

"Perhaps just a quick look," said Tasha. "Not wise to linger."

We reached the rocky cove and the gently flowing sea. It was low tide and the blocky structure in the bay was less than a hundred yards from us, with the village itself further around the cliff. There was no-one abroad and everything was still.

"We will look," I replied. "And I will hope to see my friend."

"Of course," she said. "If he's there we'll die to save him, but if he's not… we both have people to warn, and we should not linger. See what you need to see and take the wise course."

I nodded and began the walk from the rocky beach to the blocky structure. The sea was low and babbling against my feet, but it didn't get deep until near the square building in the bay. I kept looking around the headland, towards the Sunken Village, but it was too far to make out fine detail. Luckily, this made us all but invisible to any watching hybrids.

As I waded into the deeper water, with Lucas and Tasha behind me, I let wyrd flow into my limbs. It was warm and comforting, like a blanket that the world could not penetrate. Having been denied my power by the strange craft of the Nether One, I found a new appreciation for abilities I'd always taken for granted. Though I worried for other duellists who might one day fight an enemy who could rob them of wyrd.

"Tone it down, love," said Lucas, motioning to my glowing fists. "There's nothing to punch here."

"Just checking it was still there," I grunted in response, letting my power lessen. "One of the Pure Ones … took it away. It was alarming."

"That explains it," he said with a smile.

"Explains what?"

"How a frog managed to put a Sea Wolf in a cage." His smile broadened into a knowing grin and I struggled to discern how much humour was in his remark, though I was sure I was not being insulted.

I returned the smile. "Kind of you to say. Though being a Sea Wolf seems to mean something different now. Something smaller."

"Ah, that's horse-shit," he chuckled. "I don't kneel to just anyone, Mistress Brand. Now, let's hush the chatter and see what we've gotta see."

He strode ahead of me, until we were both chest-deep in brackish water. Tasha was already swimming, and the three of us glided towards the temple with barely a ripple flowing from our movement. Further east, where the cliffs rose, was the Lodge of Dagon. It lanced out into the bay, as angular stone tendrils, poking above the low tide and covered in dark green seaweed. Dozens of tunnels and chambers, looking as old as the cliffs and as fetid as the Sunken Village.

I started to swim, and we reached the base of the square building in a few minutes of gentle exertion. Lucas unfurled a rope and Tasha grabbed hold of the irregular brickwork. I'd taken a cutlass from their supplies and used it to secure myself against the stone.

"Up you go, Frog Killer," said Tasha, smiling at her companion.

Lucas, keeping hold of his knotted rope, began to climb the sheer stone wall. He was light-footed and quick, using the smallest holes to anchor himself to the wall. I'd seen dextrous men before, none more so than the Wisp, but Lucas Vane was highly skilled, able to ascend a vertical surface in moments. He disappeared over the lip, trailing the rope behind him.

"What's he fixing it to?" I asked Tasha, having seen no features atop the square structure.

"He's not," she replied. "He's going to hold it."

I raised an eyebrow. "No disrespect to your friend, but I doubt he could hold my weight."

Her smile was warm and friendly. "Lucas has a habit of gaining and losing names. He gets bored, he says. Frog Killer is just the latest to take his fancy. A few years back we called him the Anchor. He can plant his feet on the ground and use wyrd to stay put. He can't do it for long, but I've seen him stop charging horses for a few moments, just by holding his ground."

"Impressive," I replied, pulling on the rope. There was no give. It was as if the rope was tied securely at the other end. At the Severed Hand such things would be seen of a waste of wyrd. If I'd been amongst other Sea Wolves, I might even have sneered at Lucas' ability.

"Hurry now," said Tasha.

I pulled myself out of the water and wedged my feet against the stone wall. A film of seaweed travelled upwards with me, and I ascended the Temple quickly, climbing hand-over-hand. The rope didn't slacken one inch, and when I crested the lip I saw Lucas standing braced, but with no visible exertion on his brow.

"Hello," he said, happily, his moon face beaming. "If you don't mind hurrying, this isn't as easy as it looks." There was a subtle blue glow around his feet, and he appeared as one with the stone, as if he was borrowing its strength and solidity.

The roof of the Temple was a huge square, made of irregular stone blocks, and commanding a view of the Sunken Village and half the bay. There were narrow slots in the roof, from which noxious fumes snaked their way into the gloomy air. I couldn't tell if they were large enough for me to climb down, but at the very least it would be a squeeze.

"Give us a hand, love," said Lucas, suddenly showing exertion. "Tasha's an ant compared to you, but I can't keep myself rooted here long enough for both of you."

I grabbed the rope and shared the burden, as Tasha pulled herself up to join us. I took more weight than Lucas and found it strange how weak he now appeared.

"Right, let's get this done," said Tasha, once she was safely atop the structure. "If we lie flat, we can creep to the holes. Just keep it slow and quiet. The frogs don't come out at low tide, so we just have to hope the hybrids don't see us."

"And avoid those fumes," offered Lucas. "I don't know what the varn burn in there, but it smells fucking rancid."

"Language, Frog Killer," said Tasha, as the three of us dropped to our stomachs and crawled towards the nearest hole.

The gap in the roof was a slot, more than six feet in length, but barely two feet in width. The Kneeling Wolves would be able to squeeze through, but I would certainly struggle.

I tried to keep thoughts of rescuing Jaxon from my mind, and focus on the here and now, on what I had to see in the Temple of Dagon. Avoiding the fumes was my first challenge. They seemed to cling to the stone, crawling out of the hole and dissipating into the air only reluctantly. Once I'd wafted enough clear space, I peered over the lip. Tasha and Lucas were either side of me, and our three heads craned downwards.

I blinked as my eyes adjusted to the gloomy light. It was day-time, but the dense cloud armoured the Temple against the sun, and the fires within were brighter than the open sky. Across a huge square room were five burning pits, arranged in a circle. In the centre was a vile altar of bone and flotsam, with seaweed woven into the angles, and some kind of thick liquid dripping from its extremities. Around the altar were prostrate Mirralite, donned in mouldy robes of green and black. They were motionless and silent, with the only sound coming from the dozens of chained figures around all four walls of the chamber. They didn't scream, as I would have expected, and their voices were barely more than a murmur, as they awaited whatever fate the Dreaming God had for them.

"Those chained are food," said Tasha. She winced, her eyes becoming narrowed. "I don't think I'll benefit from seeing this again." She edged backwards and sat up on the stone roof. "You may have to wait a while for the good stuff, Mistress Brand."

I spared her a concerned glance, but my eyes were quickly back within the Temple. I scanned the chained figures, looking for the Wisp, but they were too distant, and the light too erratic. The only men I could see clearly were the varn. I didn't relish a long wait, skulking atop the structure, but perhaps with enough time my eyes would adjust and I'd be able to see my friend.

"Quite comfy really," said Lucas, after a few minutes of waiting.

I didn't reply or turn to face him, and the minutes stretched as we looked down into the Temple of Dagon. With the dense cloud above, I found it hard to judge the passing of time, but ten minutes turned into an hour, then two hours, and the tinges of blue at the edge of clouds dropped and lengthened, until the whole sky had a muddy dusk glow, from horizon to horizon.

"I think this is what Tasha meant by lingering. Thought we weren't going to do that," observed Lucas.

"You can leave whenever you wish, but I'm staying. Until I've seen whatever it is that you two saw. And maybe, just maybe, I'll also see my friend."

Tasha had moved away from the narrow hole, and was sitting on the edge of the roof, facing the nearby village.

She'd said nothing since she left us. Lucas made a comment every few minutes, but rarely had they elicited a reply. I'd scarcely taken my eyes from the altar, the varn, and the chained figures, though they had done little but shift position in the time I'd been watching.

"It'll be dark in less than an hour, love," said Lucas. "Not wise to stay this close when the frogs come out."

I was about to repeat that he could leave, but my voice was stalled as the varn slowly began to move. Their movements were uniform, with an accompanying chant. I'd seen Pure One rituals before, though this was different. There were ten of them, chanting in a guttural tongue and reaching for the altar.

"Eyes up, Mistress Brand," said Lucas. "Something's happening."

The chanting continued, and four more robed Mirralite appeared from arched doorways around the perimeter of the chamber. Those in chains – whom Tasha had described as food – shied away from the approaching men, burying their frail faces in their spindly limbs. My eyes were more accustomed to the light and I could now see faces. Though Jaxon was not amongst the chained, he *was* now present in the chamber, carried in by two of the new additions. The Wisp was unconscious and naked, with heavy, woollen wrappings around his left leg and part of his chest.

"A Sea Wolf!" exclaimed Lucas. "Your friend?"

Upon hearing this, Tasha rushed back to join us, lying flat on the roof of the Temple. "He's still alive?"

"Hard to tell," replied Lucas. "What do you think, Adeline?"

I watched them set Jaxon on the floor in front of the altar and remove the woollen wrappings. I took a deep breath and peered downwards, unsure of what I was seeing. There were patches of red under the wool, and scratch marks across his torso and face. He'd been flayed. Half his leg and a large patch on his chest were without skin. From the scratches, I guessed that it had been removed a piece at a time, in small strips.

My breathing became heavy and I gritted my teeth. "Ten of them, no more," I grunted. "Pure Ones with no wyrd. Lucas, your rope."

They both looked at me, but said nothing. My eyes were then drawn back to the Temple of Dagon, where a single varn had started speaking in actual language.

"The Devils of the Sea will be the first to fall," intoned the Mirralite. "Let their skin and flesh be nourishment to the chaos spawn of the Dreaming God."

The guttural chanting reached a crescendo and the air around the altar began to churn. I felt a crackle at my fingertips, as the glass around the varn shuddered. It was a spirit summoning, but not like any I had witnessed. The glass split in places, and thick mist entered from the void. It swirled into small tornadoes, before forming into dozens of chaos spirits, twisting masses of flesh and teeth. They had killed my brother and now, through the twisted craft of the varn, were somehow able to enter the realm of form.

"No tales tell of such a thing," said Tasha. "No spirit-master I've met has *ever* told of spirits entering the realms of form. Possessions and talismans, but that is all."

A piece of my brain wanted to grab the rope and descend into battle, but I was wise enough to wait, though it felt wrong to leave my friend in such a state. As I wrestled with what to do, a varn revealed a slim-bladed knife and took it to Jaxon's chest. He sliced laterally, taking a sliver of skin and making the Wisp writhe in pain. He was still alive and still needed restraining, as they moved in to hold him down. The small piece of his skin was thrown into the air, where the chaos spirits fought over it, like dogs fighting over a bone, until the largest won. Something about Jaxon's flesh, perhaps Sea Wolf flesh, was desirable to the spirits, and their gnashing mouths hungrily slobbered over the piece of skin.

My unblinking eyes were locked onto the scene below – the cackling varn, the mumbling captives, the swirling spirits, and the restrained body of the Wisp. I half-heartedly gestured to Lucas's rope, but my movements showed no conviction.

I felt a hand on my shoulder. "Patience," said Tasha, gently. "Varn we can kill, but those spirits…"

"Watching this hurts my eyes," I replied. "And makes my fists clench." I could feel an involuntary ripple of wyrd, stretching into my limbs and making me angry. I didn't know how much patience I had left.

Lucas put a hand on my other shoulder, and I imagined the two Kneeling Wolves were preparing to restrain me, thinking I would rush into an impossible fight.

"Easy," said Lucas. "The spirits will be gone in a tick. The varn, a tick after that. Then we wait a tick, and move."

"Three ticks of the clock," I muttered. "But three days when looking at my friend in pain."

The spirits finished their frenzied feeding dance, and the varn stopped chanting a moment later. Slowly, and with curious reverence, the Pure Ones swept their arms together and dismissed the spirits, sending them back through the slice in the glass, to join the multitudes, dancing in the void.

There was an audible snap as they departed, making the hair rise at the back of my neck.

"Patience," repeated Tasha, her hand still on my shoulder. "No-one profits by us dying."

The varn formed a line and slowly left the Temple, keeping their heads bowed as they glided past the altar. The other Pure Ones, re-bandaging Jaxon's body, were the last hostiles left in the chamber. The chained captives were once again silent and I involuntarily edged forwards, picturing how difficult it would be to squeeze through the hole. There were just four men left. No hybrids or varn. It was the best chance I'd have.

Three more agonizing beats of my heart, and Lucas stood. "Now!" he stated, looping his rope between two of the holes and quickly tying it off.

I stood with him and made sure my cutlass was secured in my belt. "Let me go first," I growled. "I'll deal with the remaining Pure Ones."

"I can't pull you both up," said Lucas.

"I'll tie Jaxon to the rope. Pull him up, then throw it back for me." I gave them no chance to question my order, and began squeezing through the narrow slot. If I'd been wearing armour I would never have fit. As it was, only my breasts got in the way, eliciting a girlish chuckle from Tasha. I wrapped my legs around the rope and climbed down, hand-over-hand, gritting my teeth to stay silent as I got closer and closer to my motionless friend and his captors. Heat from the fires sent a warm tingle up my body, and the noxious vapour made my nostrils sting. I was suspended in mid-air, but above the globes of light and unseen by those below. The rope ended above the heads of the Pure Ones, with Jaxon's broken body almost within reach.

I took a deep breath and let go of the rope, letting a surge of wyrd fill my limbs as I hit the stone floor, cutlass in hand. They had no chance to react. Four pairs of wild, bloodshot eyes stared at me. Then three pairs, as I severed the first man's head. The second man died as they were beginning to recover their wits, with the remaining two backing away and producing small, pincer-like knives. After days of feeling helpless, it was exhilarating to be strong again, to be able to kill my enemies again. These were nothing special. They were neither varn nor hybrids and were no match for a duellist of the Severed Hand. Perhaps Arthur's death had not made me half a person after all.

They attacked at the same time, aiming at my chest, and I easily spun away from both pincers, slicing one man across the back of the neck as I moved. He clutched the wound, with small gouts of blood pushing between his fingers, and his eyes rolled back in his head a moment later. The last man turned to run, but I roughly grabbed him by the throat and slammed him into the stone floor of the Temple. Holding him with one hand, I placed my blade on the floor and punched him in the face. Then again. And again. I punched him in the face with as much strength as I could, breaking his nose, crushing his jaw and cracking his skull. I punched him until little of his head was left.

"Adeline!" snapped Tasha from above. "Quick, quick, quick."

I pulled back my fist and balked at the slick of blood and bone, sticking to my hand. I shook it off on the floor and retrieved my cutlass. Keeping low, with an eye on the only visible entrance, I rushed to Jaxon's side.

"It's Addie," I murmured, smoothing his bloodied hair out of his battered face. He was frail, with discoloured skin. As I gathered him up, his arms fell limply at his sides. "Jaxon. You're not dead yet." There was still warmth in his chest and a faint heartbeat.

The rope was loosened and the end struck the stone floor. I grabbed it and pulled out some slack, wrapping it around Jaxon's chest and securing it under his arms.

Then a sound reached my ears and I looked to the entrance. Another Pure One stood, silhouetted in front of a fire, staring at me. "Invader!" he growled. "Devil of the Sea." The man flailed his arms in the air, and ran away, disappearing around a corner and shouting a warning to his fellows.

"Lucas, pull him up," I shouted, forgetting stealth.

The chained Pure Ones had been silent, but now a rhythmic murmur travelled amongst them, quickly rising to a screech. Elsewhere in the structure, beyond the cavernous Temple, running feet and shouting filled the tunnels.

The Wisp was pulled from the stone floor as Lucas used his prodigious wyrd to good effect. I brandished my cutlass and stood ready to repel whoever came to investigate. I was alone in the centre of a huge room, framed by blazing fires, with the abominable altar to my left. I'd not taken in the surroundings as I descended, nor had I looked around as I killed the Mirralite and rescued Jaxon. Now, with nothing to do but wait, while Jaxon was pulled out of the Temple, I found my vulnerability return. Killing the Pure Ones had been easy, but I tried not to forget that I'd already met my match. It was rare to have done so and still be whole, but the

Sunken Men and their hybrids had not yet broken Adeline Brand.

Above me, Tasha and Lucas babbled about Jaxon, assessing his wounds as he was pulled closer to freedom. I'd barely looked at his body once I heard his heart beat. He was alive and that was all I needed to know in that moment. Flaying was torturous, but not fatal. It was his mind that caused me worry, and that could not be assessed with a look.

"Nearly there," said Tasha, her words echoing around the huge chamber.

I counted the beats of the clock as I waited for the Wisp to be pulled to freedom and the rope returned for me. The shouting was close, the running feet were closer, and a dozen armed Mirralite appeared in the entrance tunnel, their outlines coming to me as swirls of smoke beyond the fire-pits. There were varn amongst them, and several grotesque hybrids, their bulk blocking the tunnel. All I could do was hold my ground and wait.

"We've got him," said Tasha. "Just hold on another tick."

I could hear Lucas grunting and doubted he'd be able to pull me up. I would have to climb, and I'd have to do it quickly. The rope made a whistling sound as it was thrown back through the hole, and struck the stone just as the first three hybrids entered the Temple. I stowed my cutlass and leapt upwards, grabbing two fistfuls of rope and pulling my legs out of reach. Slimy hands groped at my feet and ankles, leaving a sticky residue on my boots as I pulled them free. More hybrids ran into the Temple, with screeching varn behind them. A dozen or more, cursing me and every Sea Wolf, but helpless to stop me as I quickly climbed upwards.

I tried not to look down, keeping my eyes on Tasha's smiling face and Lucas's waving arms. The rope was tugged and jerked from below, but they couldn't pull it loose. Nor could they shake my grip. Stretching, hand-over-hand, with my legs coiled, I began to smile. I was angry and tired, but also exhilarated. I was a duellist of the Severed Hand and I had been tested. I had watched my brother die and been deposited, helpless, in a cage. But I was not broken. Jaxon was wounded, physically and mentally, and we would return to the First Fang with grave news. But we *would* return.

"Give us your hand, love," said Lucas, reaching down to help me up the last few feet. With his help, I clambered out of the Temple, with the varn's screeching following me into the night air.

"Quick, quick, quick," said Tasha. "We need to get out of sight."

Lucas pulled up the rope and bid a mischievous farewell to those below, winking and giving a cheeky wave.

"Will they follow?" I asked, getting my breath back and moving to where they'd placed Jaxon.

"They will," answered Lucas. "But if we get far enough away they'll get bored. They don't see us as a threat."

I nodded, making sure that the Wisp was properly bandaged. He was naked, except for the two patches where he'd been flayed, and his thin body was deeply cut from a whip or thin blade. He was never the largest Sea Wolf, but now he appeared almost frail. His eyes were closed and he showed no awareness that I was there.

Lucas coiled his rope and ran to the edge of the huge square roof. The sea had risen, and the distant beach had all but disappeared. I'd not looked up as we watched for activity within the Temple, and I was suddenly aware that it was getting dark.

"Quick, quick, quick," repeated Tasha, helping me lift Jaxon so as not to aggravate his wounds. "He'll mend."

"His body," I replied. "His mind... I don't know."

The three of us, with the Wisp held as gently as possible, made our way to the edge. The roar of the sea masked any sound from within, but the varn would certainly be mounting a pursuit. I jumped down into the water, finding it higher up the building than before and much colder. Lucas wrapped his rope around Jaxon, securing it under his arms, and held the rope taut as he lowered my unconscious friend down into my waiting arms. Tasha splashed into the water next to me, her still-smiling face a reassuring addition to our escape.

"Come on, Frog Killer," she said, waving up to her companion. "Time to go."

I held Jaxon across his chest and pushed away from the Temple, swimming on my back and keeping him above the water. Tasha swam with me, but Lucas paused, atop the huge, square roof.

"I can't leave," he said, with a shake of his head. "Harriet is still alive. If there's a fool's chance, I have to stay. At least for a little while longer."

"Unwise," I replied, treading water beneath him. "They'll be coming for us."

He chuckled. "The frogs don't scare me. They only care if you're two feet in front of them. And those half-breeds are slow. *And* I don't plan to get into any fights."

Tasha swam back to the base of the stone wall. "Lucas," she murmured. "Come with us. Harriet would understand."

"It's okay," he replied, cheerfully. "I can stay hidden on my own. You should go with Adeline to the Severed Hand. Tell the First Fang what we saw here. But I can't leave. Not yet."

I frowned, steadying myself against the stone structure. "You're an honourable Eastron, Lucas Vane," I said. "And we'll meet you *and* Harriet back at the Severed Hand."

"We'll be just in time for fish," he replied with a grin, before darting out of sight across the roof of the Temple.

19

They didn't chase us. I didn't know whether Lucas led them away, or they got bored, but we nursed Jaxon back to the coast with no further drama. Once out of the water, Tasha led us to the narrow mountain path and, with Jaxon over my shoulder, we turned our backs on the Bay of Bliss and the Lodge of Dagon. It took another hour to reach the Kneeling Wolves' cave and find suitable clothing for the Wisp, by which time night had fully descended. Tasha warmed up some leftover stew and I carefully placed Jaxon next to the low fire.

"Swordfish, carrots, potatoes and a hint of spice," said Tasha, inhaling deeply from her small cauldron. "Harriet's favourite. Nothing better to bring your friend back to the waking world."

"I hate fish," I replied. "Never developed the taste."

She looked at me as if I'd claimed to be a sea-serpent or something equally bizarre. "Never met a Sea Wolf who didn't like fish. What do you eat?"

I shrugged. "Vegetables mostly. We do have chickens and sheep too. It's not all fish."

"What about him?" she asked. "Does he like fish?"

"When he's awake he does," I replied, looking with concern at my torpid friend. He was still breathing and his heartbeat was regular, but he'd not opened his eyes or moved so much as an inch. I cradled him in my lap, smoothing back his hair. There was dried blood around his face and neck, too stubborn to be removed by our watery escape, but outside of the flayed skin, he'd suffered no significant injuries.

"Jaxon," I whispered. "You're safe. We're going home now."

"And you've made some new friends," offered Tasha. "A duellist and a cook."

I stared at her, quizzically. "You're not a duellist?"

She grinned. "Gosh, no. Kneeling Wolves never leave the Folly without a good cook. Lucas, Hector and Zorah were the duellists."

"And Harriet?"

Tasha dropped her eyes in sadness for a moment before answering. "She was a Sister. That's what we call them – Brothers and Sisters – people we take along because they make us all smile. Never underestimate the value of a hot meal and a good grin. Lucas used to joke that he was the most important and she was the second. I always thought he was right." She stirred the pot and screwed up her face, as if she wanted to ask me something, but was nervous of the answer. "So, er ... where are we bound?"

I took a bowl of the stew, noting that Tasha had just given me vegetables and separated the fish. "Dark Wing knew of this place," I replied. "I have a suspicion he knew more than he said. And if it cost the life of my brother and the mind of my friend ... well, we'll go there on our way to the Severed Hand."

Tasha took her own bowl and dampened down the fire with a handful of gravel. "He's a duellist, isn't he? A mad old man from what we heard. Not really worth killing. And

Jaxon Ice should be our main concern. Makes me sad seeing a Sea Wolf like that."

"Didn't say I was going to kill him," I replied, looking down at the Wisp. "Perhaps I just want someone to blame for my stupidity. If I think it was someone else's fault, I'm less likely to tie myself in knots worrying that it might be mine."

"Now, Mistress Brand," said Tasha, adopting the demeanour of a kindly school teacher, "I don't want to hear that kind of talk from you. Okay?"

I dropped my head and screwed up my eyes. All at once, I felt the weight of what had happened since we left the Severed Hand. I sniffed, then a tear appeared at the edge of my eye. I wiped it away, but more came, until I could no longer hide my grief and my face ran with tears. "Arthur," I whimpered. "I'm sorry. I'm so sorry."

Tasha positioned herself at my side, with her arms wrapped tenderly around my shoulders. I didn't have the energy left to push her away, so I just clung to Jaxon and cried.

We rowed around the coast until we were clear of the Mirralite Reservation, then trudged inshore across a mudbank. Jaxon had remained motionless in the back of the boat, and was equally motionless when carried in my arms. By the end of the first day we were inland, skirting the edge of the Plains of Tranquillity. By the end of the second, with weary limbs, we camped within sight of Dark Wing's skeletal forest. It was a short western diversion, and a welcome break from carrying the Wisp. My back, my neck and my shoulders throbbed, as muscles were called upon for the first time in over a week.

Tasha was a pleasant travelling companion, and was able to find glee in the smallest of things. A cloudy morning, a red-feathered hawk, a soft-boiled egg. The Kneeling Wolf handled every menial task without question – setting our camp, lighting our fire, cooking our food and somehow managing to keep my spirits from falling any further. I even heard her whispering lullabies to Jaxon when she thought I was asleep. His eyes even twitched once or twice as she sang of tall trees and gentle animals, in a low, soothing voice.

"There's more colour in his face each day," said Tasha, as we rose from our bedrolls. "Fish soup, I do declare, it could soothe the dead back to the light." She glanced at me across the remnants of our small nightly fire, appearing to realize that I could take offence at her words, if I were to be overly sensitive about Arthur's death.

"Don't worry," I replied. "I can tell well-meaning words from harsh ones."

Tasha had also taken charge of Jaxon's care as we camped. She fed him soup and massaged his throat, encouraging him to swallow, until his body began to respond and take in a little sustenance. When and if his mind reordered itself, at least he wouldn't be too malnourished.

"Are we going into that nasty forest today?" she asked, stoking the fire and cutting some thin slices from her diminishing block of salted bacon. "I think there are wild dogs in there. Heard them barking last night."

"Dark Wing is fond of them," I replied. "Apparently they liked me. Can't think why."

"I'm also fond of dogs," said Tasha, scrunching up her nose in imitation. "I'm sure they'll like me too. I have a terrier back at the Folly, called Scraps. Mischievous little thing."

As if Dark Wing's hounds could hear us, a chain of barking sounded from the edge of the dead forest. We were over a ridge, and had camped out of sight, but now I felt as if we were being watched. My time at the Bay of Bliss appeared to have chiselled the edges from my previously stoic shell, and I had to shake my head to push irrational fear from my mind.

"Watch Jaxon," I said, before striding over the ridge and standing defiant before the skeletal trees. "Anyone watching?" I shouted. "No spirits, gods or men, hold dominion over me."

"Er, Adeline," murmured Tasha. "Who are you shouting at?"

I stared at the empty treeline for a moment, before dropping my head and chuckling. "I suppose I'm shouting at myself."

Suddenly, the hairs rose at the back of my neck and my eyes were drawn to a figure approaching from the forest. He'd been unseen within the trees, but was now visible in the open ground. It was Dark Wing. Like a clothed ox he loped towards us, his massive frame and fur-covered shoulders identifying him even at a distance.

Tasha joined me over the ridge and shielded her eyes from the morning sun. "He's a big fellow. Is he friendly?"

"No, but he's not a threat," I replied, walking to meet the hulking wild-man. "Stay with Jaxon, I'll deal with the unfriendly man."

"Just try not to kill him," she replied, returning to Jaxon's motionless body.

Dark Wing was lumbering towards me, his straggly beard and mismatched cloth bouncing as he moved, but his dogs were nowhere to be seen. I could still hear them in the trees, perhaps waiting for their master's command, or perhaps unwilling to leave the forest.

"You return," he growled. "Does the sea rise?"

"Ever higher," I replied.

We came together on the flat ground between the ridge and the forest. The wild duellist was hesitant, not approaching too closely and keeping his posture hunched. He was still taller than me, but may have sensed that I was less likely to be cordial during our second encounter.

"I can feel your friend's mind, he needs aid," grunted Dark Wing.

"He does, but I need answers first. Tell me what you didn't tell us before we left... before my brother died."

His face wrinkled up and he scratched at his thick beard. "Your friend—"

"Yes, he needs help," I snapped. "Answer me first."

My choice of words was poor, and Dark Wing took a step back, imagining I was challenging him.

"Answer my question, not my blade," I stated, losing patience. "But I *will* kill you if I do not like your answer."

He frowned, his eyes moving to meet my glare. He wasn't afraid of me and I saw something of the old duellist spark back into life as I threatened him. Old and wild he might now be, but there was a time when he prowled Duellist's Yard on the Day of Challenge like the rest of us.

"I told you what I knew," he replied through gritted teeth. "I showed you the statue and I told you not to listen to the sea. If you chose to go there ... you are a Sea Wolf, take some fucking responsibility."

I seethed with anger and approached him. He didn't back away as I glared up into his dirty, bearded face, nor did he reach for a weapon or take a defensive stance. "You are a fat old man. Big, but slow. Let us establish a line of authority – I have it, you don't. Disagree with me and I will end your fascinating existence. I hope your dogs can fend for themselves."

Tasha coughed from behind us. "Adeline, perhaps your new friend can help the Wisp. Maybe. If you don't kill him."

Dark Wing's twitchy eyes shifted to the Kneeling Wolf behind me. "Is that your backup? A rat from the Folly?"

I rammed an open palm up into his throat and followed with a powerful kick to his shin. The huge wild-man tried to catch his breath, grabbing at his throat and wheezing, but when his leg gave way he crumbled to the grass in front of me. "That *rat* saved my life. Insulting her will get you hurt."

"Adeline!" snapped Tasha. "Do *not* start a fight on my account. I will kneel to you, but I will not be an excuse for you to hurt another Sea Wolf. Now, calm down and think about Jaxon."

Dark Wing lunged at me, wrapping his arms around my thighs and tackling me to the ground. I hit the grass hard, knocking the breath from my chest, but I managed to sprawl backwards and avoid a pin from the huge man. If I'd been at my best, the wild duellist would have received a kick to the face, before I choked him unconscious. But after my confinement in the Lodge of Dagon, I was barely able to avoid his paw-like hands and scramble to my feet.

"Oh dear," grumbled Tasha, just audible over my grunting and Dark Wing's growling. She ran towards us, over the ridge, flapping her hands in the air. "Stop it! Right now, stop it. You're both Sea Wolves." She stopped next to us and knelt, bowing her head and spreading her arms wide. "We have enough enemies. Adeline, you've seen them. Do they wear *his* face? Are they old duellists, living with their dogs in an old forest of dead trees? No! They are not."

Dark Wing was on all fours in front of me, his pale blue eyes showing neither aggression nor submission. He was cunning, though perhaps not wise enough to accept defeat. I backed away, allowing him to stand. "They're coming for the Severed Hand," I said. "They fear us above all Eastron. The Battle of the Depths seems to have left an impression."

"We lost," grunted Dark Wing.

"But we fought," I replied. "I don't think the Sunken Men like those who fight back. Perhaps they're not used to it."

Tasha clapped her hands together. "That's good, that's good. Talking. Talking is good."

"You don't speak here," snarled Dark Wing, shaking his hairy fist at the Kneeling Wolf, before glaring back up at me. "Yes, yes, the rat saved your life and I shouldn't insult her."

"That's right. Now, stand up!" I demanded. "And answer me this – can you help Jaxon?"

"I can," he replied, lumbering to his feet, like an overweight cow. "Bring him." He turned and jogged back across the open ground to his dead forest, his bulky shoulders bouncing and his feet making a heavy thud on the earth.

Tasha was smiling at me, and I found it irritating, as if she was congratulating me for not hurting the wild-man too badly. "Just leave it," I snapped, returning to Jaxon.

She didn't stop smiling. "I will leave anything you ask, noble Sea Wolf. Well done though." She chuckled to herself.

I picked Jaxon up, cradling him in my arms as I'd done since we left the Bay of Bliss. After time spent locked in a cage, carrying my friend back to Dark Wing's forest had done wonders for my muscles. My back, arms and legs were still sore, but at least I no longer felt weak.

"Does he have a cabin?" asked Tasha, fastening her rucksack and slinging it over a shoulder.

"He has a bone palace," I replied. "The man's been killing Mirralite for a long time."

Her eyes narrowed and her lips curved in uncertainty. "Bones? Don't his dogs eat them?"

"Apparently not. I'm not actually sure what they *do* eat. Unless he has a way of storing Pure One flesh."

"Urgh!" said Tasha, in revulsion. "He wouldn't feed men to his dogs. Would he?"

I shrugged and made my way after Dark Wing, with the Kneeling Wolf hurrying along behind me, mumbling something about feeling sick.

Dark Wing was a more skilled herbalist and healer than I expected. He unveiled a huge, wooden chest of vials and jars, each with some kind of herb or ointment. He knew what he was doing and applied a quickly assembled salve to Jaxon's forehead. I let him work, standing with Tasha at the entrance of his domed bone palace. The old duellist used wyrd, but only subtly, sending it in soothing waves across Jaxon's body. The flayed skin was covered in a brown paste of some kind, emitting a nasty smell and a noxious vapour, but Dark Wing concentrated on the Wisp's head, as if his mind required more healing than his body. After ten minutes of fast and skilful activity, the wild-man soaked a cloth in a bowl of clean water and pressed it against Jaxon's forehead.

"He'll mend," said the old duellist. "The mind of a Sea Wolf is not as strong as his body. Fighting, killing and shouting does little to strengthen the mind. But he'll mend."

The Wisp rolled over and huddled into a foetal position. His eyes remained closed, but his mouth opened and his scratchy throat emitted grunted sounds.

"The chanting," he muttered. "The varn... they fear us. The Dreaming God screams at them and they chant of the Devils of the Sea. The teeth and gums of chaos... they're meant to destroy us."

"Easy," I whispered, moving to his side. "There is time."

Dark Wing wrung out his cloth and returned it to Jaxon's forehead. The old duellist was a different man when focused on healing. His wild eyes were still and he'd made some effort to tie his hair.

"The teeth and gums," repeated Jaxon, his eyes opened – wide and staring. "Teeth like jagged glass and burning red gums. I couldn't count them, but I could feel them, scratching beyond the glass."

"Rest," I said, smiling in relief. "You're safe. We're safe."

"Arthur!" he grunted, tears appearing in his eyes. "He's gone."

My jaw tightened, but I didn't cry. I wouldn't allow myself to, not in front of Dark Wing. I'd already cried for my brother and more tears would neither bring him back nor make me feel any better. "We'll be back at the Severed

Hand soon," I murmured. "Tomas Red Fang will help you. Your mind was strong, it will be so again."

Jaxon rocked onto his back and reached for me. His hands, cold and clammy, grasped my face. "The Severed Hand," he repeated.

The Eastron found more than a kingdom when they invaded.

They found more than the Pure Ones.

They found spirits of nature and elements.

They found spirits of might and majesty.

They found the Lords and Ladies of the Quarter.

The Winterlords found the Dawn Claw.

The Dark Brethren found the Night Wing.

The Sea Wolves found the Old Bitch of the Sea.

And the Kneeling Wolves found the Kindly One.

From "An Eagle, an Owl, a Wolf and a Rat"
by Lennifer High Heart, Lore-Mistress of First Port

PART SEVEN

Duncan Greenfire on Nowhere

20

The island of Nowhere was disputed territory. Warriors had gathered here, intent to fight for it and hold it, like a recently discovered gold mine. The problem was, as I saw it, that one side didn't truly know of its value. The Sea Wolves thought they had come here to fight for their territory. They knew only one of their ships was missing. They didn't know about the doorway to a distant realm, nor of the need to flee through it. They didn't know of the pale man, or that he'd controlled the minds of Xavyer Ice and Inigo Night Walker. They didn't know that Marius Cyclone had conspired to annex the island. And, above all, they didn't know that the sea was rising, and that swords and strength would be meaningless against the breaking waves of the Sunken God. But *I* knew, and I too was a Sea Wolf. I'd been given a task by the Old Bitch of the Sea, and I was determined to honour her.

The ignorance of my people was paramount in my mind, far more prominent than my own obligations, as I looked at the four tall ships at anchor in the bay. Each had three masts, with stowed sails, tied to dark wood. I recognized the largest. It was called the *Blood Hammer* and was usually to be found at Laughing Rock. It flew a billowing flag, displaying a ravening wolf, and all the ships were filled to the railings with fully armoured warriors. They'd been there since morning, and made no effort to communicate with those on land. A party of Mirralite, led by Ten Cuts, had made themselves visible, standing in plain view on the beach, but so far the Sea Wolves had ignored them. They didn't know Vikon Blood was dead. If they had, they'd have swarmed ashore and killed every living thing on Nowhere. At least they'd have tried.

"You know you've stopped twitching," observed Loco Death Spell. "When we first met, the left side of your face looked like it was dancing. But since we got back from under the Maelstrom ... nothing."

I sat on the grass, upon a cliff to the east, reclining against a tree, with the clean-cut void legionnaire's straight sword resting on my shoulder. Any freedoms I'd been given, after the pale man restructured everyone's memories, had been swiftly taken away once we left Cold Point. They wanted to use me as a white flag of sorts, but didn't trust that I wouldn't run back to the Sea Wolves, screaming of foul treachery.

"Ignoring me, boy?" prompted Loco, tapping his blade against the bare skin of my neck.

"Will I have your sword against my throat when I talk to *them*?" I asked, nodding at the four warships.

"You will," he replied. "*And* four short bows aimed at your head."

I felt a gentle ache in my left leg, as if Twist was scoffing at Loco's implied threat. The pain spirit and I both knew that they would no longer kill me out of hand. I turned towards him, looking along the length of his sword. "I'm not a diplomat," I said. "If you want me to mediate with a blade against my throat, I'll probably fuck it up."

The young Dark Brethren never smiled, nor did he allow obvious emotion to intrude upon his face, but he relaxed his sword-arm. "*I* don't want anything," he replied. "I'm just a void legionnaire, but Lord Inigo wants whoever is aboard those ships dealt with peacefully... until he returns. You are the only Sea Wolf survivor of the *Dead Horse*. You also know that the sea rises, and have seen our only means of escape. I should think that makes you the *perfect* diplomat."

"As soon as they hear the Second Fang is dead, they'll attack," I replied.

"Don't tell them," he stated. "You need to mollify them, or every Sea Wolf who comes ashore will die. It *is* for their own good... in the short *and* long term. When Lord Inigo returns he will sit down with them, but we must achieve a parlay before that can happen. The Stranger always intended to include the Sea Wolves in his plan. Just not yet."

I'd not seen Inigo Night Walker since we left Cold Point. He, and the majority of the fifty void legionnaires, had not accompanied us to the coast. Only Loco and my four other guards were present. They stayed clear of the warriors of Ice, camped in the low ground beyond the bay. The Grim Wolf wasn't here, but he'd despatched a significant force to greet the Sea Wolves, apparently enough to defeat the crews of four warships.

I sighed. I wasn't afraid anymore, and saw wisdom in Loco's words, and Inigo's intentions, but I couldn't forget that they'd killed Vikon Blood. They'd killed Cold Man, Anthony Blitz, Lydia Hearth and the entire crew of the *Dead Horse*. I couldn't clearly remember the vision of the Sunken God, but I remembered the massacre of the crew with crystal clarity. The Old Bitch of the Sea wasn't the only one I had to honour.

Blade Smile emerged from the low ground, leading a squad of warriors. They lacked the upright uniformity of the Dark Brethren, appearing more like thugs than soldiers. The People of Ice resisted being called Sea Wolves, but they looked like them, covered in leather and steel, with heavy cutlasses and wide-bladed falchions. The only thing that united their appearance was the chip of blue ice on each chest, and the way they looked at me. Their fear of my wyrd was now tinged with anger, as if the presence of more Sea Wolves made them remember that they should hate me.

"I expected you an hour ago," said Loco, glaring coldly at the Grim Wolf's son.

"I had no plans to be here an hour ago," replied Blade Smile, grinning like a madman. "But I'm here now. I've decided your commander is probably right. Slaughtering more Sea Wolves will complicate things."

"*You've* decided?" snapped Loco. "Inigo Night Walker is Sentinel of the Dark Harbour and commander of the third void legion, his wisdom is matched only by that of Marius Cyclone. But *you've* decided he's probably right?"

The thin warrior of Ice didn't stop grinning. He enthusiastically nodded his head. "Yup, I've decided. But first we need to know who's coming ashore on those longboats."

Loco frowned, rushing to the edge of the cliff. The other Brethren went with him, and I was swept up in their movements.

"I've not been to the Severed Hand since I was a boy," said Blade Smile, calling after us. "I wouldn't know Lord Ulric or any of his dogs by sight, but I think the big guy at the front of the first boat is someone important. What do you think, Duncan?"

I shielded my eyes from the glare of the shimmering blue ocean and saw three huge longboats in the water. Oars stroked them slowly towards Ten Cuts and the Mirralite on the rocky beach below. The *big guy* was Lord Ulric Blood, First Fang of the Sea Wolves and elder of the Severed Hand. He was at least sixty years old, but still emanated an aura of indomitable power. Over his fur-clad shoulder was Jacob Hearth, captain of the *Black Wave*, and at the back of the boat was Taymund Grief. There were other faces I knew, duellists and sailors, some I could name, most I just recognized. The Brand twins weren't there, neither was the Wolf's Bastard, but Ingrid Raider and Vincent Heartfire were at the fore of the second boat. The face that grabbed my attention was Siggy Blackeye, Mistress of the *Dead Horse*. She'd escaped Nowhere and made her way back to the Severed Hand.

"Time to go," said Loco, pulling me away from the cliff's edge. "Your first diplomatic assignment will be mollifying Lord Ulric Blood. Auspicious indeed."

Since I'd arrived on Nowhere, I'd been surrounded by people who saw the Sea Wolves as villains, and few of their reasons could be genuinely challenged. The People of Ice had been oppressed and forgotten. The Dark Brethren had been demonized, whilst suffering under relentless piracy. Even the Pure Ones hated us, and their reasons were more profound than most. But still, it was the Dark Brethren and the People of Ice who'd conspired a way to save the Eastron.

Was the loss of a single ship of villains truly so significant when our very survival was at stake?

But *I* was a Sea Wolf, and I couldn't forget Lord Vikon or our totem. The pale man told me that I was too powerful for him to control. If that was true it meant I had free will. Perhaps the Sunken God *was* too powerful to fight, and our only chance of survival *was* fleeing into the void. But seeing the First Fang on the rocky beach reminded me whose side I should be on. As much as I admired his son and heir, Lord Ulric was like a god to me. He had as much right to decide upon our fate as Marius Cyclone or the pale man.

Loco and his men led me from the high cliffs, down a winding path, to approach the beach from the north. Behind us, Blade Smile commanded a mob of warriors, hidden from the beach by a grassy ridge, and above us, on the flanking cliff tops, were two wings of archers, ready to emerge and fill the Sea Wolves with arrows.

Ahead of us, sauntering from their longboats in loose formation, were a hundred warriors. The First Fang led the vanguard, with many more Sea Wolves watching from anchor. There was a significant mob of grubby-looking Kneeling Wolves with Lord Ulric, staying behind the Sea Wolves, but just as well-armed. The forces of the Severed Hand were dressed for war, and those in the front warily regarded the high cliff tops. They'd know how open to ambush they were, but they still approached Ten Cuts and the Mirralite, where a line of spears had been stuck into the ground, indicating a parlay. Everyone else was hidden from sight.

"There's no point in hiding," I told Loco. "They know the Brethren are here. They know you attacked the *Dead Horse*."

The point of his straight sword had remained in the small of my back as he'd pushed me down to the beach. The four legionnaires with short-bows were in a line behind him, their arrows nocked and ready. "And how would they know that?" he replied.

"Siggy Blackeye," I said. "She was Mistress of the *Dead Horse*, and she escaped." I glared at him. "It appears I wasn't the only Sea Wolf to survive."

The young Brethren took a moment to think, glancing out of cover to assess Lord Ulric and his warriors. He then looked inland, past Blade Smile and the massed warriors of Ice, as if waiting for his commander to give him an order. But Inigo Night Walker was not here, and Loco would have to make his own decisions.

"What you waiting for, pretty boy?" asked Blade Smile, coming to stand with us. "I got a lot of swords here, and they'll kill those Sea Wolf bastards if you wait too long." There was a collective nod from the closest People of Ice.

"I have orders," replied Loco. He clearly didn't like the Grim Wolf's son, but no hint of irritation showed on his face. "Duncan, walk." He nodded towards the beach and waved his men to follow.

I took a deep breath and made my way over the rise, to stand in clear view of the Sea Wolves. Five Dark Brethren walked with me, down loose sand and pebbles, to clatter across the rocky beach of Nowhere. Blade Smile commanded a small army, each of whom would gladly wet their blades on Sea Wolf blood, but they stayed hidden, close enough to rush from cover if needed.

Loco walked within whispering distance of me, keeping his sword at my back. "History does not always reward heroism," he muttered. "Remember what's at stake. Your job is to keep your people alive ... for today, and perhaps forever. The small picture and the big picture, both will be brighter if we find a peaceful solution on this beach."

I feigned a stumble on the rocks, so I could scratch at the thorn clinch. Twist was silenced by the glass of Nowhere, but I wanted his input. It was a strange thing to wish for pain, but I trusted no-one else. I didn't know what to do. My wisdom agreed with Inigo Night Walker, and wanted nothing more than a peaceful solution. But my instincts thought otherwise. It was as if my reason fought with my passion over the future of the Sea Wolves, but I had no earthly idea who was right and who was wrong. The sword in my back pushed me towards a confrontation I wasn't ready for.

Lord Ulric Blood, First Fang of the Sea Wolves, and elder of the Severed Hand, strolled at the front of the column. Men and women either side of him hefted cutlasses and circular shields, glaring at the small group of Dark Brethren. Their movements were controlled, but each one was a coiled spring, seconds away from violence. Most took a step forwards, ready to attack the brazen Dark Brethren, until they saw me. Siggy and Lord Ulric conferred, nodding in my direction, and the Sea Wolves lowered their blades.

Ten Cuts and the Mirralite parted, and we met in the shadow of the two overlooking cliffs. Lord Ulric, grey-haired and fierce, stood in front of Jacob Hearth, captain of the *Black Wave*, and Siggy Blackeye, Mistress of the *Dead Horse*. Loitering behind them was a Kneeling Wolf, likely their captain. He was short and muscular, with greasy black hair, braided down his back, and a coiled whip across his shoulders.

"Master Greenfire," said the First Fang, scratching at his beard. "Good to see you haven't found a way to get killed. How flows your wyrd?"

A hundred warriors, mostly Sea Wolves, stood in a mob before me, and my mind conjured a vivid memory. I thought of a day and a night, spent in the Bay of Grief, and of a cold walk to the Wolf House. I remembered a duellist, who warned me not to trip on the red carpet of the Bloody Halls, and I remembered the high table, and the elders of the Severed Hand, welcoming me as a Sea Wolf. Maron Grief had been there, and he'd made a stupid comment about my height. My father had thrown his usual scorn, but Vikon Blood and Tomas Red Fang had stuck up for me.

I stared up into the face of Lord Ulric, hoping to find some answers or, at the very least, some reassurance. I found neither. To my surprise, what I *did* find was a small surge of wyrd. Twist was warily pawing at my leg, equally surprised that the glass allowed us *any* power. Somewhere nearby, likely aboard the four ships, were Sea Wolf spirit-masters. I couldn't tell how many, but I could feel their wyrd-craft, like it was a comforting smell. It made sense that they knew about the glass of Nowhere, and had come prepared. Villains we may be, but the Sea Wolves were far from stupid.

"Duncan," snapped Ulric. "Say something. Where's my son?" He scowled at Loco. "Do the Brethren have him?"

"No," I replied. "They ... want a truce."

I didn't speak loudly, but those Sea Wolves close enough to hear erupted in laughter. The Kneeling Wolf captain threw his head back, and Siggy Blackeye chuckled, before spitting on the rocks. I felt like a fool for saying something so stupid. Twist was dancing up and down my leg, angry that I didn't just tell them the truth.

"We don't wish to fight," offered Loco Death Spell, prodding me in the back with the point of his sword. "We brought Duncan as a show of good faith. My commander, Inigo Night Walker of the third void legion, wishes to talk ... not fight. We have a tale you will want to hear."

They stopped laughing. The warriors of the Severed Hand must have known that there were additional forces waiting in ambush, but they couldn't know how many archers skulked above, nor of the small army commanded by Blade Smile. If stories were to be believed, the First Fang alone was the match of any ten men, but the vanguard was in the open and could be cut down with relative ease.

"Where's my son?" repeated Lord Ulric, now talking to Loco. "Where are the survivors of the *Dead Horse*? Siggy told us a dozen at least survived."

"Why aren't we killing them?" slurred the Kneeling Wolf captain, with a grotesque lick of the lips.

"This is Charlie Vane, called the War Rat," said Lord Ulric. "He *also* came here looking for his son. A father's rage should not be ignored."

"So, shall I kill 'em?" asked Charlie Vane. "How many more do you think there are?" He scratched his nails along the handle of his leather whip.

Loco removed his blade from my back, and pointed it at the muscular Kneeling Wolf. "Silence, rat. Men are talking."

Ulric chuckled ominously. "Give us the boy," he said. "And the other survivors. *Then* we can talk."

"No," replied Loco. "The boy stays with us. You will remain here until Lord Inigo returns. No-one needs to die on this beach."

I almost walked forwards, turning to join the Sea Wolves, but the Dark Brethren closed around me. Four short bows were now inches from my head, and I wasn't willing to gamble that they wouldn't kill me, but I wanted to tell the First Fang that Lord Vikon Blood was dead, that his son had been executed by Inigo Night Walker and the third void legion. Twist and I wanted to use my wyrd to help them reclaim Nowhere. The pain spirit was practically screaming, making me grit my teeth to stop from blurting out something stupid.

Behind us, giving in to impatience, Blade Smile appeared on the ridge, leading a single line of warriors. Most were still hidden, but the young man of Ice seemed to be reminding the First Fang who held the upper hand.

"Hmm," grumbled Lord Ulric, chewing on his lip. He again looked to the overhanging cliffs, as if planning an appropriate strategy.

I felt beads of sweat trickle down my forehead, as I struggled to bear the pain of the thorn clinch. *Honour us, Duncan.* It was Vikon's voice, but felt like it was Twist speaking. I was grateful to him for reminding me who I was, even if he had to hurt me to do it. "Vikon's dead," I announced, practically shouting. "Inigo executed him."

There was a pause, as if everyone stopped breathing for an instant. Silence erupted from the vanguard of Sea Wolves, and everyone stared at me. Loco was wide-eyed, the most expressive I'd seen him, and his men hesitated, suddenly aware they were alone on a beach with a hundred Sea

Wolves. They took a step away from the First Fang, taking me with them, as Loco interposed himself between us.

Slowly, Lord Ulric's face vibrated through a series of complex emotional states, before hardening into a mask of rage. Then he threw back his head and emptied his lungs. The sound was deep and discordant, like a dying wolf, howling defiance with its last breath. It stretched and echoed, filling the air with the anguish of a father who'd lost his only son. It travelled inland, washing over the warriors of Ice, reaching the ears of Blade Smile's archers, hiding on the cliffs. The sound made tears appear at the corners of my eyes, as I remembered Vikon's face, the moment before he died.

Before I knew what was happening, I was being bundled backwards, with Loco's sword now at my front, guarding against any Sea Wolves who gathered themselves quickly enough to attack. Luckily, none did.

"Let me go!" I snapped, fighting back tears. "I'm a Sea Wolf, I should be with them." I struggled against restraining arms, but couldn't free myself. I reached for the Sea Wolves, wanting more than anything to stand with them.

Loco growled at me over his shoulder, but kept his attention focused on the Sea Wolves. "Keep the boy safe," he ordered. "We need him. Now, move!"

As the First Fang stopped roaring, and the vanguard began a resolute advance, Blade Smile started shouting. The young man of Ice directed his warriors to form up on the ridge. He waved an arm at the cliffs, and dozens of longbows appeared. As the five Dark Brethren and I retreated, we were passed by a deep column of warriors, advancing onto the beach. The People of Ice had a huge advantage of numbers and appeared confident. At least until they saw a hundred Sea Wolves summon their wyrd.

The spirit-masters were sending wave upon wave of spiritual energy towards Lord Ulric and the vanguard. Somewhere beyond the Sea Wolves, perhaps only visible to me, small sea spirits snapped and snarled amidst the incoming waves, summoned by the spirit-masters and adding their power to the warriors of the Severed Hand. I could sense them in the void, as if a fragment of the Old Bitch of the Sea had travelled with the First Fang. I could almost feel her warm fur against my skin.

Ulric gave curt orders and his warriors split in two, each group of fifty moving to the base of the adjoining cliffs, taking cover from the longbows. I saw Taymund Grief go to the left, raising his shield above his head and pushing wyrd into his limbs. Ten Cuts and the Pure Ones melted away in alarm, grabbing their spears and running to the relative safety of the dead ground beyond the beach. Lord Ulric himself stayed in the open, throwing off his cloak and drawing two heavy cutlasses. His prodigious wyrd created a bluish glow around his outline, mixing with the low sun and causing a glare. It became an expanding star of energy, before rushing into his extremities with an audible crack.

The warriors of Ice swore in alarm, confused at the display of power. They muttered that the chaotic glass of Nowhere had forsaken them, or that the Sea Wolves were somehow able to bend the void to their will. A hundred and fifty years of submission had instilled in the People of Ice a paranoid fear of the First Fang, as if he was all their nightmares incarnate.

The void legionnaires dragged me over the ridge, and away from the beach. Loco spun me around, so I couldn't see the First Fang, and wrapped his hand around my throat. His stoic demeanour was gone, to be replaced by a homicidal glare. "You have fucked *everything* up," he shouted. "Now watch your people die."

21

I'd spent a day and night in the Bay of Grief, but I'd only felt like a Sea Wolf since the Old Bitch of the Sea visited me on the coast of Nowhere. We'd seen a vision I couldn't clearly remember, and she'd given me a task. *Greenfire must honour us all. Greenfire must let his wyrd shine.* I'd tried. I'd even gained some control, but still I'd succeeded only in getting people killed. This time I'd not even needed to use my wyrd to do it, and the people I'd killed were Sea Wolves.

From the cliffs came two sheets of arrows. They were loosed in unison and arced downwards, blanketing the vanguard. The archers targeted those warriors trying to hide under the opposite overhang, relying on weight of fire, rather than accuracy. A handful of arrows were deflected by wyrd, but two dozen at least found the mark, killing or crippling their targets. The First Fang's warriors laughed, cursed, and shouted oaths of retribution against the enemies of the Severed Hand. They behaved like Sea Wolves should, looking death in the face and telling it to fuck off. But it didn't hold the appeal it once had.

All four warships had launched boats, sending hundreds more warriors to reinforce the vanguard, but they wouldn't arrive in time to save the small force on the beach. Blade Smile's warriors of Ice outnumbered the Sea Wolves by at least five to one, and the vanguard had split into two, in an effort to protect against the archers. Lord Ulric was standing on his own in the centre of the beach, though his cloak of crackling blue wyrd deflected attempts to shoot him. I couldn't see a way for them to win. Was I going to be forced to watch the First Fang die?

"One flicker of wyrd, and I sleep you," snarled Loco, wrapping my neck in a choke-hold. He didn't tighten it, but left me in no doubt that I couldn't help Lord Ulric. We'd fallen back to the ridge separating the beach from the dead ground beyond, with a maddeningly clear view of the conflict. Loco and his four legionnaires were here to guard me, not to assist Blade Smile in killing the Sea Wolves, but their anger at what I'd done was clear.

There was wyrd on both sides, though the warriors of Ice used theirs sparingly, fully aware of how difficult it was to leach spiritual power through the glass of Nowhere. Their limbs emitted a subtle nimbus, but nothing like the surges of energy being provided by the spirit-masters at anchor. It was like looking at a mismatched chessboard, with one side having only their most powerful pieces left.

Blade Smile stayed in the centre, with a small force, to face down the First Fang, but directed his warriors into two wings, with each going to one of the cliff faces. Loco didn't let me move, and I lost sight of the two groups of Sea Wolves behind the advancing columns. All I could see was Lord Ulric, standing alone on the rocky beach, holding his twin blades across his chest, with a look of violent madness on his rugged face. A stray arrow ricocheted from his wyrd, as Blade Smile ordered his forces to kill them all. Then people started dying.

Once more for the Severed Hand. I heard it a dozen times from all quarters, as the Sea Wolves ran to meet the oncoming warriors of Ice. Individuals disappeared in a fog of steel, swearing and blood. The First Fang was the last to engage, but when he did, he killed two people. One blade was driven downwards through a man's skull. The other emerged through a twitching woman's throat. Blade Smile hung back, looking for an opening, as his warriors surrounded Lord Ulric. Either side, two larger battles took place, though I could barely see the Sea Wolves amongst the warriors of Ice. They wore the same armour, and wielded the same cutlasses, and killed each other with the ferocity of true hatred.

"*You* did this," said Loco, spitefully. "This is not what Lord Inigo wanted. Your First Fang will die, not knowing that he could have been the saviour of his people. This proves that the Sea Wolves can never be a part of Marius Cyclone's plan. You're far too barbaric."

"Once more for the Severed Hand," I whispered, with tears seeping from my eyes.

Loco tightened his arm around my neck. "What did you say? Boy!"

I didn't repeat the words. I let him jostle me left and right, as I tried to focus on the slaughter. The void legionnaire didn't choke me unconscious, but I could feel that he wanted to. His hold loosened when the First Fang drove a blade through a man's eye, and kicked another in the groin.

To the left, Taymund Grief was suddenly visible, hacking at warriors of Ice with equal amounts wyrd *and* steel. To the right, Siggy Blackeye was cackling with laughter, as she danced around blades, skewering their wielders. The weak and unskilled amongst the Sea Wolves were quickly dealt with, leaving only twenty or so of the most powerful. The air was thick with crashes of wyrd, meeting at the point of every blade, and scything through bodies. The warriors of Ice were swarming, with small circles of resistance forming around the strongest Sea Wolves. Vincent Heartfire swung a huge falchion, severing the arms and legs of anyone who got too close to him. Jacob Hearth, captain of the *Black Wave*, used strength to batter his opponents to death. Charlie Vane, the Kneeling Wolf, was freakishly skilled with his barbed whip, and used it to strangle people and steal their swords.

My eyes were suddenly drawn upwards, as the archers were dispersed by ballistae bolts, launched from the ships at anchor. A handful were killed, and the rest scattered, as the artillery reloaded and fired again.

What the People of Ice and the Dark Brethren didn't understand, was that the Sea Wolves would never surrender. They'd never submit or retreat. They'd fight and die with a smile on their faces, content that their deaths would be remembered in tales. Perhaps even written in the Bloody Halls, and immortalized in song. There was a time when I wanted nothing more than to think like them, but seeing them fight and die made everything feel so hollow. Twist certainly thought so, and the pain spirit was hunkered down on my leg, experiencing things with regret, as if the truth had suddenly changed. We'd seen the rising sea, though we couldn't remember it clearly, and everything else was suddenly petty. I'd made a huge fucking mistake.

Lord Ulric Blood, First Fang of the Severed Hand, was far more powerful than the warriors of Ice who attacked him, and he'd killed five or six, but twenty blades was a lot, even for him. His skill had waned, to be replaced by frenzy, and the huge man was now an engine of war, with insane eyes and an instinctive will to survive. But still his wyrd shone. He appeared taller and brighter than everyone around him, making his attackers hesitant.

The rocky beach was now stained red, with narrow rivers of blood snaking away from the growing piles of dead and maimed bodies. Warriors of Ice broke off from the conflict to assist wounded friends and remove the dead, but the Sea Wolves just kept fighting, even as most were overwhelmed and cut down.

Ingrid Raider and two other Sea Wolves had broken away from the battle lines, and were fighting to reach Lord Ulric. They thinned out the attackers just enough to keep Taymund Grief alive, allowing him to keep his back to the cliff face, whilst fighting the closest three attackers. Charlie Vane was surrounded, but he used his wyrd like a second whip, describing a circle through which no-one could pass.

"This is taking too long," observed Loco, his eyes betraying a flicker of concern. "Blade Smile's warriors are..."

"Weak?" I offered. "Unskilled? Relying on numbers?"

He yanked my neck, making me splutter. "Their morale is... lacking. A psychological war can be more important than a physical one. And the Sea Wolves won *that* war long ago."

Even so I struggled to find a dozen still alive. Ulric, Taymund, Charlie Vane, Ingrid Raider, they were all wounded, but still killing people. I couldn't see Vincent Heartfire, Siggy Blackeye or Jacob Hearth, but my vision was as much obscured by dead warriors of Ice as living ones. They may have outnumbered them five to one, but they now had five times more dead. The Sea Wolves would never surrender, but the People of Ice were wavering. If they pushed forwards, they'd win, but there was a reluctance in their movements. So many had died, and the remainder were looking for a reason to fall back. Their reluctance got them killed. The few remaining Sea Wolves were mighty warriors, and Lord Ulric was a legend. It was a stark reminder of how powerful an Eastron could be, if they channelled every ounce of their wyrd into combat prowess.

I started to feel light-headed. At first, I attributed it to the gruesome spectacle on the beach and Loco's restraining arm, but it was something else. Over the sounds of combat, flowing from every clash of steel and shouted word, came the thin whine of a whistle. I couldn't turn my head, but I knew Ten Cuts was close.

Is this what you wanted? It was the pale man who spoke, his voice coming from far away.

"Not *this* exactly," I replied, thinking the words, but not saying them out loud. "I wanted to be with them. I'm not sure I do anymore. I feel like a fool."

It's not your fault. It's mine. I thought you'd understand the vision, but your pain spirit protected your mind. You know the sea is rising, but you can't recall any details. And your need to be a Sea Wolf is stronger than I anticipated. I need to show you again. You need to see more. And you need to remember what you see.

My eyes were drawn upwards, above the brutal conflict, the warships at anchor, and the encircling cliffs. Twist made me flinch, with ripples of discomfort, pushing my gaze into the clouds, as if he'd finally decided we should remember. From the muddy grey sky, a shape started to form. The mirages, known to appear along the Bright Coast, were a remnant of past void battles and overuse of the glass.

This was different. Somehow I was seeing an apparition, superimposed onto the sky. At first it was just an outline of an indistinct shape. Then Twist pushed my eyes up and down, and left and right, and I saw an immense shadow, forming across the horizon. The colossal shape was lacking in colour. Everything else – the rugged, green and grey cliffs, the rolling terrain, and the massed warriors – all appeared vibrant in comparison.

Twist wouldn't let me look away, as arms and legs gradually formed in the distance, flickering at the shadowy edges, as if caught by a great wind. A giant form loomed over everything, eclipsing the light and casting a vile shadow over the insignificant creatures below. The silhouette was humanoid, with bat-like, membranous wings, and a bulbous head, dripping with tentacles.

The Sunken God strode forwards, sweeping up a warship in its clawed hand, before effortlessly crushing the vessel and flinging it at the beach. The hull splintered, sending lethal shards of wood into the bewildered Sea Wolves. The mountainous creature took a stride forwards, indiscriminately killing a hundred warriors of Ice and Mirralite Pure Ones. Each human was an ant, scattering as quickly as they could, unable to comprehend what they saw. Sea Wolves roared, warriors of Ice ran, Mirralite froze. Most died. They were crushed by its slimy feet, grabbed in its sinewy hands, or gobbled up by its twitching tentacles. Its vile body shimmered in tones of black and grey, almost unreal against the rivers of blood and flesh that now saturated my field of vision.

Twist was afraid. The spirit hugged my leg, causing me no pain, but gripping as tightly as it could, as if it were a small dog, cowed into submission by a loud noise. We'd seen it before, but it had been different. The lines weren't as clear, and we'd chosen to forget it.

"Duncan!" I wasn't sure who was talking, and was surprised that I could hear the voice above the deafening carnage below. Men and women screamed as they ran, with no-one mustering the insanity needed to stay and attack, while each footfall of the monster's flabby limbs made the earth shake.

"Duncan, what is wrong with you?" It sounded like Loco Death Spell. "Stop screaming." He was grunting with exertion, as if he held someone down.

The Sunken God swept an arm across the low ground, annihilating half the fleeing warriors with one swipe. It then tensed its colossal legs and stood upright on the beach, allowing a tidal wave to wash past its ankles and drown any mortals that remained, eclipsing the ships, the beach, the cliffs, and travelling inland for more than a mile, carrying with it utter darkness and complete destruction.

My face started to sting, as if someone had slapped me, and I realized I was lying on the grassy ridge, with Loco's hand over my mouth. I stopped screaming and fought back vomit, struggling to turn my head and look at the beach. The Dark Brethren were alarmed, and four short bows were pointed at my head. They still thought I might erupt and kill them, but Twist and I were far too distressed to lash out. I just wanted to look at the Sea Wolves and see if I'd caused the death of the First Fang.

Loco removed his hand and let me move, but only when Blade Smile and the screaming warriors of Ice began to rush past us. They'd broken in the face of the Sea Wolves, and had fled. Through the chaotic retreat, I saw a line of figures, spread out across the rocky beach. They were covered in blood, and they howled to the sky, roaring their challenges at the cowards who had run away. There were eight of them. One hundred had come ashore as the vanguard, but only eight Sea Wolves had fought hard enough to keep their lives. They were truly powerful... and utterly insignificant.

Lord Ulric, Siggy Blackeye, the War Rat and five others, unrecognizable under a second skin of blood. One of them, cheering despite the loss of an arm, looked like Taymund Grief. Another may have been Ingrid Raider, but she was too wounded to stand.

"Fall back," commanded Blade Smile, his voice crackling with panic. Fifty or so warriors of Ice were retreating in a disorganized mob, seemingly oblivious to their advantage of numbers. Hundreds of them had died, and they had no further will to fight. The Sea Wolves were some kind of evil spirit made flesh, and many of the fleeing warriors of Ice cursed their own foolishness for daring to stand against the First Fang. The Severed Hand had smashed them, and smashed them again, over and over, since Duncan Red Claw and Velya Ice first arrived with the Always King. They'd never been able to stand against the Sea Wolves. Why was now any different?

As the People of Ice retreated, Mirralite Pure Ones hastily erected barricades in the low ground beyond the ridge. They couldn't fight the Sea Wolves, but they could allow themselves the illusion of corralling them on the beach. Not that their piles of wood and debris would stop the First Fang. He'd come inshore when he wanted to.

As for Twist and I, we could barely think clearly enough to be happy that some had survived. All I could see, as if tattooed on my eyeballs, was the monstrous creature, staggering forth from the depths of the Sunken City, with seaweed and slime oozing from its flabby body. In time, my mind could recover, but it would never be the same. I'd been shown something that mortal creatures were not meant to see and I feared I would never be rid of it. This time I would remember.

Where was Inigo Night Walker? Where was the third void legion? Blade Smile practically screeched the questions, over and over again, as hundreds of Sea Wolves made camp on the beach, and began assembling funeral pyres. He asked the questions so many times that Loco retreated to the cliff tops, taking me and his four legionnaires with him. Reinforcements had arrived from Cold Point, and there were now two significant armies, facing each other across Mirralite barricades and burning bodies.

Thanks to me, the Sea Wolves knew only that Vikon Blood was dead. They knew nothing of the rising sea, nor of the importance of Nowhere. They thought they were killing rebels and traitors, not warriors who fought to keep secret a doorway into the distant void. So many had already died in ignorance, and I was tortured by my part in it. Twist dug nails of anger into my leg, and I deserved every ounce of pain the spirit caused me.

"I've seen you kill a lot of people," said Loco, perhaps gaining insight into my facial expressions. "I imagine that must be difficult to bear." He paused. "I apologize for my earlier sharpness. A void legionnaire should not allow emotion to intrude."

"I'm sorry too," I replied. "You were right. You, Inigo, the Grim Wolf, you were all right. The Sea Wolves *are* too impulsive and violent to understand why you came to Nowhere... and why you attacked the *Dead Horse*. And I'm a fool for getting so many people killed... why? Because I'm a fucking Sea Wolf." I snorted the words, angry at what they meant.

From along the cliffs came a tall Dark Brethren. I felt he'd been listening, and chosen this moment to make himself known. He wore a black steel breastplate, under a leather overcoat, and had the bearing of a void legionnaire. He came to a stop, looking down at us. Loco had been sitting next to me, leaning against a tree, with his sword resting across my shoulders. Now, the young Brethren stood and backed away. It was the furthest he'd been from me in days.

"A fucking Sea Wolf?" queried the tall man. "You shouldn't insult your own people. That's where you came from. That's who you are." He had black hair, with silver streaks, and wore a thin beard. A tattoo was just visible, creeping onto his neck from under his leather collar. It was a blue shape of some kind, but I couldn't guess at the whole design. "You can't swing a sword or shout a worthy challenge, but you can save the Eastron from extinction. I'd say you are the most important Sea Wolf who has ever lived."

Loco and the other four void legionnaires bowed their heads, as a crackling blue aura slowly faded from the tall Dark Brethren. I felt I should stand up, but Twist didn't want me to. I'd need to massage feeling back into my left leg before I could stand unaided. "You're new," I said, scratching at my leg.

"Yes," he replied, trying not to smile. "I am Marius Cyclone, called the Stranger. We would have met sooner, but there was an assassin sent after me. I believe I have *you* to thank for thwarting his efforts at the Severed Hand. I suppose I should be honoured that my brother found me as worthy of killing as Prince Oliver Dawn Claw."

He waved an arm across the cliffs and the rocky beach below, and the air changed. The hairs began to rise on my arms and I felt goose bumps all over my skin. The ambient temperature dropped sharply and mist came from my mouth. I pulled myself upright, using the tree as a crutch. I glared at the Stranger, fighting back the impulse to hate him.

"I am claiming the island of Nowhere," stated Marius Cyclone. "It must be protected at all costs."

Small arcs of lightning struck the air all around us, from the beach, across the cliffs, to the low ground. The lightning framed a blue-and-white vortex in the air, drawing hundreds of eyes upwards. Then another appeared, then another, until dozens of whirling storm clouds of fizzing energy surrounded the battlefield. Warriors on both sides showed signs of panic, though the Sea Wolves were slower to move. Even Lord Ulric had taken several backward steps and appeared unsure what was happening.

The largest vortex surged backwards, opening out and forming a tunnel of roiling energy. From the depths of the storm, surrounded by lightning and blue cloud, walked Inigo Night Walker. Behind him, slowly emerging from the tunnel, marched ranks of Dark Brethren. Each vortex became a storm tunnel, and through each came a similar column of warriors, marching in formation. They wore black armour and helms, fashioned into the likeness of an owl, with wide eyepieces. Each held a tall shield and a spear, with a straight sword at the hip. They appeared on the cliffs, the beach, and on every side of the low ground. Rank upon rank of warriors, moving as metal snakes with a rhythmic clank of steel.

There were so many of them. They filled every part of the coast, with the closest column barely twenty feet away. As the third void legion left the storm tunnels, the air slowly returned to normal, with lightning and thunder marking the closure of each vortex.

The Stranger moved to the edge of the cliff and spread his arms wide, making sure he could be seen by the Sea Wolves below. "Lord Ulric," he boomed. "Talk or fight... your choice."

The Lodge of the Rock was loyal, strong and rebellious.
The Lodge of the Tree was noble, tall and watchful.
The Lodge of the Fire was cunning, stealthy and volatile.
The Lodge of the Air was wise, gentle and flighty.

For time unknown they were balanced.
Then we arrived from the Bright Lands.
The Rock became the Severed Hand.
The Tree became the Silver Dawn.
The Fire became the Open Hand.

But the Lodge of the Air remained free.

From "The Great Theft" by
Mathew Lahandras of the Sundered Claws

PART EIGHT

Adeline Brand at the Severed Hand

22

We approached the hold from the north, breaking the treeline of the Wood of Scars and heading for the Tranquil Gate. Dark Wing had remained in his dead forest, but Tasha and Jaxon walked with me. My friend's head was bowed, and he barely registered the Severed Hand when it appeared, but Tasha was struck dumb for a moment. I assumed she'd have visited before, but her wide eyes and open mouth showed different.

Four Claw's Folly, across the Turtle Straits, was half again as big as the hold of the Sea Wolves, but the glass was more solid and the air played no tricks on Eastron eyes. On Nibonay, the distant shimmer of the sea created a thousand illusions, and I could see the Kneeling Wolf processing figures and scenes as they appeared and vanished across the stone silhouette of the hold. I stopped walking and let her look.

"A great wolf," whispered Tasha. "Leaping from wall to wall." Her face brightened into a gleeful smile. "A laughing girl, looking to the sky."

"I always see a pair of green eyes," I replied, amazed that sight of the hold made me think of one thing above all.

"Frog Killer would tell me stories about it," she said. "The Wolf House and the Bright Coast, the Bay of Grief and the Laughing Rock. I never thought a humble cook would ever look upon the Severed Hand." She turned to me and grinned. "What shall we have for dinner?"

"Probably fish," I replied, dryly. "Let us go to the Wolf House first. Rys Coldfire and the First Fang will need to hear our words."

I suddenly felt tired. I'd not slept properly since Arthur, Jaxon and I first left. I'd also barely had a change of clothes since Tasha and Lucas rescued me. My leather armour and cutlass were lost somewhere in the Lodge of Dagon. My vest and woollen underclothes had been stuck to my skin for the last few days, and the smell was becoming hard to bear. Perhaps the Wolf's Bastard could wait until I'd had a bath.

"I see blood," said Jaxon, suddenly. "Over the Wolf House, the air turns red."

"Where?" enquired Tasha. "I see no red."

"The Bright Coast plays games with your eyes," I replied, putting my arm around the Wisp's shoulders. "There is no red. You'd be the first to tell me that."

He looked at me and I feared he would never be the same man. Some spark of life had been extinguished, to be replaced by a permanent shadow across his eyes. We'd pulled his body from the Temple of Dagon, but his mind was still there.

"We're home," I said to him, blocking his view of the hold. "We're safe and we're home."

Tasha's eyes remained wide and Jaxon's remained bowed as we passed through the Tranquil Gate. The northern walls had green algae stains around the base, and jagged castellations at the top. Everything was quiet. Duellists patrolled the battlements, Pure Ones went about their business in the small settlement of Lion's End, outside the walls, but all activity was slow and sombre, as if the Severed Hand was expecting a storm.

The gates had been opened at our approach, though no significant presence greeted us within. "Ho there!" I shouted to the gate-guard – an old duellist with one glass eye. "Do you know me?"

He looked up from the slab of swordfish he was eating and poked his head out of his guard shed. "I do, Mistress Brand. Hail to you."

"And to you. We are bound for the Wolf House. How fares the hold?"

"Dark times," he replied. "The First Fang left for Nowhere. Don't know why. I expect they'll tell you." His manner was laconic and dry, likely the result of a life spent guarding a gate, rather than fighting.

"Very well." I left him and walked into the hold, taking a deep breath of air.

"Smells horrid," observed Tasha, screwing up her nose. "Like ... rotten fish."

"Smells like home to me," I replied.

We turned a corner, between two large buildings, and Tasha stopped walking. Before us was the Wolf House, towering over the northern half of the Severed Hand. Twenty-three storeys – far and away the tallest building on Nibonay.

"It's ... it's huge," she muttered. "And those black murals ..."

Jaxon, who'd been at least a step behind us the whole way back, suddenly stood next to me and joined Tasha in staring up at the seat of the First Fang. "Looks smaller to me," he said. "Smaller than when I last saw it." He looked at me. "Why would Lord Ulric go to Nowhere?"

I smiled, attempting to lighten Jaxon's mood. "Perhaps young Sharp Tongue has insulted the Grim Wolf and caused an incident. I doubt his father would be surprised. Or perhaps the assassin's second target has been revealed."

Tasha gasped. As we walked, her eyes had travelled from the black murals, down the Wolf House, to the open cloisters of the bottom level. The encircling square was usually filled to the brim with Nissalite, conducting business, and Eastron, jockeying to get inside the auction houses on the lower levels. Now it was mostly empty, with a single line of wooden stakes acting as a perimeter. Upon each stake was a dead Pure One, and before each dead Pure One was a duellist, standing guard over the Wolf House.

"There's been a purge," muttered Jaxon. "A bad one."

Tasha averted her eyes, but didn't make comment on Sea Wolf justice.

"A couple of hundred at least," I observed. "Someone must have greatly angered the Wolf's Bastard or the master-at-arms."

I quickened my pace, eager to get inside. Much needed to be said and much had changed. Jaxon and Tasha followed, both having to jog every other pace to keep up with me. We walked around the building until Jacob's Tower came into view. Lesser duellists nodded their respect at our passing, and word quickly spread that Adeline Brand and Jaxon Ice had returned to the Severed Hand. There were other whispers as well, things I couldn't quite hear or put into context. The atmosphere around the Wolf House was tense, with normally relaxed guard patterns tightened up, and duellists clearly on edge.

"Get out of my fucking way," I barked at the four lesser duellists on guard by the main entrance. They averted their eyes and moved, allowing us entry. One almost thought to stop Tasha, but I snarled at him.

"When was the last time they locked up the Wolf House like this?" mused Jaxon.

"I've never seen it locked up like *this*," I replied.

"A rather grim place," observed Tasha. "Grey and cold." She smiled at me, as if worried she'd cause offence. "But lovely all the same."

The bottom level was empty, with nothing but a whistling wind coming from vacant auction rooms and duellists' chambers. I strolled across the empty stone floor. It was a different building with no-one in it, like a giant's tomb, awaiting its occupant. My breathing echoed and my muscles tensed. I didn't know why, but I was suddenly on edge. The air was charged. I looked at Jaxon and saw his eyes flickering and his mind whirring.

"What do you see?" I asked him.

He paused before answering, looking to the wide steps that led to the Bloody Halls. "The hold feels sick," he replied. "The void, it's ill. I can feel it in the stone and the wood. The teeth and gums of chaos. Chaos spirits, they are bound here. By ... something." His hands shook, as if he was afraid of his own mind. His wyrd sight remained, but he no longer liked what he saw.

"How can those things be here?" I asked. "They're summoning them at the Bay of Bliss. How can they be bound here? So soon."

"I don't know," replied Jaxon. Though his sight remained, he lacked the clarity to explain what he saw.

I didn't have time to coddle my friend, we needed to report in, so I rushed towards the stairs, giving Jaxon and Tasha a wave to follow me. Beyond the ground level, duellists guarded every turning and chamber, standing in a solemn vigil, barely nodding at our passing. The Wolf House was like I'd never seen it. It was never a warm building, but it was usually alive with activity, and arriving within felt like coming home. But no longer.

"Adeline! Where the fuck have you been?" shouted Jonas Grief, the master-at-arms. He sat in a map chamber on the first level of the Bloody Halls, clustered with Rys Coldfire and other senior duellists. Lagertha Blood, Lord Ulric's teenage daughter, was also there.

They scanned the doorway and saw me, Jaxon, a strange Kneeling Wolf, but no Arthur Brand. "We've been imprisoned at the Bay of Bliss," I replied. "Arthur was killed by chaos spirits and we were rescued by this Kneeling Wolf and her companion."

Telling the story of our journey was harder than I thought. Seeing their faces and reactions made me feel small and weak, as if every look implied judgement. The Wolf's Bastard didn't mean to scowl as he asked about the Sunken Men, but I shrank a little under his dark eyes. Jonas Grief was kind as we spoke of chaos spirits and Arthur's death, but still I felt like a small girl addressing a full-grown man. I struggled through the whole story, paying particular attention to Jaxon's fragility and the bravery of Tasha and the Kneeling Wolves. I spoke of what we saw in the Temple of Dagon, though I didn't linger on what they intended for me.

My arms fell limply at my sides, as tiredness assaulted every inch of my body. I had to fight back tears, and was helped into a seat by Lagertha. Near the end, unable to maintain his composure any longer, Jaxon curled up in a ball on the stone floor. Spirit-masters were summoned and the Wisp was taken away, and I finished the story with Tasha's hand on my shoulder.

"Dark Wing cleared his head for a time, but he's not been the same." I watched Jaxon be helped away. "Where's Tomas Red Fang?"

"In the void," replied the Wolf's Bastard, wearing an expression halfway between pity and concern. "It's become treacherous." He sat down opposite. "Adeline, look at me. You didn't kill your brother. I'm truly sorry you had to watch him die, but you didn't spill his blood. We have much to do and your presence will help. The hold is under threat and we have many warriors absent."

"She needs to rest," said Tasha. "She's not slept properly for weeks."

Jonas Grief glared at the Kneeling Wolf. "She is a duellist of the Severed Hand and does not need you to mother her."

"Well, she needs *someone* to look after her," snapped Tasha. "Are you going to do it? Or are you just going to ask her questions, before putting a blade in her hand and pointing her at the next fight?"

The master-at-arms lowered his head at the telling-off, but a sly smile flowed across his face. "Very well, Addie can take some rest. The Kneeling Wolf may remain in the Bloody

Halls. It's not safe on the streets at the moment. But if she talks to me like that again, she'll have to answer for it."

I removed my ragged clothes in a daze. I sat in a soapy bath, unable to feel the water or smell the soap. I scrubbed dirt and dried sweat from my back, and felt blood before pain as I scrubbed too hard. I barely dried myself before falling into bed and dragging a blanket over my head. The warmth of the room, the softness of the bed and the exhaustion in my limbs, quickly lulled me into a deep, deep sleep.

If I had dreams, I didn't remember them. All I remembered, when I awoke, was that I was back at the Severed Hand. My world had been shaken, but certain anchors of my strength remained. I was not broken, just beaten ... for now at least. I was alive and still strong. That was more than could be said for the other two Sea Wolves who travelled to the Bay of Bliss.

I sat up in bed, as a clatter reached my ears. Beyond my bedroom door, someone was grumbling as they attempted to navigate the sparse kitchen. I rubbed my eyes and shielded them against the glaring sunlight, streaming through the window. My chamber was as I remembered it – warm, but barren, containing little but the accoutrements of a duellist. A wardrobe with few clothes; a cabinet of whet stones and blades; a low table, scattered with belts and undergarments.

Another clatter from the kitchen, and a male voice swore. "Fucking hell, Adeline," grunted the voice, probably unaware I was awake and listening. "Don't you ever put anything away?" It was a rhetorical question, but I felt like answering.

"I have a system," I replied, raising my voice to be heard. "And who let you in, Tomas?"

"The charming Kneeling Wolf outside your chambers," replied Tomas Red Fang, the spirit-master. "I thought to brew a pot of tea, but you have no clean cups. In fact, you have no clean crockery of any kind…actually, no, I just found a clean plate. Just the one, mind."

I rubbed sleep from my eyes and turned out of bed. The stone floor was freezing. I'd slept naked, going straight from my bath to my bed. As I emerged from beneath my blanket, I balked and pulled it back over my shoulders. It was unusually cold and I went instantly for a thick, woollen robe.

"Why's it so bloody cold?" I asked, through the door.

"Just get up," replied Tomas. "I'd rather talk to you face-to-face. I got a second-hand version of what happened from Rys, but he's lacking in subtlety."

A shiver travelled up my spine. The prospect of retelling the story of our journey mingled with the cold and made my teeth chatter. I dressed hurriedly, pulling on woollen leggings and a thick tunic. Then a leather overshirt and a cloak, pulling the fabric around my shoulders and letting the warmth travel through my limbs. When my body no longer shivered, I knelt and put on socks and leather boots. My feet were still numb, but I felt vaguely human again.

"Whenever you're ready, Mistress Brand," prompted Tomas.

"Yes, yes," I grumbled, rubbing my hands together before opening the door.

My kitchen was seldom used. It adjoined a small sitting room – also seldom used – and was disorganized in the extreme. Duellists' lodgings were on the second level of the Wolf House. They were utilitarian, but larger than you might imagine, especially for those deemed senior. I'd never paid much attention to my chambers, using them to sleep and eat, as the need arose, but I found myself strangely embarrassed when I saw Tomas Red Fang sifting through dirty crockery, with a steaming teapot in his hands.

"Seriously, Addie, this is unhealthy," said the spirit-master, flinging a layer of grime from his hand. "What would your mother say?"

"She wouldn't say anything," I replied. "She'd just spend two hours cleaning it. And I'd spend a few days undoing her work."

"Ah, you're rebelling against parental expectations," he said. "That fits your character. Though I wonder if it extends to the expectations of your station. You're a duellist, Adeline, against *that* you shouldn't rebel."

I sat opposite him, across a circular wooden table in my kitchen. "Doubting my conviction? That's bold…coming from an old man like yourself. You have no more authority over me than a tree or a rock, so keep your fucking judgements to yourself."

He set the teapot down and laughed. His face wrinkled up like paper, and his hands clapped together in amusement. "Good," he chuckled. "Good, good, good. You're still Adeline Brand. The story I was told made you sound like you were a quivering shadow of your former self."

I bowed my head. He'd been told that I'd felt fear, that I had seen Arthur die and been captured; and rescued by Kneeling Wolves. "I needed rest," I replied. "I should have slept before I gave my report. I think I meant to, but everything happened quickly. I saw the master-at-arms before I saw my bed. If it had been the other way around..."

"Well, don't worry, I can tell you don't want to tell the tale again. I won't make you. But of these chaos spawn, we must talk." He poured tea into two moderately clean cups and set the teapot aside. "Varn Gloom Scribe has been busy in your absence. In truth I believe he was busy long before you left. He's established quite a following amongst misguided Pure Ones."

"What?" I exclaimed. "He consorts with Sunken Men and follows their dreaming god. I assume he leaves that out of his preaching?"

"Seems so," replied Tomas. "Not that it would matter if he didn't. The Shackles of the Wolf hang heavily, and some would do anything...pledge to anything, just to feel the chains removed. Rys has questioned a hundred and purged a hundred more, and we're no closer to finding the slippery bastard. We just keep hearing the same thing – he listens to the sea."

"Why the purge?" I asked. "He was against it before we left."

"That was before the void... changed." His eyes darkened, as a film of wyrd caressed his face. Beneath the dark blue shimmer, the old spirit-master had a dozen small wounds across his head and neck. They appeared to be jagged bite marks. "First, the hold spirits began to disappear. A bird here, an elemental there. Then duellists started to go missing, lost somewhere beyond the glass. Then the air began to smell of chaos. It wasn't a summoning. That would have taken years. It was a binding. More and more arrive each day, no doubt from that charming village at the Bay of Bliss. How many did you see, Adeline?"

I sipped the tea and lost my focus for a moment, staring blankly at the stone wall opposite. I was tired. My body felt heavy and my head rebelled, not wanting to talk or even think.

"Mistress Brand!" snapped Tomas. "I thought we had a problem before. Now I hear that these things can break the glass! That the Mirralite were feeding them Sea Wolf flesh. So, tell me, how many are there?"

"I don't know," I replied. "Too many to count. I only got a good look at them when ..."

"When they killed your brother," offered the spirit-master. "The Adeline Brand *I* remember would want vengeance, not pity."

"Fuck off, old man!" I shouted. "You didn't see them attack. You didn't see how helpless we were. Against the hybrids, the spirits, and especially the fucking frogs."

He took a slow sip of tea and stood. "It seems you've already accepted defeat. That is disappointing. I'll see you're not disturbed until you come to me." He backed away, allowing his subtle wyrd to again obscure his wounds. "We should probably summon Lord Ulric and his warriors back from Nowhere. Dark Brethren attacked the *Dead Horse*, you know. The Second Fang is missing."

23

Halfdan Blood, called the Bloody Fang, was fond of dungeons. Before Lord Ulric took his father's place at the point of a blade, he built extensive chambers under the Wolf House. Long, dark tunnels of grey flagstones, housing two hundred cells, not tall enough to stand up in or wide enough to lie down in. The Bloody Fang called it his place of forgetting.

For most of my life its inhabitants had been skeletons and rats, and, if paranoid fisherman were to be believed, the ghosts of slain Pure Ones. I had never seen it with my own eyes. Not until two days after Tomas Red Fang left my chamber, and I saw a familiar face being dragged under the Wolf House. Two duellists led a gang of chained Pure Ones down the narrow steps, to be caged, and questioned when and if the Wolf's Bastard remembered they were there. Third in line, his face a mask of red cuts and black bruises, was Young Green Eyes.

I'd not thought of him since I returned. My blood had not risen and I'd felt no urge to visit Swordfish Bay. I'd felt no urge to do anything. I'd not left the Wolf House, nor checked on Jaxon. Yesterday I'd slept, today I drank. There was an empty seat next to me, and if I hadn't been staring at it, I wouldn't have seen the line of captive Pure Ones marched past the low bar's entrance. It was an hour or two after midday and I'd been drinking since breakfast.

"Stop there," I said to the duellists, draining my mug and rising to meet them. I was on unsteady feet, but my senses were only a little dulled.

"Mistress," said one, with a bow of his head.

"What is that one's crime?" I asked, pointing at Young Green Eyes.

The two lesser duellists looked at each other. "Not known, mistress. They are the latest group. Swordfish Bay is being purged."

I coughed and spat on the floor. "How many are dead? So far."

"Not known, mistress," he repeated. "You should speak to Master Coldfire."

I turned from them and faced Young Green Eyes. He wore only a pair of ragged trousers, with his feet and chest bare. He'd been cut and badly beaten, and his beautiful eyes were hidden behind swelling and blooded hair. He didn't acknowledge me until I put a hand under his chin and raised his head. "My world is a fragile place," he murmured, with a thin smile. "*I* knew this. And *you* knew this."

I wanted to say I could help him, that I could remove the chains with a word, but I glanced back at the two duellists and realized it was impossible.

"Don't struggle for words, Adeline," said Young Green Eyes. "There are none."

"If you know something, tell them," I whispered. "It may not save your life, but it will soften your death."

He looked at me, his face bulging and red, with bruises spreading from his chin and cheeks. "I don't especially want a soft death. All deaths are hard since the Invaders came."

"Mistress," said one of the duellists. "Is there something else you need? These men are required below."

I bowed my head. "Take them away," I said, not looking at Young Green Eyes.

"Aye, mistress." The gang of Pure Ones were led away, down the narrow stairs, until they disappeared into the darkness below.

I'd sobered up quickly and there was now a rancid taste in my mouth. I looked down, realizing that my fists were tightly clenched and numb. I rubbed feeling back into my palms and fingers, and allowed myself a single tear. I didn't know if I'd have cried for him before. Perhaps, or perhaps I would have thanked the purge for ridding me of a problem I lacked the fortitude to rid myself of.

"You don't see us as superior anymore," said Jaxon. He'd appeared silently behind me. "Neither do I." His face had some colour, but his eyes remained haunted, and his clothing was little more than a robe, with no markings to signal his station as a senior duellist.

I slowly faced him and paused, moving in for an emotional embrace when he showed me a thin smile. "I knew you'd mend," I whispered.

"And I knew I'd find you in the bar," replied the Wisp. "You always drink to forget."

I led him back inside the low bar and we took seats opposite each other. He kept his shoulders hunched, and he moved in small steps, with little strength or confidence.

"Do you know what's happening out there?" he asked. "The spirit-masters wouldn't tell me."

"I've not left the Wolf House since we returned," I replied. "I only know that the chaos sprits are being bound here and Pure Ones are being questioned and purged. I have no further information. I think Tomas Red Fang relieved me of duty ... for the time being at least."

"*That* I was told," said the Wisp. "Gossip still spreads. It is said that Adeline Brand has felt fear, and is no longer the same woman."

"Hard to disagree," I replied. "But I should belt on my blades and visit the Wolf's Bastard. I feel like knowing what is happening to the Severed Hand." I went to the bar and drew two large mugs of ale. "You should come with me."

The main chamber of the Bloody Halls was half-full. The worn red carpets were filled with duellists, spirit-masters and scribes, and around the circular table sat the hold elders, at least those that were still here. The Wolf's Bastard, Tomas Red Fang and Jonas Grief sat with Lagertha Blood and Torstein Hearth, the scroll-master. A young Kneeling Wolf was also there, though standing next to the table. Jaxon and I had not tried to join them, and we stood with Tasha Strong, next to a carved wooden pillar to the left of the high table. In total, four or five hundred Sea Wolves awaited news. Many thousands more, mostly lesser duellists, were in the hold, doing what they could to maintain order and smoke out rebellious Pure Ones.

"We have little time for gatherings," began Jonas Grief, addressing the huge chamber, "so this will be as brief as we can make it. The Severed Hand remains under martial law, with only Eastron allowed abroad after dark or to grace the stone of the Wolf House."

Rys Coldfire stood and took over from the master-at-arms. "The purge has not worked," he announced, with a sigh.

"We've killed hundreds and have not found a single varn capable of any kind of binding, let alone the shit currently squirming in the void." He looked at Tomas Red Fang.

"We're looking for one or two immensely powerful Pure Ones," offered the spirit-master. "The only name we have is a Mirralite, called Varn Gloom Scribe."

"If we do not find this man," continued Rys, "it is likely the chaos spirits will multiply until …" He gritted his teeth and looked at the floor.

Tomas Red Fang took over, and it became clear that they did not want the assembled Sea Wolves to know that the spirits would be able to break the glass and enter the realm of form.

"We have no count of missing Eastron," said the old spirit-master. "Though hundreds at the very least have disappeared in the void. Anyone breaking the glass does so at their own risk."

"Tell them of Lord Ulric?" prompted Lagertha Blood. She was only sixteen years old, and rarely seen in the Bloody Halls, but with the First and Second Fang absent, she was allowed a seat at the high table.

"As you may have heard," said Jonas Grief, "the First Fang has not yet returned from Nowhere. We have sent messengers to inform him of the dire situation here, but we've received no word of him or Lord Vikon."

I leaned into Jaxon. "How many men did he take? Do you know?" I asked.

"Four ships," replied Jaxon. "Including the *Lucretia*. Eight hundred warriors, maybe."

I frowned at him. "What was the *Lucretia* doing at the Severed Hand?"

"Don't know," he replied. "But the Kneeling Wolf by the high table is Oswald Leaf, the Friend's eldest son."

Lagertha stood from the table. Her voice was clear and precise, but it crackled slightly with nerves. "Until my father or my brother return, we have a duty to protect our people and our hold. We will find whoever is binding these spirits and we will kill them."

"Once more for the Severed Hand!" shouted the Wolf's Bastard.

The words were echoed by every other Sea Wolf in the Bloody Halls. Every other Sea Wolf except two. Neither Jaxon nor I shouted. We just looked at each other, then at the assembled warriors. Each pulsed with wyrd, from the slight vibration of the lesser duellists, to the torrent of energy from the mightiest spirit-masters. They each felt a powerful sense of their own superiority, as if they had already won and the fight was a formality. They were Sea Wolves of the Severed Hand and had never known their match. At least that is what they were told to believe. Our one true defeat had been twisted into a ghost story and the enemies forgotten. I hated myself for thinking it, but it was the truth.

Quickly, the hall emptied. Men and women, driven by conviction, exited the Bloody Halls, intent on being the one to find Gloom Scribe and secure the hold. Jaxon and I remained, with Tasha trying to stay hidden behind us.

"That was really impressive," whispered the Kneeling Wolf. "They all have very loud voices."

"Shouting a lot trains you to speak loudly," I replied.

"You two, get over here," ordered the master-at-arms, proving my point.

Neither of us were properly attired. Jaxon wore his robe, and I wore woollen leggings and a black tunic. Around the table, each of the hold elders wore armour of some kind. Rys and Jonas wore breastplates, Tomas and Torstein wore light chainmail, even Lagertha wore moulded leather armour. Only Oswald Leaf, the visiting Kneeling Wolf, was unarmoured, standing casually in a heavy, black overcoat and canvas clothing.

"I didn't want to believe it," said Jonas Grief. "Adeline Brand has felt fear."

"Easy," said Rys. "She's earned our tolerance a hundred times over, and I will hear no insult toward her *or* the Wisp."

I said nothing, intending to let them insult or dismiss me as they saw fit. Luckily, the words of the Wolf's Bastard stopped anyone else making a comment. Tomas wanted to say something clever, but even *he* was cowed into silence.

"I'm still a duellist," I said, quietly. "Just a little wiser."

They all looked at me, as if I'd just posed them a complicated riddle.

"Mistress Brand," said Oswald Leaf, with a bow of his head. "I have heard much about you. I hope you and your friend are well." He exchanged a restrained smile with Tasha. "We, at the Folly, have also seen the touch of these Sunken Men. A cathedral of flesh was found on Big Brother. The frogs were sacrificing Jorralite Pure Ones to their dreaming god and twisting their bodies into an altar. I came here with Charlie Vane to assist any way I can."

I frowned at him. The man was young and fresh-faced, and his cheeks pinched into dimples as he spoke. He was tall for a Kneeling Wolf, but still shorter than the average Eastron.

"We are not alone in our battles," said Jonas Grief. "The Friend will sail to our aid if we need him. Worry not, Adeline. You may return to your chambers and sleep. You are clearly in need of rest and your counsel is not needed."

"Fuck off!" I replied. "You have no dominion over me. I act, as I have always done, for the Severed Hand. That I am now more aware of the threat should be a boon, not a burden."

Rys chuckled. "You have words, Adeline?"

"I do, for these are not times for arrogance. Jaxon and I have seen the enemy. We have seen it in forms you'd struggle to comprehend. We have seen it in forms both terrifying and unstoppable. And we are alive. Dismiss us, and you may die sooner than you expect."

"The teeth and gums of chaos," offered Jaxon. "They have been fed on Sea Wolf flesh. *My* flesh." He parted the front of his robe and revealed a bandaged torso. "The varn have trained them to hunger for it. When they are unleashed, they will fall upon us like starving dogs. We are not their match."

"What do you want us to do," snapped the master-at-arms. "that we are not already doing? Hundreds of Pure Ones... none of them know a thing."

I sneered at him. "Perhaps cutting off their feet is not the best way to garner information." I knew the comment would mark me as weak in their eyes, but I also knew I was right.

"Adeline," said Tomas Red Fang, his eyes narrow and aware. "I do not think you are ready to resume your duties. The same goes for you, Jaxon. There is little any of us can do until Lord Ulric returns."

I turned, showing them my back and marching from the chamber. Jaxon followed a step later and, hurrying along behind, came Tasha. I was angry and didn't trust myself to stay calm. I wouldn't challenge any of them, but I'd given them ample reason to challenge me, and I wanted to avoid such foolishness. I could still help, even if I had to do so without their consent.

"What do we do now?" asked Jaxon. "I don't feel like resting... and that's all anyone tells me to do."

"We're not resting," I replied.

"So, er, what *are* we doing?" asked Tasha, hurrying along behind us.

"We're going to find Gloom Scribe," I replied.

The staircase to the Bloody Fang's place of forgetting was narrow and steep. There was no railing, just a close wall to steady myself against. Someone with shoulders larger than mine might need to descend the stairs sideways, to stop from getting stuck. There were lights at the top and the bottom, but nothing in the steep downward tunnel. As it levelled out and we entered the first globe of torchlight, we were faced with a handful of lesser duellists, standing at intervals next to dozens of tiny cells. Small passages linked more corridors and more cells, and a low moan of pain echoed from almost every angle. Men and women were being stored here until someone thought to question them. The Pure Ones wouldn't be fed or cared for. They'd either be taken away to some unpleasant fate, or forgotten about and allowed to starve to death. It reminded me of an unpleasant recent experience.

"Mistress," said one of the duellists. "How can we assist?"

"Stand aside," I replied. "I'm here to talk to someone."

The duellist frowned and looked at his fellows. They wouldn't have been told to interfere, but they'd know of my situation and that I had no business in the dungeon.

"Excuse me," said Jaxon. "If you make Adeline Brand ask you a second time, she may be inclined to hurt you."

"Oh, yes," offered Tasha. "She gets really cross."

The duellist took a final look into my eyes and stood aside. He knew I could kill him with one hand, and, though I never would, the name of Adeline Brand was still enough to cow him.

I didn't rub it in and make him feel any worse. I just wandered away from the stairs, pausing to look into each of the tiny cells in the first row. They were narrower than the staircase, and the ceilings were barely five feet from the dusty ground. I saw bronze-skinned men and women, mostly young and badly beaten, leaning against bales of straw or slumped forwards through the bars. Some were pleading for their lives, saying that they were loyal Nissalite; others were crying in pain or grumbling about the Shackles of the Wolf. I was sure that none of them knew where they were or what fate awaited them.

"Which of these poor wretches are we looking for?" whispered Tasha.

"*He* knows," I replied, pointing at the Wisp, but not slowing my pace.

"I'm not supposed to know," said Jaxon.

"But you do," I replied.

"So, er, who are we looking for?" repeated Tasha.

"Her lover," said the Wisp. "I don't know his name, but she's been trying to convince herself that she's not in love with him for a little over a year."

I nodded at the assessment, as I walked past an unconscious Nissalite woman, curled up in her cell. "His name's Young Green Eyes. He's Mirralite."

"Complicated," offered Tasha, with an accepting smile.

Halfway down the line, I stopped. Sitting in the small cell was a man I knew. His beautiful face was puffy and bruised, but his eyes still shone. He'd suffered no further beating since I last saw him, but hate and rebellion were written all over his face. He looked up with no surprise, as if he'd heard our entrance. There was a thin smile, but nothing more.

"Adeline," he whispered. "I hope you've been ordered to kill me."

Jaxon and Tasha stood either side of me, peering into the cell. The lesser duellists had melted away, confining themselves to gossiping at the base of the stairs.

"I've not been ordered to do anything," I replied. "Things are… different now. You told me it wasn't my world and you were right. I should have died, but I was cursed to come back with what I know."

"You hear the sea," he said, with a slight nod. "I *did* warn you. For all your advantages, Sea Wolves can be fragile."

I stepped towards him and grasped the cell bars. "You're right. You *are*. But I can still save the Severed Hand. If you help me."

"What do you think I've held back? I've already been beaten and burned. You call it *questioning*. You apparently call murder *purging*."

I tightened my grip around the bars. "Yes, we're terrible people. We always have been and we always will be. We are pirates and killers and should pay for our arrogance. But if you believe every Eastron at the Severed Hand should be eaten by chaos spirits, tell me now. Or fucking help me."

24

Threatening a handful of lesser duellists was easy. Persuading the Wolf's Bastard to let me release a captive Mirralite was difficult, especially as Tasha kept quietly insisting that all the captives should be released, or at least *treated gently*.

"He's already been questioned?" asked Rys, from behind a map table in the Bloody Halls.

"He has," I replied. "Burned and cut."

"*And* beaten up," offered Tasha, eliciting a scowl from the Wolf's Bastard.

"Don't tell her not to speak," I said, drawing Rys's scowl to me. "I don't want to fall out with you."

"Nor I you," he replied. He sighed and bowed his head. "I didn't get the chance to say sorry for Arthur. He was a fine Sea Wolf, and a better duellist. And don't think I value *you* any less because of his death *or* your fear."

"I like this one," said Tasha, with a smile.

He scowled at her again. "You shouldn't like me, Mistress Strong, I'm not a very nice man. I've killed more people than you've met in your life." His eyes were still and penetrating, making the Kneeling Wolf cook avert her eyes. "So, this prisoner..."

"He can help," I said. "But I don't think hurting him will get anything other than defiance. He's not bound by the Shackles of the Wolf."

"So he's Mirralite, living in secret? And you've known this?"

"Indeed," I replied.

"If it was another time and you were another duellist, I'd probably call your name and kill you," said the Wolf's Bastard. "But I can't spare you, or a potential source of information."

"So he can be given into my care?" I prompted.

"Slow down, Addie," replied Rys. "Perhaps further questioning first. If we know he's a source of information, it's only a matter of time."

I banged my fist on the table. "Did you not listen? Have people stopped listening since I left?"

Rys remained calm, raising his eyebrows and looking at me. "Bark at me again ..." he whispered, threateningly.

Tasha coughed. "Please don't fight," she whimpered. "I'm not sure I could bear to see two more Sea Wolves fighting."

"We're not going to fight," offered the Wolf's Bastard. "Adeline just needs reminding that there are those she can't intimidate. Isn't that correct, Mistress Brand?"

He was right. I'd acted in anger to a man I needed as an ally. A man who could and would kill me if he thought it justified. "I apologize. But I *am* right. Please trust me."

"Give me the food and open the fucking cage," I barked to the lesser duellist. I now wore leather armour, with a heavy cutlass at my waist. Jaxon stood behind me, similarly dressed, and even Tasha had found a nasty-looking knife to sheath in her belt.

The duellist wanted to argue, but he wasn't confident enough to do so. He produced a large key and unlocked the cell, before hurrying away, towards the stairs and a dozen similarly cowed guards. They wouldn't have been told to comply, but Rys knew I was capable of exercising authority, with or without his name to back me up.

Tasha pulled the cell door outwards and reached in, offering her hand to Young Green Eyes. He slowly took it, showing a slight smile of appreciation, and the Pure One pulled himself to his feet. He ducked under the cell door and straightened his back. His torn and bloody clothing covered barely half his torso, and blackened burn marks were visible on his chest. The scars would soften in time, but they would never fully heal.

"Where are you from?" asked Jaxon, helping him away from the cell. "I've never really spoken to a Mirralite that I didn't subsequently kill."

Young Green Eyes kept his eyes on me as he answered. "South-east of Mirra. A fishing village on the Red Straits."

"A nice place?" asked the Wisp.

The Pure One rubbed his bruised face and stood to his full height. "A peaceful place," he replied. "We looked to the sun and the sea, barely aware of the Shackles of the Wolf."

"Sounds lovely," offered Tasha. "I'm sure you'll get to go back there."

"It's not there anymore," he replied. "It was destroyed by Sea Wolves. They salted the fields and polluted the bay, so no plants grow and no fish swim." It was said with no bitterness and little emotion, as if his wounds were not the kind that ever really healed, but stayed as a part of you forever.

Tasha's eyes fell into a puppy-dog look of sadness, and Jaxon bowed his head. I just walked away from the cell, silently angry at myself for never having asked him where he was from. Raids like that were common. Whenever Sea Wolves got bored, or when the plunder in the Inner Sea was at a low ebb, they would spend a few destructive months reminding the Pure Ones of their place.

"Where are we going?" asked Young Green Eyes, as we passed the guards and left the place of forgetting.

"We're going to get you cleaned up," replied Tasha. "A nice hot bath, and a nicer hot meal. If I can wrestle Adeline's kitchen into shape, I should be able to rustle up a spicy fish stew. The swordfish here is to die for. Nice meaty texture."

We walked through the cavernous, lower chambers of the Wolf House, past duellists and closed doors, until we emerged on the third floor, and approached my quarters. Young Green Eyes would never have been in the Wolf House, and his head kept moving from side to side, as he tried to take in the architecture and scale of the huge building.

Once inside, Tasha went to battle with my kitchen, and Jaxon helped Young Green Eyes into my bathroom. Water was pumped up from beneath the streets, and the Wisp drew a bath for the injured Pure One, before closing the door and letting him wash in peace.

"You trust him?" asked Jaxon.

"Up to a point," I replied.

He smiled at me. "It's okay to admit that you just wanted to free him, Addie. If he can help us, that's a bonus."

"Do you remember that shack on Swordfish Bay? Where we first fought the hybrid? Well, that location came from Young Green Eyes. If he knew *that*..."

"Hmm," mused Jaxon, thoughtfully. "This is almost a social experiment, you know? Can kindness beat torture?"

"Every time," offered Tasha, from the kitchen. "I'd never think to question the Sea Wolves, but torture has led you to this point, maybe kindness will lead you somewhere new."

"And what about Oswald Leaf?" the Wisp asked her. "Why's he here? He mentioned a cathedral of flesh."

Tasha balked at the term. "Yes, Lucas told me about that before we left. Hidden in caves, along the west coast. Kessalite were abducting people and boiling their bones. Some kind of worship. It was one of the reasons the Friend sent us north. We didn't find out about it through torture though. I believe it was through hiding in alleyways and eavesdropping."

The Kneeling Wolves were our closest allies. They'd stood at our side since Antonius Mud declared his allegiance during the Friendly War, but I'd never truly valued them until now. My shaken confidence had allowed me to look beyond the blunt methods of the Sea Wolves. Perhaps kindness wasn't so bad. Though hiding in alleys and eavesdropping would take some getting used to, and I'd always be better at fighting. Perhaps just toning down the torture would be a good start.

Tasha had cleaned enough pots and pans to prepare her fish stew, while Young Green Eyes washed and dressed in the next room. Jaxon had provided clothes, though I imagined they'd be too big for the slender Pure One. He was big for his people, but not as tall nor muscular as the Wisp, who, ironically, was rather small for a Sea Wolf.

"Ready!" announced Tasha, happily. "Now, Adeline, I know you're not fond of fish, but I urge you to try this." She placed a steaming casserole dish in the middle of the table and removed the lid with a flourish. A waft of sweet tomato and fruity chilli caressed my nostrils. It was a deep red colour, with flecks of green, and chunks of white fish, poking through the surface. "It's not too spicy, but this swordfish can take some nice, strong flavours. We have peppers, onions and lovely tomatoes."

"Smells delicious," said Young Green Eyes from the bathroom door. He was dressed in Sea Wolf leather, with a woollen overshirt. The clothing was slightly too big, but not terribly so, and he appeared strange in such attire. His battered body was defiantly upright, though his face was covered in red patches.

"And we have some lovely wholemeal bread to mop up the sauce," added Tasha, producing four deep bowls and taking her seat at the table.

I sat opposite the Pure One, but the awkwardness quickly degraded to nothing but loaded glances, as Tasha ladled out large portions of fish stew. She babbled about marinating the swordfish in chilli, garlic and oil, and how the sea-salt at the Severed Hand really brought out the flavour of the tomatoes.

"Tuck in," she said, handing out spoons and placing a basket of brown bread on the table. "There's plenty for seconds."

Jaxon and Tasha ate hungrily, but the Pure One and I maintained eye contact for another moment. I wanted to smile at him. In fact, I wanted to kiss him, but I did neither. I just bit my lip and looked down at my bowl. His eyes were still beautiful, even framed with swollen flesh and bruises.

"Adeline," said Tasha, as she blew on a spoonful of steaming fish. "Just try it. If you don't like it, I'll rustle up a nice omelette for you."

I chuckled, wondering why cooks weren't held in high regard at the Severed Hand. I prodded at the stew, turning over tomatoes, soft peppers and chunks of fish. It *did* smell nice, and I hesitantly ate a spoonful. The chilli was sweet and fruity, as well as hot, and the sauce was deep and rich. The swordfish was meaty and well seasoned, and I found myself tingling with warmth as I ate a second spoonful. "Arthur would be pissing himself laughing," I said, with another chuckle. "He used to wave fish under my nose until I punched him."

"He'd have loved this stew," said Jaxon, tearing off a chunk of bread and dipping it in his bowl.

"You like?" Tasha asked me, as if my response was the most important thing in the world.

I sighed in resignation. "It's fucking delicious," I replied. "The fish doesn't taste like fish. It's not slimy and there aren't any bones."

The Kneeling Wolf grinned. "Stick with me, Mistress Brand. Within a month you'll love food more than fighting."

Jaxon and I laughed. It was loud and genuine, and made me feel alive for the first time in weeks. I looked up and saw Young Green Eyes smiling, as he ate a mouthful of stew. Even the cynical Pure One could enjoy a moment of levity amongst the death and suffering. The laughter didn't stop. Tasha regaled us with a menu of delights, from a hearty mutton hotpot to a fresh salad of prawns and chilli. She knew more about food that I knew about killing, and I began to wonder which sphere of knowledge held more worth.

We ate and we laughed until the casserole dish was empty and all four of us leant back in our chairs with full bellies. Young Green Eyes had not joined in the chatter, but he'd smiled warmly at me while eating his stew, and his usually prickly demeanour had softened considerably. Perhaps even *he* saw the value of a good meal.

"Do we have to talk business now?" asked Tasha, standing to clear away the bowls.

"Unfortunately," I replied. "Just when I was starting to feel human again."

"Perhaps tomorrow then," joked the Wisp. "Tomas Red Fang can persuade the chaos spirits to wait."

"I'd rather talk now," said Young Green Eyes. "When I'm also starting to feel human. Tomorrow I'll just be a Pure One again." It was the most he'd said since we'd all sat down. "I've never shared a meal with a single Eastron, let alone three. If we wait, you'll remember who you are ... and who I am."

Jaxon lent forwards and rested his arms on the table. "My life and my mind have been changed by what I saw at the Bay of Bliss. I flatter myself that I also know Adeline's mind in this matter ... and it has also been changed. But think what you will of us and the Sea Wolves. As long as you help us."

"Well put," I added. It was the sort of thing I would have said, had my tongue not been tied.

"So," continued the Wisp, perhaps sensing my unease at questioning the Pure One. "You know about shacks with frog-hybrids living in. What else do you know? Gloom Scribe, the varn?"

"You asked about Gloom Scribe once before," he replied, looking at me. "And I gave him to you, Addie. Admittedly, you weren't burning my feet whilst asking. The shack on Swordfish Bay, I assume you didn't explore thoroughly."

I leaned in. "The hybrid needed to be taken to the Wolf House. We didn't think to."

"Underneath," said Young Green Eyes. "There are tidal caves. I went there once and didn't like what I saw." His eyes went faraway, as if fighting an unpleasant memory.

"Why did you go there?" asked Jaxon. "You must have known you were betraying the hold."

"This isn't your world," he snapped. "You just invaded." He glared at the Wisp. "There was a time when I'd have done anything to kill both of you. You destroyed my family and everything I loved. You are the fists of an arrogant, hateful giant, called the Sea Wolves, and you are my enemy." He leant back, smiling to himself. "When a varn offers an opportunity to fight back, I listen. On this particular occasion, I didn't like what I heard."

Tasha came back and resumed her seat. "So much hate," she said, with sadness. "The Jorralite on Big Brother aren't so angry."

"The Mirralite on Nibonay are," replied Young Green Eyes, again looking at me. "Don't worry, I didn't betray the hold. At least not that time."

"You're pushing it," I said, through gritted teeth.

"So beat me," he replied. "Use the one weapon you have and summon your wyrd."

"No-one's beating anyone," said Tasha. "We're co-operating. Aren't we, Adeline?"

"We are," said Jaxon, interrupting my response. "Our wickedness aside, there are caverns under that shack?"

In that moment, I wanted to hug the Wisp. He'd managed to pull things back to the present, and given me another opportunity to keep my fucking mouth shut and awkwardly glance at Young Green Eyes.

"When the tides are low, three shafts lead to dry caves," said the Pure One. "They take Mirralite *and* Nissalite down there, with promises of power and rebellion. But many leave... when they start talking about a dreaming god who will destroy the Devils of the Sea. Pure Ones agree with the Eastron on *that* point – if gods exist, they're not worthy of worship."

"But some don't leave," said Jaxon.

Young Green Eyes smiled again, a sparkle appearing in his eyes. "Does it surprise you that people hate you *that* much?"

"The Sea Wolves are practised at being both wise *and* oblivious," replied the Wisp. "But you need to show us these caves."

"Let your dinner go down first," interjected Tasha. "I find that a nice nap aids digestion."

25

The shack was unoccupied, as was the nearby brothel and most of Swordfish Bay. Duellists had swept through the Pure One mansions like an intractable tide, displacing or killing as they saw fit. The markets were empty, with fruit and vegetables left out to rot. The homes – those still with occupants – were locked up tight, filled with terrified families, thanking their nature spirits that they were still alive. South of the Pup Yards, it had all been like this. The Severed Hand had never been united, but neither had I seen it so divided. It was like two totally different cities, and I struggled to remember how peace had been maintained for so long.

"At least we don't have to hide this time," observed Jaxon.

Young Green Eyes and Tasha were both with us, wandering through the strange ghost town on the Bright Coast. It was low tide, and the rocky coast fell away from us in a sheer drop of twenty feet or more. The muddy banks we'd skulked along on our previous visit were now high terraces, well above the water and revealing dozens of small tidal caves, some half-submerged, others draped in dry seaweed.

We'd come alone. Primarily because the Wolf's Bastard didn't really understand subtlety. But also because Young Green Eyes agreed to show only us. It said something about my change of heart that I'd not argued. Jaxon had even agreed with the Pure One, that a subtle approach was best. So we came alone. Two duellists, a Mirralite and a cook.

We stopped in front of the dilapidated shack, with our backs to the sea. The roof and walls were covered in holes, far more so than when we'd first come here. Barely fit for habitation before, *now* it was little more than a pile of wood and rubble. I pushed through an open section of wall and ducked under several exposed ceiling beams. Jaxon entered through an adjacent hole, while the other two hung back.

"Why didn't we search it?" I mused.

"The frog," he replied. "Don't you remember? Arthur nearly had a panic attack. We were shaken, Addie. I suppose it was the first step on the strangest of roads."

"What threat could the Pure Ones ever truly pose to the Sea Wolves." The words sounded hollow and I was angry at how long I'd believed them. Thoroughly searching a hovel on Swordfish Bay was beneath a duellist of the Severed Hand. The idea wouldn't even have occurred to me.

We pushed inside, through broken walls and smashed furniture, to the central chamber, where we'd fought the hybrid. "What are we looking for?" I asked, surveying the debris-strewn floor and partial walls.

Young Green Eyes was a step behind us, with Tasha bringing up the rear. "The fireplace," said the Pure One.

I crouched down next to the only stone construction in the hovel, and prodded at the hearth. It was cracked down the centre, with the stone base positioned at an irregular angle. "Again, what am I looking for?"

"Excuse me," said Young Green Eyes, gently nudging me to one side. "Looks like it's not been used for a while." He braced his arms against the fireplace and pushed. It slid backwards, just an inch, revealing that the hearth was on two runners. I added my strength to his and we pushed it all the way back. Underneath, covered in dust, was a recessed hatch in the floor.

"You've been down there?" I asked.

He nodded. "It seems your raid made them find an alternative entrance to the caves. But the shaft will still be open. The tides will have seen to that."

I looked across at him. Jaxon and Tasha were behind us, and it was the closest I'd been to being alone with him since we'd opened his cell. "I'm sorry," I whispered. "For everything."

His deep green eyes softened. "I'm in love with you, Adeline. And I hate myself for it." He turned back to the hatch and brushed his hand across the wooden surface, clearing it of debris. Jaxon knelt down to help him, robbing me of any opportunity to respond. In my head, I told him that I didn't understand love and that I wanted to.

Jaxon wedged his cutlass between the wood and the stone, and pried the hatch outwards. A sharp, salty smell rose from the opening and the slosh of the ocean became louder. The Wisp looked at me, smiled, and swung his legs around. His foot met the top rung of a ladder, and he began to climb down. Young Green Eyes followed, and they soon disappeared below. Tasha came to sit next to me, crossing her legs on the dusty floor.

"I don't mean to pry," began the Kneeling Wolf, "but there's nothing wrong with what you're feeling. Why run from it?"

"Get down the hatch," I replied, angry that my emotions were so transparent.

She nodded her head and obeyed, slowly climbing down the ladder, towards the sound of rushing water. I followed after a moment of quietly grumbling to myself. The ladder was fixed to the base of a damp, rocky tunnel, with one end open to the ocean, and the other dropping away into darkness. I landed in a thin film of stagnant water and seaweed, set to be swept away by the tides, and followed Young Green Eyes down the tunnel. Jaxon summoned a globe of wyrd into the palm of his hand, illuminating the tunnel, and revealing a walkway of wooden planks, just above the water.

"It leads inland," said the Pure One. "There's another ladder and a series of caves. A little way ahead."

"Then that's where we're going," I replied.

"Slow down," said Jaxon. "There must be other ways in and out. How many people could we find down here?"

"I didn't see the whole complex," said Young Green Eyes. "Just a big central chamber. A dozen varn, maybe a handful of Mirralite. With your purges, there could be a lot more. Not devotees, just people trying to hide."

"Hybrids?" I asked.

"I didn't know what those were until you told me," he replied.

"So any one of them could be disguised as Mirralite," said the Wisp. "We need more warriors. It doesn't serve the hold if we die down here."

"My thoughts exactly," agreed Tasha, smiling nervously. "I might be able to help." She looked at Young Green Eyes. "In a way that won't upset anyone."

"Explain," I prompted.

"Well, a dozen Sea Wolf duellists would stomp down here like a battering ram against a paper door." She looked down, as if she felt she might cause offence. "But a dozen Kneeling Wolf duellists ... well, *we* walk more softly." She produced a small wooden whistle and put it against her lips. "One blow and a spirit tells Oswald Leaf that we need him."

"That's a spirit-whistle," said Jaxon. "He's beyond the glass?"

"No, but the rat spirit following us is," she replied. "Never hurts to have a spirit watching over you. He had to eat his way through a few chaos spirits though."

"You told Oswald Leaf we were coming here?" I asked, finding it strange that I wasn't angry.

"Not *here*," she replied. "But I told him we might need help."

I grinned and gave her a hug. "We should value cooks far more highly. Blow the whistle. When they arrive, we'll move ahead."

•

The thin film of water became a steady slosh as we waited. Beyond the first wooden walkway was a dry platform, leading to the next ladder, and the four of us rested against the stone, near the hatch, letting Tasha whisper our options for dinner. A meticulously described fish pie was her favourite, and she was halfway through the description of her apparently world-famous crispy pork belly, when we heard the hatch open.

Jaxon and I quietly jumped from the platform and drew our blades. Our feet were underwater and we hugged the wall either side of the ladder.

"I believe I'm expected," said a voice from above.

"Show yourself," I replied. "And keep quiet."

The folds of a long overcoat emerged in the shack above, and a dimpled face peered down at me. It was Oswald Leaf.

"It's a shame you didn't arrive earlier," said the Kneeling Wolf. "Charlie Vane likes skulking around in tunnels. He'd have enjoyed this. May I come down?"

"You may," I replied. "How many warriors did you bring?"

He climbed down the ladder, revealing a set of bladed knuckle-dusters hanging at his belt. "A dozen," he replied. "My father insists on a guard whenever I leave the Folly. They're holding position in the shack and will follow behind us. Everyone else was on the *Lucretia*."

"So, what do they call you?" I asked. "The Second Friend?"

"Ozzie," he replied. "And you're Adeline. Any nickname?"

I shook my head.

"Well, we'll have to find you one," he said with a smile, before gliding through the water to give Tasha a hug. "Still no sign of Lucas or Harriet, but I'm sure they'll appear over the hill any day now. Just in time for fish."

"We should move," I said, gently. "This is Young Green Eyes, he's our ... guide."

"A pleasure," said Ozzie Leaf. "Lead the way."

We moved further down the tunnel, as a gang of well-armed Kneeling Wolves descended the ladder, their tanned, canvas clothing virtually disappearing into the darkness. They followed at a distance, as we slowed to a crawl, keeping our steps light and our mouths shut. Jaxon had closed his hand around the globe of light and it was now just a dull glow, but enough to reveal another ladder at the end of an upward-sloping tunnel. More passageways went left and right, above the waterline and snaking away under the hold.

Young Green Eyes placed a finger to his mouth and pointed upwards.

Jaxon leaned in to me and whispered, "Lots of spirits here. And men too." His eyes twitched and his breathing had quickened. "Teeth and gums."

"Not in the realm of form," I replied, putting a hand on his shoulder. "Not yet. Not if we stop them."

He gulped and his teeth began to chatter. "I trust you," he replied. "Just not sure I trust myself. You may need me … and I may fail you."

"No," I stated. "No, you won't. Because you're all I've got now. And I'm all you've got."

I began to climb the ladder, motioning for the Wisp to follow. Tasha came next, with Young Green Eyes and Oswald Leaf at the rear. I worried for my friend, but didn't want to admit it, especially not to him. He'd played the part of a duellist, keeping his fear in check, but I knew he was still fragile. I was gambling that, if *I* pretended to be confident, it would give him some strength. Unless of course he could tell I was shitting myself.

The ladder ended in another recessed hatch. This one showed signs of recent use and I could see flickers of light at its edges. I paused and tried to filter out the deep rumble of the sea. After a moment, I could hear a voice. Then two more. I let a tiny ripple of wyrd into my arms and gently pushed the hatch open. Just a crack, but enough to send a beam of light down the stairs. The voices continued, but I could now see to who they belonged. Three Pure Ones, each holding a short spear, reclined against a cave wall. There were two wooden doors either side of them, leading further into the caves, and they seemed relaxed.

I held up three fingers to those below and narrowed my eyes at Jaxon, indicating they were likely guards. I paused, to make sure there was no-one else in the small cave, then sprang upwards, with the Wisp barely a step behind me. It was strange to hold my cutlass again. And stranger still to attack with it. But the wyrd in my limbs and the fear on the Pure Ones' faces drove me forwards. Before they could stand I'd punched one unconscious with the basket-hilt of my blade. As one tried to heft his spear, I rammed his head into the wall with my off-hand. The third was kicked in the face by Jaxon, and all three were silent within four seconds.

The others emerged from the hatch, as Jaxon and I sat the three Pure Ones back against the cave wall. We'd been quick and quiet, though a clatter or two may have travelled to the adjacent chambers. Oswald Leaf darted to the left-hand door, drawing his bladed knuckle-dusters and hugging the wall. Tasha and Young Green Eyes were slower to react, and the Pure One stayed still, looking at the unconscious bodies. Below, a dozen more Kneeling Wolves waited.

The doors had no locks, and the frames were only partially fixed to the cave walls. A solid kick would dislodge them, but I elected to continue with stealth. I grasped the wooden handle and pulled it ajar. The cave beyond was large, with a low ceiling and torches placed around the irregular walls. Clustered in small groups across the bare floor were Pure Ones, perhaps a hundred, though mostly the old and the very young. They had small cook-fires and makeshift beds, and there was little chatter. Oswald Leaf had opened the other door, and I could see they led to the same room. There were four or five other entrances to the large cave, some with doors, others just cave openings. It appeared to be a large complex.

“I count two spears,” said Jaxon, appearing over my shoulder. “By the opposite door. Most of these are just hiding from the duellists above. They’re not our quarry.”

“We can’t get past them quietly,” I replied. “And there’s no way around.”

“Short order,” whispered Oswald Leaf, from the other door. “We can’t go around, so let’s go through as quickly as possible. These Pure Ones don’t want to fight, so we use that. Just run past them.”

“It has merits,” agreed the Wisp. “If there’s a varn in here, he’s not in that room. Rushing the guards at the door will put them on the back foot.”

“Okay, get the Kneeling Wolves up here,” I ordered, eliciting a nod from Oswald. He hopped back to the hatch and signalled to his men. Within a few seconds they’d scuttled up the ladder to join us in the small cave. They wore no armour, but wielded a variety of small blades, from hand-axes to sickles, and everything in between. They were silent, but looked ready to fight, with a slight surge of wyrd in each pair of eyes.

“We move quickly,” I whispered. “Through the cave and onwards. There are two guards by one of the doors – that’s where we’re going. We’re looking for a varn or two who’ve been binding spirits, let’s find them before they have a chance to bind anymore.”

We moved quickly. Jaxon opened the left door and I opened the right. Behind us, a small force of warriors flooded into the cave, with a cook and a Pure One bringing up the rear. The cowering masses jumped, screamed, gathered up their children in their arms, and prayed to their nature spirits that their end, when it came, would be quick. I ran around a cluster of terrified women, standing on an elderly Pure One's skirt as I did so. The Kneeling Wolves behind me fanned out, darting through the cave and homing in on the one guarded door.

"Invaders!" screamed one of two spear-wielders, banging on the door with his fist. I charged him, wrapping my arms around his waist and tackling him into the stone wall. I heard breath leave his body and felt several of his ribs break.

Jaxon punched the other one into unconsciousness, and a split-second later, Oswald Leaf dropped his shoulder into the door. A nimbus of wyrd marked the contact point and he sent the door into splinters. Beyond, a young Pure One was running away from the door, glancing back over his shoulder with terror.

"Stop him," I ordered.

I heard the whistle of a bolas from behind, and a Kneeling Wolf threw at the fleeing man's legs. The weapon was a long length of rope, between two round weights, and it entangled the man's ankles, sending him tumbling forwards, to hit his head on the tunnel floor.

"Good throw," said Jaxon, moving into the tunnel.

The Kneeling Wolf just nodded professionally.

"And these people?" asked Young Green Eyes, moving around the last few clusters of terrified Pure Ones. His eyes were moist, and he hesitated, wanting to reach for them.

"We're moving on," I replied, curtly, motioning for the others to follow.

We passed the unconscious Pure One, with Jaxon and I in the lead. The tunnel forked and we stopped. To the left was another door, to the right another ladder.

"Two men hold position at the ladder," I whispered behind me. "We go for the door."

Our advantage of speed and surprise would disappear quickly, but I was back in my element and felt a rumble of confidence return.

"Power ahead," mumbled Jaxon. "Be cautious."

"If we're tested again," I replied, in a whisper, "we'll pass. You and I."

"Once more for the Severed Hand," he said, with a weak smile.

We approached the door. It was more solid than the others, with metal rivets and frame, and a conspicuous keyhole. Ozzie and his men hugged the walls of the tunnel behind us, with two skulking at the bottom of the nearby ladder. I tried the door handle. It was locked. I signalled everyone else to make ready and summoned wyrd into my limbs, feeling strength and speed infuse my body. Jaxon did the same, and each one of the Kneeling Wolves was now a small concentration of wyrd, pulsing with power. With a kick and a flash of energy I sent the door flying off its hinges, and we rushed in, half going left, half going right.

It was a circular chamber with a low, domed ceiling. In the centre, prostrate around a still pool of sea water, were robed Pure Ones. Around them were two dozen warriors, turning towards us in surprise and lowering long-spears. There were other doors, but my vision was focused on the robed figures. I felt fear again. Perhaps there were hybrids amongst them. Creatures who were a match for three Sea

Wolves. My palms began to sweat, but my wyrd remained strong.

"You have no place here, Invaders," intoned the robed figures. "*Here* we listen to the sea." I took them to be varn.

"I've not killed anyone today," I announced. "I've been careful not to ... not until I know who the enemy is. But you *will* surrender or die!"

To my left, I could see Jaxon shaking. His hands flexed open and closed, and his eyes twitched. There was power here, and I did not need his wyrd sight to see it.

"We are one of many," said one of the varn. "Too many for you to stop. We summon the sea to wipe your taint from the Lodge of the Rock. Gloom Scribe has willed it." He stood up, leaving his fellows kneeling over a large pool of water, rippling over the edges of a circular hole in the middle of the cave. "When the void is full, the glass breaks."

I balked at the implication, but tried to keep my focus on what needed to be done. There were no signs of surrender and most of the varn had yet to stand. Any number of them could be hybrids, and any number of things could emerge from the pool of water. Paranoia crept up the back of my neck, and my hands began to shake. We'd surprised them, yet I felt as if *we* were the ones in danger.

"Not like this!" announced Young Green Eyes, standing by the door with Tasha. "We can't beat the Invaders like this."

"You have yet to hear the sea," replied the varn, his voice rising into a shriek.

I hesitated. I should have ordered an attack, or at least a command to subdue them, but I couldn't find my voice ... or my courage. Jaxon was worse. He could hear the chaos spirits bulging beyond the glass. I could almost hear them myself, but to the Wisp they would be deafening. Two duellists of the Severed Hand, unable to attack their enemies. What good were we if we could not fight for the hold?

"Forward for the Eastron!" roared Oswald Leaf, drawing his bladed knuckle-dusters and bounding forwards. The Kneeling Wolves joined him, and they attacked the spearmen with speed, wyrd and ferocity. They stayed low to the ground, thrusting upwards with knives, hand-axes and sickles. One even used a barbed whip. They fought in close, harassing the Pure Ones and nullifying their spears. Ozzie tackled the standing varn, using his bladed hands to pin the man's throat to the ground. Wyrd surged up his arms and I was shocked by his power. He had the might of a duellist in the body of a lesser Eastron. Kneeling Wolves did not usually have such powerful wyrd. But he *was* the Friend's son.

Perhaps it was shame that made me act, or the fact that none of the varn had twisted into grotesque hybrid forms. Either way, my hands stopped shaking and I advanced to join the Kneeling Wolves in battle.

With a casual swing of my cutlass, I killed a Pure One, slicing across his chest. It was so easy. One movement flowed into another, and men died with minimal effort. It was as if nothing had changed. I was Adeline Brand, duellist of the Severed Hand, and these were lesser men. Then I glanced across at the Wisp. His was on his knees, with his hands against his temples and his face twisted into a scream of terror. Tasha was trying to help him up, but he shook her off and lay prostate on the ground.

I'd turned away from the Pure Ones and dropped my arms, paying for it with a spear thrust to the stomach. I spun away and it deflected downwards off my leather armour, slicing a chunk of flesh from my side. I dropped to one knee and killed the man with an upward thrust. Around me, the Kneeling Wolves were finishing off the spearmen, and closing in to surround the varn.

"Adeline," said Tasha, from across the chamber. "We need your help."

I burned my wounded side with a surge of wyrd and turned back to Jaxon. He was convulsing on the floor, with white drool frothing from his mouth. Young Green Eyes had joined Tasha in trying to control the Wisp, but the Kneeling Wolf had little wyrd and the Pure One had none. He thrashed and bucked, as vile gurgling belched forth from his throat.

Then the varn stood, as if they'd been compelled to continue their rituals until the last possible moment. That moment came when Oswald Leaf sliced the leader's throat with the curved blades on his knuckle-dusters.

"You are outmatched," said the Friend's son. "Surrender."

The death of their leader caused the remaining varn to shriek and drop to the floor, as blood began to seep from their mouths, eyes and ears. It was as if the killing blow on one varn had somehow struck all of them at once.

"That was unexpected," said Oswald Leaf, his hands dropping to his sides, as if the wind had suddenly been taken from his sails.

"Adeline!" snapped Tasha.

I ran back to Jaxon, leaving the Kneeling Wolves to stand around the pool of water, wearing a variety of confused looks on their faces.

Back at the door, Young Green Eyes lay across the Wisp, trying to stop him from convulsing. Tasha had placed the hilt of her knife in his mouth and was trying to clear the froth from his face. I dropped my cutlass and pushed Young Green Eyes away. Straddling the Wisp, I held his shoulders to the cave floor and tried to discern any hint of sanity in his eyes. All I saw was chaos. Something was happening to him. I could feel the glass buckling around him, as something tried to press through from the void.

"A spirit is trying to possess him," I announced, just as wyrd flowed through his torso and he flung me aside.

The Wisp stood, blazing green wyrd shining in his eyes, and his mouth twisted to obscene proportions. The teeth and gums of chaos. Somehow a chaos spirit had possessed Jaxon Ice, a duellist of the Severed Hand. He battered Young Green Eyes into the wall and a jolt of wyrd turned Tasha into a rag doll. Then he hissed at me through his distended jaw. I could see the outline of the spirit, superimposed upon my friend. One of the creatures that had killed my brother, with its blubbery body and gnashing mouth.

"Oswald... eyes up," I shouted, retrieving my blade and backing away from the possessed Sea Wolf.

The Kneeling Wolves all turned from the scattered dead bodies and their eyes went wide in surprise. The first thing they saw was the Wisp advancing on me. The spirit was using every ounce of Jaxon's wyrd, turning him into a churning shape of crackling energy. He was using more than I would have needed to commit suicide in the Lodge of Dagon. The spirit was going to kill him. He had no weapon, but his arms flashed out, sending tentacles of barbed energy towards me. I ducked, and rolled to the side, looking for an opening. Could I subdue him? Would the spirit leave if Jaxon was rendered unconscious?

"What do we do?" asked Ozzie Leaf, directing his men to surround the possessed Sea Wolf.

"Hold!" I commanded, pressing more wyrd into my wounded side and nullifying any handicap.

The Wisp attacked again. This time, he leaped from the rocky floor and spread his glowing arms wide in mid-air, attempting to envelop me. I fought the impulse to attack and dove under him, just as he landed, rolling back to my feet behind him. I grunted and took a chance, leaping forwards and wrapping an arm around his neck, securing him in a tight choke. If he still needed to breathe, I'd put him out in a matter of seconds. If not, I may have been fucked.

I noticed Young Green Eyes, slumped against the wall, and Tasha, motionless on the floor. Either could have been dead, but I gritted my teeth and focused on keeping Jaxon alive. The wyrd, pulsing from his body, burned my arms and face, but I didn't let go. The chaos spirit, writhing within him, screamed in my head. I felt its primal hatred and its desire to consume. Its kind had been fed Jaxon's flesh, and it was hungry. It was so very hungry.

I heard him splutter. Underneath the ferocious intent, the voracious appetite and the combustible wyrd, it was a human body that needed to breathe. I tightened my arms around his neck, ignoring the burned skin on my forearms and cheeks. I arched my back and hefted him upwards. "Jaxon, you're all I've got!"

"That wyrd is going to detonate," warned Oswald Leaf. "Adeline, back away."

His body went limp, but the surge of wyrd remained. I pulled my arms away, wincing at the scarred flesh, and let his body fall to the ground. My friend was merely unconscious, but the chaos spirit hadn't left him, nor had it stopped using his wyrd. I stood over him, the light surrounding his body getting brighter and brighter. As the light became a blinding curtain of blue energy, I leapt backwards.

Jaxon Ice, called the Wisp, duellist of the Severed Hand, died in an explosion of his own wyrd. His power had always been subtle and precise. He'd always known things I could never know, and been wiser than I could ever be. He was my friend and I had to watch him die.

The Friendly War lasted sixteen years
  The Wolves fought the Dark Brethren to a standstill
Those who sail and those who kneel were united
  The Year of Slaughter, when the Bloody Fang burned the Open Hand
The Emerald Massacre, where the Friend declared his allegiance
  The Battle of Moon Rock, where fell Piedro Cyclone.

The Wolves killed the Brethren until the Winterlords spoke
  A new Always King, Christophe Dawn Claw, the Shining Sword
In a two-hour void duel, he killed Lucio Eclipse, and the war was ended
  Peace reigned for a time.

Written on the highest level of the Wolf House

PART NINE

Duncan Greenfire on Nowhere

26

Twist was angry, but quiet, and I felt as if we were waiting for something. I could feel my wyrd pulsing, but not flaring too high. The spirit-masters aboard the four warships allowed every Sea Wolf to feel their wyrd, and I was no exception. I *was* a Sea Wolf, but fighting to the death held no appeal. Wisdom was hard won, and I felt as if I'd fought a dozen battles to realize the horse-shit of my own people. The last battle had been seeing the Sunken God crush a hundred Eastron beneath his colossal foot.

But Lord Ulric Blood hadn't seen that, and he didn't answer the Stranger's question. Talk or fight? It was a simple question, with a simple answer, made complicated only by the third void legion, who'd suddenly appeared on the coast of Nowhere. Twist let me stand unaided, and I saw the spectacle as a vibrant painting, depicting the military might of the Sea Wolves and the Dark Brethren. Eight hundred pirates and killers, facing down five thousand void legionnaires.

"Loco, bring the boy," said Marius Cyclone, called the Stranger, elder of the Dark Harbour. "Perhaps Lord Ulric will answer if we're face to face."

"He'll probably fight," I stated, as Loco led me from the cliffs.

The Stranger paused, looking down at me. The blue tattoo, creeping from under his leather collar, was clearer, and I saw the design of a rampant horse. He didn't say anything, just looked at me through open, brown eyes, his expression neutral, but fierce.

"Are you trying to intimidate me?" I asked. "Because I don't think that will work anymore. Don't kill them... I wouldn't like it."

His eyes narrowed, but he stayed silent. From his balled fist, a globe of wyrd pulsed, elongated, and hardened. He held his other hand out, and a bastard sword appeared out of nowhere. Marius Cyclone stroked a hand along the blade and sheathed it across his back. He didn't smile, but I sensed that he wanted to. He just walked off, leading the way down to the beach.

"Marius," grunted the First Fang, by way of greeting.

"Ulric," responded the Stranger.

They stood, facing each other, close enough for either to attack if they wished. Neither of them did. The Brethren were in columns, facing their opponents with shields and spears. The Sea Wolves were in a mob, coiled and ready to die. Lord Ulric stood in the centre, his eyes down-cast and his fists clenched. Behind him, Ingrid Raider and Siggy Blackeye scowled their way forwards, leaving the swaggering form of Charlie Vane at the rear. Weathervane Will's father had his whip coiled over his shoulders, and an unfocused grin on his face.

Ulric registered my presence, but was preoccupied with Inigo Night Walker. The First Fang did not appear impressed with the commander of the third void legion, and thanks to me, he knew Inigo had killed the Second Fang. He sneered as he sized him up, judging his stature and weaponry to be insignificant, like an alpha wolf looking down at a young challenger. "You didn't kill him in a fair fight then?" mused Lord Ulric. "Tell me, was he on his knees? Did you execute him?"

"Address *me*," said Marius Cyclone. "I have claimed the island of Nowhere. Vengeance for your son will have to wait."

"And the Grim Wolf?" countered Ulric, not turning his gaze from Inigo. "Where does *he* skulk?"

"Xavyer Ice and I have come to an accord. You will submit and sit with us in peace. I want no more of your people to die." He stepped to his left, blocking the First Fang's view of Inigo. "I have a story to tell you, Lord Ulric. You *will* listen, for it is all that matters. You and I can save the Sea Wolves, the Winterlords, the Dark Brethren, even the Kneeling Wolves."

The Sea Wolf elder grimaced and bowed his head, nodding angrily. "You shouldn't have stood in front of him, Cyclone," he snarled, flexing his huge shoulders and striding forwards. There was nothing but rage in his eyes, as if he'd barely heard what was said to him. He suddenly pulsed with wyrd, ignoring the army before him, and lunging at Inigo Night Walker.

Even the Stranger, standing between the two men, appeared startled by Lord Ulric's sudden ferocity. Loco dragged me backwards, as the First Fang struck, sending a thunderous right-hook at Marius' jaw. The Dark Brethren didn't fall, but he staggered enough to expose Inigo. Ulric barrelled past the Stranger and tackled the commander of the third void legion, using superior size and strength to drag him to the ground. He didn't even draw his twin blades, instead relying on his fists. It was a bizarre scene. Two men wrestled on rugged ground, between massed warriors. One man was huge and snarling, the other lithe and concentrated.

Marius Cyclone waved an arm at his warriors, signalling them forwards, though his throat was snared by Charlie Vane's whip. Ingrid Raider and Siggy Blackeye both drew heavy cutlasses and stood ready, and the massed Sea Wolves roared in defiance. I found myself musing upon their arrogance. Or was it just foolishness? They couldn't win and they were all going to die. They'd tell themselves that they fought for honour, that they were Sea Wolves of the Severed Hand, the finest warriors in the Kingdom of the Four Claws, and their wyrd alone would see them victorious. I didn't know if I'd *ever* really believed it myself, but I certainly didn't now. Killing warriors of Ice was one thing, but I'd seen them squashed like ants, swept aside by a creature of true power, and I believed what I'd seen.

"Advance!" choked Marius, struggling with the whip around his throat.

"I choose to fight!" boomed Lord Ulric, between fierce blows to Inigo Night Walker's face.

The third void legion advanced in a single line, shields snapping together and spears levelled, whereas the Sea Wolves broke into loose formation and simply ran at the enemy, the sound of their leather and steel armour, and heavy cutlasses, lost amidst shouting. The men were mostly bearded, the women mostly tattooed, or wearing red face-paint. They showed prodigious wyrd, but no fear. Eight hundred Sea Wolves, with a few Kneeling Wolves, charging five thousand Dark Brethren, with more than a few warriors of Ice in reserve.

I stood off-centre, with Loco's forearm pressed into my throat, and Twist insisting I watch every movement. I occupied a rapidly shrinking space. I saw Marius Cyclone coil his arm into the whip and fling Charlie Vane aside. I saw the two forces close, and I saw Ulric Blood pummel Inigo Night Walker to death. The Brethren's skull had been split open by repeated blows, until only a pulpy, red mask remained. The man who'd killed the Second Fang, and kept me captive, was helpless as he died, his stiff formality and military bearing crushed as easily as his head. Ulric howled with anger and cried with pain, appearing as little more than a frenzied madman. The death of their commander, more than the threat of the Sea Wolves, drove the Dark Brethren forwards. They were more skilled than Blade Smile's warriors had been, and far more disciplined.

Looking to my left, I saw an impenetrable line of shields and spears; to my right was an irregular mob of killers. The two groups bore down on me like the closing of a vice, but I found myself interested, rather than afraid. Twist was interested too, giving me subtle nudges in the leg, as if the spirit wondered what would happen next. He didn't fling me aside, or demand that I run away. If anything, he wasn't certain that the conflict was actually happening at all, or perhaps he was just grateful that we were not being forced to view any more primal destruction. Mortals killing mortals was trivial compared to the truth of the world. The truth of what actually existed in this realm of form, hidden between dreams and reality, waiting for its time. Again, I wished I could talk to my pain spirit, perhaps ask him what we should do, or whether we were still totally sane.

As the two forces clashed, I found myself enveloped in a circle of steel and blood. No-one attacked me, but everyone attacked everyone else. Sea Wolves vaulted over rectangular shields, flailing with their wyrd and their cutlasses. Void legionnaires drove their spears into flesh, attacking in a persistent rhythm, and advancing. Ulric Blood was a focus of attention, as was Marius Cyclone. Both sides wanted to kill the opposing elder above all things, and their efforts focused on the central ground, where lay the bloodied corpse of Inigo Night Walker.

I wasn't hurt, or barrelled to the ground. The battle happened around me, staying out of arm's reach. I occupied a small circle of pebbles and sand, across which no blade was swung. For a moment I smiled, thinking everything was a dream. The death and destruction was played out in dull shades of black and grey, with every actor moving, killing, and dying in slow motion. None of it touched me. None of the warriors even looked at me. My smile turned to a frown, as I saw the involuntary nimbus of wyrd I'd summoned.

I looked at my arms. I was glowing a subtle blue from every inch of my body, and I could feel tiny thorns caressing my face and hands. I hadn't pushed it outwards on purpose, but I'd somehow removed myself from danger, using my wyrd to stay isolated. I looked upon the battle from another place, and I suddenly felt sad.

The Sea Wolves were losing, but their ferocity, and disregard for their own lives, gave a false impression of their might. They fought as individuals, using their wyrd to kill the enemy any way they could. I saw Siggy Blackeye tear out a legionnaire's throat with her teeth, and Taymund Grief repeatedly head-butt another until both their faces were covered in blood. I saw it all through a lens of sadness, that gradually turned to anger.

The Stranger flickered from place to place, killing as he desired, before holding position and allowing his warriors to advance past him. The First Fang described an arc of death with his twin blades, cleaving shields and heads, and creating a bulge in the legion's line. But none of it really mattered. The Sea Wolves couldn't win. They were my people and they were all going to die.

"I want them to stop fighting," I whispered to Twist. "I really want them to stop fighting... and stop dying." My hands started to shake. "Why won't they stop fighting? Why won't they surrender? They need to know of the Sunken City, they need to know of the Sunken God."

A few feet away, Taymund Grief received a spear thrust to the face, sending a slow-motion spray of blood across my field of vision. The tip emerged through the back of his head, and was withdrawn, sending his twitching body to the ground. Through my shield of wyrd, the blood appeared black, and Taymund hit the ground like a limp fish.

Greenfire must honour us.

"Please," I cried. "Stop fighting." No-one heard me, and people kept dying. Through sheer weight of numbers the void legionnaires pushed forwards, marching over piles of dead Sea Wolves, and my small, isolated world was enveloped by thousands of Dark Brethren.

Greenfire must let his wyrd shine.

"Twist, help me," I muttered. "They have to stop fighting." The pain spirit scurried around my leg, causing little pain, but sharing my distress. "I don't know what to do. Help me. Please."

Our control was minimal. We could keep our wyrd restrained, or we could unleash it. We decided to unleash it. "Stop fighting," I shrieked. "Now!"

My shield of wyrd pulsed, flaring in and out, like a crackling bonfire of pale blue. It jumped around me, dancing in the air and growing in size. Tiny twigs and thorns wove themselves into the nimbus, before it erupted outwards as a globe of energy. The battle slowed down even further, though the nearby void legionnaires now registered my presence. They pointed, and spoke in alarm, though their mouths moved too slowly for me to make out what they were saying. I saw Loco Death Spell, his mouth formed into a shout as he tried to reach me, but he couldn't penetrate the expanding globe of wyrd. As his arm reached through, I saw his fingertips smoulder and burn, then the skin of his arm peel backwards and the bones disintegrate. As my expanding wyrd flowed over the young void legionnaire, his armour was reduced to rusted flakes, and his skin fell into a blackened mess.

"Loco," I whimpered, wishing I could undo what I'd done. The young man had been my guardian for weeks, and though we'd not bonded, I found myself upset that I'd caused his death... again without meaning to. I'd torn him apart, from his armour, down to his bones, until nothing remained but red and black mist. But he was just one of many.

People started to run, and I realized they were running from me. The Sea Wolves were lost amidst a forest of black-armoured void legionnaires, most of whom were caught by a violent shockwave, pulsing away from me. I screamed and grabbed my head, half in anguish, half in pain. I couldn't look, for fear of what I'd see, but neither could I stop. I kept seeing the Sunken God behind my eyes, towering over the island of Nowhere, and stepping on Eastron as if they were ants.

I used all the wyrd I had. I used too much, and I felt my mind break.

My vision was foggy. My head was throbbing. My body was numb. I was lying down, with two shadowy figures standing over me. It was night-time ... no, it was still day, but I was inside somewhere. I tried to blink, but my eyes wouldn't co-operate. I tried to move, but my muscles wouldn't work. Everything was grey and glaring, with no fine detail or texture.

"Is he alive?" asked one of the figures.

"Still breathing," replied the other. "But unresponsive." A hand was waved in front of my face. "He's been staring for hours. Just ... staring. I've been talking to him, but ... nothing."

The first figure knelt down next to me. My head was jostled to the side as if he'd slapped my face, but I felt nothing. "Do you think he knows how many people he killed?"

"I'm not sure he knows anything anymore," was the response.

I shouted internally. *How many? How many people did I kill?*

"But he's known pain," continued the second man. "It may have been all he's *ever* known. The pain's keeping him alive."

He was right. Twist was encircling my mind, like a stalking animal, prowling around his wounded cub. He trusted no-one and nothing, but wouldn't let us die. *He* didn't know how many people we'd killed either. The pain spirit couldn't comprehend such things. We wanted them to stop fighting, so we made them stop fighting.

"If he'd been born a Dark Brethren, he'd have been trained as a wyrd-master. The fucking Sea Wolves cause me to be weary. So powerful, but so very primitive. They've ruined this boy. I would wager that, even now, he just wants to be accepted as one of them."

The man stood from my side, and I saw the shape of a large sword, slung across his back. It was the Stranger. He'd survived the eruption of my wyrd, and not yet thought to execute me. What was he waiting for? I couldn't be any good to them like *this*, and I was guilty of killing...I didn't know how many of the third void legion. I knew I'd killed Sea Wolves too, but tried not to think about it. If I thought about it, I'd have to consider that I might have killed the First Fang.

"It's time," said Marius Cyclone, putting his hand on the shoulder of the other man. The Stranger was much taller, and I realized he was talking to Ten Cuts, the speaker of the Mirralite and the pale man's closest ally. "We need to take him *now*, before the pain stops keeping him alive."

I was in a tent with a coned roof, and two more figures entered. They picked me up, though I couldn't feel their hands. My head swam, as I was thrown over someone's shoulder. I felt like I was falling into water, with no control over my limbs. Everything was black and white, and crackling at the edges. Outside the tent was an endless sea of shifting grey shapes. The sky, the ground, the cliffs, the sea, it was all monochrome.

"Back to the Maelstrom, my lord Marius?" asked the man who held me.

"Indeed," replied the Stranger. "As quickly as we can. This whole place stinks of death."

"In the years not yet lived," offered Ten Cuts, "this place will be called Duncan's Fall, and will be sung about in mournful songs."

"We need to get his body to the doorway," stated Marius Cyclone. "Hurry."

I was falling away, as if my mind was giving up. Twist was shaking me, but I couldn't cling to consciousness. I couldn't feel my body, so I couldn't feel the pain. I wondered if this was death, madness, or some new part of my journey. My eyes closed on the grey landscape, and I lost all sensation. But I wasn't dead. Slowly, like waking from the deepest sleep, my senses were reordered. I rose above myself, squeezing out of my body, until I was unfettered by the realm of form. I felt the warm caress of soft fur, and I heard a distant howl.

Pinpoints of sensation returned, though everything was vague and hard to discern. I felt as if I was moving, maybe even flying, but without a physical form it was impossible to tell. All I could be certain of was that whatever was left of me was clinging to something. Something large, and something benevolent. I heard another howl, this time low and sorrowful. It was the Old Bitch of the Sea, and she carried me above my body, into the void sky, and towards the Maelstrom.

I couldn't see the huge, blue wolf, but I could feel her. As we soared away from the realm of form, the totem of the Sea Wolves looked back, and showed me what she saw. There was a circle, visible beneath us. It nestled between cliffs, set back from the shimmering water of the Red Straits. In the centre, rocks and sand had been churned into a crater, with rings of red and black dust piled around it. Beyond the dust were larger rings of piled bodies, broken into arms, legs, heads and twisted metal. Further outwards, the circles were less distinct and flickered, as if fires were burning all around the circumference of the circle. How many people had I killed? More than I could count.

27

In my dreams I saw the teeth and gums of chaos. Writhing amoebas of pulpy flesh and gnashing teeth. They fell from the Dreaming God like parasites, consuming everything in their path. There was an alien intelligence about them, a primal drive that didn't understand light and dark, up and down, left and right, or any rational concept. They descended upon me like an impenetrable cloud of chaos.

I was standing at the Severed Hand, looking up at the Wolf House, with wave upon wave of chaos spirits rushing towards me. Then a mantle of thorns descended, as an angry pain spirit rushed to my defence. The chaos spawn struck barbed and tangled brambles, and were cut to pieces by a thousand tiny thorns. Twist was a fearsome opponent, able to protect me from all angles at once. Not only that, the pain spirit's resolve was shielding my mind, angry that madness was trying to consume me.

"Wake up, Duncan," said a distant voice. "You are once again whole."

I opened my eyes and saw grey stone. I was back in the small stone room, stretched out on a soft couch. My skin was clammy and my eyes itched, though the air was fresh as a summer field, and the hoppy smell of ale filled my nostrils. I sat up and patted my legs and arms, reassuring myself that I was whole. I absently fiddled with the thorn clinch, making sure Twist was okay. The spirit hugged my leg, warming me with familiar pain.

"It's good you are becoming friends," said the pale man, though only his voice was present. "You and your spirit have seen the same things. It's afraid, probably more so than you."

I tried to speak, but my mouth was dry and my throat scratchy. I swung my legs from the couch and coughed, hacking up a globule of phlegm. "How?" I spluttered. "How did I get here?"

"Your mind was delivered by a spectral wolf," he replied. "Your body by Marius Cyclone. It took effort to put you back together. For all practical reality, you killed yourself."

I took a deep breath, holding my head in my hands. "How many Sea Wolves did I kill?" I whispered.

"I don't know *who* you killed, or how many," replied the pale man. "You should put such concerns from your mind. We have things to discuss. We'll soon arrive at my hall beyond the world."

Put it from my mind? It seemed inconceivable after what I'd done on the coast of Nowhere, but it was all so distant and cloudy, as if Twist and I *wanted* to put it from our minds. "Where in the void is this?" I asked.

"It's a sanctuary," replied the voice. "A way of bridging the gap between your realm of form and my hall. That's where I'm taking you. Without this room, you'd be open to attack from infinite layers of the far void. Nasty things dwell out here."

"Void beasts?"

"Dholes, Byakhee, Mi-go, immense segmented slugs with cruel spiders for blood. If you travel far enough you'll find the boundless nuclear chaos that slumbers at the heart of all things, and be forced to sign your name in the black book. But we're not going that far. Just to the shadow halls beyond the world."

I rose from the couch. The floor was covered in thick, red carpet, and warm air rolled subtly from every angle. A mug of frothy ale sat on a small wooden table, but the square room was otherwise bare. I was travelling through the void, but everything was still. I'd exploded in a ball of wyrd, but I was still alive, no matter what *practical reality* said. Twist and I were closer than ever, and we needed to keep our wits about us. After everything we'd seen, and every hammer-blow to my mind, I could still feel the young man who wanted, above all things, to be a Sea Wolf. Duncan Greenfire, called Sharp Tongue, son of the High Captain, was still in there somewhere. He was broken, but far wiser, and he still had a task to do. I *would* honour them all. I *would* save the Eastron from annihilation.

"We've arrived," said the strange voice. "You'll like my hall, it's beautiful. You'll be the third mortal from your realm to have seen it. One day soon, when I stabilize the Maelstrom and open a gateway, thousands will walk through the glass to safety, and it will take no more than a minute. Salvation for your people, Duncan. Each and every one."

A solid door of old wood appeared in the one of the walls. Black metal hinges secured it to the stone, and a ring of burnished brass acted as a door handle. I barely hesitated before reaching out and grasping the handle. The metal was cold and my hand tingled as I opened the door inwards. Then a blinding light.

I blinked and saw a carpet of green and grey, stretching away from my eyes as forests, grasslands and mountains. There was a dark void sky overhead, but a blanket of pale blue cast a warm light across a huge, fertile land. A wide river cut through a wooded valley, leading to a pasture, and beyond was green country as far as the eye could see. It didn't feel like the void, except for the sky. Everything was solid and textured. Smells and sounds were sharp, as if we had somehow returned to the realm of form.

I stood on a wide, stone terrace of multiple levels, part of a palatial citadel of white stone and ornate railings. The architecture was like nothing I'd seen in the Kingdom of the Four Claws. The building blocks were enormous, and I struggled to fathom the kind of engineering required to move them, let alone construct a castle from them.

"It took me a long time to build," said a gentle voice.

Leaning against the closest railing was a man. He was of slightly below average height, with huge shoulders and well-muscled arms. His skin was so pale that small, red veins were visible on his face, and his eyes were a deep shade of pink. Down his back was a long braid of bone-white hair, half-obscuring an ugly scar across the side of his neck. He was clean-shaven, though his peculiar complexion made it difficult to guess his age.

"You look like a man," I observed, certain I was seeing the pale man for the first time. "Just a man with white skin."

"I *was* a man," he replied, in his precise, clipped accent. "Long, long ago."

"What are you now?" I asked, aware that Twist was coiled protectively around my leg.

He smiled. There was a benevolence to his face, cutting through the pale skin and pink eyes. “If I told you my name was Utha the Ghost, would you truly be any wiser? If I said I was a god, would you believe me? A shadow giant, an old blood? These terms mean nothing to your people.” He smiled again, this time mournfully, as if in remembrance. “I want you to trust me, Duncan. You’ve seen the Sunken God. You know what the Eastron face, and you need to trust that I *can* help. That *we* can help. I’ve told this to no-one but Ten Cuts and Marius, but my hall beyond the world is large enough for all. Your civilization *can* survive, in any one of a million other realms of form. *Your* realm is but one of many, floating in the void sea.”

I looked down the valley, and saw another world. It wasn’t the Kingdom of the Four Claws, but it was just as real.

“This is just a fraction,” said the pale man, seeing my wonder at his hall. “There are beautiful, rolling blue oceans to the south, and snow-capped mountains to the north. I’m sure there are great cartographers amongst your people who will delight in mapping its extent. I’m not even sure *I* could tell you how big it is. Life has a way of expanding on its own. Even in the halls beyond the world.”

He approached me, looking like nothing more than a mortal man, cursed with white skin. He wore a simple robe of black fabric, gathered at the waist, and a silvery cord woven into his long, braided hair. He put a hand on my shoulder and was flung backwards by an aggressive flash of my wyrd. I didn’t mean to, but Twist reacted to him touching me.

“I’m sorry,” I muttered. “He doesn’t trust you.”

The pale man had struck the terrace, ten feet away, and didn't appear hurt. He was flat on his back, but a knowing chuckle removed any tension.

My wyrd pulsed to the surface, becoming a cloak of tangled thorns. I'd never seen Twist physically manifest, but then I'd never been to a void realm before. Perhaps the rules were different. I wasn't stung, but slowly felt something crawling within the knotted brambles.

"Say hello to him," said the pale man, rising to his feet.

Over my shoulder, pulling itself through thorns, was a small imp. It had dark green skin and sharp ears, rising to two points either side of its round head. Its mischievous, angular eyes covered half its face, and around the spirit's waist was my thorn clinch, worn like a belt. The twisted brambles flowed around it, allowing the imp to perch on a narrow branch and face me. We looked at each other for the first time.

"Hello, Twist," I whispered, tentatively raising my hand, and reaching for the spirit. The imp flinched for an instant, before nuzzling into my hand and closing his eyes. It felt as if our nerves were connected. We were wrapped in a warm blanket of wyrd, but I couldn't tell where *I* ended and Twist began. Our thoughts mingled. Shared fear, confusion and anger, but also gratitude and relief. The pain spirit loved me. I loved him too. We were each other's worlds. We'd grown together and shared everything, until we were one being.

Twist had been a juvenile spirit, floating through the void of Moon Rock, when Clatterfoot dragged him into the thorn clinch. A pain spirit knows only pain, and he'd lashed out, unsure what else to do. For years he'd raged against me, trying to free himself from bondage, seeing me as his enemy.

We'd made each other strong. Then we'd seen the Sunken God, and had become one.

"I don't know who bound him to you," said the pale man, looking with amusement at the imp. "But he did you a great service. You and your pain spirit have made each other truly powerful. Unchecked, chaotic, but powerful. Perhaps more powerful than any other Eastron in your Kingdom."

Twist opened his eyes and glared at the pale man. Thorns and nettles sprouted from his body, and he snarled a deep rumble of distrust.

"We don't like you," I observed. "You control people's minds. You made them attack the *Dead Horse*. We think you're dangerous. We know you can help, but Twist might try to kill you if you don't tell us who you really are, and how we can honour the Sea Wolves ... and why you care."

The pain spirit whined, his pointed ears drooping slightly, and his tiny fingers sprouting bright green nettles. My discomfort affected him, just as his suspicion affected me. The spirit and I shook our heads in unison, trying to find a peaceful middle ground, where we could happily exist together. There were a thousand differences between us, but we'd grown into a single being. With time, the join between us would be invisible. We faced each other, sharing a smile.

"I haven't controlled *you*," replied the pale man. "Come and sit. Let us talk."

Twist darted to my shoulder, pulling the thorns back into himself and tugging on my ear. He only cared about *us*, and wanted to keep us safe. The void realm allowed him to manifest, but did nothing to soften his suspicions. We couldn't scratch the image of the Sunken God from our mind, and he blamed the pale man. We blamed him for Lord

Vikon too, and for bringing Marius Cyclone and the third void legion to Nowhere. Our collective mind was a whirl, with all of our concerns mingling together.

By the railing, positioned at the head of the green valley, were two chairs. The pale man squeezed his bulky shoulders into one of them and produced a small keg from beneath the table. We narrowed our eyes, but decided to take the second chair. The view from the citadel was spectacular. We were a hundred feet from the ground, and the scale of everything was enormous. From our vantage point, the mountains, the river and the trees were like a painting of a perfect wilderness.

Twist jumped up and down, muttering in my ear. "I know you have use for us," I said. "And you want us to trust you ... but how *can* we? And if *we* can't, after what you've shown us, how will you persuade the Sea Wolves and the Winterlords? Or will you just control as many minds as you can?"

The pale man grumbled to himself, his strange voice forming a string of curses and barely intelligible invective. None of it was directed at me, but I felt uncomfortable nonetheless, perhaps even regretful that I'd pushed him.

"My name *is* Utha," he said, when he'd finished muttering under his breath. "And I know I've made mistakes. And I've got people killed." He drew two mugs of dark brown ale from the cask and handed me one.

Twist smacked his lips together and snatched the ale from Utha's grasp. The pain spirit cackled and wrapped its arms around the mug, taking several deep gulps. We both felt the effects, and I swallowed contentedly. It was the same delicious ale I'd tasted before, and had the same refreshing effect.

"Where did you say this ale was from?" I asked, trying to avoid further grumbling from the pale man.

"A city called Ro Leith," he replied. "A long, long way from here. It's built on six hills, near a huge forest, called the Fell. Leith's famous for its wine, but the ale ... best hangover I ever had." He spoke like he was a normal man, but with a sadness behind his words. He *looked* like a normal man, but with an eldritch aura, hanging like a cloak over his white skin. Then he smiled. "Thank you. It's pleasant to talk of ordinary things. It's rare I get the chance."

"How old are you?" we asked.

He was reluctant, and we sensed a vulnerability, as if the pale man was more fragile than he wanted people to believe. He bowed his head. "I was born a mortal man. I discovered I was an old blood. I slowly became a shadow giant. One day soon I will be a god. As for how old I am ... I thought a few hundred years, but that was a few hundred years ago. Time doesn't mean a lot here, so I only get a sense of its passing when I return to the realms of form. But there's no guarantee that time moves at the same pace in each realm. So, I don't know how old I am."

Twist burbled in my ear. "We don't really know what it means to be a god," I said. "I once heard Adeline Brand say that, if the Eastron ever had a god, we killed them before we left the Bright Lands. Gods have no place in the Kingdom of the Four Claws. No-one would worship them."

He flexed his neck, looking off into the distance. "The gods of old were our freedom's woe, and we were freedom's fool. The Bright Lands they gave us, but our thrones of wyrd we stole. Upon their graves the Eastron were born, and the Eastron sailed across the sea."

"What's that?" I asked.

"It's written in the Strange Manse at the Dark Harbour. Marius showed me. I think he was trying to tell me the same thing as you... that gods have no place in the Kingdom of the Four Claws." He looked at me, the smallest hint of a smile appearing as his eyes flicked to the green imp, perched on my shoulder. "I care about the Eastron because I am to be your god. You are to be my followers. That is the last step on *my* journey, and the first step on yours. But it means nothing if I can't save you from the sleeping Old One."

I balked at the idea. The Sea Wolves would sooner die, throwing themselves at the Sunken City, than kneel before the pale man. They'd believe they could win, until they were faced with the reality of the creature, and then it would be too late. Though I couldn't speak for the rest of the Eastron.

"Is that why the Stranger knelt to you?" I asked. "Are you the new god of the Dark Brethren?"

He appeared surprised at the suggestion, snorting ironically and swigging from his mug of ale. "No," he stated. "I am not. There are three Cyclone brothers, each commanding a third of the Dark Brethren. Unfortunately, I only trust *Marius* Cyclone. He follows me because he believes I am the only hope for your civilization. If I prove to be so, he will be my first cleric. But not before."

Twist gnashed his teeth together, absently scratching at my shoulder. The spirit understood no more about divinity than me, and just wanted to know where *we* fit into the almost-a-god's scheme to save the Eastron. "And us?" I asked. "Are *we* expected to worship you? We were powerful enough to see you, but what does that mean? What do you want from us?"

He bowed his head, setting aside the ale, and sitting forwards. "You are the only Eastron I've met who can survive what I need doing. To use any other mortal would mean killing them... in great pain. Probably a dozen or so people. But your pain spirit has amassed more than enough power for both of you. I can take your wyrd without killing you. And I will need no-one else."

I awoke in a bed, laid on smooth sheets and enveloped in a soft quilt. The air was fresh, and my throat and nostrils felt cleansed, pulling in soothing breaths as I blinked myself awake. My body was rested and our mind felt clear. In fact, our mind felt calm and rational, as if Twist and I had been allowed time to acclimatize to each other.

I shook my head and came fully awake. We didn't remember finishing the conversation, nor leaving the terrace and descending into Utha's citadel. We hadn't even *seen* a citadel, just the suggestion of one, stretching beneath the multilayered terraces and immense views. Curiosity drove us to sit upright immediately, rather than lounge around in the unnaturally comfortable bed. Around us was a small bedroom, made of stone blocks with wooden framing. A cold hearth sat next to a door, and my clothes were on a chair beneath a single window, through which shone a clear void sky. At every angle and at every corner was a shadow, forming vibrant lines. They cut into the room, wherever the light couldn't reach.

Twist flung back a corner of the thick, woollen quilt and yawned, making a low, burbling sound. Our thoughts and concerns were now shared, and both of us felt content, as if a years-old war had ended in an amicable peace. A bit of Duncan wanted to shout *fuck you* to Clatterfoot and my father, but Twist thought we should shut up and be grateful. As a single being, we decided to be smug, but not shout.

The imp grinned, his huge, angular eyes sparkling as he darted to my shoulder. A prickle of thorns glided across my arms, but caused no pain. We had control of the thorn clinch. Twist no longer needed to lash out, and Duncan no longer needed to feel pain. We couldn't exist without each other, and there was a sensation of unbreakable love between us.

"I know," I said, standing from bed. "He wants to take our wyrd. Or is it just *my* wyrd?" Twist burbled again. "Okay, your wyrd is mine and my wyrd is yours."

The spirit gave a contented murmur and settled into the crook of my neck, summoning a small nest of thorns in which to recline. He continued making quiet noises as I dressed, observing everything I did with interest.

"Helping him means helping the Eastron," I mused. "But who *are* we without wyrd?"

The murmuring flowed into a low whine, like a puppy who sensed distress. I felt a small pinprick of pain in my neck as Twist pawed at me, his spiky ears drooping. Our power flowed in a circle between the man and the spirit, amplifying what each possessed. Our collective power was staggering. The deaths we'd caused had largely been accidents, but if we wanted to, Twist and I could best *any* mortal, no matter how mighty their wyrd. It was a strange feeling to be in possession of so much power. We imagined smashing the door open, or pulling down the stone room entirely, just because we could. Tendrils of wyrd snaked outwards, appearing as thick brambles, twisting together and emitting a dark blue glow.

"*That's* ncw," I obscrvcd, looking down at thc thorny mass of wyrd that we now collectively controlled. "Maybe we should call Rys Coldfire's name on the Day of Challenge." I bowed my head, pulling in our power. "If we get the chance... if we're not dead."

Our world had changed, and not just because we'd found each other. Twist was as afraid and confused as Duncan, perhaps more so. But maybe this was our chance to shine. We would win no battles, conquer no wildernesses, defend no holds, but we could save millions of people. Sebastian Dawn Claw had brought the Eastron from across the sea. Could Duncan Greenfire bring them into the void?

28

We found a doorway and a set of enormous white brick steps, and walked from the citadel. Down and away from the stone terraces, and along a lush valley, with snow-capped mountains in the distance. The air was fresh and clear, and the sound of birds and game echoed down the valley. There were deer in the woods and fish in the crystal blue river, marking the centre of the valley. If it weren't for the sky, I could believe I was somewhere in the realm of form. But, far above me, a void sky looked down on Utha's hall beyond the world. It was blue and black, with glinting lines and flashes of energy. Somehow, the far green land had grown and flourished, as if a sun shone overhead. In the time I'd been here, I'd seen at least a day and night, though the sky had never changed. It had got dark, creatures had slept or hunted, then morning had come. I wondered it if rained here, if clouds formed, and if so, how it was maintained.

We were alone in a vast new world. The pale man hadn't appeared since our conversation. He was either occupied in the realm of form, or giving Twist and me time to wander. We conjured a hundred images across the landscape. The forests encircling mighty holds, the mountains looking down on fertile pastures and grazing livestock. There were oceans somewhere, upon which a fleet of Sea Wolf ships could prowl. Stone could be mined, trees could be felled, cloth could be woven. Perhaps rebuilding in a new land would even lead to a prolonged peace. That would certainly be the fairy-tale ending, but there was an infinite list of things that could go wrong before that happened. The least of which was persuading the Sea Wolves that there was a fight they couldn't win. Though Twist was more concerned with how the pale man intended to use our wyrd.

Our wandering had taken us far from the citadel, and into a series of wide, rugged gullies, pushing away from the river like fingers. The earth was dark brown, with patches of weeds and herbs sprouting every few feet. Then Twist scratched my neck and I stopped walking. We stood in front of a pitted rock face and a jagged cave, creating an overhang that obscured the void sky. Oddly, the shadows were thin here, as if they were wary of the cave. Where they ended, dense web began, undulating gently in the wind and framing the black opening.

I'd seen bugs and flies in the void realm, but no spiders. Perhaps they all lived in a single cave. Twist jumped from my shoulder and scampered towards the darkness, trailing a line of thorns from his perch. He grumbled at the cave, and we felt something cruel and potent within. A single being – old and bitter, angry at things beyond our comprehension. It knew we were here, and it didn't like us. It was the first hostility we'd sensed in the realm, though not enough to cause us fear.

Fetid air rolled from the cave, and Twist burbled, letting the line of thorns pull him back to my shoulder. We backed away, but only slowly, determined to show our newly discovered power to whatever skulked within. Our determination rapidly diminished as an enormous, hairy spider squirmed from the cave. Its grey, mangled face appeared first, then it gathered up thick legs of faded red and green hair, and pushed itself through the opening, spreading its body across the rocky ground. Patches of rot covered its abdomen and face, and several of its eight eyes were welded shut with some kind of mould.

We'd been startled by the creature, but were powerful enough to react without thinking. We conjured thorns and dense brambles at the tip of each of its legs, anchoring the spider to the ground. We caused it pain, pushing nettles into its remaining eyes, and we armoured our self with an impenetrable layer of spiritual barbs.

"Don't kill her!" demanded the pale man, appearing through a slice of shadowy air.

"We're defending our self," I replied. "It was going to attack us. We can feel its hostility." The sudden intervention had not surprised us. It was likely the pale man had been observing, maybe self-conscious of his realm, or worried we'd encounter its other denizens. "Did you make this thing?"

He approached, interposing himself between me and the spider. The enormous beast hunkered down, arching its grotesque head towards the pale man. One of its fangs was snapped in half, and the other was dry and cracked, like badly sunburned skin.

"This *thing* is called Ryuthula," said the pale man. "And she's far older than me. Long, long ago she could assume mortal form, but the void changes all things." He gently reached for the spider, placing his hand on its huge head. The creature reacted, twitching in appreciation. "She saw the beginning. She helped me build everything you see. She will be safe with me for as long as she needs. When the Eastron arrive, Ruth will descend into endless caves, beneath the earth. There she will weave her web for all eternity, in peace."

We released the creature, weaving the thorns and nettles into a single green mass and pulling it back into our body. "Did you *want* us to meet her?" I asked.

"She wanted to meet *you*," he replied. "She will give up her cave, but only if I'm right about you. Only if you're powerful enough to help me."

"Are we?" I asked, knowing the answer.

The immense spider crept backwards, staying low to the ground and pulling in its mottled legs. There was an aura of diseased power and eldritch wisdom, but also a deep sadness, shown through gentle movements and quiet, expressive clicking sounds. "Go back to sleep," whispered Utha, ignoring my question. "Peace awaits. Think of your sons, and find comfort in their strength. Torian and Leon will outlive us both."

Ryuthula turned her spiteful eyes to us, then flared her grotesque legs and rippled back into her cave, able to fit through the small opening with amazing dexterity. The pale man then inhaled deeply and turned to face us.

"What do you need us to do?" I demanded, letting Twist flare across my shoulders, creating a cloak of thorns. "We're ready to help, but our wyrd will not be given without good reason. What do we need to do to save the Eastron from extinction?"

The pale man stood before me, his black robe flowing over a muscular torso. His pink eyes were narrow and focused, as if he was about to do something that he dreaded. He was hard to read, but we sensed his vulnerability again. The pale man knew where his path would take him, but he was afraid of what he didn't know. Fear of the unknown was just as strong in a god as it was in a mortal.

"My realm is missing one thing," said Utha, doing an admirable job of hiding his trepidation. "The one thing that will allow the Eastron to live here. The one thing *you* can provide. My realm needs a sun. You are a mighty being, Duncan. For seventeen years, you've resisted every attempt to cage your power. Your people channel everything into their sword arms, but Twist didn't want you to learn the wrong lesson... so you learned nothing."

We looked at him, then up at the black and blue sky. It was an alien vista of shooting lights and sparkling shapes, there one moment, gone the next. "A sun?" I queried. "How is that possible?"

The pale man walked away, waving for me to follow. Twist was getting irritated by his manner and reluctance to give us straight answers. Without Duncan's approval, the pain spirit conjured a rope of brambles and flung it around the pale man's chest, holding him in place. "Sorry," I said, half-heartedly. "Sometimes we just react when we're threatened... or frustrated."

Utha remained calm, looking down at the ropy tendril, wrapped tightly around his torso. "Remove it. Now!"

Twist screwed up his impish face, and Duncan frowned. We were about to respond, but apparently not fast enough for the pale man. He dispelled the brambles with a wave of his hand and dragged us to him, until we were face to face. We tried to summon more wyrd, but it wasn't there. We tried to struggle, but were overcome by weakness.

"Never raise your wyrd to me," whispered Utha. "This realm and I are one, and I cannot be harmed here. If you push me, my hall will kill you before I get a chance to stop it. And I need you alive."

"So we can be a sun?" I asked, with Twist hopping up and down on my shoulder. "Explain."

He tried to smile, but the expression faded into a grimace. "Greenfire must let his wyrd shine."

"I will be a god. The great turtle spirits of the Father have seen it, and I've always known it. I hate the word *destiny*, but my path demands I accept it. I will have mighty clerics and devout followers, each blessing my name and following my will. Eventually, your people and I will return to the realms of form. They are greater than most mortals and will rule wherever they choose to dwell.

"But that may be the endeavour of centuries. The endeavour of *now* is saving the Eastron. The threat grows with every tick of the clock. Even now, the dreams of the Sunken God infect the rotten corners of your realm, sending forth chaos to herald its awakening. The time when the stars are aligned. I can't defeat the Old One... I wish I could. All I can do is follow my path and trust that we are not too late."

We stood in a vast hall of white stone blocks, with arched wooden vaults high above. Distorted corridors of dizzying infinity crept away from the hall, each more difficult to comprehend than the last. It was wider than the central chamber of the Bloody Halls, and four times higher, with strange architecture. Everything was straight and flush, as if constructed over centuries by master craftsmen. There were no dust or cobwebs, gaps in the stonework, or birds nesting in the rafters. In front of us, more finite than the hall, but still immense, was a set of wooden doors. They pulsed, as if struck by a great wind from the other side. Opposite the doors was a smaller archway, pointed directly down the valley.

We didn't remember coming here, and felt as if everything was happening in our head. The pale man was controlling what we saw and what we heard, but it was more than an illusion. We could look down and see our body, we could look left and see Utha, but we'd not physically moved anywhere.

The pale man placed a hand against the wood, and the doors faded from view. A rushing wind threw us backwards, as charged energy crackled through the huge opening. We scuttled away and shielded our eyes against the wind. Beyond was the Maelstrom, rolling down and away. We were at the top of the void storm, though the angles were indistinct. We felt as if we were looking up, down and across all at the same time. Twist yelped, and disappeared into a clump of brambles.

"We're at the very top," said Utha. "A pinprick in the glass that stretches from my hall to Nowhere. Too small and unstable to bring people through, but the only place in your Kingdom of the Four Claws where it's possible. If there had been a void storm near the Dark Harbour we may never have met, young Duncan. Though I'd have needed to find another Eastron of your power. I'm sure one or two exist."

I stood, coaxing Twist out of hiding with a gentle scratch of our thorn clinch. "How do we make the gap bigger?" we asked.

"With shadows," replied the pale man. "And light. The Eastron will slowly succumb to the void without something to anchor them. In time each will fall into madness and death. This is a realm of void, not of form, and mortals cannot survive here indefinitely. Unless it is powered by the unfettered wyrd of an Eastron. When I say I need a sun, imagine I am an engineer of the spirit realm, building a suitable home for a fragile people, with specific needs. Your wyrd will be a small, but essential, part of my construction. The last part. The most important part. Everything is about to change."

We stood on the banks of the glittering river, looking back down the valley, towards the palatial expanse of the citadel. White brick and grey stone formed a barrier across the valley, with nothing visible beyond but a shimmering void sky. It was hard to gauge the size of the building. It was wider than it was tall, but the void distorted everything, making the structure appear intimidating and humble at the same time.

"What happens to the Pure Ones?" we asked. "Are *they* invited? Or does the Sunken God get to kill them?"

The pale man looked at us, his strange features falling into a complicated mask of emotions. "They are far wiser than the Eastron," he replied. "Their sword arms are not as strong, but they have lived in harmony with this world for millennia. They will stay in the Pure Lands. They say they will repair it after the Invaders leave. In *their* stories the Sunken God falls asleep once more. Ten Cuts and the spirit child will lead them into peace. Relax now, Duncan."

Twist pawed at my face, burbling in a low voice. The spirit hugged me with a warm embrace of thorns, trying to lock our wyrd within and keep us safe. We were caught in a loop of power, helpless against the might of the pale man, with both of us feeling confused and vulnerable. We wanted to lash out, but everything was muted and numb, like trying to run underwater. We looked around, but all directions were suddenly cloaked in the same impenetrable shadow. All we were permitted to see were the pale man, and his huge, stone citadel.

Was this it? Were we about to become a sun? Would he drag our wyrd from our form in pieces, or make us give it willingly? These questions concerned Twist more than Duncan, whose thoughts turned back to the Severed Hand and the Sea Wolves. Our collective worry was almost overwhelming. Two beings, concerned with different things, smashed together into a single mind. Neither of us wanted to be a hero. Twist wanted to be safe and Duncan wanted to honour his people.

The pain spirit and Duncan looked deeply into each other's eyes. Then up at the pale man. The flowing shadows formed a cloak across his shoulders, and his long, white braid fluttered in the wind.

"I don't twitch anymore," I said. "And Twist doesn't feel like a prisoner." The imp disappeared back into thorns, and the thorns disappeared into the man. "*We* feel no pain. We are safe together and we belong together. And we will do what needs to be done to save our people. Do what you need to do to complete your void realm."

"Thank you," intoned the shadowy figure. "The Eastron will all know your name. You will honour each and every one of them."

He pulled our wyrd to the surface. All of our wyrd. Miniscule pins scratched across the surface of our skin, and all our muscles tensed at once. From every tiny reservoir of power rushed a spider's web of wyrd, leaving a scratchy pain in its wake. Thorns and brambles were pulled outwards, making Twist squeal, as every tendril of our wyrd was drained into a nimbus of subtle red and blue, seeping from our body like sweat.

"I only need Duncan's power," said the pale man. "The spirit's energy will flow behind it, leaving more than enough wyrd to sustain you."

His words did nothing to stall the pain, causing a tight embrace between the spirit and the man. Twist cried and Duncan wailed, as we were battered by powerful surges of energy and a complete lack of control.

A conflagration of wyrd boomed from our body, displacing the dense shadows and causing the air to catch fire. Shadowy trees blasted backwards and the river retreated in a violent wave. We stood in the centre of a crackling orb, growing and churning through different shades of blue, green and yellow, like a concentrated void storm. Behind the orb, clinging to our body, came a skin of brambles. Twist remained fastened to my shoulder, making sure our spiritual power stayed behind. It flowed into our extremities, replacing Duncan's wyrd like a transfusion, as the crackling orb rose and expanded. Already its mass was four or five times bigger than my own, and it continued to grow.

We fell to the ground, staring up at the expanding ball of pulsing wyrd. "Stay where you are," said the pale man, his glowing pink eyes narrowing and his hands weaving shapes in the air. He pulled the orb away from us, moulding it like clay, and changing its colour to a fiery golden red. "This is raw, divine energy, acquired long ago by the Eastron from across the sea. How mighty your people could have been ... if you'd *all* resisted training."

We were slouched on soft grass, next to the riverbank. The air itself was now charged, and the globe of wyrd reacted by sending crackling shards of lightning from its mass. We felt as if we were watching a negotiation of sorts, as the void-stuff of the hall beyond the world tried to reason with my wyrd. It was now a huge ball of roiling fire, angrier and more volatile than any storm.

The pale man, still cloaked in shadows, studied the orb, his face contorting as he crafted a sun from Duncan Greenfire's wyrd. Conflict shone in his eyes, indicating the enormity of what he was doing, until the orb flared, shooting upwards, as if repelled by gravity. The fiery red softened to a warm gold, causing a glare at ground level and displacing the unnatural light of the void sky. The new sun stopped moving and hung low in the distance, providing the bright glow of a sunlit dawn. Shadows crept from every texture around me. Trees, hills, water and mountains, everything cast a dense black carpet across the realm.

The void sky flickered, as if becoming accustomed to the new sun. Then, with a blinding flash, it was blue, with flowing clouds of muddy grey and white. We shielded our eyes from the glare, and felt the last building block of the void realm fall into place. The sun acted in concert with everything else, woven into place and creating a perfect home for the Eastron.

Utha smiled and appeared to rise above the ground, his legs becoming indistinct as they strode across a blanket of shadow. I watched him rise higher and grow larger. The shadows clung to him, tripling his mass and making him appear as a giant of shadow, with a window on the cosmos replacing his face. The giant stepped over the wide river as if it were a tiny stream. He rose into the path of the sunlight, bringing an immense shadow with him. His back, rippling with power, was bathed in light, but the blackness beyond him was total.

"My design is finished," intoned the giant.

The distant stone structure was now bathed in shadows. Then, with an immense pulse of energy and a deafening roar, the pale man destroyed his citadel. The stone broke and flew backwards in waves, enveloped in an otherworldly tidal wave of wyrd. In its place was a building of solid shadow, rising as black obsidian across the head of the valley. But the shadow didn't end there. The burning golden sun struck every nook and cranny of the realm, sending an endless spike of blackness away from Utha. He was now even larger, walking slowly down the valley.

We stumbled to our feet and staggered from rock to tree, using anything we could to stay standing and follow in the giant's wake. He used tendrils of shadow as fine tools, to shape and build the black castle, moulding it around a central archway, leading to the Maelstrom. We tried to run, wanting to see more, but could manage only a zigzag trot.

The new building was awesome, formed of castellated towers and shining black balconies. Everything was smooth, flowing from one surface to the next, as if it was all formed from the same enormous shadow.

We steadied our self and followed in the god's huge footsteps, getting closer and closer to the black castle and the central archway. As it came into view and I found a suitable rock to lean against, the Maelstrom began to quieten. The void storm appeared to be the centrepiece of the construction, and tendrils of shadow crept down and away. There was no wooden doorway or stone tunnel, just a plunging curtain of black, overwhelming the raging storm. Somewhere below us, across unimaginable layers of void, the People of Ice would be looking up into a darkening sky, and see a shadow cast across the Maelstrom.

The pale man had talked of a gateway, large enough for a hundred men to march abreast. What we saw, forming in the heart of the hall, was wide enough to eclipse all of Cold Point. A solid, permanent connection between the distant void and the realm of form. Twist and I were elated, as if the Kingdom of the Four Claws might actually have a future. A future we'd helped create.

From the hall it was a plunging black shaft, but when we stepped on it, it was an enormous, horizontal bridge, complete with beautifully knotted railings. Though everything was black, there were hundreds of different tones and shades, playing across each other, as if aesthetic beauty was still a concern for the shadow giant.

Twist capered across the railings, hopping up and down excitedly. The imp poked thorns at the shadow bridge, and burbled with glee when it appeared solid. We were still powerful, but would be forever tied to this void realm. In the realm of form, we had died, but in the shadow hall beyond the world, we were second only to the pale man himself.

The pain spirit hopped back to sit on my shoulder, stroking my face and grinning. After all the pain we'd caused each other, we now felt free. The Eastron would act according to their nature, but we'd given them every chance to survive. Perhaps one day we'd confront Wilhelm Greenfire and Clatterfoot, laughing that their cruelty had led to our salvation. But, as we sat against the railing of the shadow bridge, our smugness felt petty. We'd seen cosmic immensity, in forms both malign and benevolent. We'd known fear and madness, but had found strength in each other. What happened next was out of our control.

The pale man appeared, standing over us. His form was that of a muscular man, with ghostly skin and white hair. The shadow giant was gone, replaced by a simple man with a grateful expression on his face. "In your realm of form it's been three days," he said. "It has taken a day for the shadow bridge to touch the earth of Nowhere. A few hundred Sea Wolves, a few thousand Dark Brethren and People of Ice, and many Pure Ones, have looked up and seen the Maelstrom change."

Twist screwed up his green features and hopped back to the bridge, approaching the pale man. The tiny imp looked up at him, his sharp ears twitching. The spirit and I had agreed that, though Utha might not be worthy of worship, he was certainly worthy of respect.

"You have a home in this hall for as long as you desire," said Utha, addressing the spirit *and* the man.

We looked along the bridge, but it fell away into the horizon within a hundred feet. The other side led directly to the lush, green valley of the shadow hall. "How long would it take to walk to Nowhere?" we asked.

"A friend approaches," replied the pale man. "You can ask *him*."

From across the bridge came a column of men. Twist squealed, springing back to my shoulder, and we stood from the railing. The men clanked rhythmically, marching towards us only slowly. Marius Cyclone, called the Stranger, was in the centre, with a phalanx of void legionnaires behind him. Each warrior tried to maintain their discipline as they wondered at the otherworldly construction of the shadow bridge. There were no Sea Wolves, Pure Ones or People of Ice, just the staring eyes of the Night Wing on each tabard.

"It's done, my friend," said Utha, coming to a stop before the Stranger and the column of Dark Brethren. "Now *your* task begins. Convince your people to leave."

Marius Cyclone bowed his head and they grasped forearms. "My faith is again rewarded," said the Brethren. "But the Silver Parliament and the Always King will have to wait. There is a situation on Nibonay. Spirits and men say the glass of the Severed Hand will soon break. I pray for your help, my lord Utha."

The holds were all we had.

Our beacons of strength amidst an endlessly hostile land.

We built them, named them, and began to revere them.

They were a sanctuary, a fortress and an identity.

The Always King saw a silver dawn.

The Bloodied Harp opened his hand.

The First Fang severed it.

And the Friend saw their folly.

Manos Bowyer, Spirit-Master of Four Claw's Folly

PART TEN

Adeline Brand at the Severed Hand

29

The hold was dark, with mist hanging as a grey curtain above all but the tallest structures. It was approaching midnight and few feet walked the streets. Just duellists, stationed at every intersection. We'd killed some varn, stopped one binding, and perhaps slowed them down, but nothing had changed. Gloom Scribe had not been found, Pure Ones were still being purged, and the Severed Hand still held its breath. The underground tunnels were being searched, and multiple engagements had been reported, but the glass still strained against pressure from beyond.

When the void is full, the glass breaks. I'd told Tomas Red Fang, but there was little we could do. He'd scratched his head, consulted a few books, and ultimately punched a wall. The void was bursting at the seams with voracious chaos spirits. Sooner or later, with a push from the varn, they'd burst through. The old man had consulted everyone he could, but given us no answers, except to say that somewhere the varn were enacting an immensely powerful ritual. At least we hoped it was the varn.

I stood at the top of Brand's Tower, looking down into Duellist's Yard. The hold looked huge, even at night. I could hear waves, but not see them, and everything was black and grey. Thousands of people lived here, though many Pure Ones had left or been killed. The remainder were either hidden underground or caged in the Wolf House; with a grateful few allowed to remain in their homes.

"Are you still there?" I asked.

"As things stand," he replied. "I think I'll be here for a while. I'm not sure how this works."

"Well, you're dead," I stated. "So, you must be ... I don't know, something more than a man."

"I think I'm a spirit," said the Wisp. "I can feel the void ... but not the realm of form. But I don't know how much of me remains. And I feel ... angry. Like I've been wronged."

"Can I see you?" I asked. "Do you have any form?"

"I can see myself," he replied. "But I'm ..."

"What?" I prompted, wrapping my cloak around my shoulders, as a sharp wind flowed over the top of the tower.

"I can see through myself and I'm shimmering," he said, reluctantly. "And I'm a long way above the Severed Hand. I can see it below me, surrounded by those fucking chaos spirits. The glass is swollen, but it's holding."

"What?" I said, with a frown. "You died two days ago, and are talking to me about the hold?"

"What else matters?" he replied. "They killed me. They will not kill you. Not if I have power left. You are all I've got, Addie."

I bowed my head and took a deep breath, looking south across the hold. I'd have to fight soon. I'd have to join other duellists and shout *once more for the Severed Hand*.

"Did I kill anyone?" asked the Wisp, his voice crisp and clear in my head.

"Not yet," I replied, tears forming in my eyes. "Tasha's fine. She's making a big pot of soup for men on duty at the Wolf House. They think it's going to be a long night."

"And Young Green Eyes?" asked Jaxon.

"You slammed his head into a wall. He's not woken up. I had to threaten half a dozen Sea Wolves to get him proper care, but it's his head, so wyrd can only do so much. They say he could die or wake up any moment."

I heard him crying. That, more than anything, convinced me that Jaxon Ice was still there. I'd never heard of Eastron becoming spirits, but if the Wisp was the first, I would not be surprised.

"I met him, after so long, then I killed him."

"It wasn't you," I said. "It was the spirit that possessed you. And he's not dead yet."

He was quiet for a moment, perhaps looking at his incorporeal body, and wondering what he was. "The glass will break tonight," he whispered. "The hold will be flooded with chaos spirits. A few will possess willing Pure Ones, and they'll try to consume the Severed Hand. I don't know what will be left. Perhaps another Maelstrom, or just a place of chaos."

I looked across rooftops, smoking chimneys and smaller towers. I imagined I could stay atop Brand's Tower and watch the glass break all across the hold. Perhaps they wouldn't even need me below and I could see my world end at a distance, with Jaxon's spirit for company. Or perhaps I was dreaming, and couldn't imagine carrying on without my friend.

The balcony was on the lowest level of the Bloody Halls, looking south over the hold. To my left was Rys Coldfire, to my right was Tomas Red Fang. Jonas Grief and Lagertha

Blood were further along the railing, and Tasha Strong stood by the door. Beneath us, thousands of duellists stood guard. The greatest concentration encircled the Wolf House, but large patrols fanned out into the hold, like a web of armed warriors. Tomas Red Fang and his spirit-masters had conversed with any spirit they could find, squeezed every piece of insight from their wyrd, and they concurred. The glass would break tonight.

A dozen duellists had been sent after the First Fang, but no ships had returned to the hold. Speculation was rife that something had happened on Nowhere. Something more than just a Brethren raiding party. Something that left us without Ulric, Vikon, *or* the warriors they took with them. But even young Lagertha accepted that the security of the Severed Hand was more important than sending a force after her father and brother.

"I hate waiting," said Rys Coldfire. "It's a kind of helplessness. Something out of my control."

It was after midnight, and the only light came from hearths and street lanterns. The cloud was low and dense, rolling in black and grey waves across the Severed Hand. In places it crackled and released arcs of lightning, illuminating shrouded streets and shadowy yards. The glass felt angry, and the void was beginning to bleed through. There was a pervasive silence that seemed to infect everyone and everything, just waiting for a loud noise to make us all jump.

"Perhaps I should tell a joke," said Tomas Red Fang. "A Winterlord, a Brethren and a Sea Wolf walk into a tavern—"

"Shut up," I replied. "I prefer silence."

"It's a funny joke," offered the spirit-master.

"Don't make me punch an old man," I said. "You wouldn't enjoy it."

"Enough," said Lagertha Blood. "Remember who you are. This is not the time for jokes *or* threats."

Tomas and I both looked at her. She was serious and used a deliberately commanding tone of voice. "Very well, my lady," I said with a shallow nod. "We will show more respect as we wait to die."

She became flustered, clearly unsure how to address me. Jonas Grief, the master-at-arms, was about to speak up, no doubt to tell me to watch my tone when addressing the First Fang's daughter, but he was interrupted by a loud noise.

A sharp crack, like two panes of glass smashing together, assaulted my ears. It grated and lengthened, making my teeth itch. I covered my ears and turned towards the south. A jagged line of rotten green energy split the sky, from the Tranquil Gate to the Bright Coast, bulging downwards, as if a wineskin had burst. The realm of form parted its clouds, its lightning and its sky, and allowed the void to rush through. I held my breath as one world invaded another. At first it looked like thick mist, then dense rain. Finally, I saw them, tumbling, as balls of teeth and eyes, from an accursed sky. Thousands upon thousands of them, flopping down onto stone buildings and terrified duellists. No spirits fell on the Wolf House, but a bubbling concentration landed near Jacob's Tower beneath us. The Severed Hand was covered in the chaos spawn of the Dreaming God, like a dusting of fetid snow. There were too many. We couldn't win and that truth was writ large on every face.

"The glass breaks," murmured Tomas Red Fang.

"To arms," whispered the Wolf's Bastard. "It is time to fight and to kill. Remove other thoughts from your mind, they do not belong in this place. This is now a place of war."

"Once more for the Severed Hand," said Lagertha Blood, unable to shout or even raise her voice.

"Oh dear," said Tasha, moving forwards to peer around my left shoulder.

I'd never been to war. I'd killed more men than I could count, fought against overwhelming odds more *times* than I could count, but I'd never charged into battle with an army of Sea Wolves. It wasn't right. This wasn't how we fought. We were raiders and skirmishers, warriors who could attack faster and more ferociously than anyone. But we weren't attacking now. We were defending, and this was apparent in everything I saw at the base of the Wolf House.

Duellists, formed into circular mobs, engaged floating masses of spirits. The spawn remained in clusters, hovering just above the ground, though lacking wings or any obvious method of flight. They each had a large central mouth, splitting their amoeba-like bodies, and joined by dozens of smaller orifices, forming and un-forming as the need arose. They were shorter than the Sea Wolves they attacked, but wider and comprised of strange void-stuff, rather than flesh and blood. They gnashed and flailed, cutting through warriors like water. Some smaller clusters gnawed through wooden walls and roofs, turning buildings to splinters in moments. It was as if they were trying to consume everything of the Severed Hand.

Bells rang and horns sounded throughout the hold, as commands were given and duellists rushed to their duty.

Once more for the Severed Hand. The words echoed through dark and bloody streets, as warriors tried to hold their ground. Gargles of pain accompanied the shouted words, and I saw a dozen warriors torn apart in the first few minutes of the battle.

The Wolf's Bastard drew his falchion and summoned a torrent of powerful wyrd into his limbs. "We prevail or we die," he roared, rushing at the nearest cluster of chaos spawn.

Jonas Grief and a dozen senior duellists followed him, erupting into a wave of power, scything forwards like the edge of an axe. Rys was unafraid, using huge amounts of his power with each swing of his blade. A spirit was cut in two, to dissipate in a fog of green mist. Two more pounced on him, but both were sliced out of existence by his wyrd. "They die," he roared. "They can all die." He was using far too much power, but his example spurred on the defenders.

"Clear the ground around the Wolf House," commanded Jonas Grief. "Get everyone to fall back here. Eastron, Pure One, I don't care, get 'em behind stone."

I'd remained behind, but guilt now caused me to draw my cutlass and move to join them, until Tomas Red Fang put a hand on my shoulder. "No," said the old spirit-master. "*You* come with me. We have a spirit to meet. The void's finally clear."

"What? No, I'm needed."

"Adeline!" he spat. "You *are* needed. The Old Bitch of the Sea needs you. Now!"

I tried to pull away from him and join the fight, but his grip was like iron, and I felt him gradually break the glass and pull us both to the void. The barrier was like tissue paper and we fell from one world to another as easily as you'd sink into a bath. We appeared on uneven ground, rolling back and forth, as if an earthquake was happening in the void. The tear was less visible and appeared to be a storm-filled valley, cutting a line through the shimmering blue landscape. There were no spirits of any kind, just the last few clusters of chaos spawn, bubbling through the tear. Any friendly spirits would have been consumed or driven off, and the void was offensively silent when compared to the battle taking place in the realm of form.

I turned sharply and grabbed Tomas around the throat. The loose skin of his neck wrinkled over my hand and his arms went wide, signalling submission. "You don't do that to me," I growled. "You ask my fucking permission. Now, tell me why I shouldn't go straight back and join the fight."

His eyes shone blue in the void and I was reminded that, though he may appear to be a frail old man, his connection to the spirits was unparalleled. "The Lady of the Quarter wants to meet you. She was forced to retreat from the chaos spirits, and was needed elsewhere, but the Old Bitch of the Sea is far from powerless. She has been regaining her strength."

I released him and stepped away. "Why me? I'm better at killing. I should be where killing is important."

"Not anymore," he replied. "Now you're wise, and you should be where wisdom is important."

It was painful to be standing in the void, unable to see the battle, but I didn't go back. I wanted to, I felt that I should. Perhaps Tomas had cut the last tendril of who I used to be, to reveal a new Adeline Brand. She'd been slowly pushing the duellist aside since I left the Bay of Bliss, strengthened by fear, defeat, but ultimately wisdom. "Okay," I conceded. "Lead the way."

The reflection of the Severed Hand was emptier than usual, no doubt eclipsed by the chaos spawn, but the Wolf House remained. The building held such significance to the Sea Wolves that it was twice as tall beyond the glass. I'd not seen the spawn gnaw through stone and hoped that their teeth could only handle flesh, bone and wood. To see so mighty a building brought low would crush each and every Eastron who survived the battle. It was more than a building, it was our heart.

"We're going up," said Tomas. "Unless you've developed the ability to fly in the void, you should hold on to me."

I looked up at the shimmering red building, towering over us. It was a long way up, and I closed my eyes as I wrapped my arms around Tomas's neck. My feet left the ground and the rush of wind stung my face. I'd flown with Jaxon a time or two, but never at such speed. Tomas Red Fang was striding up the crackling air like a mountain goat.

Atop the void reflection of the Wolf House was a mound of earth and wood, forming a huge den. Thick moss lined the floor, and the smell of wet dog and salt water hung in the air. My boots sank into the moss, like walking on a particularly soft mattress, with frothy water bubbling up from each step. Tomas led the way, silhouetted against the turbulent void sky, towards the huge den entrance.

"My Lady of the Quarter," shouted Tomas. "We beseech you to rise. Our hold is falling."

A deep growl came from the dark opening, followed by a waft of musty air, as if an enormous creature was breathing out.

"The Alpha Wolf accompanies me," continued the spirit-master. "The Sea Wolf who has fought the Sunken Men."

I strode past him to stand at the foot of the entrance, with a wall of pitch blackness in front of me. "Help or don't," I commanded. "I will not beg a spirit for aid."

Another growl, closer this time, and a huge snout poked out of the darkness. I backed away as the spirit's muzzle emerged from its den. Sparkling blue eyes followed and the head of an enormous wolf regarded us with suspicion. Its ears twitched upwards, with a rippling crest of sea water framing its sleek head. I'd never seen the totem before, and was surprised to find that it impressed me. It pulsed with wyrd, its blue and white fur forming a soft skin of power across its huge head. It could swallow me whole, but it didn't bare its teeth and I saw no anger in its eyes.

"Will you help us?" I asked, stepping forwards to stand under its left eye. "*Can* you help us?"

It snarled, its sparkling, pale blue gums parting to reveal huge teeth. I backed away and looked to Tomas Red Fang. The old man raised his arms and approached the spirit. "Easy," said Tomas, stroking a hand along its muzzle.

The wolf craned out of the darkness and I saw small bite marks across its shoulders and front legs. It stopped growling and started whining, nuzzling against the spirit-master's hand. The totem had already been to war. It had survived, but wore numerous scars from the chaos spawn. Would it truly fare so much better if it rejoined the fight now? As more of her emerged, I saw bald patches across her flanks, where the totem was almost entirely see-through. It had far from regained its full power.

Tomas continued stroking the huge wolf, until it lay down and stopped whining, though its emotional blue eyes stayed focused on me. “We need time,” the spirit-master whispered. “Time to get everyone behind stone. Or there may be no Sea Wolves left, my old friend.” The wolf flexed its jaw, again revealing huge teeth and a mouth that could swallow Tomas and me at the same time.

“She’ll die,” I said. “There’re too many of them.” The spirit and the old Sea Wolf now *both* looked at me, and I began to understand that death was exactly what was being discussed.

The Old Bitch of the Sea loped out of her den and approached me. She was beautiful; shimmering blue and white, with a kind face and intelligent eyes. Each of her paws ended in a small wash of sea water, bubbling up over her fur and spraying my face.

You see Sunken Men?

The question formed in my head and I nodded.

You know of Dreaming God?

Again, I gave a shallow nod.

You are Alpha Wolf. Lead fight back. I die to give you hope. No Sea Wolves means no fight. Must be fight... fight back. All others can be saved if Sea Wolves fight back.

30

The Severed Hand had erupted into chaos. Homes were fled, barricades were erected, and people died. Eastron families and many remaining Pure Ones had gathered in the Pup Yards, defended by hundreds of warriors. For the first time, I saw Sea Wolves and Nissalite fighting side by side. So many people were cut off. Gangs of ten, or five thousand. The hold was sliced to pieces by the chaos spawn of the Dreaming God, forming lines of destruction and reducing anything in their way to a bloody mist or a splintered ruin. They moved in floating waves, with no order or tactics to their senseless destruction. All that stopped them was stone. The Wolf House was the only refuge for hundreds of thousands of people. Less the thousands who had already died.

"Another group broke through," said Jonas Grief. "A few hundred. Get them a place to sleep."

We were at the front entrance to the Wolf House, underneath huge archways and behind a thick column of duellists. The master-at-arms was in charge, ordering men and women to help where they could. He was a combat general, but surprisingly good under the current circumstances. Rys Coldfire had fallen in and out of consciousness as he exhausted his wyrd with every sortie into the hold. He'd rescued hundreds, and ignored calls for him to rest, but he could only keep himself alive for so long at such a pace.

Tomas Red Fang and I had conveyed nothing of the totem's intentions, and for us, the wait was torturous, as the Old Bitch of the Sea regained sufficient strength to attack. Time meant little to spirits, and *soon* was the closest timeframe we'd been given. It had so far been two hours.

Lagertha Blood tapped me on the shoulder. Like me, she'd not yet advanced into the hold, nor drawn her blade against the chaos spawn. "You're waiting for something, Mistress Brand," said the young girl. "What?"

"You'll know it when it happens," I replied. "You'll see me draw my cutlass and rush into the hold. From that point, we either save the Severed Hand or we watch it die."

"We have many behind the walls already," said Lagertha.

I smiled down at the girl, somewhat charmed by her naivety. "We have ten thousand ... maybe. That's not a hold. That's a village." I felt a tingle travel up my spine, and a pleasant tang of salt water caressed my nostrils. "The true battle is about to start."

A lyrical growl filled the air. It echoed around stone buildings and caused thousands of eyes to look up at the break in the glass. The chaos spawn, gnashing in waves of pulpy flesh, paused, the waves of destruction suddenly still. Then an enormous wolf's head appeared above. The Old Bitch of the Sea was slavering, with drool coating its huge teeth. Its claws hung from the edge of the tear as it looked into the realm of form for the first time.

I drew my cutlass and smiled at Lagertha. "It's time."

The wolf pounced, jumping through the tear and landing in the realm of form. It stood on buildings and crushed chaos spawn beneath its paws, growling with murderous intent. The spawn hissed a discordant sound of defiance and massed together, clearing a dozen routes of safety for the citizens of the hold.

I parted the ranks of duellists guarding the Wolf House, and advanced into the open. I heard whispers from those around me, speculating on why Adeline Brand had suddenly acted. They beheld the totem of the Severed Hand, and one of its most powerful duellists, and they moved to flank me, forming a phalanx of swords and wyrd.

"I am Adeline Brand," I shouted, "called the Alpha Wolf." I walked forwards, not turning to address those behind me. I knew they listened. "I will save as many people of the hold as I can, for this night will *not* be our last. Who will come with me?"

A cheer sounded behind me, rising as a guttural snarl of agreement, and flowing into hundreds of battle cries and oaths of fidelity.

"Once more for the Severed Hand," I roared, charging forwards. The words suddenly meant something again, and I released my wyrd, running west to Jacob's Tower and the Pup Yards.

"All of you, on Mistress Brand," commanded Jonas Grief, backed up by a shout and a raised sword from Lagertha Blood. I heard running feet and clanking metal, moving in my wake. I heard them call me *the Alpha Wolf*.

The churning chaos spawn cut our path, but were beginning to move away, as many tried to swarm the Old Bitch of the Sea, who towered over Fisherman's Yard, devouring any enemy that got close. The wolf was more of a threat than the Sea Wolves. The totem couldn't win, however immense and powerful it was, but its savagery bought us time. Not to mention the mouthfuls of chaos spawn it tore apart. But dozens of spirits still blocked my path.

I skewered the first, penetrating its bubbling body just below its largest mouth. I withdrew the blade and followed up with a powerful downward swing, turning the spawn to green mist. Rys had made killing them look easy, but their bodies were dense, and made of some form other than flesh and bone. They vibrated in the air, hovering a foot above the ground, but their reach was minimal. At sword length, they were a grotesque bubble of eyes and teeth, lunging at anything they could eat. And I was no longer afraid. The Wolf's Bastard had said it best – *they die*. Other duellists were hesitant, finding their minds assaulted by the raw chaos before them. But they followed my example, taking strength in my ferocity, and covering my back as we cut into the mob of chaos spawn. These things had killed Arthur *and* Jaxon, and my rage had returned.

The wolf howled. The sound was beautiful and mournful, as the Old Bitch of the Sea weathered bites, and crushed gangs of spirits. Buildings shook and dust fell, as her huge paws struggled for grip. Her presence, from her bulky tail, swishing overhead, to her sorrowful howl, added more to the duellists' confidence than anything *I* could do. But I was on the ground, and I had a sword in my hand. And they followed me into battle.

From the Pup Yards, I heard the survivors rally. From Red Claw's Rise and Fool's Town, mobs of Eastron and Pure Ones rushed towards us. Some had been barricaded in stone buildings, others had been fighting, but all wore scars of pain or loss. They'd seen friends and family die. They'd seen the refuge of the Severed Hand turned into a nightmare, in a flash of teeth and chaos. Hundreds, then thousands, they ran, walked and crawled towards the safety of the Wolf House. They would live, as would the hold. I believed it. For the first time since I was caged at the Bay of Bliss, I felt powerful. I felt like Adeline Brand, called the Alpha Wolf, duellist of the Severed Hand.

Soon I die.

The words were soft and didn't distract me, though I felt a pang of regret.

I will re-form. One day, far from now. Want to know Sea Wolves when I return. Lead them. Lead them in fight. Save Eastron. Alpha Wolf.

We reached the Pup Yards. Ahead, countless people allowed themselves to believe they'd survive the night. Behind, the road to the Wolf House was clear. The last few chaos spawn formed a floating barrier between us and the survivors. But above our heads, the wolf howled in pain. Almost all the spirits had enveloped her, gnawing at her fur and diminishing her power with every bite.

I leave you fragment. Keep it safe.

I felt a dull pain in my head, and my surroundings suddenly sharpened. My wyrd was more focused and my attacks more precise. I killed a spawn with one strike, slicing it in two. The green mist parted to join the sickly cloud above, and the next bubbling mound of teeth died as quickly. It felt as if my cutlass was suddenly razor sharp, meeting no resistance from the void-stuff of the spirits. She'd lodged a fragment of herself in me, amplifying my wyrd, and strengthening my body.

Then the road was clear, and I was enveloped in running Eastron and Pure Ones. Thousands fled the Pup Yards, and thousands more ran to safety from other roads. I stopped, breathing deeply and letting my wyrd retreat. The hanging green mist quickly disappeared, but the multitudes still swarmed above us. Jonas Grief reached my side, both of us looking up at the dying wolf.

"Don't stop now, Adeline," said the master-at-arms. "We haven't got long until those things need something more to eat."

"Get them to the Wolf House," I ordered. "As many as you can."

He obeyed, finding some new deference that I'd not previously seen. "Alpha Wolf," he replied. "This gives us time. Until they breach the Wolf House."

I ignored him and strode forwards, getting as clear a view as I could of the Old Bitch of the Sea. Towering above buildings, shimmering blue against the black sky, the totem of the Severed Hand writhed in pain. Her form was mostly eclipsed by writhing chaos spawn, with only her rampant muzzle visible, pointed up towards the break in the glass. The multitudes had been dented, but the wolf had spent its power. She tried to scratch the gnawing creatures from her body, but her strength waned more and more with each movement. With a final lunge upwards, she extended her neck and howled back at the void. Then she slumped, dissipating into a huge cloud of white and blue mist, and the Old Bitch of the Sea was gone. But the part of her she'd gifted to me remained strong.

"Addie, time to move," snapped Jonas, grabbing my shoulder.

I scanned my surroundings, looking at things in detail for the first time. Men and women, rushing in a panicked wave, streamed towards the Wolf House. Duellists flanked the streets, encouraging the citizens of the hold to get behind the huge stone walls as quickly as possible. Above, the immense cloud of chaos spawn began to move back to ground level, reforming into its destructive whirlwind. It became a race. Eastron and Pure Ones shouted at each other to hurry up, as the spawn descended ever closer.

I'd begun jogging back, shepherding the fleeing folk from the rear. I now started to sprint. "Move! All of you," I shouted, stowing my cutlass.

More shouting and more fleeing folk, joining the mob from every adjoining street. I turned the corner at the base of Jacob's Tower and faced the Wolf House. The ground level and the huge central entrance were filled with beckoning duellists, preparing to drop the portcullis when everyone was inside. Other, smaller entrances were at choking point, unable to contain the sudden thousands who fled the destruction. The entire hold wanted entrance to the Wolf House. More survivors remained in the city, barricaded within other stone buildings, but the majority were swarming in front of me.

"Master-at-arms," I shouted, making Jonas Grief face me across the line of fleeing folk. "Assemble every duellist to protect these people. The portcullis drops when I say. Not before."

He nodded and snapped orders to those near him. The command was relayed and duellists assembled. Multiple lines of people were slowly squeezed into the Wolf House, as the warriors of the Severed Hand formed a protective line behind them. I saw faces locked in fear, and others fighting to keep control, but no duellist ran or abandoned their duty.

The hovering mass of chaos spawn had returned to ground level, and they bubbled their way through empty streets and back alleys, stretching out like the fingers of an abominable hand. They were close and getting closer.

"Hold this ground," I commanded, striding down the line of duellists. "This is *our* ground. If we must die, we will die hard, giving these fuckers nothing."

"Column!" ordered Jonas Grief, making the duellists re-deploy into a formation, three warriors deep, facing Fisherman's Yard and the rapidly approaching spirits.

My mind was assaulted by numbers, too large for me to process. The fleeing citizens, the swarming chaos spawn, the fearful duellists. Thousands upon thousands of friends *and* enemies, all focused on the Wolf House. I'd never seen so many people *or* spirits in one place, though I didn't feel small or insignificant. I would lead these warriors. We couldn't win by defeating the chaos spawn, but saving the hold was the greater victory. I would honour the Old Bitch of the Sea, and the strength she'd given me.

"This just solves the first problem," said a voice in my head, sounding like the Wisp. "They can't eat through stone, but *you* can't defend every entrance. We've lost too many duellists. Too many foolish men have thrown their lives away, believing a Sea Wolf could never be defeated. We need help."

"Not now," I replied. "Now we need to deal with the first problem."

I stepped in front of the column, facing the oncoming spirits. Jonas joined me, hefting twin cutlasses and gritting his teeth. The Wolf's Bastard had not emerged, and the two of us were alone, the only elders of the hold able to stand and fight.

Tomas Red Fang was elsewhere, Lagertha Blood was not a seasoned warrior and many more were either absent or dead. Lord Ulric's blade in particular would be sorely missed. The First Fang, his son, and the senior duellists still on Nowhere, would not be enough to turn the fight, but they'd make a hell of a mess before the hold fell. The Sea Wolves had earned that much. We'd at least earned a good death.

"No spirits, gods or men hold dominion over me." No-one heard my whispered words. "I fight now to honour our totem. To preserve what I know... and to avenge those I've lost."

The chaos spawn of the Dreaming God rushed forwards, frothing out of every conceivable opening before us. Alleys, roads, windows, rooftops, everything was eclipsed by a tide of mouths, eyes and pulpy flesh. The column of duellists took a step back, gawking up at the approaching surge. Jonas Grief was about to join them, until *I* took a step to the front.

"Stand!" I roared. "We die *hard*!"

The line steadied behind me, as duellists remembered their oaths. They pulsed with wyrd and hefted weapons, each man and woman fighting fear to stand with Adeline Brand, called the Alpha Wolf, duellist of the Severed Hand.

The buildings disappeared behind a wall of spirits. They massed into an enormous amoeba, bubbling with teeth and eyes, but their fleshy forms met only steel. I cut a dent in the middle, then Jonas Grief sliced through two bulging eyes to my left. Then the column of duellists attacked. We met the wave of chaos a hundred feet from the base of the Wolf House, with screaming folk behind us. We were their last line of defence, and we threw everything at the chaos spawn.

Every cut and thrust meant another handful of people could get beyond the walls of the Wolf House. Every duellist who died, torn apart by whirling teeth and flesh, bought the lives of dozens.

We died hard. The column was fighting a flowing tide of chaos, at every turn trying to flow around us or envelop us. The wave stretched out again, reforming into bulbous fingers, where it was impossible to discern individual spirits. Our formation broke up as duellists fought to stop the spawn getting past us. I acquired a second cutlass from a fallen duellist, and Jonas and I held the centre, using range to kill, and keep the spirits at bay. As long as our wyrd remained strong, we received only glancing bites, but neither we nor the duellists at our back could keep up the defence forever.

I chanced a look behind us, momentarily taking my eyes from the front. The lines of fleeing folk had been whittled down to the last few groups, struggling to clear the portcullis. The smaller doors had been closed and would be barricaded from within. It was time to fall back. Any longer and we'd have no duellists left. As I was about to order a retreat, my shoulder was snared by a gummy mouth, filled with gnashing teeth. Its weight sent me to the ground and its lines of wicked teeth dug deeply into my flesh. More mouths loomed, as I struggled to move away. I roared, wildly stabbing my remaining blade into the void-stuff of the spirit. My shoulder and arm went numb just as the spirit dissipated into green mist.

"Get up," shouted Jonas, dragging me to my feet. Behind us, rushing forwards in a rescue effort, were Oswald Leaf and his Kneeling Wolves. Tasha Strong was with them, and they screamed at us to fall back.

"Back to the Wolf House," I croaked, as a nearby duellist had his head bitten off in a single gluttonous gulp.

"Fall back! Fall back!" The command was shouted again and again, but there were few left to hear it. The Kneeling Wolves didn't cover us or join the attack. They just grabbed us in a wave of retreat, and all remaining duellists broke, running as fast as they could away from the bubbling wave of chaos.

My arm hung limp and my wyrd was spent, but I could still run. Jonas ran next to me, and Tasha rushed to give me her assistance, as reaching arms of chaos spawn attempted to envelop us. The Wolf House was close, with Lagertha Blood, Tomas Red Fang, and hundreds of others beckoning us to safety.

"Drop the portcullis," I commanded, as the survivors sprinted across open ground, with stone streets beneath our blood-soaked boots. The heavy steel framing poked out from an arch above the main entrance, as those within prepared to release the chains that held it up. We reached the wide, main entranceway and I locked eyes with a fleeing girl, part of the last group to be pulled inside. She was young and skinny, with innocent eyes, and I almost needed to tackle her through the falling portcullis.

Warriors with spears formed within the ground level, skilfully keeping the chaos spawn at bay through the heavy steel framing. All of a sudden there was a kind of calm. I couldn't hear the shouting and screaming, though I could see twisted and ashen faces, trying to process what was happening to the Severed Hand. All I could hear was a high-pitched whine that started at my extremities and enveloped my head. I found myself slumped against a pillar, whilst people rushed around me. Then I turned and looked at my shoulder.

"Oh, fuck," I muttered, fighting to stay conscious. I'd lost a chunk of my left arm, ripped from my bicep and shoulder. My forearm and hand were limp, hanging by tendons and bone, and what remained of my leather armour.

I saw Tomas Red Fang appear over me. He was talking, but I couldn't hear the words. Tasha joined him, with tears falling down her face.

I smiled, feeling no pain. "It's okay," I whispered. "I fight with my right hand."

I awoke in silence, with a rhythmic pounding in my head. My first thoughts were of Jaxon and my brother, and whether they'd be proud of me. Then I wondered about the silence and the state of the hold. How many were safe and how many had died? My third thought was about the emptiness I felt. The totem spirit of the Severed Hand had been destroyed, and she left an intangible hole in my heart. I doubted the Sea Wolves would ever be the same, no matter how many cowered within the Wolf House. But she'd made sure I'd never forget her, by giving me a chunk of her power.

"You can sleep as long as you need," said Tomas Red Fang. The spirit-master sat on a wooden stool, and I realized *I* was lying on a low table, covered by a simple blanket. "There's a cot in the corner. Might be more comfortable." He sounded weary, with a catch in his voice.

"What news?" I murmured, still not fully awake.

He sighed, heavily. "The sun comes up in three hours. The sky is clear… aside from the jagged tear in the glass.

A woman gave birth, not ten minutes ago, on the carpet next to the First Fang's table. The Bloody Halls are now a miasma of terrified families... and I cut off your left arm two hours ago."

I took a deep breath. The pounding in my head slowly retreated, to be replaced by a light-headed calm. "I'm quite fucking angry about that," I whispered. "But I want to know if the Sea Wolves still exist, or are we still to be dinner for chaos spirits?" I turned my head to look at him, and saw a heavily bandaged stump where my arm used to be. I could feel that wyrd had been used to burn the wound, removing any chance of infection.

Tomas leant away from the table, his wrinkly folds of skin undulating as he sighed again. "They're like ants," he replied. "They crawl over everything, searching for holes, weaknesses, anything made of wood. We can hold them at the portcullis, but they realized quickly that wasn't the easiest way in. Windows and balconies are our problem. And food. We'll break before we lose the fight. We don't have the numbers."

"The numbers," I repeated, in a weary rumble. "How many? How many survived?"

He paused, rubbing his deep-set eyes. "One-third. Give or take. The Kneeling Wolves are listing the dead and missing, but it's a slow process. And we have no idea how many Pure Ones are dead. *They* won't even talk to us. They're on the second level, nursing their own wounds."

"They've never seen the inside of the Wolf House," I murmured. "Men and women, who've lived within sight of it all their lives, but never set foot within. Give them time. Is Rys awake?"

Tomas nodded. "Though not yet able to walk. The fool nearly killed himself."

"We'll need his blade," I grumbled, struggling to keep my eyes open. "We're not finished yet. How long until I can fight?"

31

Everything I knew was gone. My brother, my best friend, my lover. Even the Severed Hand. The hold was a shell of stone, with rubble and splinters marking every street. The Wolf House remained, but it was changed. It was a vertical town, with families crammed into every stone corner large enough to hold them. Only the highest level of the Bloody Halls remained off-limits. Even my humble apartment had been turned into a triage, where those with minor wounds were assessed and passed on. All the time, anyone able to wield a blade or point a spear was frantically keeping the chaos spawn at bay. The Bloody Halls had windows and balconies, and every other level was a potential point of ingress. And I kept hearing the same phrase – *it's only a matter of time*.

It was hard to process what was happening. The only way to get a complete view of the hold was to travel to the void, and Tomas Red Fang had advised against it for all but the most seasoned spirit-masters. But word had filtered throughout the Wolf House. Everything but stone buildings and walls had been destroyed. The wooden jetties of Laughing Rock remained intact, as if the spawn couldn't traverse the water, but everywhere else was now their domain. At least for now. The sad reality was that, even if Lord Ulric returned with his ships, we'd still be hopelessly outnumbered.

And it was hard not to stare at the stump of my left arm. It had been my least favourite arm, but still not something I would have willingly sacrificed. I'd risen from bed earlier than Tomas had advised and needed help to dress. I was weighted down by what had happened, but no-one dared to question me or send me back to bed. The blood I'd lost, and the sheer trauma of being crippled, made me light-headed, but the Old Bitch of the Sea had strengthened my will as well as my body and my wyrd.

I'd made my way to a map room – one of the few empty chambers remaining – poring over plans of underground tunnels and possible escape routes. Most were old and unusable, built in the days when Sea Wolves still had things to fear, and the remainder were narrow, and led no further than the treeline of the Wood of Scars. Escape wasn't an option.

I leaned against the map table and took a few deep breaths. I wore only a woollen robe and sandals, and was barely strong enough to walk unaided. I couldn't fight, but I could still think. Unfortunately, all my thoughts led me to the same phrase – it was only a matter of time. All I could think to do was struggle on with my sword belt, limp to where there was fighting, and flail painfully at the chaos spawn. It wasn't much of a plan. Currently, a healthy fisherman would be a better addition to our defences than me. The power I'd been given had stopped the wound from ending my fight, but it wouldn't grow back my arm, or give me a week's rest.

"Would you accept help?" asked the voice of my friend.

"Do you mean advice? Because *that* I would accept."

"No, I mean help. And not from me. Would you accept it?"

"Help from who?" I asked.

For a moment there was no answer and I again wondered if I was merely hallucinating. Then I heard Jaxon sigh. "You won't like it," he replied. "But it'll soon be dawn, and the sunrise will bring powerful shadows."

I scratched at the bandaged stump of my left arm. "Having your voice in my head is not entirely unpleasant, but please make sense."

"I can see strange things in the void," he replied. "The air is close and charged with energy. It's as if something is waiting for the dawn. Something powerful."

"Some kind of help I won't like?"

"There are owl spirits, circling far overhead," said Jaxon. "Somehow the Dark Brethren are involved."

I snarled, a hundred potential conspiracies entering my head. "They're here to help finish the job," I muttered, wondering how long it would take me to don my armour.

"No," replied the voice of the Wisp. "They are here as allies. There is a benevolent power behind them. A shadow."

I snorted my scepticism and hobbled out of the map room. In the corridor were lines of huddled young men and women, mostly those who had lost parents. They all knew who I was, but my demeanour was clearly not conducive to conversation, as none of them spoke to me. At the end of the passage, where stairs led down to the First Fang's table, I was met by two duellists, flanking Jonas Grief.

"Addie, if you're going to get out of bed, please tell someone where you're going," said the master-at-arms. "These halls are more crowded than usual."

"My presence doesn't add up to much," I replied, thankful to have someone to lean against. "Give me a few days and I'll be almost back to my old self. Do we have a few days?"

He bowed his head. It was first time I'd seen fear in his eyes. The same could be said of the duellists behind him and every other Sea Wolf, licking their wounds in the Wolf House.

"Jonas," I said, gently. "It took *me* weeks to get over it. Now answer the question."

"No," he replied. "We don't have a few days. They'll breach soon after dawn.

"Then let us hope the dawn is an ally," I said, letting him help me down the stairs. "I want to see the hold. Clear a balcony."

"Easier said than done," he replied. "The fucking spirits reform within a minute or two. There're just too many of them."

At the bottom of the stairs, the huge, red-carpeted hall of Lord Ulric Blood was filled to the brim with huddled folk. Around the high table, wounded and screaming people were tended to by spirit-masters and herbalists. And sitting alone by the far door, with tear-filled eyes, was Rys Coldfire. The Wolf's Bastard wore battered armour and his fist was still locked around the hilt of his falchion. He'd lost no limbs and suffered no serious wounds, but the defeat in his eyes was almost crippling.

I stood, looking at him, for several moments, until Jonas led me across the hall.

"Mistress Brand," said Rys, trying to smile. "You look well." He nodded at the stump of my arm. "Lucky it was the left. You'll be just as dangerous with practice."

"Practice takes time," I replied. "We don't have time."

"It seems not. One hundred and sixty-seven years. Hardly a long time in the grand scheme of the world. I thought the

Sea Wolves would last longer. But I heard what you did, and you should be commended ... Alpha Wolf."

We shared a nod of respect. "The dawn may yet have a surprise for us," I said. "Let us stand and greet it."

The Wolf's Bastard stood from his chair, grunting at sore limbs and minor wounds. "I've made my peace with lady death. She can no longer do anything to me. Send for Tomas Red Fang to join us."

Jonas, Rys and I made our way down two more flights of stairs, bringing duellists in our wake. Where the Bloody Halls ended, the defence of the Wolf House began. Wide corridors, leading to windows and balconies, were now the frontline. Columns of spearmen worked in rotation, keeping the chaos spawn at bay, with water, food and medicine constantly flowing through the lower levels. But attrition was slowly killing us.

We were greeted with salutes and faltering oaths of loyalty. These men and woman were broken, but were too brave to admit it. They saluted our names and asked if they could assist us, but each pair of eyes was slowly dying. Jonas offered kind words of encouragement, but Rys and I remained silent. I was the only Eastron here not wearing armour and I leant on his shoulder, tuning out the discomfort.

"The balcony," I muttered, pointing down the largest corridor. "We need to see the dawn."

"Be light soon," roared Jonas. "Let's clear those bastards, so we can see the sun one last time."

It was enough. The defending Sea Wolves were functioning on their last nerve, just needing one reason to carry on fighting. Perhaps seeing this endless night make way for dawn was enough. Once more for the Severed Hand – the words had never been more true.

At the end of the corridor, framed by mahogany beams, was a wide balcony. It pointed south across the hold, but the view was of eyes, flesh, mouths and death. There was no portcullis, just a narrowing of the stone passageway, allowing a line of five spears to hold the ground. The spawn were patient, testing each and every defender until they made a mistake and died. It was a pattern repeated across hundreds of windows and dozens of balconies. But at *this* balcony the defenders rallied.

Five spears became ten, then the column advanced. Two more surges, and the chaos spawn were pushed back. The mass of teeth and eyes snapped at spears, and splintered wood, but only three warriors died getting us to the balcony. Rys and Jonas stayed either side of me, as the last embers of defiance showed us a dark sky and a distant glow. A window opened through the curtain of gnashing teeth and thrusting spears, and we saw the sun begin to rise across the Severed Hand.

"In this realm, there are monsters we should fear," said Jaxon's voice. "But there are other realms and other powers, in front of which even monsters would do well to cower."

I was helped onto the balcony, and a ring of spears quickly lined the railing before me. Jonas directed the warriors to hold the ground, and Rys stood at my left shoulder. Up and down, the stone of the Wolf House was covered with crawling amoeba. A cocoon of pulpy flesh, rising above the Severed Hand. When I managed to pull my eyes from the chaos spawn, all I saw was a ruined hold. Everything wooden was gone. Towers, walls, and thousands of buildings. The outline of stone remained, providing a strange sketch of what the Severed Hand used to look like. The tear in the glass was still there, though it was now more of a slice than a gaping wound.

Tomas Red Fang appeared next to Rys and me. "Something comes with the dawn," said the anxious spirit-master.

"A shadow," I replied, smiling at the old man. "Perhaps our last hope."

The sun poked over the horizon for the first time, beaming a blanket of golden light from the Bright Coast to the Wolf House. As it struck stone, dense black shadows cut through the hold. Every feature, every ruin, they each contributed to the lengthening carpet of black. It was as if the shadows of dawn had been waiting, and now sprinted to cover the hold. They appeared to need just a glint of light, dancing forwards, unnaturally large and shimmering.

"Is this wyrd?" queried Rys, stepping to the edge of the balcony. "Look! The spirits pause."

We all cast our eyes around the Wolf House. The chaos spawn had stopped gnashing at our defences, and slowly pivoted, as if the shadows called to them, or represented some kind of threat. They backed away from the stone walls, allowing the defenders respite. Every window and balcony was now filled with gawking men and women. They were tired, bloodied and restless, with the encroaching shadows drawing every set of eyes.

The blackness danced, rising from the ground and forming into sinuous whirlwinds of shadow. Small at first, the whirlwinds gently roiled in the charged air of the hold. A thousand different tones of black, plunging backwards and becoming tunnels.

"Be ready," I commanded. "Something is about to happen. For good or for ill, we must be prepared."

"Those aren't void bridges," said Tomas. "But something's definitely coming."

The spawn came together as a single, enormous ball of polypous flesh, teeth and eyes. They left the Wolf House and rippled through the air to meet the lengthening tunnels of shadow.

From my vantage point, on a high balcony, I imagined some incomprehensible spirit-war was taking place. That was until I heard the clank of metal. The closest shadow tunnel was also the largest, and from its depths came a column of warriors. They were indistinct and marched in some kind of close formation. Similar columns emerged from every shadow tunnel. They were all angled downwards, encircling the stone around the Wolf House.

Spears came into view, followed by chainmail and rectangular shields. Finally, black helmets, styled in the likeness of an owl. Dark Brethren void legionnaires, though too distant for me to identify which legion. Around me, the Sea Wolf defenders gasped, too confused to be angry and too tired to move. Everyone just stood in silence. Even Jonas Grief and the Wolf's Bastard. They stood with me and Tomas Red Fang – four elders of the hold, watching our oldest enemies strike the stone of the Severed Hand, and unable to react. My remaining hand tensed, as if it felt strange not being around the hilt of a sword, and I saw similar signals from those around me.

The Dark Brethren exited the shadow tunnels and formed into dense columns, with shields locked together and spears held low. They saw the huge chaos amoeba, but took no steps back. Their helmets masked their emotions, allowing no fear or confusion to show. Each warrior was a perfect copy of the next, with only minor differences in stature.

"How many men is a legion?" asked Tomas Red Fang.

"Five thousand," I replied. "Not enough."

Almost before I'd finished speaking, the shadow tunnels coalesced into a single sheet of blackness. As if alive, the shimmering darkness glided through the air, wrapping itself around the chaos spawn. For a moment, the Wolf House was again enveloped in night, as the shadow passed in front of the balcony. I imagined an enormous hand, half-closing around the bubbling spirits and pulling them towards the waiting spears. The spawn gnashed and squirmed, trying to bite their way free, but every time a mouth closed over shadow, a spirit hissed and blinked out of existence. Thousands died, somehow crushed by a closing hand of shadow. Others tried to flee, buzzing away from the mass, but meeting only a carpet of spears.

In moments, the shadow had killed more chaos spawn than the collective might of the Sea Wolves *and* their totem. Any spirits that were attacked by the Dark Brethren were already trying to run, and were a fraction compared to those crushed by the shadow creature. I was stunned, as was everyone who watched from the Wolf House. Suddenly, the presence of the void legionnaires was trivial. I didn't understand what I was seeing. Was it another kind of spirit? Or some twisted weapon of the Dark Brethren?

"I think it's a god," said the Wisp. "I see a being of form *and* void, but belonging to neither. And they worship it… some of them."

The hand closed into a ball, slowly crushing the spawn into nothingness. A few thousand stray spirits were driven into the path of the legion, and quickly corralled into a killing ground between advancing spearmen. Then the air was still. The chaos spawn were all gone and the shadow had pulsed down into a single tight orb of darkness.

I craned my neck around the balcony and saw thousands of Sea Wolves, bearing silent witness to the rising sun. Exhausted and wounded defenders were roused, helped to windows and balconies, and shown that they no longer needed to fight. They understood nothing else of what they saw. Just that they would live another day.

The orb of shadow continued to shrink, until it disappeared below, amidst lock-step legionnaires. They lowered their spears and stowed their shields. I heard commands to *stand-at-ease*, and they formed a disciplined column of owl faces, looking up to the Wolf House.

"We should go below," said Rys Coldfire. "At least greet them and their shadow with a modicum of respect."

"That thing could annihilate us," said Tomas Red Fang.

"These people have fought enough," said Jonas Grief, gesturing to the battered citizens of the Severed Hand.

All three of them looked at me. They would never openly show deference, but each now felt they should seek my counsel. Something, other than my arm, had changed, and they instinctively reacted to it. I straightened, finding that the stump of my arm barely hurt and my legs again had strength.

"We greet them below," I said. "With swords peace-tied. Whatever it was ... whatever they brought, it saved the hold. Remember that."

*

The portcullis had been raised, and the ground level was packed with stunned citizens. Some whispered of victory, some of soon being able to return home. But most were in shock. Sea Wolves were hard people, and this would either break us or make us harder. As for me... I was strangely focused. Nothing had made sense when I returned from the Bay of Bliss. I'd seen things I didn't understand, and lost too many people. But I was somehow changed. One arm or no, I was now called the Alpha Wolf.

Rys Coldfire stood over my left shoulder and Tomas stood over my right. Jonas Grief led a cohort of toughened duellists behind us, with Lagertha Blood holding a place of honour in the middle. We left the Wolf House, followed by a gang of Kneeling Wolves, with Oswald Leaf and Tasha Strong amongst them. Before us was a mass of black armour and spears, parting in the middle to allow their leaders to meet us.

"Peace!" shouted a gravelly voice. "We have done our killing for this morning."

I was at the centre, striding away from the Wolf House, with a broken hold and five thousand Dark Brethren in front of me. I stopped, within a respectful distance of the void legionnaires, and allowed the duellists of the Severed Hand to form a line either side of me.

"To whom do I speak?" I replied, raising my voice.

Two men approached from the mass of shields and spears. A Dark Brethren and a hulking Sea Wolf. The Brethren wore a long leather coat over a breastplate, and an intractable look in his intelligent eyes. The Sea Wolf twitched manically, but hid it behind a fierce scowl. It was Xavyer Ice, called the Grim Wolf, elder of Nowhere, and his presence was almost as confusing as a dozen other things that had happened since the sun came up.

"My name is Marius Cyclone, I'm called the Stranger," said the Brethren commander. "Who are you?"

A thousand Sea Wolves growled. None of them would know the Stranger's face, just his name and reputation. Most would have served aboard ships that pillaged the Dark Harbour's trade routes, or seen friends die at the flash of a Brethren void path. Of all the people who could have saved the hold, Marius Cyclone was the least likely. As we hated *him*, he was renowned for his contempt for the Sea Wolves.

I reduced my reply to a curt nod at the Dark Brethren. The Stranger wore a bastard sword across his back, and a blue tattoo poked up from his leather collar.

"Her name is Adeline Brand," offered the Grim Wolf. "*That* one is Rys Coldfire, the Wolf's Bastard. I don't know the others."

"Xavyer Ice," said Rys. "Are you a traitor now? Because if you're not, you'd better tell me quickly." His hand went to his falchion. He could advance, draw his weapon, and kill, all in the blink of an eye. If he chose to.

"He's no traitor," said Marius Cyclone.

"Silence!" I commanded. "You saved the Severed Hand, so I won't fillet you for daring to speak here, but your opinion of Xavyer Ice is not relevant." I turned to the Grim Wolf. "Answer the fucking question."

The old man of Ice was almost as large as the First Fang, and his sparkling blue eyes shone with almost as much wyrd. "I don't want to fight either of you," he replied. "But question my honour again, and you'll leave me no choice."

Rys assessed him, gritting his teeth and trying to decide whether or not he liked the answer. A mob of Sea Wolves stood behind him, ready to act, but there was little fight left in their limbs.

I decided to show some leadership, and perhaps stay Rys's falchion. "If you're not a traitor, why do you stand alone with one of the Cyclone brothers?"

Marius smiled and drew a fingertip across his lips, indicating that he planned to remain silent. The Grim Wolf twitched at the lack of help, glancing at the Wolf's Bastard and me. He appeared to be struggling with an answer, as if his thoughts were conflicted. "I don't know," he muttered, looking at the ground. "I just know that we are all going to die if we don't flee this realm of form."

Rys looked at me, trying to convey something. I sensed that he was unconvinced by the answer, and felt gratified that he checked with me before killing the Grim Wolf. The hold was a ruin, and thousands were dead, but the Wolf's Bastard was still strong enough to punish treachery when he saw it.

"I've had enough of this," snapped Marius Cyclone, interrupting Rys, as he reached for his falchion. "Sea Wolves are ignorant brutes, unable to see beyond their blades. If strength is all you understand, I will show you strength."

I heard the thin whine of a distant whistle, and saw shadows gather around my feet. The cold morning sun danced off ruined buildings and statue-like warriors, creating fingers of darkness at every angle. Whatever shadow beast the Dark Brethren had unleashed, appeared to be returning.

"Show respect," said the Wisp, murmuring in my head. "You are about to address a god."

I reached out with my remaining arm, catching Rys before he could draw his blade and kill anyone. "Let it play out," I ordered, causing a shallow nod from the Wolf's Bastard.

Marius Cyclone raised his arms, as if summoning the shadows to him. The carpet of black rose from the ground, but didn't envelop the Stranger. It coalesced behind him, eclipsing my view of the void legion, and forming into a shape. It happened slowly, giving the Sea Wolves at my back time to retreat a step. Even Jonas Grief and Tomas Red Fang took an involuntary stride away from the rising monolith of shadow. Only Rys and I stood our ground, facing down whatever the Stranger had summoned.

"We've had enough of conflict," said Marius, allowing the immense shadow to form arms and legs behind him. "I detest your people. Your arrogance, your pettiness, your lack of sophistication. But my fear of the Sunken God is stronger than my hatred of the Sea Wolves." His eyes were dark and sunken, as if plagued by memories. "I am not my brothers. I sent no assassin to your hold, nor do I wish to kill you now. I forgo the vengeance I am due for all your acts of brutal piracy ... but you *will* listen."

His words were given gravitas by the looming shadow behind him. It formed into a giant, thirty feet tall, with a mirror of stars where its face should have been. The limbs oozed and flowed, as if made of thick, black liquid, dripping onto the stone and vanishing. The towering shadow creature blocked out the morning sun, casting a blanket of darkness over thousands of duellists.

"Stand your ground," I shouted. "We are Sea Wolves of the Severed Hand."

My words stopped them fleeing, but did nothing to alleviate their fear. The air became still. No-one whispered or shared ideas about what they were seeing and hearing. Questions of what the shadow giant *was* remained internal.

"Our Kingdom of the Four Claws will fall," said Marius Cyclone. "You've seen a fingernail of the enemy, but there is more to come. The Sunken God awakens and the Eastron are a doomed people. I offer you a chance to leave this realm and rebuild your lives in safety and peace. Many of your people are dead. But the rest *can* live. This creature..." he waved his arm at the shadow giant, "...is our friend."

I spat on the floor in front of him, and looked up at the shadow giant. "Is this Dark Brethren your slave?" I asked, approaching the looming figure. "Answer me!"

The Wolf's Bastard moved with me, but the two of us were alone, our resolve clearly stronger than the rest of our people. I couldn't speak for Rys, but *I'd* certainly seen scarier things than a sentient shadow. If it was truly a god, as Jaxon believed, I was not impressed.

"Answer me!" I repeated, this time in an aggressive snarl.

The shadow giant pointed its glassy face downwards, and I saw infinite layers of cosmic immensity. My teeth were gritted, and my remaining hand clenched tightly around the hilt of my cutlass. I would *not* be cowed by fear. Not now. Not again. The Old Bitch of the Sea had given me strength enough to resist any kind of terror.

"He won't answer you," said Marius Cyclone, keeping his face neutral. "Your question *or* your pointless Sea Wolf challenge." The Stranger looked up at the shadow giant, his eyes soft and grateful. "But he *is* our friend, and we have not finished you off... when we could easily have done so." He snorted, letting anger get the better of him. "Try to let that penetrate your vacuous head."

Rys punched him in the face. The Brethren elder staggered backwards, and was dropped to the ground by an additional left hook and right cross. "Stand up and I cut off your fucking cock," growled the Wolf's Bastard. "We're talking to the master, not the lackey."

The shadow giant reacted, swatting a heavy hand at Rys, like a cat pawing at a ball of string. He flew backwards, landing next to Lagertha Blood. Tomas rushed to his side, but the Wolf's Bastard quickly sat up, coughing blood from a bruised mouth and grasping his chest.

"I said," grunted Marius, gingerly getting to his feet, "that he won't answer you. And thank you for confirming my assessment of your character." The Stranger didn't appear angry, or even concerned. He didn't touch his bleeding face, or glare at Rys Coldfire. He just looked at me. "Showing you strength, Adeline Brand, is clearly not enough."

The shadow giant took a step towards me, its astral face tilting downwards. In my mind, creeping to my ears from a great distance, came a strange voice. It was clipped at the edges, but clear and precise. "Listen well, Sea Wolf. You will open your mind to me, and your people will follow you to safety. You will feel no pain, and I will force you to do nothing that damages your honour."

The voice was easy to listen to, like the comforting sound of a trusted relative. I felt a warmth envelop my mind, as if ceding control was the simplest, most natural thing in the world. Then I heard a growl, and the Old Bitch of the Sea reminded me who I was.

Must be fight…fight back against Sunken God. Not enough time to save all. The Sea Wolves must fight. The Sea Wolves' fight will save the Eastron.

The shadow giant balked, as if it had heard the she-wolf. It straightened back to its full height, towering over thousands of gawking warriors, and removing its influence from my mind. I became angry.

"No!" I roared, glaring daggers at the giant. "No gods, spirits, or men hold dominion over me."

My words carried far, but only Rys, clutching his wounded chest, moved to flank me. Tomas Red Fang, Jonas Grief, and the assembled duellists were still struggling to explain what they saw.

"Strike me if you wish, but my mind and my wyrd are my own." I turned my back on the shadow beast, and thrust out my chin, addressing the Sea Wolves. "I am Adeline Brand, called the Alpha Wolf. Listen to my words." I drew many eyes to me, but most were still fixed on the huge creature.

"Listen!" I boomed. "It you want to fear something, fear *me*." I pushed a fragment of the Old Bitch of the Sea outwards, framing my body and appearing as an opaque she-wolf, ravening above my head. Suddenly, *all* eyes were on me, and all ears listened. Faces hardened, and terrified people remembered they were Sea Wolves. The old spirit-master and the master-at-arms joined the Wolf's Bastard, their backs turned to the shadow giant, and their might added to my own. Together, with the she-wolf poised above me, the four of us produced enough wyrd to almost eclipse the shadow creature.

"We are Sea Wolves of the Severed Hand," I shouted, letting a growl follow every other word. "Send word to Moon Rock, to Rathwater, to Four Claw's Folly, and to Last Port. Tell them the Sunken Men and their dreaming god have returned … that they brought the teeth and gums of chaos to the Severed Hand." I paused, pulsing with rage. "But we are still here, and we *will* strike back." I bowed my head, trying to control my surging emotions. "Men, women, children and spirits are dead. Too many for me alone to mourn. I ask each of you to mourn with me … and then to fight with me."

"Once more for the Severed Hand," boomed Rys Coldfire, spraying blood and spit across the ground. "One more fight for the Severed Hand."

Some people cheered, some cried, others shouted or dropped to their knees. It was as if the entire hold used *that* moment, with our words echoing in their ears, to release tension. They'd fought for their homes, their futures and their loved ones. Each and every one would have seen someone they knew die. But, in this time and this place, each would pledge their lives to fight for the Severed Hand.

I turned from the crowd and addressed Marius Cyclone directly, keeping my eyes fixed on the Stranger, and away from the hulking shadow creature who'd tried to control my mind. "Run if you wish," I said. "But *our* path will lead us south. To the Sea of Stars and the Sunken City. If you have the will to fight, I invite you to bring your legions, your outrider knights, your void walkers. I may even let you sail with us. But if your will is … lacking. If your path is retreat." I frowned at him, shaking my head. "Then you should go, for cowardice has no place here."

"We are both Eastron from across the sea," replied Marius. "I wish you and your people the best. May your wyrd flow freely, for you cannot win."

I growled, taking a step towards the Dark Brethren. "There *will* be a fight back," I replied. "But do *not* think me a fool. For me, wisdom was hard won. I will attack this Sunken God, and I will war against his servants. If the wisdom of my totem means anything, you and I will help save the Eastron from extinction. Me with a blade, you with cowardice. Now, take your god and leave."

EPILOGUE

The man was Varn Gloom Scribe of the Mirralite. He stood on the deck of a small ship, gliding gently west through the Turtle Straits. It was early morning, and the sea winds were fresh and biting. He could see the Bright Coast of Nibonay to the north, but nothing but blue ocean to the south, east and west. The ship had full sails and ample speed. He'd be well clear of the island within a few hours.

He'd escaped the Severed Hand less than a day ago, leaving acolytes to complete the bindings, and he doubted the Sea Wolves would mount any kind of pursuit. They'd be too busy licking their wounds and crying over lost Invaders. They were short-sighted brutes, unaware of their own insignificance. He could slip away and continue his struggle, hopefully able to return to the Bay of Bliss as soon as possible.

Bells rang across the deck, and the Mirralite sailors called to each other that a sail approached. "Varn, you should stay out of sight," said the captain, a haggard man from the Bay of Bliss. "Few Invaders sail these waters. Just Sea Wolves."

Gloom Scribe took the warning and ignored it, moving to the starboard rail. From the west, cutting a large silhouette, was a warship. It had a low draft and three angular sails. As it sped forwards, the varn could discern a flag being raised from the deck. A black owl, with wide silver eyes.

"It's the *Claudia*," said Gloom Scribe. "From the Open Hand. Pull in the sails and raise a flag of submission. They meet us sooner than expected."

"Dark Brethren?" queried the captain. "They don't sail the Turtle Straits. And are not to be trusted."

The varn looked at him, letting a flicker of madness glint across his eyes. "Submit," he commanded. "Now!"

The captain backed away in terror and hastily ordered a white flag to be raised. The sailors responded with equal fear, going about their duties quickly, but muttering to each other about ill omens and bad luck. They were useful pawns, but remained superstitious children.

He looked up at the *Claudia*, towering over the small Mirralite ship. It trimmed its sails and turned into the wind, quickly coming to a complete stop. Armed legionnaires lined the railings, their spears held upwards, forming a solemn fence on both sides of the warship. Faces were grim, looking down on the Pure Ones as a farmer would look upon cattle. The Dark Brethren vessel gave no commands, nor did it react to the white flag. As the two hulls bobbed together, all he saw were impassive faces.

Ropes were flung and hooks dug into wood, securing the lesser ship and allowing a gangplank to thud down amidships. The legionnaires parted, to reveal a man and a woman, standing proud on the *Claudia*'s deck. They were young, and had olive skin and brown eyes. They held hands, with fingers interlocked, but were dressed for war. Gloom Scribe knew them to be Lucio and Alexis Wind Claw of the Open Hand. They were brother and sister, of an old noble family, and they marched confidently down the gangplank, followed by a dozen void legionnaires.

"There are still Sea Wolves alive," said Alexis, purring the words. "Many, many Sea Wolves. How did this happen?"

Gloom Scribe was unafraid, knowing that his faith was beyond reproach. "They had help from the Stranger. But the chaos spawn reduced their hold to rubble and killed many of them. The Dreaming God has been well served. I feel his twisted gratitude, grasping my heart."

Lucio Wind Claw smiled, his young face showing dimples. "They should have been the first to fall. The Devils of the Sea haunt his dreams." The young man pouted, looking at the varn through narrow eyes. "His dreams should be of beautiful chaos."

"And the rising sea," offered Alexis, reaching up to stroke her brother's face. "We gave you everything to destroy them. How do they yet exist?"

Gloom Scribe threw his head back in laughter. "You are arrogant children. You gave me nothing. The Dreaming God spoke to me long before you came to the Bay of Bliss. We worship him for our own reasons. You are Invader scum and are useful ... but can never hope to understand."

Lucio and Alexis smiled. The void legionnaires behind them stood ready to act, but Gloom Scribe was still unafraid. "How delightful," said Alexis. "Look at us ... we argue over who is the more faithful servant. But, let me pose you a question. Who told you his name? And who summoned your first chaos spawn?"

"It was us," continued Lucio. "We gave you the means to wipe the Invader scum from Nibonay. Before we arrived, you could barely understand the Sleeping Whip. You just let its children fuck your people, making dull-witted mixed-bloods. *We* gave you direction."

"Sooner or later we'd have enough hybrids to retake the Lodge of the Rock," said Gloom Scribe. "And we still can. When you're done chiding me, I will return to the Bay of Bliss and continue my work."

"No!" snapped Alexis. "It serves us better if you simply disappear."

Gloom Scribe was about to return a barbed insult when the deck of the small ship violently juddered. The Dark Brethren legionnaires remained stoic, though Alexis gritted her teeth in an intense grin. They slowly backed away to the gangplank, as the juddering stopped and the Pure One ship began to list, as if something was anchoring it from below.

"Varn," said the captain, through a quivering mouth. "Are we to die?"

From the port side, the small ship tilted, as a section of dark blue water began to churn. Then a huge spiny crest rose from beneath the ocean, followed by segmented scales of green and blue. At first, the seaweed and strange colours made it hard to discern. Then two blubbery hands, dripping with slime, grasped the port railing, and the creature pulled itself upwards.

The mottled colours blended together, making light dance across its surface in bizarre patterns. It was a huge, bloated Sunken Man. The head of a fish and the grotesquely bulbous torso of a frog, with sickly-green slime across its body, and pallid, bubbling saliva, popping from its mouth.

Gloom Scribe had encountered one almost as large, sleeping beneath the Red Straits. But, even when awoken, it had been too bloated to move. They were the Whips, eldest servitors of the Dreaming God, who had existed since their master last ruled.

"I can't pronounce his name," called Lucio, from the deck of the *Claudia*. "We've taken to calling him the Gluttonous Whip."

The legionnaires, standing at attention, didn't react. Their faces showed neither surprise nor fear, as the huge creature pulled itself onto the Mirralite ship. Of the Dark Brethren, only Alexis and Lucio were animated, giggling to each other and pointing to the terrified Mirralite.

Three slimy toes, attached to a foot five feet across, slammed down amidships. Its legs were gangly and sinuous, with opaque layers of sickly-white skin, revealing tendons and blood vessels. Its arms wrapped around the hull of the ship and its belly crushed two men.

The Pure Ones didn't run. They were fixed in place, looking through wide, bloodshot eyes, as the Gluttonous Whip gobbled up their friends. It thrashed its layered neck, sucking up men through globules of saliva, until only Gloom Scribe was left.

"Worry not," shouted Alexis Wind Claw. "It's not female. It wants to eat you, not fuck you."

The creature now enveloped the ship in a crippling embrace. The wood splintered, the sails fell, and water flooded the decks. Gloom Scribe couldn't run or shout. He could only feel betrayed. He'd given everything to the Dreaming God, doing unspeakable things for the good of his people. The Sleeping Whip had sung to him in his sleep, decrying the Devils of the Sea and giving the Mirralite a path to freedom. In his last moment, the varn knew he'd been tricked. There was no freedom for the Pure Ones, there was just submission to a worse master.

To be continued.

APPENDIX

SEA WOLVES

The hold of the Severed Hand, where sits the First Fang. Raised by Duncan Red Claw in the fourteenth year of the dark age. The First Battle of Tranquillity won the island of Nibonay from the Pure Ones, supplanting the Lodge of the Rock.

Lagertha Blood	Daughter of Ulric Blood
Ulric Blood, the First Fang	Elder of the Hold
Vikon Blood, the Second Fang	Protector of the Hold
Mefford Blitz	Pup-master
Jonas Grief	Master-at-arms
Torstein Hearth	Scroll-master
Tomas Red Fang	Spirit-master

DUELLISTS

Siggy Blackeye
Adeline Brand, called the Alpha Wolf
Arthur Brand
Rys Coldfire, called the Wolf's Bastard
Maron Grief
Taymund Grief
Vincent Heartfire
Jaxon Ice, called the Wisp
Roland Lahandras, called Dark Wing
Ingrid Raider

OTHERS

Lys Blackeye	Bosun of the *Black Wave*
Anthony Blitz	Bosun of the *Dead Horse*
Ronald Blitz, called Clatter-foot	Spirit-master of Moon Rock
Duncan Greenfire, called Sharp Tongue	
Wilhelm Greenfire, the High Captain	Elder of Moon Rock
Jacob Hearth	Captain of the *Black Wave*
Lydia Hearth	Lookout of the *Dead Horse*

THE PEOPLE OF ICE

Roderick Ice, called Cold Man	Captain of the *Dead Horse*
Xavyer Ice, called the Grim Wolf	Elder of Cold Point
Xymon Ice, called Blade Smile	Protector of Cold Point
Zia Lahandras, called Freeze	Commander of Cold Point

KNEELING WOLVES

The hold of Four Claw's Folly, where sits the Friend. Raised by Mathew Lone Claw in the fifteenth year of the dark age. Big Brother remained wild, with Jorralite Pure Ones assisting in the hold's construction.

Oswald Leaf	Protector of Four Claw's Folly
Harriet Mud	Sister of Four Claw's Folly
Tasha Strong	Cook of Four Claw's Folly
Charlie Vane, called the War Rat	Captain of the *Lucretia*
Lucas Vane, called Frog Killer	Duellist of Four Claw's Folly
William Vane, called Weathervane Will	Rig-rat of the *Dead Horse*

DARK BRETHREN

The hold of the Open Hand, where sits the Bloodied Harp. Raised by Medina Wind Claw in the thirteenth year of the dark age, supplanting the Lodge of the Fire. Records are not kept as to how many Pure Ones died during its construction.

The Dark Harbour, where sits the Stranger. Raised by Markus Eclipse, in the twentieth year of the dark age. Claimed by the outrider knights in defiance of the Bloodied Harp.

Marius Cyclone, the Stranger	Elder of the Dark Harbour
Santago Cyclone, the Bloodied Harp	Elder of the Open Hand
Trego Cyclone, the Deathless	First Minister of the Silver Parliament
Jessimion Death Spell	First Lord of the Dark Harbour
Loco Death Spell	Void legionnaire
Inigo Night Walker	Sentinel of the Dark Harbour
Santos Spirit Killer	Commander of the second void legion
Alexis Wind Claw	
Lucio Wind Claw	

WINTERLORDS

The hold of First Port, where sits the Always King. Raised by Isabel Defiant in the second year of the dark age. Claimed by Hector Dawn Claw in the eighty-first year of the dark age. The Isle of the Setting Sun was the first to submit to the might of the Eastron.

The hold of the Silver Dawn, where sits the Silver Parliament. Raised by King Sebastian Dawn Claw in the thirteenth year of the dark age, supplanting the Lodge of the Tree.

Christophe Dawn Claw	Always King, Elder of First Port
Natasha Dawn Claw	Aunt of Oliver Dawn Claw
Oliver Dawn Claw	Protector of First Port
David Falcon's Fang	Duellist of First Port

PURE ONES

The boundless native tribes of Rock, Fire and Tree, divided into numerous camps.

Snake Charmer	Spirit child of the Rykalite
Ten Cuts	Speaker of the Rykalite
Young Green Eyes	Mirralite
The Nether One	Varn of the Mirralite
Gloom Scribe	Varn of the Mirralite

THOSE WHO HAVE BEEN CLAWS

The Always King

The highest office in the Kingdom of the Four Claws. Elder of the Winterlords. The title is strictly hereditary.

Sebastian Dawn Claw	1–20DA
Arnulf Dawn Claw	21–52DA
Gaspar Dawn Claw	52–73DA
Hector Dawn Claw	73–96DA
Gustav Dawn Claw	96–130DA
Christophe Dawn Claw, the Shining Sword	130DA–?

The First Fang

Elder of the Sea Wolves. Usually hereditary, though a Day of Challenge frequently causes problems.

Duncan Red Claw	1–40DA
Vincent Red Claw	40DA
Jacob Ice	40–41DA
Ragnar Ice	41–43DA
Heinrich Ice	43–46DA
Darius Blood	46–50DA
Valen Ice	50–52DA
Robert Greenfire	52–80DA
Mathias Blood, the Lost Pirate	80–93DA
Victor Blood, the Half Heart	93–113DA
Halfdan Blood, the Bloody Fang	113–139DA
Ulric Blood	139DA–?

The Friend

Elder of the Kneeling Wolves. The High Families vote.

Mathew Lone Claw, the Last Claw	1–63DA
Sorrin Leaf	63–80DA
Antonius Mud	80–101DA
Jeremiah Strong	101–106DA
Isaiah Leaf	106–130DA

The Bloodied Harp

Elder of the Dark Brethren. No laws of ascension have been established.

Medina Wind Claw	1–20DA
Esteban Death Spell, the Full Moon	21–80DA
Marco Death Spell, the No Moon	80–90DA
Yaago Wind Claw, the True Harp	90–99DA
Gogol Cyclone	99–112DA
Piedro Eclipse	112–129DA
Lucio Eclipse	129–131DA
Santago Cyclone	131DA–?

ACKNOWLEDGEMENTS

It's hard to put the following people in order. Each one has helped me, through advice, support, humour, and occasional slaps to my stupid face. But there's one person who should be mentioned above all. A friend who's no longer around to read this. This book is for her. I love you, Carrie.

Carrie Hall, Kathleen Kitsell, Simon Hall, Marcus Holland, Benjamin Hesford, Scott Ilnicki, Mark Allen, Tony Carew, Martin Cubberley, Mathilda Imlah, Terry and Cathy Smith.

ABOUT THE AUTHOR

A.J. Smith is the author of *The Black Guard*, *The Dark Blood*, *The Red Prince* and *The World Raven*. When not writing fiction, he works in secondary education as a youth worker.